Holding T
Coppe... eads

MW00640587

By

Joe Nobody

Edited by:
E. T. Ivester
D. Allen

PrepperPress

Post-apocalyptic Fiction & Survival Nonfiction

www.PrepperPress.com

Holding Their Own XII: Copperheads
ISBN 978-1-939473-44-8

Copyright © 2016
Kemah Bay Marketing, LLC
All rights reserved.
www.joenobodybooks.com

Other Books by Joe Nobody:

Holding Their Own: A Story of Survival
Holding Their Own II: The Independents
Holding Their Own III: Pedestals of Ash
Holding Their Own IV: The Ascent
Holding Their Own V: The Alpha Chronicles
Holding Their Own VI: Bishop's Song
Holding Their Own VII: Phoenix Star
Holding Their Own VII: The Directives
Holding Their Own IX: The Salt War
Holding Their Own X: The Toymaker
Holding Their Own XI: Hearts and Minds
Apocalypse Drift
The Little River Otter
The Olympus Device: Book One
The Olympus Device: Book Two
The Olympus Device: Book Three
Secession: The Storm
Secession II: The Flood
Secession III: The Surge
The Ebola Wall
Holding Your Ground: Preparing for Defense if it All Falls Apart
The TEOTWAWKI Tuxedo: Formal Survival Attire
Without Rule of Law: Advanced Skills to Help You Survive
The Home Schooled Shootist: Training to Fight with a Carbine

Find more titles at
www.JoeNobodyBooks.com

and

www.PrepperPress.com

Chapter 1

"I'll never go back, Lord," Jeb prayed as his beefy right arm worked the Freightliner's gearshift. "I swear it. Once I get across this river, I'm never going to set foot south of the Rio Grande as long as I draw breath. I don't care how much money they offer me. I don't care how much they beg. If your good graces will protect me long enough to reach Texas, God, I'll never leave her again."

The trucker's eyes were burning tired but remained in constant motion, motivated by both habit and fear. After verifying the road ahead appeared clear, the next stop on his visual inventory was the 12-gauge shotgun riding beside him. It was right where it should be, but provided little comfort.

His eyes moved to the side mirrors, scanning to make sure Jake's white Peterbilt was still behind him and double-checking that the now-familiar grill of his friend's 18-wheeler was the *only* thing on his tail.

Next, he surveyed the Freightliner's dash, Jeb's experienced eye sweeping the cluster of gauges in less than a second, satisfied all were reporting normal levels and outputs. The exercise confirmed what his ears already knew – the powerful Cummins diesel under the hood was humming like a sewing machine.

He began repeating the cycle.

A roadside sign answered his next question; the Amistad Dam was only 14 kilometers ahead. Despite his exhaustion, his brain managed to calculate the distance at just over seven miles until they were home.

Jeb's mind reverted to events three weeks prior. He'd just finished fueling his over the road truck and gulping down a quick lunch when a well-dressed man had approached.

"Would you be Jeb Hewitt?" the stranger had inquired.

"Yeah. Who's asking?" responded the trucker, his frame tensing for either fight or flight.

"Relax," the gent had smiled, showing his open palms in a peaceful, 'don't shoot' stance. "My name is McCarthy, and I work for the government. I just want to offer you a job."

Driving a semi in the post-apocalyptic world of southern Texas wasn't the safest occupation. Despite the recovery, teamsters still encountered a few highwaymen, scavengers, and the occasional outlaw gang. An ambush could occur anywhere, at any time.

"The Alliance?" Jeb questioned.

"No, not *that* government. The United States of America. I'm here for Washington, to hire truckers for a special haul. I hear you're one of the best around."

With a wave of his hand, Jeb dismissed the man. After all, it paid to know who you were working with during these dubious times. "Nah. I've got plenty of work, Mister. Right now, I'm taking this load of lumber to El Paso, and then bringing back several tons of lettuce. I'm all booked up. Thanks, though."

Thinking the conversation was over, the driver pivoted and made for his cab. The sound of footfalls behind him forced another jolt of concern through his now alert mind.

Jeb flipped around to see the stranger was following him, and that pissed the big trucker off. "You wanting trouble, Mister?"

"No," the bureaucrat responded in a calm, stoic voice. "I was just curious what kind of truck you drove."

"It's a Freightliner," Jeb replied, an obvious edge to his voice. "Anything else?"

The man from Washington seemed to be checking out the vehicle as if he were in the market for his own rig. "How many hours on the engine?"

Jeb didn't know whether to be alarmed or exasperated. "Too damn many," he spat. "She's due for a rebuild but try and find a competent mechanic around here these days. What's this all about, man? What is your endgame? 'Cause right now, I gotta tell you … you're beginning to annoy the hell out of me."

The civil servant smirked as if he were privy to a secret. "How would you like a brand new semi? Same model? Updated diesel, and the new generation of magnetic suspension," he baited the driver, grinning ear to ear. Finally, to seal the deal, he added, "Even in the dusty Texas plains, you could see yourself in her chrome."

For the first time since the odd conversation had started, Jeb's full attention was now completely focused on the stranger. "You're kidding me? Right?"

"Nope. Up north, in the worst hit areas, there are hundreds and hundreds of rigs sitting on the dealers' lots. I'm authorized to offer you and 14 other drivers free and clear title on a new tractor – if you'll make a series of runs for the U.S. government."

The mention of a new transfer truck had the driver's attention, the Alliance's recently implemented rules of property ownership putting an immediate halt to scavenging the car lots. Besides, he wasn't the sort to take what he didn't earn, no matter how bad things got.

Rubbing his chin, Jeb was skeptical. After all, his dad had taught his that if an offer seemed too good to be true, it probably was. "And just what kind of haul would you be talking about?"

"We need 15 trucks to go to Central Mexico, about 100 miles south of Monterrey. Agents of the U.S. government have made an agreement with the local farmers there to purchase badly needed foodstuffs. We are recruiting drivers who know this region, speak Spanish, and can take care of themselves and their cargo. I was told you were the best."

"Food? Like produce and stuff? You don't need to go all the way to Mexico to get groceries, Mister. You can get that here on the north side of the river," Jeb countered, pointing toward a nearby trailer full of greens.

It was Mr. McCarthy's turn to grunt, "Washington would be happy to buy locally, but we were told in no uncertain terms by the Alliance leadership that Texas-grown commodities weren't for sale in the quantities we require. According to the people in Alpha, this region's population needs every calorie they can produce. They don't have any surplus to export to our hungry citizenry."

The trucker had to admit there were a significant number of "bone bags," walking around. Still, it had been a while since he'd seen anyone with the swollen stomach associated with severe malnutrition. Progress was being made; it was just slow.

"I suppose that's up to them," Jeb replied, "I'm just a truck driver. I go where someone will pay me to haul a load."

"Does that include Mexico?" McCarthy asked.

It was a fair question. Jeb was a man who spent his days crisscrossing the territory and his travels often included meeting and talking with a variety of people. News was always in high demand for those who pulled a trailer. The difference between profit and loss might hinge on word of a downed bridge or blocked road. Diesel fuel was always in short supply, as were spare parts and the men who could install them. A driver's life might depend on hearing about bushwhackers or raiders working a certain section of the roadway.

Rubbing his chin, the huge trucker thought about McCarthy's question for quite a while. "There are always rumors and gossip about life south of the river. According to some, it's pretty dangerous in places, not so bad in others."

In fact, Jeb had heard it all. He knew most of it had to be bullshit, made up stories told by blowhards who'd like nothing more than to see a man piss down his leg when a funny noise reached the sleeper's bunk alongside a desolate stretch of road.

3

Uncle Sam's representative beamed, "So you'd be willing to accept the job?"

"I didn't say that," Jeb answered. "I don't know enough to say yes or no. Did you mention 15 trucks? A convoy?" A group of trucks might mean safety in numbers. But on the other hand, if its route were general knowledge, it might become a target for the starving and desperate.

"Yes. So far, I've recruited a grand total of three drivers."

While he wasn't a sophisticated man, Jeb was no fool when it came to negotiations. He sensed desperation on the other side of the table. "And how much does this trip pay?"

McCarthy acted puzzled by the question. "Like I said, a new truck upon delivery of the freight."

"No, no," Jeb responded, shaking his head. "That's the bonus. How much per mile?"

Indeed, the trucker's read had been accurate. McCarthy was becoming discouraged by his lack of success. There had been a drought in Ohio and West Virginia, the lack of rainfall reducing the anticipated harvest by over 50%. If Washington didn't procure a ready source of nutrition soon, the food riots would start all over again.

"I'm sure we can arrange suitable compensation for this first venture," the government's business broker stated, hoping to entice the driver even more. "And this could prove to be a lucrative business. We're planning on this being a long-term relationship with our neighbors to the south. Make this a regular run, and you would become a very prosperous man, indeed."

It occurred to Jeb that Mexico was only part of the problem. According to some people, parts of the U.S. were far more dangerous. "How far north do we have to go to deliver the freight?"

McCarthy shook his head, dismissing the concern. "Only to Texarkana. Our drivers will take it from there."

The two men haggled for another hour, eventually arriving at an agreement. Jeb, as well as any of his friends he recruited, would each receive a new truck, 200 gallons of diesel, and two ounces of solid gold. The fuel would be delivered up front, the remainder paid upon delivery. The drivers would commit to ten trips and receive legal title to their rig after the final leg.

Jeb spent the next week talking to his trucker buddies, bringing as many hearty souls into the fold as he could manage. After a week and a half, he had rounded out the 15-rig convoy.

Next came the security.

Jeb was no fool. The U.S.A., or anybody else for that matter, wouldn't offer such a huge payday for a round trip to Disneyland. Jeb figured they would run into more than just Minnie and

4

Mickey. They were going to need some serious hombres to ride shotgun, and the driver knew just the men to come along for the trip. The fact that he had survived the downfall was in no small part due to having cultivated such acquaintances.

Now, as he drove like a maniac for the Texas border, Jeb wished he'd hired more rifles. Of the five armed shooters that had entered Mexico with the convoy, only one could still draw breath. Again, his eyes sought the shotgun wedged between the console and the passenger seat. They had lost three drivers and four rigs as well.

The shining waters of Lake Amistad filled the driver's soul with relief, a signal they were almost out of Indian country. Texas, and the safety of Alliance territory, were on the other side of the man-made body of water. The blacktop between his truck and the bridge appeared free of roadblock or barricade. They were almost home.

Jake's voice sounded over the CB, "Woohooo! Ain't that a sight for these sore eyes. We did it!"

The convoy of 11 trucks began the ascent from the south, the final leg of the harrowing journey taking them onto the lake's massive dam that also served as a bridge. One of the rigs behind Jeb was laying on its horn in celebration.

At the apex of the bridge, Jeb spotted movement alongside the road ahead, but his concern was only minor. They were rolling into Texas now, and while law and order weren't guaranteed, the Alliance territory was a far more secure environment than the blood-soaked madhouse of chaos and anarchy looming in their rear-view mirrors.

As the line of semis started the descent across the bridge, Jeb let his right foot relax off the gas pedal. Diesel was still a precious commodity, and they no longer had to drive like the devil riding their asses. A few moments later, that same foot was slamming on the brake.

A series of spider webs exploded across the windshield, sending a blizzard of safety glass flying through the cab. At the same moment, an earthmover appeared from nowhere, its bright yellow mass pulling onto the road from a gully next to the dam.

The huge construction machine strategically blocked the highway in the narrowest section of road. Despite his tires smoking from locked brakes, Jeb knew he wasn't going to make it. There was no place to go around, not enough room to stop.

The Freightliner's front bumper slammed into one of the scraper's massive rear tires, the impact of the barreling semi barely prompting a shudder through the 250,000-pound machine's frame. Jeb was killed instantly.

5

The trailer jackknifed into the air, flipping in a nearly perfect summersault over the cab and landing on the earthmover's rear engine with a screeching explosion of compacting metal.

A fraction of an instant later, the second truck in the convoy skidded into what remained of Jeb's rig, and then the third truck in line continued the chain reaction of destruction.

Before the billowing, grey clouds of burning rubber had begun to drift skyward, two dozen armed men rose up from both sides of the dam. With battle cries booming a song of fury and rage, they began firing into the disarrayed line of trucks, a maelstrom of lead pelting the shocked and confused drivers.

Volley after merciless volley of high-velocity death raked the convoy, the frenzied assault seemingly fueled by hatred and unbridled spite.

The truckers tried to defend themselves, a few managing to return one or two shots from their cabs before being slaughtered. Just as abruptly as it had started, the thunderous roar of gunfire stopped, its echo rolling across the otherwise calm surface of the lake.

The ambushers had needed no more than 20 seconds before all of the drivers were dead, the kill zone now covered in crushed sheet metal and a snow-like blanket of glass.

One by one, each of the surviving trailers was torched, common road flares tossed into puddles of leaking diesel that mixed with smaller, purple pools of human blood.

As the multiple columns of dark, black smoke boiled into the Texas sky, a sole raider approached the earthmover and withdrew a can of spray paint from his pocket.

"SET THEM FREE!" he scrawled in bold, black letters across the yellow canvas of the scraper's body.

Bishop scanned the nearly vertical walls of the canyon below and flashed Butter a knowing grin. "Let's see how our comrades do with this little wrinkle, shall we?"

The SAINT team's largest member grunted his approval and nodded toward the valley beyond. "How far are you going to make them move, sir?"

Judging the terrain as just short of impassable, the Texan rubbed his chin. Then, his gaze travelled back up the mountain they had just crested two hours ago. Grim and Kevin were up there, assuming the role of a two-man sniper team that was providing cover.

As he considered the question, Bishop shifted his burning legs and then adjusted his pack. The straps had started eating his shoulders an hour ago, and he was sure ice packs were in his lower spine's future. "I'd think two hundred meters would be a fair test. If they can get set up in time to cover us, then I'd say they were both fit enough to return to duty. Wouldn't you?"

Butter shook his head, "Grim is going to be pissed to high heaven, sir. Kevin won't say anything, but that old man is going to chew on you like a cheap steak."

Shrugging, Bishop responded nonchalantly, "I've been married to a mean woman for a long time, my young friend. I've had my ass chewed by the best. Compared to Terri, Grim is a soft, purring kitten."

A flash of confusion crossed Butter's face, "Miss Terri isn't a mean woman, sir. Why do you say things like that?"

Bishop's expression and voice turned fatherly, "After you've been married a few years, come back and we'll have a beer. You can tell me then if you're still perplexed by my insight."

Before Butter could explore the topic further, Bishop reached for the radio microphone clipped to his shoulder. "Lead to overlord, lead to overlord, we've got contact. I repeat, contact. Count 15, no, make that 30 armed men moving on our original route. Do you copy – over?"

"Copy, lead," came Grim's voice, the ex-contractor's tone making it clear he already smelled a rat. "What's the call, boss?"

Winking at Butter, Bishop keyed his mic, "We're going to have to go around these guys. I need you to set up on the other side of that canyon to cover us. Over."

High above their teammates, Grim and Kevin scanned the canyon in question, seeing more pain, sweat, and tears in the rugged rock formations and sheer faces of stone.

"What the hell is he trying to do to us?" Grim complained, wiping a sleeve's worth of perspiration from his forehead. "If he wants us dead, why not just sink a bullet in our heads and get it over with? I think that sadistic bastard is enjoying our slow, agonizing demise."

Kevin didn't respond at first, still riding a wave of joy over the doctor's approving his return to the team. He knew exactly what Bishop was doing and didn't blame the SAINT leader. "He's just making sure we're ready to go back to work, Grim. That's all."

"Grim? Did you faint?" Bishop's voice taunted over the air-waves. "Hello? Overlord? Did you two decide to take your toys and go home? Or do I need to call in a medevac copter?"

"We're scouting the new route," Grim hissed into the radio. "Trying to estimate the impact to our timeline, over."

"You've got 20 minutes," Bishop's command-like voice boomed through the speaker.

Grim's eyes grew large at the deadline, his gaze returning across the treacherous terrain before settling on Kevin. "Are you shitting me? I couldn't cross that deathtrap in 20 minutes before my leg got shot to hell. He *is* trying to kill us!"

"We better get moving," Kevin urged, rising from their hide and hefting his sniper rifle and pack.

"I think we need to inform that crazy son bitch that he's suffering from heat exhaustion and that we need at least an hour!"

Kevin pivoted and shrugged, "Up to you. But… do you really want him telling my dad that we're not able to return to duty?"

The grizzled, old veteran had to think about that. Finally shaking his head in disgust, he keyed the mic, "Roger that, lead. We'll be ready."

Traversing the rocky, downhill terrain with over 50 pounds of gear stressed their muscles unlike any gym workout or weight routine. Grim felt like his knees were rusty joints, screeching the protest of pain with every step. His calves cramped up, his lungs burned from the high altitude and lack of oxygen. Still, they kept moving, climbing, scrambling, and pressing the limits. While he would never admit it, deep down inside he knew Bishop was right. Their lives depended on each other, the four-man team only as strong as its weakest member. He was determined not to be the link of the chain that failed.

Finally, they reached the bottom of the canyon, both men drenched in sweat, both gasping like marathon runners at the finish line. Kevin checked his watch, "We've got eight minutes to get up the other side and find a good spot."

Glancing at the steep wall to be negotiated, Grim began having second thoughts. *Maybe it's time to hang up this rifle and let them put me out to pasture,* he considered. *I'm too old for this shit. It's taking me longer and longer to recover. Maybe the wife is right. Maybe it's time.*

The fact that Kevin, 20 years his junior, seemed to be suffering just as badly did little to console the old warrior. *His injuries were twice as bad as mine,* he thought. *Besides, there is no age discrimination on the teams. Either I can do this job or not. Period. End of story. I can't keep up, and I will get one of these guys killed if I pretend otherwise.*

8

Just as Grim was reaching for the mic to report he couldn't achieve the objective, the packed earth of an animal trail caught his eye.

He followed the path with a steady gaze, a knowing smile crossing his face as he realized Bishop hadn't seen it from across the canyon. "Well lookie there," he whispered to Kevin while indicating the path frequented by local white tailed deer. "Let's take the easy route."

The youngest member hesitated, knowing that Bishop had ordered them to cross as a test. Grim detected Kevin's pause. "Sometimes it's not how strong you are but how smart you are. Sometimes experience will save your ass when muscles won't." Noting his partner's persistent hesitation, he continued his sales pitch, "Besides, trail hikes can represent their own set of dangers. Come on, and I'll regale you with stories about how I wrestled a bear on the Appalachian Trail when I was just a lad."

A full minute before the deadline, Grim keyed his mic. "In position, sir. Your new route is clear of tangos."

Down in the valley, Bishop heard Grim's report and flashed Butter a look of surprise. "No fucking way," he mumbled, turning to glance toward where his men should be. Sure enough, Grim stood from behind a thicket of brush, his arm waving in wide strokes. He then flipped his boss a one-fingered salute.

The Texan was partially mystified, mostly pleased. He had no idea how Grim had pulled off what was surely a minor miracle, but in reality, he didn't care. What really mattered was that his team was back together, and that gave Bishop a feeling of satisfaction he hadn't experienced in months.

Just as the SAINT leader was reaching for his mic to give Grim a rough time about sprouting wings and flying across the canyon, the thump-thump-thump of a helicopter echoed through the valley. Nick's voice in his earpiece soon followed. "SAINT One, SAINT One, this is Honcho. Do you copy?"

"Did you decide to deliver a picnic lunch, boss?" Bishop responded. "Butter is dying for some fried chicken and potato salad."

Nick, however, wasn't in a joking mood. "Get your people together, Bishop. There's been an incident."

Frowning, the Texan turned to Butter and halfheartedly mocked his friend, "Well, of course, there has been an *incident*. We wouldn't want to take a few days to rest and recover, now would we?"

Butter shook his head and then seemed inspired. Fanning his nose, the young man teased, "Mr. Bishop, I hope they at least let *you* take a shower before we deploy, sir."

9

Taken aback by the kid's attempt at banter, Bishop scanned his teammate up and down for a moment. Butter, having ventured onto an unfamiliar limb, suddenly looked unsure and guilty.

Bishop started laughing, "You've been hanging around Terri too much."

"Go on, show Aunt Diana what a big boy you are," Terri cooed to Hunter, trying to coax the child away from the couch that supported his wobbly legs. "Come on," coached the proud mother, holding out her arms a short distance away. "You can do it."

Hunter's face lit in a broad grin, his glowing eyes traveling between his mom and Diana to make sure he was the center of attention. It soon became clear, however, that he wasn't going to let loose of the sofa, no matter how appealing his mother's promised embrace.

"Come on," Terri continued, waving her outstretched hands in welcome. "Take that step, big fella. Just one step."

Taking a deep breath, Hunter lifted his leg, but then a look of pained confusion painted across his face. He decided to plop down instead.

"Oh, no," Diana snickered. "Maybe next time."

"Dang it," Terri chuckled, "I wanted him to take that first step before Bishop and the guys left. Dad needs to be here for that."

Diana bent and scooped Hunter from the floor much to the child's delight. Bouncing him on her hip, she said, "I wanted to be in on the big event, too. I thought for sure he'd do it for his favorite auntie."

Terri began packing the diaper bag while the Alliance's top official entertained and snuggled with the cackling babe. "He's such a happy boy," Diana noted.

"Bishop spoils him rotten when he's home," Terri confessed with a sigh. "Then all of a sudden my hero-of-a-husband is off on some grand adventure, and I'm left with a kiddo who thinks I should spend every waking moment playing and attending to him."

"Why don't you leave him here with me and go along with Bishop on this trip? I could use the distraction, and other than this brewing international incident, there's not a lot going on right now."

Terri momentarily brightened at the idea of a mom's day out, but then flashed a coy smile at her friend. "You're just wanting me to go along because the Colonel is pissed about his food convoy getting torched."

Feigning innocence, Diana countered, "What? Nooo. Not me. I was just thinking my friend could use a break from her routine. Besides, this mission isn't dangerous. Nick wouldn't be sending Bishop's team down south if it weren't for your husband's relationship with the President of those United States. Leave Hunter here with me for a few days and go with Bishop.... Get out of the house ... change up your day a little."

Terri was still skeptical, "Uh-huh. The fact that my husband doesn't have a diplomatic bone in his body wouldn't have anything to do with your offer – would it?"

A tinge of guilt colored the Alliance leader's expression. "Well ... err ... maybe a little. I would feel a whole lot better about the situation if you were going along."

Before Terri could respond, the door to Diana's office opened in a rush, Nick and Bishop barging in, serious business on their minds. Both of the men pulled up short when they spotted Terri and Hunter.

"Hiya, big guy!" Bishop greeted his son, moving to take the little one from Diana. "How's my best buddy doing this morning?"

Hunter, obviously thrilled to see his primary playmate, reached for his father's embrace while screaming, "Daddy!"

"Diana wants me to tag along with your SAINT team, Bishop. She's worried that Washington is going to try and put the blame for the massacre on the Alliance," Terri casually announced.

"That's one hell of an idea," Nick interjected before Bishop could respond. "Sheriff Watts has at least 20 deputies down there right now, so it's probably one of the safest places in the entire territory."

Bishop stopped flying his Hunter-airplane, much to the dismay of the tot. The Texan became serious in an instant, "Terri, how many times do we have to go over this? New Mexico and the Toymaker were an exception. I thought we agreed not to endanger our son anymore?"

"Oh, I'm going to babysit Hunter," Diana chimed in. "You and Terri can go check out the convoy and make nice with the U.S. representative for a few days. After that, why don't you take a little time together and enjoy Lake Amistad? I'm sure there's at least one functioning boat left. I'll even requisition some gasoline."

11

"It would be a chance for some alone time," Terri added, seductively moving to hook arms with her husband and flashing a sultry look.

Bishop's eyes moved from each of his friends and then landed on his wife. "I can see that I'm a victim of a conspiracy here," he mumbled. "Not only am I hopelessly outnumbered, but you're using intimacy as a weapon of mass destruction. What possible choice do I really have? I guess Terri's going along on this trip."

Diana and Nick exchanged knowing looks, and then the Alliance's top elected official reached for Hunter. "I'm going to spoil you rotten, little man. I know where the best ice cream is in all of Alpha, and we're going to put a serious dent in their inventory."

"Be careful there, lady," Bishop teased. "That's my son you're now in charge of."

Nick grunted, "I'll say the same to you, sir. Be careful, my friend. That's my son you're now in charge of."

Chapter 2

Bishop could see whiffs of smoke from a considerable distance as the Blackhawk began a gradual descent toward the scene of the massacre. It wasn't long before the scope of the tragedy came into focus.

The lake laid to the west, an impressive reservoir commanding over 800 miles of shoreline. Bishop remembered reading that it was the fourth largest body of water in all of Texas.

To the east flowed the Rio Grande, a narrow stream compared to the mass of the basin. Separating the two was a roadway with waterfront on one side and farmland on the other. The dam, along with its spill gates, rested in the middle. Just on the Texas side of the river, the blackened, charred remains of several trucks spoiled the otherwise picturesque view.

"Wow," the Texan mouthed, turning to give Terri a look of wonderment. "That was a serious ass ambush if I've ever seen one."

"That's going to take weeks to clean up," she shouted over the helicopter's roar. "Those poor truck drivers never had a chance."

The bird landed next to what had been the old U.S. Border Patrol station, a choking cloud of South Texas dust rising into the air. Grim and Kevin exited first, habit prompting both men to take up defensive positions. Bishop hopped out next, followed by Butter who helped Miss Terri out of the chopper.

"Suck up," Bishop sneered as the big kid passed.

As quickly as possible, all of them moved away from the whirlybird and the fog of sand and grit being catapulted skyward. At the edge of clear air stood Sheriff Watts, complete with mirrored sunglasses and Smokey the Bear hat.

The lawman was all business, "If you'll come this way, I'll brief you on what we know and what we suspect."

As the group trudged toward the bridge, Bishop pulled Butter aside. "I have a special job for you. I want you to guard Terri like a hawk. You are now her personal bodyguard. Anything happens to her, and you and I will have an unpleasant encounter. Is that clear?"

"Yes, sir. You know I'd die for Miss Terri, sir," Butter guaranteed.

"I'm probably being paranoid, big guy, but somebody shot up this caravan and did a damn fine job of it at that. Stick to that woman like glue, and keep your eyes open. If something even looks slightly out of place, I want her out of here. Immediately. Without delay. Post haste."

"With two of us watching out for her, she'll be fine," the team member whispered. Bishop observed as Butter hustled to catch up with his wife while she strolled along with Watts.

As the entourage approached the bridge, a single man appeared from the wreckage and waved to Watts. "That would be one Mr. McCarthy," the sheriff announced. "He works for Washington and was the individual who commissioned these food trucks."

Deputies were crawling all over the area, most of the law enforcement personnel concentrating along both sides of the road. "We're searching for any evidence that would explain where the bushwhackers were hiding," Watts explained. "The trucks ... or what is left of them, have already been processed."

"And?" Bishop inquired.

"We know that a variety of weapons were used in the ambush. We've found at least five different calibers, most of them sizable. From what we can tell, there were approximately 20 shooters. We have no idea how they got to the bridge or how they left though."

"Maybe by boat?" Terri asked, glancing at the water.

"Could be, ma'am. At this point, your guess is as good as mine."

Bishop pointed toward the massive, yellow earthmover, "Where did that come from?"

"We believe it was hotwired and driven here from just outside Del Rio. The Alliance was in the early stages of trying to repair the dam's hydroelectric generators that were damaged during the collapse. A lot of silting has occurred in front of the intake, and the engineers were drawing up plans to redirect the flow and sent in huge machines like that to clean up the mess."

"Had the project started?" Bishop asked.

"No, sir," replied the officer. "This area is still a bit unsettled. We're making inroads into reestablishing the rule of law, but our progress has been slow along the river."

"Why?" Terri asked, now intrigued.

Watts paused, wanting to pick his words carefully. "This area was being pulled apart at the seams before the collapse, ma'am. We had pronounced racial and cultural tensions. Not to mention the cartels creating havoc just on the other side of the river and their determination to smuggle drugs and people into the States. A huge economic divide between the populations of the two countries made a definitive border a necessity. You know, I think whoever said, 'Good fences make good neighbors,' surely had the southern Texas boundary in mind," the sheriff paused as he continued. "But then, the border kind of evaporated, and the various factions hereabouts determined to tear each other to shreds."

Bishop's first reaction to the lawman's words was to tighten the grip on his carbine. Then, glancing at his wife with concern for her safety, he inquired, "Has order been reestablished, Sheriff?"

"Mostly, yes. We've had a few corruption issues with some of the leadership, and from what I'm told by the locals, there has been a lot of cross-border activity originating from both sides. The big shots in Alpha informed me a few days ago that the Eastern Rio Grande Valley will be one of the last areas of Texas to be fully reintegrated, mainly because there's hardly anybody left alive down here."

McCarthy arrived just then, prompting Terri to put on her diplomatic hat after handshakes and introductions had been accomplished. "Sir, I can't express the Alliance's sadness and regret over this incident. I know I speak for everyone in Alpha when I say that we are all deeply troubled by this tragedy and want to assure you and the President that our government is doing everything in its power to find the criminals who perpetrated this atrocity and bring them to justice."

It became immediately obvious that the man representing the interests of the United States wasn't a happy camper. "Thank you for those words, ma'am, but I'm only interested in results." He then turned to Sheriff Watts and barked, "Are any of these new arrivals the forensic specialists my government requested?"

Bishop didn't like the man's attitude nor the fact that he had dismissed Terri's words without even a polite consideration. Still, the Texan checked his reaction. Mr. McCarthy's last few days surely had been a nightmare.

Watts seemed to have had his fill of the man as well. "No, sir, these people are not law enforcement. As I explained before, sir, the Alliance doesn't have any forensic specialists available, and even if we did, this really isn't the type of crime scene where those skills could be utilized."

"So why are they here, Sheriff?"

"I've pulled in deputies from over 50 miles away, Mr. McCarthy. Even at that, if the vigilantes who executed this ambush return, my people aren't equipped to handle a para-military force of any size. The Alliance mobilizes SAINT teams for situations like this."

McCarthy's voice became louder as he mounted his tirade. "I can't believe that in all of Texas there isn't a qualified CSI team. I feel like this incident isn't a high priority for your government."

The statement was yet another example of the rhetoric coming out of Washington. Diana had been warned by the newly appointed Alliance ambassador that such conversations were taking place in the hallowed halls of the U.S. capital. Some legislators had even gone so far as to insinuate that the Alliance had been responsible for the attack.

Terri stepped in, flexing charm instead of muscle. "If you have access to such a team from the U.S., I'll grant permission for them to enter Alliance territory and examine the scene, sir. We have nothing to hide … nothing whatsoever. While our lack of resources is somewhat embarrassing, we'll gladly accept any help available in solving this crime."

Her countermove stunned McCarthy, who suddenly found himself at a loss for words. Terri had essentially cut the verbal legs out from under the man, and everyone watching the conversation knew it. It was common knowledge that such specialized personnel were extremely rare in either nation, and she had just shut down his main argument in less than five seconds. Terri didn't rub it in or gloat, however, keeping a look of pure, innocent sincerity on her face as she waited for a response.

"I'll take that offer under advisement and contact my superiors as soon as possible," McCarthy finally grumbled.

Bishop leaned close to Butter and whispered, "See? I told you so. A mean woman. Grim ain't shit compared to that."

A few hours passed as the new arrivals received a tour of the gruesome site and surrounding area. It was clear to Bishop that the ambushers had arrived by boat, hidden alongside the road, and waited for the trucks to enter the kill zone. Simple. Effective. Deadly as hell.

From a purely professional aspect, the Texan had to admire the planning that had gone into the action, especially the simplicity.

Old adages abounded, infantry wisdom that postulated even the best battle plans changed as soon as the first shot was fired. Bishop's experience reaffirmed those proverbs.

In reality, the best plan was always the easiest to communicate to the troops. Effective leaders understood the fear, panic, bedlam, and confusion that average humans experienced when other people were trying to kill them. Being able to recall when, where, and what you were supposed to do became nearly impossible during intense combat. Complex coordination among multiple groups of people just wasn't practical.

Good generals played checkers, not chess.

Whoever had planned the convoy's demise had obviously had his shit in one, single, neat bag. While Bishop deplored the slaughter of "innocent" life, he had to respect the forethought that had gone into the operation.

"We're dealing with professionals here," he stated calmly to Watts and his team. "They used a minimum of ammunition, exposed themselves for a matter of seconds, and had an excellent path of regress if things went horribly wrong."

Grim agreed, "This was well done. Probably one of the best ambushes I've ever seen, and I've been on both sides of the equation more times than I care to remember."

Watts rubbed his chin, "So we're looking for a military unit of some sort?"

"Not necessarily," Bishop responded, sweeping the length of the bridge with his arm. "There wasn't a lot of skill required by the average rifleman here, and that's the brilliance of the thing. In this spot, with good intelligence, pretty much any group of men could have pulled this off. The leadership, however, knew what they were doing. Probably military, or cartel combat experience … a guy sporting a resume heavy on fighting with a dash of leadership experience was giving the orders here."

Terri, growing bored with the soldierly aspects of the massacre, pointed toward the message scrawled on the yellow, commercial grader. "If they were such precise, professional killers, why did they take the time to paint that?"

No one seemed to have an answer. Still, she couldn't help but think the graffiti was a key piece of the puzzle. "Set them free," she read aloud, unwilling to let the subject go. "Set who free?"

"Prisoners?" Watts offered. "Captives being held that someone wants to be released?"

"Hostages?" Bishop asked when no one responded to Watts offering.

Terri shook her head, "The Alliance would know if either of those two scenarios existed. We've only recently started incarcerating criminals. Sheriff, you would know if any large group of hostages were being held. No, this is something different."

"The Alliance would know if it was happening in our territory," Bishop offered, staring south toward Mexico. "Who knows what's happening on the other side of the river?"

"But the attack came on our side of the bridge," Watts countered.

Terri tilted her head in thought, smiling at her husband's observation. Without warning, she pivoted quickly, her eyes boring into Mr. McCarthy. "Exactly what is going on south of the border, sir? You sent those truckers down there. Your government negotiated some sort of arrangement, and you've been awfully quiet about the subject."

Flashing the classic "deer in the headlights" gaze, McCarthy managed a half-hearted shrug.

"We've been assuming that someone from Texas was involved," Watts chimed in, happy to get on Terri's bandwagon. "Perhaps that was in error. Where were these drivers picking up their loads, Mr. McCarthy?"

"I didn't personally travel to Mexico or participate in any of the negotiations with the leadership down there," he countered. "I gave the drivers a map and information about whom they were to contact once they arrived. Their trailers were to have been preloaded and ready when the semis arrived. It wasn't a complex arrangement."

Terri stepped forward, her eyes like laser beams on the man from Washington. "Who did cut the deal? How was payment made? You seem content to put the blame on the Alliance, but not willing to offer any details. Why?"

McCarthy was more prepared this time. When Terri had first arrived, he'd written her off as just another pretty face. Now he knew why she was here and was ready for her verbal onslaught. "I can't provide what I don't know, ma'am. I was told to hire 15 truckers and given authority to offer them various forms of payment. Their destination was a fertile valley 40 miles north of Monterrey where the loaded trailers were to be waiting. That's all I know."

Watts stiffened at the statement, "Did you say 15 truckers? There were only 11 here on the bridge. What happened to the other four?"

"I don't know that either, Sheriff. I do know that Jeb Hewitt, the man that recruited most of the drivers, also hired five security men. They were to ... how did he phrase it? Oh, yes, they were to ride shotgun."

Watts was notably displeased with the update. "I wish you had divulged that tidbit a little sooner, son. My men and I have been scratching our heads why we had 12 bodies, but only 11 trucks."

Bishop exchanged knowing looks with Grim. The truckers had been nervous or warned of the hazards of making the trip. Hired guns had been enlisted to provide security, and some of them had been killed. Despite the precautions, the convoy had still lost vehicles and freight before reaching the Texas side of the river. Those facts shouted a message to men who understood combat, and it wasn't comforting.

There were always rumors about life south of the Rio Grande, the SAINT teams having been exposed to snapshots here and there. Texas had even annexed one, small village during the Salt War.

What little information that did wander across the border was mixed. Some refugees claimed that the drug cartels had taken over certain regions of the country, terrorizing natives and commandeering whole settlements. Other Mexican citizens showed up with fresh vegetables and locally produced goods and were eager to barter and trade. In fact, rumor had it that Pete's seemingly endless supply of coffee was via just such a relationship.

The Alliance's agricultural breadbasket along the Rio Grande had developed strong ties with similar farming operations just on the other side of the river. Most of the Mexican farms ventured north to sell their produce in exchange for fuel and other necessities.

Little was known of central and southern Mexico. Like so many distant lands, tales of ghastly suffering, tyrannical dictators, and brutal living conditions abounded. Over the lifespan of the apocalypse, folks tended to develop an immunity to such sagas. Facts were often exaggerated and embellished, bad news having always been more interesting than good. The line between grim reality and pure exaggeration was murky at best.

Yet, a broker representing the U.S. government had chanced a trip to Mexico and negotiated a deal with the people there. There must be some level of authority and control because the trailers had indeed been loaded and hitched to the semis. It was obvious from the charred remains scattered on the bridge that excess food was being grown and exported.

Bishop toured the truck boneyard, studying the scorched remains of the contents. The variety of foodstuffs was impressive. There were bags of rice, some sort of flour, and at least three different trailers full of corn ears. Whoever had selected the inventory knew what they had been doing, maximizing the number of calories per pound of freight, shipping items that wouldn't easily spoil.

The scrape of a footstep interrupted the Texan's survey.

"I don't like this one bit," Grim announced, walking up behind his commander.

"You and me both, brother. There has to be a small fortune in food here. I could understand the convoy being a prime target for banditos, but these trailers were torched after the ambush was over," Bishop noted.

"And," the Texan continued, stepping over to kick the grey ashes of a road flare with his boot, "charbroiling the food was planned from the start. Somebody didn't want the U.S.A. getting this shipment. This was perpetrated by somebody who isn't desperate, hungry, or a simple criminal. This was a political ambush from the get-go."

The old warrior's gaze worked up and down the gruesome line of trucks, "Even that doesn't track though. If the highwaymen had a political agenda, why not take a hostage or two? Or line them up and execute the poor bastards? Hang them from the bridge? Watts said none of the bodies had been mutilated or disturbed, and we don't have any evidence of captives being taken. It's almost as if the people who did this were more upset with the food than the drivers. How is that political?"

Bishop nodded in silence, his only acknowledgment of Grim's astute observations.

The two men continued trekking south, toward the Mexican side. At the apex of the bridge/dam, Bishop noted the large, brass plaque that marked the physical border and then turned to face the foreign, unknown horizon to the south.

Grim watched his friend closely, sensing a change in the man's normally mellow demeanor. The seasoned contractor had seen it before ... first a tightening of Bishop's jawline, immediately followed by the slightest narrowing of the eyes. The weight shifted a bit forward to the balls of the Texan's feet, his grip on the carbine tensing as every muscle grew taut, coiled for violence.

It was the eyes that bothered Grim the most. All humanity vanished from Bishop's suddenly cold stare. There was no hint of intelligence, not a sign friendliness, reasoning, or curiosity. It was if the civilized person standing on the bridge had morphed into some sort of wild animal – a predator that was ready, willing, and fully capable of unleashing unspeakable ferocity. It was enough to send a shudder down even the most hardened man's spine.

So intense was Bishop's projection, Grim's own mind sought to scan the surrounding area, thinking his boss had seen something ... had detected some previously unnoticed threat.

A light breeze chose that moment to swell up from the south, its warmth flowing across their faces. "There's trouble on that wind," Bishop whispered to his friend. "I can feel it."

Acknowledging that Watts and his unit had the crime scene under control, Bishop, Terri, and the team hitched a ride to the marina via two deputies and their SUVs.

"My mom warned me that I'd end up in the back of a police car if I hung out with you," Terri teased.

"You know I was your mom's favorite 'child,'" Bishop responded with a grin.

"Her judgement went to hell in a handbasket after she became ill," she countered.

Skirting the shoreline took a considerable amount of driving, the shimmering surface of the reservoir always visible in the distance. The melancholy feeling left by the carnage they had just witnessed was somewhat offset by the blue water, clear skies, and gentle breeze.

"I think a change of scenery will do us both good," Bishop noted, his gaze fixed out the window at the lake. "I just hope our sleeping accommodations aren't a letdown."

"That's always a crapshoot when traveling these days," Terri said. "Heaven help us if there's only a twin bed available, and we have to sleep in each other's arms."

Eventually, they pulled into the marina, a sign announcing Northshore Rentals and Boat Ramp. Like most post-collapse businesses, the place had obviously seen better days.

The two squad cars were met in the parking lot by a middle-aged woman who wore a large revolver on her belt and a semi-permanent scowl on her face. Bishop wasn't sure if the pistol was a post-apocalyptic addition or not.

The first phrase that popped into Bishop's mind as Hannah Lee Hogan introduced herself as the proprietor was "one tough, old bird."

She was in her early 50's, with wrinkled skin no doubt caused by years of exposure to the sun, wind, and cigarettes. She had the gravelly, sandpaper voice of a long-term smoker and the grit of a survivor.

Hannah Lee's first statement was an apology. "I'm sorry, but some scoundrel made off with my best houseboat a few days ago. I knew I should have trusted my gut when he wanted to rent her. I kept asking myself why a single man would need such a big vessel, but he was insistent. He left me an ounce of gold and $500 in greenbacks as a deposit, but he never brought it back."

"How big was the boat?" Bishop asked, scanning the nearby watercraft tied up along the piers.

"She was 52 feet stem to stern," Hannah replied, pulling a drag from her hand-rolled cigarette. "We bought her three years before the collapse ... right before the economy slid into the

21

depression. My late husband and I lived on her for a while after the world went to hell. We anchored out in the lake until things settled down a bit."

"And somebody rented it a few days ago but didn't bring it back?" Terri inquired.

"Yes, sweetie. That's exactly what that no-good man did. Always trust your gut, honey. Always."

Bishop was interested now. "Was this fellow by himself?"

"Yup. He said he had some friends that were coming to the lake later," Hannah answered, blowing out a grey cloud of exhaled smoke.

Terri's eyes moved back to the lake, "Where would someone go with a stolen boat that big? I mean it's not like they can just back up a pickup with a hitch and pull it out with a trailer."

Hannah nodded, "Oh, I'm sure I'll find it one of these days. It's probably over on the Mexican side, being stripped to the bare bones even as we speak. They'll take the engines, fuel, appliances, even the deck chairs and fishing poles. I'll just have to suffer the loss and carry on. What choice do I have? I mean it's not as if I can just file an insurance claim on the damages these days. You know? "

Bishop and Terri exchanged a troubled look and conducted a hushed sidebar. "I think I know what the ambushers used for transportation now. A machine of that size would ferry a lot of riflemen," Bishop reasoned.

Grim had caught on as well and continued the inquiry. "Had you ever seen this man before?"

"Nope," Hannah declared. "He seemed nice enough, but something in the back of my mind kept telling me he was up to no good."

Terri turned the conversation back to the present issue, "So there's no place for us to stay tonight?"

Hannah flashed at the mere suggestion that she couldn't take care of her customers. "Oh my goodness, darling, of course, there is. That man took my biggest rental, but there is still Belle Blue. She's only a 50-footer, but she's plenty big for just the five of you. Come on, I'll show you her accommodations."

Indeed, Belle Blue was a fine craft with four staterooms, a well-equipped galley, and tons of comfortable seating. "I guess it's called a houseboat for good reason," Bishop chuckled. "Heck, this is bigger than our first house."

Grim provided the next surprise, peppering Hannah with a series of questions about the mechanicals. After several inquiries about the engines, rudders, propellers, and how the proprietor had managed to keep the boat in such good condition, the old contractor announced, "I used to have a vessel a lot like this one. They don't handle very well, but you don't need an ocean-going hull just to putter around on the lake."

"We have a captain!" Terri cheered. Bishop was noticeably relieved as well, hoping that his wife wasn't actually expecting him to commandeer the boat out on the lake. He had no idea how to pilot such a machine.

Hannah was excited as well, "Thank God one of you knows how to handle this little dinghy. I was afraid you were going to ask me to do it, and I don't have anyone to stay here and watch my place until my daughter returns."

The deputies helped unload the team's equipment, promising to return the following morning so Bishop and his men could finish the investigation by scouting the Mexican side of the bridge. Neither the Texan nor Grim expected to find anything, but duty was duty. Diana and the bigwigs in Alpha wanted to send a message to Washington that the Alliance was taking the matter seriously.

Bishop had just finished stowing his gear in the master stateroom when a massive splash sounded outside. Thinking someone had already managed to fall overboard, the Texan rushed to the outside deck while trying to remember if he'd seen any life preservers.

No sooner had he reached the rail than a quick shadow blocked out the sun, next a flash of something flying by, followed by another tremendous eruption of water.

"Good one!" Butter yelled, treading water off the port side. "For a little fella, that was one heck of a splash."

Kevin surfaced nearby, shaking his head to clear the water from his eyes. Both of them were soon paddling for the ladder.

"Did someone fall in?" Grim yelled, rushing to the rail a few moments later, an orange life preserver in his hands.

"No," Bishop laughed. "It's just the kids high diving from the bridge."

Grim leaned out to look at the higher deck right when Butter's massive frame sailed by. Again, a huge geyser of water erupted, the splash chasing Grim away from the edge. "Damn it!" he snarled, looking at his soaked shirt. "I knew those two, little shits would get into trouble sooner rather than later!"

"What did you say, Grim?" Butter asked, only his head breaking the surface.

Once more, Grim leaned over the rail, intent on giving his teammate an ear full. Before the old warrior could inhale, Kevin's body soared past, impacting the surface and launching another wall of water that found their friend.

23

Both of the lads were hooting up a storm, pointing and laughing at their buddy's drenched clothing and red face. "Why you little shits!" Grim bellowed.

In a flash, Grim dove over the side in a perfect swan, his body disappearing into the depths. Bishop, laughing so hard his ribs were aching, knew the hunters were about to become the hunted.

As the Texan watched, Kevin and Butter's heads were pivoting right and left, wondering where Grim had gone. It was the big man who shrieked first.

"Something's got me! Something's got me!" Butter screamed in terror. "It's an alligator ... or maybe a shark! Somebody help!"

As Kevin moved closer to his friend, Butter went under, his flapping, desperate hands flaying at the water as his head disappeared beneath the surface.

Before Kevin could even take a deep breath, Grim and Butter surfaced at the same time, the old man waving Butter's swimming trunks in the air like it was the greatest trophy he'd ever earned.

Bishop was now howling up on the deck, Terri rushing to help, thinking something was badly wrong. Just as she rounded the bulkhead, Butter's dripping trunks plopped down in her path.

Kevin might have been the one of the younger members of the team, but that didn't mean the boy couldn't figure out what was coming next.

Gulping a lungful of air, the unit's marksman bolted for his escape. He managed one overhand stroke before Grim caught him from behind and pulled him under. The lad's last words, "Oh, shit! Nooooo!" frantically thundered before his body vanished from sight.

Again, a few seconds later, both Grim and his victim surfaced, Kevin's trunks soon joining Butter's up on the deck.

"Laugh at the old man, will ya?" Grim chuckled, now swimming gracefully toward the ladder. "Little shits. That'll teach 'em to mess with their betters."

Terri, catching on quickly to what had just transpired, sauntered up to her husband and whispered, "I take it that I shouldn't go back below deck just yet?"

Bishop glanced at Kevin and Butter's anxious faces, both of them wanting desperately to retrieve their swimwear, neither willing to expose themselves to the lady. "Absolutely, my love. You should stay right here for a bit and enjoy the view ... err ... the sunset, I mean."

Terri snorted, "Yeah, it's probably best if I don't get any 'view.'"

Grim, rubbing out his hair in a towel, soon joined the couple. "How long do you think those two can tread water?" he laughed.

"I keep waiting on one of them to figure out they can go to the back of the boat and climb out without being seen," Bishop replied.

"Nope. Hannah is back there, fixing something on the pier," Grim answered with pride.

The trio had another good laugh, which was soon interrupted by Butter's pleading voice, "Mister Bishop, sir, could you please toss us our trunks, sir, please?"

"What did you say, Butter?" Bishop shouted back, cupping his hand behind his ear.

"Sir, could you please throw our trunks back to us?" Kevin repeated, knowing good and well that they were the butt of a very well played joke.

"What happened to your shorts?" Terri asked from the rail, her voice laced with innocence. "Don't tell me you two fine, young gentlemen were skinny dipping? Not in the presence of a lady?"

Bishop had never seen Kevin and Butter's faces so red. "No ma'am," they both pleaded at once. "We kind of … well … we lost them."

"Give them back their trunks, Grim," Bishop ordered. "Unless you want to explain to Nick why his son drowned."

For a moment, Bishop thought the team's senior member was going to protest the command. Shrugging, he merely replied, "Yes, sir. I suppose we might need those boys tomorrow."

A moment later, the swimwear was airborne, landing a short distance away from the two tiring paddlers. Just as Butter reached his floating clothing, Grim couldn't help himself. "By the way, guys, that water is crystal clear. You can see *everything* from up here."

Both kids' eyes immediately darted to Terri, who simply nodded and smiled. "I'm going to go finish unpacking, Bishop," she announced loud enough for the team's youngest members to hear. "Let me know when it's safe to come back up on deck."

Chapter 3

Bishop awoke to the aroma of frying eggs.

In all his years, travels, and adventures, he'd never slept so well as the previous night. Rolling over in hopes of encountering Terri's shoulder and a warm embrace, the Texan was only slightly disappointed to find that his wife had already risen.

In his half-awake state, he found it odd that she had managed to exit the berth without his knowing it. Another whiff from the ship's kitchen interrupted that thought with a more troubling idea. Butter and Kevin might be up as well. There could only be so many eggs. He'd better hop out of bed before those two bottomless pits consumed every morsel in the galley.

It was, however, easy to ignore the urge. The comfortable mattress and fresh air were fighting the good fight, the soft, morning-warm blankets adding their weight to the forces that opposed rising and shining. The vessel's gentle sway was like a mother's arms rocking her child to sleep.

What really sealed the deal was that the pillows still carried the easy fragrance of his wife's hair and skin. Last night had been a good night, worthy of replaying in his mind a few more times before pulling back the sheets and hitting the deck.

He was glad she came along – this time. Despite Nick and Diana's reassurances that this assignment was benign, images of Hunter being raised without his mother and father disturbed the Texan.

Yet, he understood her need to change what was surely a mundane routine. He knew his wife loved Hunter with every ounce of her being, but that didn't mean being a full-time mother in the post-apocalyptic world was an easy task. Beyond the physical dangers and overt threats, their current environment didn't embolden two-career families. From Bishop's way of thinking, his wife would have had a much better chance before the collapse of continuing her professional pursuits.

Communication was one of the biggest issues. Bishop could remember thinking about Hunter three times yesterday. Had his firstborn taken that first step yet? Or had he fallen in the attempt and bumped his noggin? Maybe that slight sniffle had developed into a cold or flu. Would Diana know what to do? Would their son's babysitter be up to the task?

Before modern society had dropped off a cliff, a phone call or text could reassure a worried parent. Diana would have posted news and pics on social media. Terri and Bishop could keep in touch in a dozen different ways. Communication was instantaneous and abundant. Not now.

Then there was state of medical care. Back in the good old days, Hunter might have had a live-in nanny or spent some time in a daycare center while Terri worked. In that age, if Hunter choked or fell or even had an allergic reaction, an ambulance could be called. There would be blood tests and labs and emergency rooms. Not now.

Yes, there was a doctor in Alpha, but no one could be sure what medicines and skills were at his disposal. It was a certainty that the tests he could order were limited. He definitely didn't have the internet and phone system to call in a specialist or consult with a teaching university.

Bishop trusted Nick and Diana more than anyone on earth except his wife. He knew both of them would treat Hunter as their own. Most times, those facts smoothed over the concerns of leaving their only child behind. Most ... but not always.

Now, however, Terri's lingering scent made Bishop appreciate having his partner along. Her eyes had twinkled like stars, looking up with love from that pillow last night. Her face had twisted in compassion and release on these sheets. They had passed from not being able to get close enough to each other into the warm afterglow of satiated lovers right here. It was enough to make a man consider missing breakfast.

"Wakie, wakie, eggs and bakie," Terri's cheerful voice rang from the cabin's threshold. "Well, eggs and toast anyway. Hannah didn't have any bacon."

She came to him with a kiss, lingering just a little longer than usual to admire her husband.

"What are you doing up so early?" he asked. "I figured you would sleep in without the Hunter alarm clock."

"Early?" she grinned. "The sun has been up for over an hour, Bishop. I did sleep in, but not as long as *some* people I know," she continued, poking him playfully in the chest.

Before he could defend himself, she lowered her voice and poured it on, "I'm worried about you, Bishop. Did I wear you out last night? Cause if I did, we may have material issues in our future. Last night was nothing compared to what I've got in store for you later, and if you're this tuckered after the warm-up, there's no way you'll survive the main course."

With the speed of a striking cobra, Bishop's arms came from under the blankets, effortlessly lifting her from the deck. Before Terri could even yelp in protest, she was pinned against

27

his chest. "I'll show you exhausted, young lady. We'll see who needs to sleep in after I've had my way with you."

She struggled, pushing against his grip with all her might, but it was hopeless. Bishop's arms were like two steel bands holding her close, his eyes were filled with pure adoration.

As usual, Terri had to resort to intellect to win the fight. "Your eggs are going to get cold. That, and I saw Butter pacing outside the galley. He might not be able to resist the aroma for long," she beamed, gently touching his lower lip with her finger.

"You little shit," Bishop whispered, releasing his grip.

"Don't pout," she reassured. "They'll be plenty of time for fun later. Besides, you've got to earn your pay today. The deputies will be here in an hour."

He started to reach for her again, mumbling something about an hour was plenty of time, but she scurried away with a giggle. "Get up, Mr. Lazy Bones. There's even an orange. Or there was five minutes ago."

Bishop wolfed down his morning meal, thanked the cook, and set about preparing his gear. He and the team were going to cross into Mexico today, and while no one knew what kind of reception they would receive, he was pretty sure it was going to be a boring day.

It was the typical SAINT mission, earning the acronym - Scout, Approach, INtroduce, and Transition.

While the transition stage was questionable in this case, Bishop knew Alpha was always looking for new trading partners and expanding what little was known of the areas outside of Texas. Other than that minor difference, they were going to handle the investigation professionally and err on the side of caution. The Texan was especially worried about the approach and introduction phases. Language and custom were going to be an issue. Old racial divides might also play a role. Any folks they encountered south of the border might not like armed gringos intruding into their territory.

It was with no small amount of pride that he inspected his team before loading into the deputy's car. No one expected much trouble today, yet his guys were acting like professionals. They knew the drill, embodied their roles, and had selected their kit accordingly.

Today's loadout wasn't intended for diplomatic relations, unless he counted gun barrel diplomacy as a legitimate option. Bishop noted that everyone was carrying the maximum amount of ammunition and the largest bug-out bags and medical kits available. They weren't going to make friends, no negotiations were slated, nor would there be waving of the Alliance flag. The agenda was simple. Get in, find out as much information as possible, and get out with all hands present and accounted for.

There were no flyers or propaganda sheets touting the benefits of joining the Alliance, nor was the SAINT team bearing gifts. There were times when such items were strategically important, but today the weight of those diplomatic tools had been replaced with bullets.

This was also intended to be a one-day mission, two at the worst. That meant the heavy packs worn by each member were not encumbered with sleeping apparatus or extra rations. In and out, fighting both ways if need be.

In reality, Grim had already inspected both of the younger men 10 minutes before Bishop's arrival. No one minded repeating the brief routine a second time. Leaving something behind … some forgotten detail or missing piece of equipment might endanger them all.

"Did you pack extra batteries for your optic?" Bishop asked Kevin.

"Yes, sir."

"Backup iron sights are zeroed?"

"Yes, sir. They're actually co-witnessed. Dad showed me how, sir."

And so it continued, everyone trying to make sure no preparation had been neglected, shortchanged, or overlooked. There weren't any corner drug stores or gun shops where they were going.

Bishop had just finished verifying the contents of Butter's load vest when Grim cleared his throat, trying to get the boss's attention. Before he could grasp what was happening, Terri's voice sounded from over the team leader's shoulder. "I got my rifle, a canteen, and a couple of extra magazines. Anything else I need?"

Bishop pivoted smartly, eyes flying wide as he realized his wife intended to join them. "Umm … err …. What are you doing?" he stuttered.

"I'm going to Mexico with the team," she announced with a matter-of-fact tone. "Why? Is there a problem with that?"

Hooking arms with his bride, Bishop pulled her out of earshot. In a low voice, he said, "Yes, there is a problem with that. We have no idea who or what we'll encounter over there. This isn't a diplomatic mission. We're going to see if we can find any evidence of who shot up the trucks or why they did it, not to negotiate a treaty or integrate a new town into the Alliance."

"I know that," she replied. "But I didn't come along on this trip to lay around the marina and work on my tan. Mr. McCarthy is proving to be a colossal asshole and will certainly make all sorts of trouble if he can. If I'm not in the loop front-to-back and top-to-bottom, I won't be able to handle him ... or Washington ... as well."

Bishop shook his head in frustration, "Terri, seriously, this isn't a good idea. We have no clue what, who, or how many hostile people might be waiting for us. SAINT teams are shot at more often than not. Today isn't a good day for you to go along and see what your husband does at the office."

"I've got my rifle," she countered, "and I've proven I know how to use it. Besides, after you and Nick pulled that little stunt with all your secret 'need to know' bullshit, you promised me there wouldn't be any more boys' club shenanigans."

Bishop wasn't buying the argument, "This has nothing to do with your being my wife or the mother of my child or a female. Those three men over there worked their asses off, training for months on how to function as an integrated team. We all know how the others are thinking without a word being exchanged. This assignment will be challenging enough with four of us, let alone a new member who hasn't been exposed to our methods and procedures."

"You said this wouldn't be an overly dangerous trip. You said you were going to try and avoid the locals. You told me not to worry."

"I always tell you not to worry."

"So you always lie to me?"

Bishop shook his head, unwilling to play verbal judo at the moment. "Why do you want to go so badly?"

"I want to learn. I want to serve the Alliance. I want to be with you. I promise, I'll do exactly what you tell me once we're in the field," she said, making an X motion across her chest. "Cross my heart and hope not to die. Besides, from the look of those trucks we saw yesterday, staying around here isn't exactly the safest place in the Alliance. Wouldn't I be safer with you and the guys?"

Bishop glanced back at his team, all three of them curious what the outcome was going to be ... all of them trying desperately not to appear nosey.

Terri then played her ace. "I speak pretty good Spanish."

"You don't speak Spanish!"

With a sultry pout of her lips and a look that would melt iron, Terri rasped, "Hola, buen hombre, quieres pasar un buen rato?"

Bishop didn't know what she had just rattled off, but he had a feeling now wasn't the time to request a translation. Sighing, he asked, "High school Spanish?"

"Two years in high school. Plus, my roommate at A&M was from Mexico. I can get by," she crowed.

The Texan's gaze went south in thought, his mind trying to find the winning point of logic or reasoning why Terri shouldn't go. Nothing came to him.

Shrugging, he capitulated, "Okay, go grab your pack, body armor, and as many magazines as you can carry."

"Body armor? I have to wear that hot, heavy vest?"

"Terri …" he scowled.

"Okay, okay. Give me a minute," she responded.

After she sped away, Grim approached with great caution. "I take it the missus is tagging along for our little stroll today."

Bishop didn't want to discuss it. Answering the question with merely a nod, he approached Butter and proclaimed, "Terri is joining us today. Your bodyguard duties have just been extended."

"Yes, sir," the operator responded anxiously. "Was she mean about it, sir?"

"You have no concept, son. No concept whatsoever."

Bishop asked the deputies to let the team unload almost a mile from the dam so that anyone who happened to be watching from the southern side wouldn't notice them deploy.

Grim took point, as usual. Next came Bishop, followed by Terri and Butter. Kevin, with his long-range rifle, brought up the rear.

If Bishop had been suspicious at all, they would have crossed before first light. As it were, Grim played it as safe as possible given the open terrain, staying off the roadway and hugging the water line.

It wasn't any big deal crossing into the foreign land. The landscape didn't change, nor did the vegetation. Other than a roadside sign that declared the speed limit in kilometers rather than miles per hour, the team didn't notice any difference. "Stay close to the water's edge, but give us some room to move if the locals aren't welcoming," Bishop had instructed Grim the night before as they studied a map.

The shoreline was mainly arid, with one rock-strewn gully after another. The undulations weren't canyons, but more than big ditches, and the going was slow. After two miles, Terri needed a break.

"Miss Terri's leg is cramping," Butter reported over the radio.

"Take 10 on the other side of that next ridge," Bishop ordered into his microphone.

When the team had found a good spot to take a breather, Bishop went with Kevin to set up a lookout. After identifying just the right overlook, he returned to check on his wife.

As he approached, the look on Terri's face indicated she was prepared for the "I told you so," speech, but it didn't come. "You okay?" he asked with genuine sincerity.

"Yes. I'm just out of shape. I'm not used to carrying this much gear. I guess I should have stayed back on the boat. I'm sorry."

"Don't worry about it. I agreed with your coming along. That means you're now part of the team, just like Grim or Butter. Any of us could be having a bad day. It happens. Drink lots of water, and if you want, I'll take some of your load."

"No," she said with a defiant scowl. "I can do it. I've got this."

"Suit yourself," he shrugged, moving off to relieve Kevin without another word.

It was actually 20 minutes before the Texan ordered everyone to move out, but no one protested the extra rest. Less than 300 meters later, Grim signaled he had contact. With a series of brisk hand motions, the point man indicated there were two people ahead; they carried no visible weapons, and they were near the shoreline.

After making sure everyone had gone to ground in a strategic spot, the Texan hustled forward to see for himself. Going prone next to Grim, Bishop adjusted his carbine's optic to study the locals.

"I imagine the people around this lake didn't suffer nearly as much malnutrition as those folks inland. For sure, they had better access to water and food," the Texan noted. He spied two boys, the oldest no more than 14 or 15 years old. Both had what appeared to be very expensive fishing poles, complete with shiny, new-looking bobbers drifting on the reservoir's surface.

"I have to say that equipment looks a little out of place," Bishop observed.

"I wonder if they're biting today," Grim whispered, suddenly mesmerized by the thought of getting a line wet himself.

Bishop, sensing his friend's distraction, decided to play along, "I don't see a stringer, but it could be in the water. Sounds like you are more interested in baiting a hook than walking point."

Grim retorted, "Well, it has been a while since I landed a big one, but it can wait. What's the call, boss?"

Bishop frowned, "Notice the fishing tackle? Those look just like the fancy, stainless steel reels we have on our rental boat. I wonder where those young men acquired such expensive equipment."

"You're not thinking those two are part of the crew that ambushed the convoy?"

Shrugging, Bishop said, "There's no way to know. Hell, you and I have both seen child warriors in several parts of the world. Why should our post-apocalyptic environment be any different than Africa or the Middle East? I want to have a chat with those fishermen, but I don't want to freak them out. Any ideas?"

"Terri?" Grim suggested with hesitation. "We can cover her approach. A woman wouldn't be as frightening."

Bishop's first flash was to reject the idea, his mind justifying that it was too risky for Terri to make contact with the unknowns. Then honesty reared its unwelcome head, the Texan realizing that his initial reaction had more to do with his wife being right about joining the team than there being any true danger. Finally, professionalism won out. They had a job to do, and Terri was the best tool.

"I want you, Butter, and Kevin on a three-vector spread covering her approach from every possible angle. Do it," he barked, clearly still uncomfortable with exposing his wife.

"We're on it," Grim answered without further comment, immediately moving to execute Bishop's order.

Bishop gave his people plenty of time to get into position before explaining to his wife the exact route she was to take and how it was all going to go down. "If either of them pulls a weapon, you go prone and stay that way – there will be a wall of lead flying over your head. If they run, let them go. If they appear hostile in any way, shape, or form, hurry like hell back the exact path you took in. I'll be within 50 yards of you at all times. Got it?"

"You're really uptight about this, aren't you?"

"Yes, I am … but we would take the same precautions no matter who was encountering strangers."

She seemed to accept the explanation, and without another word, handed Bishop her rifle and headed for the two boys. "Terri," Bishop whispered, "I love you."

Stopping, she pivoted and returned to him. "Am I allowed to kiss the team leader?"

"Only you."

"I'm glad to hear that," she giggled and then gave him a peck on the cheek. "See you in a bit."

33

"Do you have your pistol?"

"Of course," she smirked as she made her way through the rocks.

"See you in a bit."

As Terri wove her way toward the shoreline, she found it difficult not to look for the guys. Not once did she hear Bishop, see Grim, or detect any of the other SAINT members. It was discomforting in a way.

Despite all of her bravado, Terri was nervous about the encounter. The last 100 steps passed quickly as she practiced her Spanish greeting over and over again. The distance closed, and before she knew it, she was standing 20 feet behind the two boys on a slight rise.

"Hello, there," she called out in the foreign tongue. "Are the fish biting?"

Both of the youth were startled by the sound of her voice, panic flashing in their eyes. For a moment, Terri was sure they were going to run.

"Don't be afraid," she cooed softly. "I'm not going to hurt you."

"What do you want?" asked the oldest.

"Just to talk. I was passing by, enjoying the serene water and wildflowers, and spotted you fishing. I thought I would come over and say hello."

The two kids exchanged a look that could only be described as "disbelieving." The older of the pair then scanned the area behind the strange woman who had magically appeared. He didn't see any threat.

"So ... are the fish biting?" she asked again, trying to settle the obviously jittery kids.

"We've caught a couple of little ones," the younger of the two reported.

"Yeah? What kind?"

"They are sunfish," answered the older, still-skeptical boy. "Where did you come from? You're a gringo, right?"

"Yes, I roamed over this way from Texas. I've never been to Mexico before."

Again, the older boy surveyed the area around the woman from Texas, a look of skepticism evident in his expression. "By yourself?"

Terri didn't want to lie but knew the truth would cause both of them to flee. "Why do you ask that? Is it dangerous around here? I haven't seen anybody else for hours."

"Yes, Señorita, it is very dangerous here. You should go back to Tejas – right now," warned one of the youth.

34

"You didn't seem to be very worried about things before I wandered over here. Why is it dangerous for me and not for you?"

It was clear from both of their faces that Terri was being naive or stupid, or perhaps both. "There are bad men that come through here all the time," the younger stated. "They won't bother us because we're too small.... But you are older ... and pretty ... and a girl."

The larger lad's eyes opened wide, almost as if he expected mentioning the devil would summon the demons. "Shut up," he barked at his friend. "You talk too much."

Terri decided to change the subject, letting out a low wolf whistle. "Ni-i-ice fishing poles. Where did you get those?" she asked, nodding at the high-end equipment with her head.

"Our uncle gave them to us," stated the older boy with pride.

"Wow, your uncle must like both of you very much. Those look like very expensive reels."

"My mom thinks he got them off the ghost boat," the little one stated.

"Ghost boat?"

The older boy shrugged, "That's what the people in our village call it. There was a big boat stuck on the shore this morning. There weren't any people onboard, and everyone started calling it a ghost boat."

"Where is this boat?" Terri inquired. "One of my friends from Texas is missing her boat."

The little one pointed to the south. "It's still there. Keep walking that direction, and you'll see it. But watch out for the bad men. They take older people like you, and we never see them again."

Trying to look frightened, Terri lowered her voice to a near whisper, "Where do they take them?"

"We have to go," snapped the older fisherman. "Come on," he continued, grabbing his smaller friend by the arm. "We should go home – right now."

"Wait," Terri implored, trying to get them to stay and talk. "Please, don't leave!"

Her pleading didn't do any good. Grabbing their fish and tackle, the two kids scampered south, both of them checking over their shoulders to make sure Terri wasn't going to follow.

Helpless, she stood and watched until they had disappeared a few minutes later. She started to turn and jumped with fright when she nearly bumped into her husband.

"You scared the shit out of me!" she inhaled.

35

"I've been standing here since they left," he shrugged, handing back her rifle. "What did you learn?"

It took Terri two minutes to repeat the conversation, her frustration at not uncovering more information obvious in her tone.

"It's looking more and more like Hannah's boat was used in the ambush," the Texan stated. He then turned and began waving in the rest of the team.

As each of the remaining men rose from their hides, Terri was stunned at how close they all were. "How in the hell did you manage to...," she began, but then dropped the question. "What now?"

"I want to look at that boat," Bishop replied. "But first, let's grab some quick chow before we head out."

Each of the SAINT members took turns at sentry duty while the others gulped down a few bites. Terri welcomed the chance to gather her second wind.

With a nod from the team's leader, Grim was moving out, soon followed by the rest of guys. It was less than 15 minutes later when the point man radioed that he was looking at the houseboat.

"Seems empty, boss," Grim reported. "I see zero activity either onboard or in the vicinity."

"Grim, Butter, form up and give me a 300-meter sweep all around," Bishop ordered. "Let's make sure somebody's not set a mousetrap using a big hunk of tempting boat-cheese. Kevin, find the high ground and give them some cover."

Bishop then turned to his wife and said, "Read between the lines for me. What was your impression of the two fishermen?"

She had to ponder the question before answering. "They were scared. That's for sure."

"Did they steal the fishing equipment?"

"No. Despite the language difference, I'm pretty sure they did not."

"Movement!" came Kevin's excited voice over the radio. "I have 8-10 unknowns, armed, bearing 170 degrees from my position. They are headed toward Bishop."

"Shit!" Bishop barked at his wife. "Move ... that way.... Now!"

Terri took a moment to react, quickly scanning the direction her husband was pointing. A second later, they were hustling straight east, away from the shoreline and toward the area where she sensed Grim and Butter had been scouting.

"Give me more, Kevin," Bishop broadcast as he followed Terri.

"Variety of ages and weapons," Kevin's now-calm voice expounded. "One of the two boys who was fishing is with them. Irregular formation. They're not trying to stalk or hide whatsoever. My call, sir, is that they're more frightened than aggressive."

Bishop didn't respond for a moment, his mind creating a map of everyone's position and direction of movement. "Grim, prepare to flank them, but do not ... repeat ... do not engage unless they hit us first."

"Roger that," came the ex-contractor's acknowledgement.

The couple approached a drainage gully that suited Bishop. "This will do," he motioned Terri to move hastily behind two of the larger rocks scattered throughout the area. "Take cover right there. Get that weapon loaded and charged."

Bishop watched as his wife went prone behind the two rocks. With a practiced motion, she pulled the M4's charging handle to chamber a round and then tilted the carbine to make sure the weapon had functioned properly. A flash of pride pulsed through the Texan's core. She would fight like hell if necessary, and any man would be a fool not to respect her capabilities.

"Okay. Ready. Are we going to have to kill the boy's uncle?" she asked, glancing up as a shadow of sadness passed behind her eyes.

Bishop frowned, "I sure as hell hope not." Then with his eyes boring in the direction of the locals, the Texan keyed his mic, "Update, Kevin."

"They appear to be heading toward the spot where Terri spoke to the boys. No change in posture."

"Are we sure they're alone?" Bishop asked.

Kevin's voice almost sounded like the question was insulting, "I've performed two detailed sweeps, sir. No other contacts."

Bishop took a knee beside his wife, his eyes still scanning in the direction of the threat. "So your two friends ran back to their little town and told everyone that a woman from Texas was down by the lake, asking questions about the ghost boat. Are the pitchforks and torches to shoo you away, protect you, or kill you?"

Before she could speculate, Kevin's nervous voice sounded over the airwaves, "Movement! Pickup truck, two in the cab, two in the bed. Armed. Going slow. 120 degrees, 1,100 meters, my position. Looks like they're heading for the first group."

"Shit!" Bishop snapped, adding yet another moving piece to his mental chessboard. His first thought was that someone was trying to spring another ambush, this time with his team in the kill zone. Problem was no one on either side was in the right position to pull off such a maneuver.

37

"Reinforcements?" Terri asked, now frowning in concern.

"Unknown," Bishop answered honestly. "One thing for certain is that this little piece of luxury real estate has suddenly gotten very popular. Me, I'm a country boy and like wide-open spaces. There are too many damn people around here. I think we should egress our asses right back across the river … maybe come back during the offseason."

"Group one has seen group two's dust cloud," came Kevin's voice. "Looks like group one is preparing an ambush."

Bishop gave his wife a look that said, "What the hell?" and then pressed his radio's button, "Grim, you and Butter well out of the way?"

"Yes, sir. We're in a good spot."

Kevin again, "Group two appears to be looking for something, sir. The two men in the bed have binoculars and keep scanning the desert. They also have AKs or SKS weapons."

"The bad guys my little friends were talking about?" Terri offered.

"We need to see this for ourselves. Let's move forward to Kevin's perch," Bishop decided.

The couple advanced with caution, Bishop telling his wife that even with Kevin's super-sharp eye, it was possible that someone had entered the area without their knowledge. A few minutes later, they joined the team's long-distance shooter.

Kevin knew what Bishop wanted without a word, handing over his sniper rifle with its massive scope. Not wasting a second, the Texan began scanning the terrain.

It was easy to find the small rooster tail of dust produced by the slow-moving pickup's wheels. Just as Kevin had reported, there were two men in the bed with large optics, scanning the surrounding desert as if they were looking for game or trespassers or some other target. Whoever was driving clearly wasn't in a hurry, the fairly new model Dodge rolling along as if it were passing through a school zone.

Finding the angler's friends was far more difficult, but eventually, Bishop zeroed in on the larger party of locals. Again, just as Kevin had reported, they had gone to ground on both sides of what appeared to be a path or trail, their faces and weapons facing toward the approaching pickup.

"They were pretty freaked out when they saw the dust cloud," Kevin said, trying to anticipate his boss's questions. "There were a lot of waving arms, and everyone was rushing around for a minute."

"So they're scared of the men in the truck?" Terri asked.

"I don't think the fisherman's group can see the truck just yet," Bishop answered. "I think they saw the dust trail and aren't taking any chances. We would do the same thing."

The SAINT team maintained their defensive position, watching from afar as the two local forces barely avoided a collision. It soon became obvious that the men in the truck were heading for the boat.

"They'll strip everything of value off Hannah's party barge in a matter of minutes," Grim broadcast, watching as the men from the pickup climbed aboard the abandoned boat. "Are we going to stop them?"

Bishop peered at his wife and stated, "That's not why we're here. That's not our job."

"She is a citizen of the Alliance," Terri countered. "The boat is her property."

The Texan didn't like it. "So? We'll tell Sheriff Watts where it's located when we get back. Technically, we are an invading force, leaning way over the edge without a safety net. I don't want to get my team shot up over some damn boat."

"Didn't you and Nick just *invade* Oklahoma not long ago?" she reasoned.

"That was different."

"How so?"

"We were after known ... we went to ... aww ... damn it!" Bishop looked at Kevin, the team leader's face colored with his obvious frustration. "Let's form up at Grim and Butter's location. Let them know we're all coming in."

"Roger that, sir."

A few minutes later, the SAINT team had gathered less than 50 yards from the pickup parked near the bow of Hannah's houseboat.

Bishop detected one of the four locals had remained next to the truck while the other three scouted the beached vessel. "Butter, take out the sentry next to the truck. Don't kill him, but don't let him warn the others."

"Can I give him a headache, sir?"

"If necessary. I'm sure your rifle barrel against his ear will do the job. It not, convince him with a bit more enthusiasm."

The big man turned to move but then froze when a voice called from the boat back to the pickup. The words were in Spanish.

"What's he saying?" Bishop asked his wife.

Terri started a running commentary, translating the words in a whisper. "This is how they did it!" shouted the man on the boat.

"There are boot marks all over the deck. This is how those bastards hit the convoy and got around our people."

The man beside the pickup rubbed his chin, obviously deep in thought. Finally, he shouted back, "Torch it," and then calmly moved for the cab.

"Torch it? Are you sure?" Bishop asked his wife.

Terri nodded with enthusiasm. "Yes."

"Butter, I've got the driver. You stay here with Terri."

"Yes, sir," the junior team member replied, but Bishop was already moving.

With the driver behind the wheel, Bishop's job was more difficult. Despite every vehicle having a blind spot in its mirror system, it was nearly impossible to tell exactly where that opportune avenue of approach was located.

Fortunately for the SAINT team, the vehicle hadn't been parked in a spot selected for its defensive attributes. There was a significant growth of mesquite and scrub elm less than 10 feet from the driver's door. Bishop was soon behind that patch of shrubbery, keeping the head-high vegetation between him and the truck's occupant during the approach.

The last bit of open space, he decided after a chest full of air, was best crossed with a full head of steam.

Pulling down his balaclava and snapping the carbine to his shoulder, Bishop unsafed the weapon and moved toward the pickup at an extremely brisk walk. The occupant never saw him coming, the driver's attention focused on his comrades and the boat.

That quickly changed when Bishop's rifle barrel pressed against the man's temple. "Did I just hear you order those men to torch my boat?" the Texan growled.

The man jerked, but not too much, his hand automatically reaching for the pistol lying in the nearby seat. He stopped the movement just as Bishop's finger tightened on the trigger. "Don't do it, my friend. You'll never make it."

"No hablo English, Señor," the driver mumbled.

Bishop didn't believe him. "That's too bad, because if I see smoke coming from my boat, I'm going to scatter your brains all over the inside of this nice Dodge truck."

The man inhaled and then shouted a string of orders in Spanish. Grim's voice sounded in Bishop's ear, "Terri says he told his men to stop and come to the front of the boat."

"I want you and Butter up here with me. Kevin and Terri are to stay back and cover us," Bishop ordered in a whisper.

The Texan then pushed the barrel of his weapon tighter against his prisoner's head, "Don't be stupid and you'll live another day. Test me and you will die. Clear?"

"Yes, Señor. Are you one of the vigilantes? Are your men the ones who killed the truckers?"

The question caused a deep frown to furrow Bishop's face. Surely, the man pinned by his blaster was one of the culprits? The Texan decided the guy was already cooking up an alibi.

The three men on the boat appeared just then, moving toward the bow cautiously, their AK47 battle rifles up and ready. Bishop was about to give his hostage instructions concerning those weapons when first one and then an entire salvo of shots rang out.

Bishop knew in an instant that the angler's friends had arrived.

One of the boatmen fell in withering agony as incoming rounds pinged and slapped the vessel's fiberglass hull and steel railings.

More lead slammed into the pickup, the Texan diving for cover as the Dodge's sheet metal and glass absorbed a wave of high-velocity punishment.

Bishop rolled hard, tiny eruptions of Mexican soil chasing him as he scrambled for the lowest spot he could see.

Now the AKs from the boat were singing their song, the return fire drawing the attention of new arrivals, prompting others to duck for cover. Sensing a lull, the Texan gathered himself for a mad dash back to the safety of his team. He had just reached a knee when his former hostage hit the ground beside the truck in a tangled heap. Blood poured from the man's shoulder, his face cringing in pain.

For half a second, Bishop didn't care. He was convinced the wounded man was a murdering son-of-a-bitch and wasn't worth risking a hangnail, let alone getting shot.

Then a flash of memory rolled through the Texan's mind. He remembered the exchange between the wounded man and his men on the boat. "This is how those bastards hit the convoy...."

Frustrated, wanting badly to go home, and desperate to get Terri out of what now had become an active combat zone, Bishop made up his mind to get some answers and *then* get the hell out of Dodge.

With three quick steps, he grabbed the wounded guy's good arm and pulled the bleeding fellow to his feet. "Come on," Bishop barked. "This way."

A blizzard of lead was flying between Hannah's boat and the local villagers. While outnumbered three to one, the water-borne shooters were far better armed.

All of this passed through the background of Bishop's consciousness as he pulled, pushed, and helped his wounded hostage back toward friendly lines. Halfway there, the man's legs gave out, his complexion as gray as the local sands. "You're going into shock from blood loss," the Texan informed his prisoner.

Doing a quick check of the man's soaked shirt and shattered shoulder, Bishop grumbled, "Fuck! Am I going to have to carry your big, smelly ass?"

There wasn't any response. With a deep sigh, the Texan swung his carbine around to his back and hissed, "I sure hope you are worth the effort."

Growing angrier by the second, Bishop took a deep breath, bending in preparation to heft the sizeable bandito onto his shoulder. The sound of a boot scraping across the soil caused the Texan to pause.

Butter was there, Grim right beside him. As the senior SAINT member covered their egress, Butter scooped up the prisoner like he was a small child and then glanced at his leader. "You okay, Boss?"

Before Bishop could answer, a bullet cracked by the team's heads, their movements evidently drawing unwanted attention.

"Yeah. I'm good. Let's go!" Bishop responded, hustling for cover.

Two minutes later, the panting trio, along with their prisoner, arrived to find a diligent, worried, Terri with Kevin. Her smile made it was clear the missus was happy to see her husband unscathed.

"Talk to him," Bishop said to his wife. "Find out what in the hell is going on around here. Butter, see if you can slow down his bleeding long enough for us to get some Intel."

Terri studied the stranger for a moment as Butter tore open the blood-soaked shirt.

"Why are the villagers shooting at you?" her first question fired.

"They do not like us, pretty lady. Are you an angel? Have I already passed to the other side?"

"And why don't they like you?"

The wounded fellow actually tried a shrug but regretted it. Sucking a chest full of air, he winced from the pain. "Why? I'm not sure. I don't think they like any strangers."

"Why did you attack the convoy of trucks?" Terri pressed.

For the first time, the fellow on the ground seemed to be taking her seriously, his eyes boring into Terri with an intense focus. "We did not shoot up the trucks! They were our customers. We sold them the food."

Terri kept her expression neutral, reacting with no more than a tilt of her head. "So did the villagers ambush the trucks?" she asked, nodding in the direction of the distant gunfire.

Again, his movement caused the stranger a gasp of pain. "No," he finally managed as Butter's hands moved quickly trying to stem the flow of blood pouring from the wound. "They are not capable of such a thing," he continued with a dismissive tone.

Terri wasn't sure why, but she believed him. "Then who murdered those men on the dam?"

Before he could answer, Kevin's voice sounded with urgency, "Sir! I've got movement ... a third party ... at least 20 men. It looks like the village is sending reinforcements."

Bishop's head snapped around, his gaze moving in the direction where Kevin's sniper rifle pointed. Again, the Texan took control of the big optic, scanning a larger group of very old and very young men, all carrying an assortment of ragtag weapons. It reminded him of pictures of the German Army toward the end of WWII when all of that nation's prime manpower had been consumed – the village was scraping the bottom of the barrel. It didn't matter, however. A rusty shotgun was as deadly as a well-oiled blaster. "Shit, we're going to get caught in the middle."

The team's leader then turned to watch Butter work. "Can he be moved?"

The big man didn't speak, instead flashing a look that said, "No. He's not going to make it much longer anyway."

Terri caught it as well, moving closer to the dying man's face and demanding his attention. "So who attacked the truckers?"

"Qu ... Quay," sounded a weak gasp.

"Who?" Terri asked.

There wasn't any answer. The light had left the man's eyes.

"He's gone," Butter announced, shaking his head and then moving to repack his medical gear.

"Damn it," Terri hissed. "Who are the Quays?"

"Vigilantes," Bishop responded, his eyes scanning the perimeter. "That's what one of the guys on the boat said."

"I know that," Terri replied. "But *who* are they? Where are they?"

Her husband didn't answer, his head pivoting between the gunfight at the boat and the approaching men from the village. "We have to move."

"No shit," Grim snapped. "This place is getting crowded. Which way, boss?"

Bishop was about to announce his decision when the distant gunfire abruptly stopped. Every Alliance ear focused toward the shore, waiting and hoping for another round to ignite the next phase of the battle. Nothing but the light morning breeze reached their ears.

Grim and Bishop exchanged knowing looks. "This ain't good," the ex-contractor warned.

"No kidding," the Texan concurred.

"What?" Terri asked, not understanding.

"One side or the other has won," her husband explained. "If it was our dead friend's compadres, they're going to come looking for him. If his enemies claimed victory, they're going to come looking for him. Either way, we're in the wrong place at a very bad time."

"East," Bishop then announced. "Grim, take point. Same formation we used on the way in. We'll go east for a mile or two and then cut north for Texas."

"Roger that," Grim said, hefting his pack and weapon. "Give me five minutes' head start. I assume you want to cover some ground until we're clear of the local festivities."

Bishop nodded, "Yup. Get us out of here. Speed is life right now."

Without another word, Grim moved off.

Only a few minutes had passed before the veteran's voice sounded on the radio. "Too late, Bishop. They've already cut us off. We can't go east unless you want to fight your way through."

"Damn it! I was afraid of that," the Texan hissed into his mic. "Get back here."

"What's going on?" Terri questioned, her husband's expression causing even more concern.

"We can't go west because of the reservoir," Bishop pointed. "We can't go north because of the fisherman's uncle and his friends. It's a bad idea to head south and deeper into Mexico. Now the new group of villagers has us cut off. We're surrounded … in a way."

Grim reappeared, running at a slow jog. "There are at least 20 of them, spread out in a picket line and heading our direction. We've got three, maybe four minutes before they spot us."

Nodding his understanding, Bishop turned back toward the north and then slowly scanned the lake area. "Hope somebody brought sunscreen, 'cause we are heading out for a boat ride."

"Huh?" Grim questioned.

"Let's take Hannah back her boat ... or at least what's left of it. The engines should be okay – right?"

Grim had to think about that one for a bit, finally nodding his head. "I suppose. But what about the villagers? I don't think they're just going to let us sail away into the sunset."

"Maybe, maybe not. If anybody has a better idea, I'm all ears," Bishop countered.

"What are you doing, Bishop? We're not going to kill those people, are we?" Terri asked.

"No. We'll see if we can sneak past them, and if not, Kevin will slow them down long enough so we can get by," Bishop said, then added, "at least that's the plan."

Just then, an excited voice sounded behind the SAINT team, a quick burst of Spanish announcing the arrival of the larger group.

"Time to move!" Bishop barked, waving everyone toward the lake.

Hustling ahead, Grim took his standard position at point. He was soon followed by the short column of Alliance personnel.

They passed through a series of drainage gullies, large ditches cut by runoff pulled toward the reservoir. "Let's hope we can stay out of their sights until we reach the boat...."

His words were cut off by the whiz and crack of two bullets snapping overhead, immediately followed by a series of excited, shouting men.

Diving for cover, the team from Texas crawled and scurried to the nearest cover, weapons coming into play as everyone searched for a target.

Bishop almost shot Grim as he came flying over a low crest, a string of bullets chasing the ex-contractor as he hit the ground sliding like a baseball player trying to steal a base.

"Fuck!" Grim snarled, rolling back to face the enemy and wiping a thick coating of Mexican soil from his face. "We ran right into them."

"So I see," Bishop responded, ducking as someone up the draw managed a close shot. "Nice job picking the route, old buddy."

After spitting a mouthful of grit, Grim threw a scowl at his friend, "What? What the hell do you mean, 'nice job?' It sure as shit wasn't my idea to try and hijack the boat."

Before Bishop could return the banter, the incoming fire increased in tempo, pushing the Alliance members lower into the sandy earth. Butter, watching their rear, made things worse.

"They're coming up behind us, sir. The gunshots are guiding them in."

Bishop locked eyes with his wife, sending an unspoken message – we're in trouble here. Serious trouble. Instead of vocalizing the obvious, he said, "I didn't want this. You know I tried to avoid it – right?"

She nodded.

The pain was obvious in Bishop's eyes. Regret. The look of a man who was about to do something evil and was already asking for forgiveness.

Terri understood immediately. The nightmares. The memories that haunted her husband every night. Yet, like so many times before, he had no choice.

Bishop got down to business. "Kevin, push them back and keep them down. Try to scare them for the first few shots … chase them away. Terri, you and Butter hold off the guys on our ass. Keep them back. Grim and I are going to flank the gentlemen to our front. Remember, people, we only want to break through, not be the cause of the second massacre this week. Questions?"

There were none.

Terri was rolling to join the big kid while Kevin found good support for his rifle. Grim looked at Bishop and said, "Right or left?"

"Left … south … they'll be expecting us to try and go north."

With the exchange of a simple nod, the two SAINT men pushed off just as Kevin's rifle roared its first shot.

Bishop and Grim moved quickly, both men instinctively using their ears to track the escalating firefight behind while using their eyes to scan for trouble ahead.

Crawling up rises and sliding down into trenches, the duo worked in perfect unison, one always covering the other's movements and ready to engage. Never were both exposed, seldom were both moving at the same moment.

Behind them, Bishop tracked Terri and Butter's rate of fire. He knew if either side of the pincher were going to overrun his team, it would be the larger group.

For a split second, the Texan was again filled with pride. He knew that even the best-trained soldiers would find it difficult to control their rate of fire when finding themselves in such a tight spot. His wife and the kid were in the fight, but their shots were regulated, disciplined, and hopefully selected with care. There was no rhythm of panic, no hailstorm of wasted ammunition.

Poking his head above the next rise, Bishop spotted the first villager. Actually, it was the dust cloud kicked up by the man shooting at his team that gave away the Mexican's position.

Waving Grim back to the lower ground, the Texan studied the terrain ahead, looking to ensure that they had indeed managed to find the end of their foe's line.

There are about 10 of them, he thought. *They're not disciplined soldiers. They'll bunch up. Safety in numbers. Trouble likes company.*

The calculation of how much territory the approaching force would cover took Bishop only a second. There was a reasonably good chance he and Grim had managed to flank their opponents.

After flashing the older man a quick series of hand signals, the duo backed slowly away and then rushed off at an angle that would bring them into the group of attackers at a right angle.

Both of the Alliance men knew that in combat, it is difficult enough to maintain an alert, concentrated diligence to one's front. When the lead is flying, all of a fighter's senses are primed and focused in the known direction of the enemy. Are they counterattacking? Are they retreating? Where is my next target? Am I already in somebody's sights?

This was the reason why flanking maneuvers were one of the most devastating of all military tactics.

When faced with an enemy on two fronts, the human tendency for flight gains momentum over any desire to fight. Now death is coming from two directions. There are twice as many variables to process.

For the vast majority, having a foe at your front while being attacked from the side was overwhelming. Generals and great leaders called the results "being rolled," or "rolling up the enemy's line."

Less than two minutes had passed before Bishop and Grim were sure they'd found the right spot to hit the villagers from the side.

"Freak their shit," Bishop whispered. "We want them to run, not die."

It was clear that Grim didn't like firing warning shots, but nodded his understanding.

In unison, the two Alliance shooters rose from their trench, Bishop's carbine sending a stream of blistering fire into the dirt around the local.

The man reacted a little faster than either man from Texas anticipated, pausing only a second before rolling to his side and snap-firing a couple of return shots. Then, much to Bishop's relief, he scrambled upright and ran.

Bishop and Grim slammed into the villagers' line, pushing back one, then two, and finally three of the men who were firing at their friends.

47

Kevin's big rifle had already baffled and confused the locals, one of his heavy bullets seeming to impact every time they had tried to advance. Now, with intense fire coming from the south, absolute bedlam swept through their ranks.

Bishop and Grim's fire was coordinated, accurate, and intentionally non-lethal. Yet, from the villagers' perspective, it seemed as though an entire infantry platoon was hitting them from the south.

As the fourth escaping local reached a full run, Bishop keyed his microphone. "Make for the boat! Now! We've opened the route, but they may regroup quickly. Go! Go! Go!"

The two Alliance men found good positions and set up to provide a blocking force until the team passed them by on the way to Hannah's boat.

It was only seconds before Bishop could hear a decline in Butter and Terri's rate of fire. Less than a minute passed before the Texan saw his wife's hair flying in the wind, and she scurried down the gully. There was no time for words.

Looking at Grim, Bishop ordered, "Go with them. Get that damn boat running and let Butter and Kevin keep them at bay. I'll hang back and be the rear guard just in case our friends get frisky."

Grim didn't like it and started to protest. Bishop's expression, however, made it clear any debate was a fruitless waste of precious time.

Watching Grim rise and rush off to join the rest of the team, Bishop returned to the business of scanning for any locals whose bravery managed to override their common sense.

He didn't have to wait long.

The large group of reinforcements evidently interpreted the Alliance team's all-out rush for the boat as a retreat. Emboldened by seeing their foes pick up and run, they decided to pursue with all haste.

Bishop was surprised when at least 10 individuals rushed the gulley, hot on the heels of his fleeing team members.

The hunters were just as shocked when the Texan's carbine opened fire.

Bodies were scrambling, diving, and bounding in all directions as Bishop's rounds raised a wall of sand and grit to their front.

One man went down, howling in pain as he ran directly into Bishop's line of fire. Another, older assaulter twisted his ankle, howling in agony as he fell. All the while, the Texan was backing away, his weapon spitting bullets to buy time for his friends.

It took the villagers almost two minutes to regroup. Perhaps it was anger at one of their own going down or pride and honor overriding any sense of self-preservation.

This time, they advanced with caution, heads poking over rocks, weapons up and ready. They moved with short, quick jumps, scrambling from rock to rock, cover to cover.

Bishop, however, was no longer there.

Hearing their comrades take up the fight encouraged the locals who had been rolled up by the Alliance team's flanking maneuver. They stopped running and turned, rushing back to join the fray. Now Bishop was about to receive a dose of his own medicine – fighting in two directions at the same time.

"We're on the boat," Grim's welcome report crackled over the radio. "Get your ass back here, boss."

"On my way," Bishop breathlessly responded.

In the distance, Bishop heard the big vessel's engines thunder to life, the sound generating a wave of relief through his core. Terri and his men were safe. Any thoughts of providing a rear guard vacated his mind. In a flash, his boots were pounding for the shore.

Reaching the flat stretch of sand next to the reservoir, the Texan was surprised to see Butter and Kevin still in the water while Grim and his wife watched from the bridge.

The houseboat's engine roared, water boiling to the surface from the vessel's stern.

It took Bishop a few steps to realize the boat was aground – stuck in the mud at the lake's edge. As his boot splashed into the shallow water, he watched as Butter and Kevin put their backs into the massive hull, straining to push her out into deeper water while Grim gunned the engines for all they were worth.

The boat didn't budge.

A few seconds later, Bishop joined his men, muscles straining with gritted teeth as he threw his weight into the struggle to free their ride home.

A bullet propelled a geyser of water skyward beside Kevin's leg, another forcing shards of fiberglass into Bishop's cheek as the pursuers caught up.

Terri proved her gumption yet again, grabbing her rifle and returning fire in order to buy them time. Again and again, her weapon gave the chasing villagers something to think about.

She heard Grim's yell before she actually felt the boat move, for a moment thinking the old timer had taken a bullet. It quickly dawned, however, that he was shouting in celebration as the houseboat lurched backward, free from the mire.

Dropping her rifle, Terri rushed for the steps leading down to the deck. She was there when Kevin came splashing around the hull, extending a hand for help climbing aboard.

Next came Butter, the big kid grinning as his boot found the bottom rung of the swim ladder.

For a moment, Terri's heart stopped when Bishop didn't appear. Grim had stopped applying power, but the huge vessel's momentum was now forcing it away from the shore. Where was Bishop?

More bullets now peppered the water, a few cracking into the boat with heavy thumps and whacks. Still no Bishop.

She was turning to scream for help when a small wave of water rolled from the surface, drenching her above the waist. Behind the mini-tsunami were her husband's smiling face and cupped hands.

After pulling him aboard and finding no wounds, a fleeting sense of anger overrode her relief. "What was that all about, big boy? I am worried sick about you and you spout out of the water and splash me like we had just been playing 'Marco Polo' in the city pool?"

The SAINT team leader flashed her a boyish grin and replied, "I always thought you'd look hot as hell in a wet T-shirt. Now seemed like as good a time as any to test that theory."

Chapter 4

The nightmare tormented her.

She was on the verandah, feet gently pushing to keep the old swing in motion. It wasn't a conscious effort, more of a habit she'd developed since she had been old enough to climb onto the faded, white slats of painted pine and grip the lengths of chain that suspended the prized perch. Her toes barely touched the ground, such was her youth.

Air conditioning was unheard of at the time in Central Mexico. The sway of the porch swing was often the only place where a little girl could feel the cooling brush of air against her cheek. It was a refuge of sorts, providing sanctuary no matter how suffocating the blanket of hot, thick air inside the hacienda.

The view from the swing was inspiring.

Rolling green hills of neatly planted rows stood and fell for as far as the eye could see, creating a patchwork of emerald, jade, and mantis.

From a very early age, she had understood that the colors represented security, wealth, and privilege. Avocados, limes, peppers, and maize created the hues, all of which would soon morph into a more profitable shade of green – money.

People in brightly dyed shirts and wide-brimmed, white straw hats shared the countryside. Their tiny, ant-sized bodies moving here and there, sometimes harvesting, sometimes planting, always engaged in the chores demanded by her father's agricultural empire.

Little Bella Dona watched it all, rocking back and forth, enjoying the breeze against her skin. The landscape felt well-worn and comfortable, a scene relatively unchanged for almost a hundred years.

The tranquil vision of her dream blurred momentarily, the passage of time reaffirmed by her feet now easily reaching the worn planks of the porch. She was older now, a teen who was beginning to understand more of the world.

A man joined her on the verandah, his uniform resplendent with patches and medals awarded for military achievements. Her brother ... off to yet another posting. Despite Mexico being at peace with the world, a war raged internally. Bella didn't understand violence, couldn't grasp the existence of the cartels that flourished outside the protective bubble of her plantation world. Her father forbade all discussion of the topic. Dialog on that subject in her presence would have drawn a harsh reprimand.

Again, the crisp image blurred. When it cleared, she was a young woman contemplating the world before her while unwinding in the rhythm of the swing.

The workers were closer now, gathered around the big house with heads low, humble hands clasped in remorse. There was a spotless hearse at the head of the massive, circular driveway, the courtyard overflowing with family and friends garbed in black and dabbing misty eyes with brilliant white handkerchiefs. Muted sounds of sobbing and that special hush of voices trying to show respect drifted on the soft breeze. Her father's funeral. The passing of the plantation to yet another generation.

As always, Bella Dona's nocturnal visions began rushing at an ever increasing pace. Now, the sage hills were cast in a different light. Gone was the innocent beholding of a child's mind. In its stead responsibility, fiscal concerns, and the keen eye of a manager. Were the limes getting enough moisture? Was that a brown patch in the avocado field?

The dream-people looked at her differently now. There was a smidge of fear in their eyes. The hint of respect. A pinch of trepidation. She was authority. The one in charge. And she liked it. The air, however, still felt cool on her cheeks as the swing swayed back and forth.

Then a darkness appeared on the horizon. It was far more daunting than any storm.

Rain was always welcome. It cooled the air, nourished the soil, and turned the hills green. But this was something more … foreboding … evil … massive.

Bella Dona knew what was coming but was powerless to stop it. The horrific images of her sleep were as inevitable as the rising sun. Coursing faster and faster, they were streaming by now. Harsh. Loud. The dream was changing into a nightmare, and she was helpless to do anything but watch and endure.

Next, thunder roared, followed by her brother's voice shrieking in a frantic pitch. She knew that no storm clouds were responsible for the rumblings, fully understood that her sibling's cries were of life and death. A battle was raging. Tanks, cannon, artillery, and bombs made the ground shake under the porch. Men screamed, prayed, and withered in pain. They were dying by the scores, their throats filled with agony, competing with the concussion of explosions and walls of fire and hot metal.

The precious emerald fields were replaced with rolling waves of white-hot flame, machines of war, and the crimson of blood. Aircraft roared overhead. Helicopters banked, hovered, and darted, all the while breathing a dragon's fire of missiles and machine guns from their bellies.

At first, a trickle of red appeared beside the porch, soon building to a stream. In just moments, a river of purple blood was flowing beside her refuge, its copper smell fouling the breeze. Arms, legs, torsos, and the heads of men and women soon polluted the runoff, the appendages bobbing like flotsam as the crimson torrent passed by.

Some recess of Bella's mind realized that no battle had taken place at the plantation. The food riots and anarchy had erupted in large urban areas like Mexico City and nearby Monterrey. Millions had died in the brutality, overwhelming the military in a matter of days. Once the government had evaporated, the starving, desperate throngs had turned on each other. Yet, her dream was accurate in a way – her brother had succumbed to the violence.

When the nightmare again refocused, the river of blood and human debris had vanished, leaving the lush green of the plantation's hills a barren wasteland of brown stalks and lifeless vegetation. For the first time during the entire nocturnal affair, Bella Dona felt the dampness of a tear rolling down her cheek.

Her land was barren, desolate, and dead. The main house, what the locals called El Castillo, or Castle, sat in the midst of a wasteland.

Bella Dona's dream vision changed perspectives. Now she was no longer on the porch, but floating over the land, fixated on the only home she had ever known. Like a brilliant white diamond floating in a pool of tainted mud, the castle towered in stark contrast to its surroundings.

The heavenly view again became blurred. When it cleared, she was back on the porch, rocking in a gentle sway.

The lifeless, dry-brown stalks of corn began to change, swelling and jerking with the transition. She couldn't close her eyes or look away as the painful, agonizing process continued. Her heart was beating as fast as the images flashing through her mind.

The dead stalks became stick figures, with arms and legs. Bone-thin and tormented, faces began to form as the old roots extracted themselves from the ground and began to stumble toward El Castillo and its queen who could do nothing more than sit and rock on the porch.

As they drew closer, the monsters became people. Grotesque, misshapen human beings struggled toward the castle, each step seeming to draw more life from their already taxed existence.

Thin from starvation, weak from malnutrition, they continued marching toward Bella Dona's swaying perch. "Help us," they moaned. "Feed us. You are the lady of this land. Lead us out of this misery."

The horde stopped at the edge of the porch, stick-like arms swaying in time with the swing, pleading for food … any morsel … any mercy from the hunger that racked their souls.

Bella Dona shouted at them, "Plant the fields! They are fertile and will grow more than you can consume."

The throng wouldn't listen, waving their boney arms in unison with her swing and crying for her to feed them.

"Plant the fields, you fools!" she screamed. "Use your backs and feed yourselves!"

"We can't," they whined. "We don't know how. Fill our stomachs! You are the lady of this house. Feed us! We will do anything!"

She became angry, frustrated at their inability to help themselves. "You are like helpless children!" she yelled. She rose from the swing and then was in the barn. The throng surrounded her, still begging to be fed. She took a hoe and rake from the wall, determined to show them how to plant the seeds.

She stomped to the field, dug a hole and held out a handful of yellow kernels. "These are seeds!" she shouted over their miserable pleas. "You throw them into the ground where they will grow and then fill your bellies!"

Tossing them into the earth, she prepared to cover the planting but was pushed aside as the starving mass dove for the corn. "Stay back!" she commanded. "Don't eat the seeds! You won't have anything to plant."

They didn't listen. Now they were fighting, shoving, clawing, and surging against each other in a desperate scramble to unearth the seeds. Bella Dona lifted the hoe, preparing to strike. She had to keep them back … had to let the crop grow and mature or no one would ever eat again.

Like always before, Bella Dona woke at that moment, her chest heaving to draw air as her heart hammered inside her chest.

Lying on her back, she stared with wide eyes at the lofty ceiling of the master suite. After only a few moments, the nightmare's rush began to waiver.

Bella Dona quickly gathered her composure. It was easier now, the dream having reoccurred so many times in the past. After a few moments, she rose to sit on the edge of the massive bed, the floor cool on the bottom of her feet. A gentle sigh and rustle reminded the plantation's mistress that she wasn't alone.

Glancing at the raven-black head of hair splayed over the pillowcase, Bella tried to remember the young girl's name. The

54

plantation's matriarch scanned the girl's exposed, high breasts, noting their rise and fall in the depths of slumber. "You were willing enough last night, but inexperienced," the older woman whispered. "You have potential, and certainly there is no substitute for youth. I have to wonder, though – were you motivated to please me or to avoid toiling in the fields?"

Shaking her head to clear her thoughts, Bella Dona decided some air would help to clear the last remnants of the nightmare from her mind. Taking one last glance at the previous evening's entertainment, she smiled knowingly and then pulled a robe from the nightstand. After splashing some water on her face and pulling a brush through her hair, she made for the porch.

Despite the early hour, the guard posted outside the master suite was awake and alert. That wasn't surprising. Being assigned to house duty was the ultimate career path at the plantation. Besides, everyone knew that sentries who were caught sleeping would be whipped until no flesh remained on their backs. Most died during the administration, and even if they survived the lashes, the almost-certain infection that followed was the ultimate punishment.

"Good morning, Señorita. Is everything okay?" the burly guard inquired.

"Yes, everything is fine. I just need some air," Bella Dona replied with a matter of fact tone.

The house was absolutely silent as she navigated the long hall and then descended the massive staircase that dominated the great room. The hardwood beneath her bare feet was as solid as the day it had been laid over 200 years prior.

The plantation's matriarch knew the morning's tranquility wouldn't last long. Word of her waking would rapidly spread through the servants' quarters. The aroma of coffee and breakfast would soon waft through the air as the news of her pre-dawn rising spread.

The hands of slaves had built El Castillo well, the estate having weathered sun, storm, revolution, and apocalypse with grace and dignity. Built in the early 1800s to mimic the massive plantations that dotted the Deep South of the U.S., Bella's forefathers had wanted to imitate what were the most economically successful agro-businesses in the world at the time. That had included antebellum architecture and forced labor.

The castle had initially drawn scorn and skepticism from her neighbors who believed the massive structure was an eyesore at worst, visual oddity at best. Over the years, that sentiment disappeared as those competing operations were bought out or absorbed by the estate's expansion.

Bella Dona's ancestors had been ruthless, sage business-men who thrived while others failed. Neither drought, nor war, nor recession seemed to slow the plantation's relentless spread. When Mexico abolished slavery in 1830, the Castle's masters had been ready to purchase neighboring operations as they plunged into financial ruin. Opportunists to their core, El Castillo's kitchens had produced baguettes as well as tortillas when the French cavalry pillaged the countryside.

The front door opened before she could reach for the knob, another sentry trying to impress her with his alertness.

She stepped out onto the verandah, still having trouble shaking the foreboding residue of the nightmare. In the early light of pre-dawn, she immediately verified that the fields were indeed green and that no river of blood flowed across the volcanic-rich soil.

There was still something in the air, however ... something that polluted the normally refreshing richness of thriving crops and freshly tilled earth.

"Is everything all right, madam?" the guard asked, seeming to sense her discomfort.

"Has the night been quiet?"

"Yes, madam. All is well," he replied with confidence.

She wandered to the end of the porch and surveyed the hills, still unable to shake the nightmare's echo. As her gaze swept the horizon, a pair of headlights radiated in the distance, their bouncing beams obviously heading for the big house.

After exchanging troubled looks with the attending guard, Bella Dona watched the approaching truck with apprehension. While the plantation's operations often included motor vehicles of all shapes and sizes, the hour and driver's urgency were out of the ordinary.

Ignoring the additional sentries summoned by the unusual occurrence, Bella Dona waited patiently as the pickup closed the distance.

A ring of security men encircled El Castillo's mistress when the truck finally came to a stop in the main drive. While it was extremely unlikely that any unauthorized person could get within five kilometers of the big house, Bella Dona's bodyguards weren't taking any chances.

A familiar face exited the truck, and for a moment, Bella Dona thought the event would prove anticlimactic.

Castro's appearance engendered a wave of relief through the gathered security men, but that quickly dissipated. "You're already awake, my lady. Good. I was dreading the thought of interrupting your rest," announced Bella Dona's top lieutenant.

"What's wrong?" she asked, now wondering if the dream had truly been a premonition or if she even believed in such nonsense.

Castro waited until the throng of guards dissipated, marching toward the porch wearing the scowl of a man who was dreading the delivery of bad news. For an instant, he considered couching his report. Perhaps delaying his proclamation until the kitchen offered coffee might be the wiser course.

After brief consideration, he decided to get it over with. Bella was famous for her lack of patience. "There's been an incident," he stated, trying to temper the apprehension in his voice.

"Go on."

"One of the teams searching for the banditos has been ambushed. All of them are dead."

A fire blazed in Bella Dona's eyes, and for a moment, Castro braced his hefty frame for the eruption that was sure to follow. The plantation's mistress was well known for a blistering temper, such outbursts often resulting in an extremely painful death for those who displeased her.

Instead, a cool anger filled Bella Dona's throat. "The villagers?"

"Yes, they were involved."

"Burn that shithole to the ground. I don't want there to be two bricks left standing. Wipe that slum off the face of the earth. Send men and exterminate them all. They have been warned," she commanded with an icy tone.

"There's more."

"Yes?"

"Gringos," Castro replied, again preparing for the fiery outburst.

Now Bella Dona understood Castro's hesitation. "From the United States?"

"No, mistress. The villagers we interrogated claimed a group of Tejas crossed the river and were involved in the gunfight."

"Military?"

"That is unclear. The peasants claim that a woman was with the Texans. Another of the men we questioned stated that the intruders had military grade weapons and fought like demons. He even went so far as to claim that the Tejas attacked both our men and those from the village."

As anticipated, Castro's words troubled his boss deeply. Rumors and wild stories of a new organization called the Alliance had reached Central Mexico several months ago. As Bella Dona's influence and control expanded, the plantation's managers had encountered several farmers, traders, and others who spoke of a government reorganizing north of the Rio Grande.

These accounts had been confused by the arrival of a representative from Washington. When the Americans had first arrived at the plantation, Bella Dona and her men had assumed that the U.S. government was doing its best to reestablish the rule of law across the anarchical landscape that dominated the once-great superpower.

Bella Dona and her extensive management team didn't trust the Yankees for many reasons.

First, like any predator, there was a natural tendency to protect territory. Since the apocalypse, the ecosystem of the plantation was reinvented, delicate, and far from established. Like all immature organizations, the men and woman who ran El Castillo's ever-expanding operations feared competition, influence, and any outside meddling that might interfere with their recovery and growth.

Central Mexico's people had suffered as badly as any on the planet, and the memories of the apocalypse's aftermath were still fresh in the survivors' minds. All of them had lost family members to the starvation and violence. Millions had perished horribly, with children and the elderly suffering the worst. Over half of the population had succumbed to disease or malnutrition … or worse yet, at the hand of their fellow man.

Bella's leadership, brutal discipline, and shrewd management had pulled the local people away from the edge of the abyss. Word spread like the firestorms that ravaged Mexico City and other metropolitan areas. Food, shelter, and sanctuary were available at the plantation.

That news brought both those who desperately needed help as well as those who lived by the barrel of a gun. The plantation had to defend itself almost daily. Bella Dona and her men survived, but barely.

There were too many starving souls, the sheer numbers constantly threatening to overwhelm Bella Dona's resources. Those multitudes, combined with the roving bands of armed raiders and nomadic gangs, had nearly spelled the end on more occasions than she could remember.

Early on, she tried to frighten the people away. She and her men became harsh, grew mean and intolerant. Still, the metro cities' refugees streamed to the plantation and stayed no matter how miserable things became. Indentured servitude was better than starvation, rape gangs, dehydration, or the illnesses that flourished outside of Bella Dona's territory.

Anyone who was willing to work ... to do anything for a full belly and a roof overhead, was welcome at the plantation. Even then, people tried to game the communal system. Many arrived at the edge of her property too weak for labor. Bella had lost count of the thousands that she had fed and nursed back to health only to find that they had snuck away in the night, often stealing anything they could carry. Again, the rules were tightened to the point where a long-term commitment was required to stay. Breaking that promise carried the penalty of death. There were no rights, no pay, no privileges – only servitude, hard labor, and unflinching loyalty to Bella Dona and her managers.

Many called it slavery, and the world had hardened Bella Dona to the point where she was comfortable with the term. History was thick with great civilizations that had survived, and even thrived, on forced labor after cataclysmic events. Why should Central Mexico be any different?

Terri and Bishop found a comfortable spot in the sun and settled in as Grim piloted them north across the lake. Using the bright rays and warm air to dry, the couple tried to digest what had just happened.

"We have more questions now than we did before crossing the border," Bishop complained. "Rather than solve the mystery, we've only managed to wander deeper into murky waters."

"That's not entirely true," Terri refuted. "We know that there are at least two organized groups in Mexico and that they don't like each other very much."

"I think there are at least three groups. I 'm pretty sure we haven't met the people who shot up the convoy."

Terri had to consider her husband's comment for a bit before finally agreeing. "You're right about that. And we still don't have a clear motive for their attack."

"Set them free," Bishop mumbled, barely audible over the big boat's motors. "We have no idea why the attackers scrawled that on the earthmover. It just doesn't make any sense. Why burn the food instead of stealing it? Why massacre the truckers when they could have just robbed them at gunpoint?"

Butter appeared just then, relaying a message from the bridge that they were almost back to the marina. "Grim wants everyone ready to help with the dock lines. He's never driven a boat this big, and he is worried because the wind has picked up a bit."

Evidently, Hannah had spotted them gliding across the lake, the marina's owner and a young woman waving Grim toward an open pier. A few minutes later, the dock lines were being pulled tight as the captain shut down the massive engines.

"You found her!" Hannah shouted as the SAINT team disembarked. "Where was she? Where did all these bullet holes come from?"

Without going into a lot of detail, Bishop explained the approximate location where they'd discovered the boat. "Sorry about all the holes," he added. "We weren't the one doing the shooting ... at least not in the direction of your boat."

With an experienced eye, Hannah scanned her vessel fore to aft, finally pronouncing, "We'll have her ship shape and good as new in less than a month. My sincere thanks to all of you for bringing her back to me."

As Hannah boarded the damaged houseboat to take an inventory of its contents, Bishop decided it was a good time to debrief his team. It was always productive to discuss what had gone wrong, what could be done better, and to compliment his men on what they had done well.

He found Grim and Kevin taking their equipment to their home-boat, but Butter was nowhere to be found. "Anybody seen the big guy?" he asked his teammates.

"He was here a minute ago," Grim responded, looking up and down the pier with just a hint of concern in his voice. "Not like him to wander off unless he discovered an all-you-can-eat buffet."

"Maybe he fell overboard?" Bishop offered, his eyes scanning the water despite the comment being mostly in jest.

"He was talking to that girl with Hannah a minute ago," Kevin added.

Bishop and Grim exchanged knowing, fatherly looks. "Who is that young lady, anyway?"

"That is Hannah's daughter, May," Kevin answered.

Again, Bishop and Grim exchanged a knowing glance. "At least we solved one mystery today," the Texan chuckled.

Grim obviously didn't like it, mumbling something about kids, and how somebody ought to pass a law as he disappeared below deck with an armful of equipment.

Terri sauntered up a moment later. "Who's that girl I just saw sashaying around with Butter?"

Before Bishop could answer his wife's question, Grim rumbled up the steps, his boisterous voice belting out, "I once knew a girl named May, who was rumored to be good in the hay...."

"Grim!" Bishop snapped, stopping the old soldier's limerick before things got out of hand.

Seeing Terri, Grim's face flashed red before he mumbled, "I'll go retrieve our wayward team member. If it's not food or arm wrestling, it's a damn girl. Kids. Until that boy's frontal lobe finishes developing, he's likely to get in trouble without my sage guidance. Someone needs to have a word with him about...."

Bishop shook his head, "No, let him go. He did well today. You all did. The debriefing can wait."

Grim paused, throwing a confused stare that said, "Are you sure?"

"He may die tomorrow, my friend. Any of us can be carried out in a bag on any given day. Let him go," Bishop added in a low, but friendly tone.

For a moment, Bishop thought Grim was going to debate the decision, but the older man merely shrugged. "You're the boss. I suppose nature is going to take its course no matter how pervasive my argument against such distractions."

There had been a fair share of females around the Beltran Ranch where Butter had been raised. Many of the hands were married, some of the hired help being of the fairer sex. There were girls his age who attended the private school erected to educate the sons and daughters of the outfit's small army of employees. Still, he'd never encountered anyone who looked, smelled, or moved quite like May.

She asked questions about his work and mission, seemed genuinely interested in what he had to say, and looked at him with eyes that bewildered the big man unlike anything he'd ever experienced.

Butter's mother had died during childbirth, his father killed by a loco mare before he was four years old. Other than a worn, black and white photograph, he had no memory of either parent. Yet, it wasn't a sad story. He felt no remorse, had never considered himself shortchanged in any way. Carlos Beltran may have ramrodded his spread with an iron fist, but the ranch was a community. The people who worked there were family.

An orphaned child wasn't all that rare. Life on a working spread was difficult at best and often dangerous. In additional to laboring around large, unpredictable animals and deadly machines, Beltran men went to war when their country called. Many never returned. When such tragedies did occur, the young ones were absorbed without question, accepted into the loving, social fabric of what was essentially a small town in the vast isolation of the West Texas desert.

Like many boys, Butter had neither the time nor the inclination for female companionship. His world revolved around rugged men, horses, cattle, and the modern machinery used on a working ranch. His life was the land, his environment the great outdoors, his heroes the multitude of father figures who treated the young lad like one of their own.

Puberty's arrival modified that behavior somewhat, the oversized teen finding his eye drifting toward the hourglass shape, softer hair, and smoother skin of the women who operated in various roles around the ranch. He began to listen more intently to the stories and conversations of the older men, dialog that just a few short years before wouldn't have held his interest.

Secondary school meant leaving the ranch's friendly confines and entering the Alpha, Texas Independent School District. Butter's amazing size, herculean strength, and nimble agility immediately drew the eye of every coach at the small school. Within hours, he was being recruited for football and wrestling.

Intense training regiments, private instruction, national competitions, and doing his fair share around the ranch left little time for the now-massive youth to develop social skills or chase girls. Still, Butter was happy and content. His co-workers often consumed a majority of the bleacher seats during home matches. Even Mr. Beltran had taken to setting his beef-empire aside and attending the events.

By the time his senior year was rolling around, every major college west of the Mississippi offered scholarships and promises of professional football recruitment or Olympic-level participation in wrestling. Butter had never been bested on the high school mat and had exhausted all of the competition his coaches could provide.

The natural athlete was about to start touring college campuses when the terrorist attacks crippled America. Like most of the extended Beltran family, he retreated to the familiarity of the ranch when society began its slide into the abyss. There he stayed, his hand-to-hand combat skills making him a natural bodyguard for the expansive outfit's owner.

It was in this role that the big kid first encountered Nick, Bishop, and Miss Terri. Their "fight" on Meraton's Main Street was now the stuff of legend and tall tales ... the oft-debated details filling the walls of Pete's Place with fierce, libation-induced discussions.

Butter had simply never had the time to pursue female companionship, always far too engaged with sports, work, or earning a place on Bishop's SAINT team. An inherent element of shyness also played a significant role in the big kid's lack of courting experience.

Now, May's doe-like eyes, buxom shape, and feminine graces were elevating all sorts of chemicals and hormones throughout Butter's oversized frame. It was as if his testosterone floodgates had been opened, and the young man from West Texas had quite the reservoir of emotional waters.

In reality, Terri was as much to blame as the big kid's new-found interest in the opposite sex as May. Butter had spent considerable amounts of time studying Bishop's interaction with his wife. His conclusion was that his boss was stronger and lived a far better life with a mate at his side.

Butter had lost count of the number of campfire tales where Terri had saved Bishop or vice versa. They were known far and wide across Alliance territory as an unbeatable duo ... an insepa-rable team ... a force to be respected.

Despite all of Bishop's grumblings about his wife being mean or demanding or difficult, Butter knew the truth. His role model adored his mate, and every ounce of that affection was returned in kind. The whole of their marriage was far greater than the sum of their individual parts. The fact that Hunter was a by-product of that union sealed the deal.

Now, right in the middle of a mission, Butter had met May.

"Tell me what this SAINT ... or whatever you call it ... team of yours is doing over in Mexico? It sounds awfully dangerous," she inquired.

Butter's attention was so focused on the young girl, that he nearly stepped off the edge of the pier. After regaining his composure, he answered, "Mr. Bishop took us across the border to see if we could find any evidence of who ambushed the truckers and why."

"Mr. Bishop? You mean you're not in charge of the team?"

With his face flashing red, Butter rushed to correct her mis-conception, "Oh, no, no, ma'am. Mr. Bishop is in command, then Grim. Kevin is next in seniority, and then, well, umm, me."

A look of disbelief formed on her face, "You're the biggest and the strongest and are so self-confident. I just thought you would be the man in charge."

A different hotness flushed through Butter's core, her compliments making him feel the warmth of a campfire – only from deep inside. "Size and strength aren't as important on a SAINT team as experience and judgment. Besides, I don't know anyone who could best Mr. Bishop in an all-out fight."

May needed to digest his response, remaining silent as they continued their stroll around the marina. Finally, "And did you?"

"And did I what?"

"Find any evidence of who ambushed the truck drivers or why?"

Shaking his head, Butter admitted, "No, not really."

A second period of awkward silence followed as the couple continued sauntering along the old, wooden piers. May seemed to arrive at disappointment, "So does that mean you'll be leaving the lake and heading back home?"

Again, Butter shook his head, "No, probably not for a while. I think we'll be here at least a few more days. Miss Terri isn't one to be chased off by a little gunfight."

"Miss Terri? I thought you said Bishop was in charge?"

"He is unless Miss Terri is along, and then, well, uhm, they kind of make decisions together … sometimes … it's a little hard to explain how it all works," Butter stammered.

Despite the contradiction, May's face seem to brighten. "Whatever the reason, I'm glad you'll be staying for a while. I want to cook something nice for you for bringing back my mom's boat. I want to make you my specialty."

The lady's offer struck a chord near and dear to Butter's heart – food. "That would be great! I love to eat, but you probably had already guessed that, right?"

May shrugged and then smiled wide, "You're a very large guy. I assumed you have an appetite to match."

"Butter! Butter!" called Bishop's voice across the water. "Hate to interrupt, big fella, but we have to finish debriefing and run through an equipment check before it gets dark."

A quick glance at his watch brought a frown to Butter's face, "Oh lordy, I lost track of time. I'm sorry, but I have to go." Then without another word, he was hustling back toward the houseboat, leaving May standing with a confused, almost hurt expression.

As an afterthought, Butter spun around, and while jogging backward, said, "But I really enjoyed our talk. I look forward to having dinner and talking some more. Thank you!"

May waved and smiled, watching as he turned away and then broke out into a full sprint across the marina. "Innocence," she whispered with a knowing smirk. "I had no idea it still existed in this world. We'll have dinner, and we'll talk some more. A *lot* more."

Chapter 5

Bishop's best boots were soaked. So were his favorite pack and load vest.

As the Texan laid out his equipment to dry on the deck, the rest of the SAINT team joined him.

"At least it's not salt water," Grim noted, running a cleaning rod through his carbine's barrel. "That shit is nasty on gear. You have to rinse it out and get everything wet all over again. It stinks and corrodes metal like crazy. Nasty, nasty stuff."

"Why Grim," Bishop smiled, "I really appreciate your taking such a positive attitude this evening. Are you feeling okay?"

Before the old soldier could respond, Terri arrived on deck, grunting under the strain from carrying her husband's hefty duffle bag. "Here are your spares, babe. How do you carrying all this ... this stuff?"

Bishop didn't respond, trying to decide if his load rig and armor would dry in the night air. His scowl deepened after feeling the damp lining of his boots. No chance. The realization wrinkled his face in a full-on frown. "Now is not the time to break in a new pair of horseshoes," he grumbled. "I see blisters in my future."

Merely finding the spare pair of footwear in his size had been a serious stroke of luck. The fact that he had found the military-issued jump boots for a reasonable price had been nothing short of a miracle. Other than rawhide moccasins in the Meraton market, no one was making shoes anymore. Still, he wasn't happy. "I should have broken these in while we were training in the mountains," he said, pulling the new units from the duffle bag. "Just once, I'd like to get away with being lazy."

Terri chuckled, "Ain't going to happen, my love. It's just not our lot in life. Maybe we should build a fire on shore? That might help dry some of our stuff out."

"Somebody's already thought of that," Grim advised.

Everybody followed the older man's line of sight to the horizon south of the marina, spotting a huge column of smoke winding upward into the dusk sky. A moment later, the pulsing orange glow of growing flames followed.

"The village," Kevin noted aloud. "Somebody's burning something really big at the village. Maybe they're having a bonfire?"

"I don't think that's a bonfire," Grim mumbled, his voice thick with worry.

"Oh, no," Terri whispered, exchanging troubled looks with her husband. "You don't think …."

As Bishop opened his mouth to answer, a series of faint popping noises drifted across the lake, the distant gunfire instantly recognizable. "Not good," Bishop said, shaking his head but unable to look away from the now billowing blaze. "Not good at all."

"We have to go help them," Terri announced, glancing between Grim and Bishop.

"We can't," Bishop answered sadly. "I'm sorry, but there just no way…."

"Bishop, please," Terri pleaded. "Those little boys … the fishermen … they were only kids…."

With a sigh, Bishop expounded, "We can't, Terri. It's impossible. Whatever is happening over there is going to be over before we could even load up our gear and get across the dam. Besides, we're in no condition to hike to the corner gas station, let alone rush into a foreign country looking for trouble."

"But Bishop," she began to protest, now nearing tears.

He took her gently by the shoulders and responded, "Terri, stop, please. Listen to me. The guys haven't eaten anything all day. Out equipment is in tatters and requires maintenance. We have to restock our ammo and oil our weapons. We are bone tired and need to rest. Even if we were primed and ready to go, it would take us over two hours to reach the village, and then what would we do? How would we know what was going on? We can't do anything tonight…. I'm sorry, but we just can't."

Her eyes glowed white-hot with anger, and the Texan braced for the tempest that was sure to follow. He knew his wife loathed injustice more than anything, despised the strong preying on the weak to the very center of her core.

Terri exhaled, moving her intense gaze from the glowing sky and zeroing in on Grim, clearly asking without words if the ex-contractor could offer any alternative.

"He's right," Grim answered with disappointment. "I don't like it any better than you do, Miss Terri, but Bishop's spot on with that assessment. We're in no condition to mount any sort of patrol or interference. At best, we would get there after it was over, at worst we would get ourselves killed. I'm sorry, ma'am."

"We'll go back over first thing in the morning, I promise," Bishop added.

Terri managed to get control of her anger, taking a deep breath and nodding. "Thanks," she whispered. "I can't stand up here and look at that sky. I'm going below."

After she left, Bishop stood and watched the swelling flames as the pop of gunfire intensified from the south. The distant battle motivated the SAINT team, the men moving with more energy as they sorted, cleaned, dried, and prepared for what was surely going to be a dangerous mission in the morning.

Then, less than 15 minutes after it had started, the shooting from across the lake stopped, followed by an eerie silence.

Turning to Grim, the Texan motioned toward the still-glowing horizon with his head, "I can't help but believe we're on the edge of something a lot bigger than just a shot-up convoy and the locals not liking each other very much. Those villagers weren't exactly crack troops, but they were clearly willing to fight. Who rolls in and takes out an entire community in less than 15 minutes? Who is strong enough to pull that off? I don't like it … not one bit."

Grim nodded, "My guess would be the guys in the pickup have some friends. Strong, well-armed friends and a lot of them. Somebody is getting their payback tonight."

"I don't know about that," Bishop answered, his eyes never leaving the red and orange illuminating the night sky. "Why would the villagers have kicked a sleeping lion? Surely, they know the players in their own schoolyard. Why pick a fight with the biggest kid?"

Grim shrugged, "Hell if I know, boss. Maybe they were sick and tired of being bullied? There's no way you and I can stand here and know for certain. Hell, we may never figure it out."

Returning to his packing, Bishop's face was still sour. "And that, my friend, is what I fear the most."

They came out of the pre-dawn light, cutting through the choking clouds of smoke with effortless energy and making no sound.

Chico was beyond pain or fear, the last of those physical sensations having passed hours ago in the new morning. Only thirst registered in his young brain, the undying need for water overriding any other message making it through his tortured mind.

He was helpless beneath the collapsed wall of his uncle's home, the unmovable pile of stone pinning his chest to the earth while a smoldering beam had nearly burned its way through his leg. He had no concept of how many times he had passed out from the pain, couldn't conceptualize how many hours he had screamed for help, begged for mercy, and finally prayed for death to come and take him away from the agony that ravaged his soul.

The blurred outlines were coming, moving through the outskirts of his village, their grace and power drawing his exhausted eyes. "Angels," he managed through dry, cracked lips. "The Holy Father has sent them to take me to heaven."

"Aqua!" he tried to shout. "Water! Please! Water!"

The effort was both exhausting and disappointing. The bricks on his chest wouldn't let him draw in enough air to ask for help. The spirits wouldn't hear him. How would they find him?

But they were drawing closer, darting here, rushing there, and moving through the main street of his village with speed and stealth that was certainly supernatural.

One of the shapes stepped into a red pool of light cast by a burning roof. When he managed to focus, the imaged shocked Chico into drawing in a sharp but shallow breath. He spied a grotesque, frightening figure with huge, insect-like eyes, no face, and a body that bulged with an inhuman form. A demon! Not an angel. He whimpered in fear.

Satan's servant heard the noise, his bug-eyes instantly snapping in Chico's direction, his weapon pointing directly at the wounded child's face.

Fear returned to the Chico's tortured mind, panic rushing through his synapses as the unholy creature moved closer. The beast spoke but used words that sounded strange. Another soon joined it, and then a third. The young villager was sure the demons were going to gnaw the flesh from his bones.

They surrounded him, evil-looking weapons sweeping what little remained of the surrounding buildings. Then another form appeared, this one completely different in the firelight.

Confused, near death, and having suffered through a night of unbearable pain, it took what was left of Chico's mental capabilities a moment before something familiar registered. He had seen the newest demon before, but where?

The vision that appeared above him cleared, his fear vanishing as quickly as the clouds of toxic smoke that still rolled through the streets. It *was* an angel, he decided as Terri's smiling face came into focus. God did love him! He had sent this cherubic spirit to recuse Chico from the army of demons that surrounded him.

Another human face appeared beside her, this one a man.

"Can you hear me," the woman said in peculiar Spanish. "How badly are you hurt?"

"Aqua," Chico said weakly. "Please. Water."

Something touched Chico's lips, and then a cool sensation flowed into his mouth. It was a feeling unlike any the young boy had ever experienced, a liquid fountain of ice, sugar, joy, and life flowing across his tongue and down his throat. He couldn't get enough. He couldn't swallow fast enough. He hoped it would never end.

But it did, convulsions racking the child's tiny frame and forcing Terri to remove her canteen.

Then Butter was under the beam, groaning with the strain, putting his back into lifting the thick wood that trapped the child. Veins of exertion popped on the big man's forehead as his massive arms and legs trembled from the effort.

Still, the timber wouldn't budge. Grim and Bishop pitched in, desperately trying to remove the bricks and rubble accomplishing little other than prompting new spasms of agony through Chico's frame.

"It's no use, Terri," Bishop finally grimaced. "We're only hurting him more. He's got hundreds of pounds of weight compressing his chest, and his leg is gone. Even if I could get a copter down here from Fort Hood, I don't think it would do any good."

Terri nodded, having already surmised that they were too late. "Let's make it as easy for him as we can," she muttered in a dejected voice as she lifted the water to the child's parched lips.

Grim appeared at the edge of the light, the old warrior resting a reassuring hand on Terri's shoulder. "The kids are always the worst of it. No matter how many times I've seen it, it still rips my guts out."

Bishop nodded his agreement, his face smeared with the same combination of anger and remorse they all felt, "I've seen war zones that weren't this disturbing. This sucks. Butter, Grim, give her a perimeter. We'll stay with him until it's over."

As his team members rushed off, Bishop turned to his wife and gently insisted, "Ask him who did this."

"The Copperheads," the child weakly croaked his answer. "They are evil. They killed my brother and uncle and everyone I know."

Terri wasn't sure she understood the words correctly. "Copperheads? Snakes?"

"The Copperheads," Chico rasped, the effort causing a spasm of coughing and choking.

Before Terri could return the water to his lips, Chico smiled at her … and then closed his eyes as a last breath rattled out of his lungs.

With tears streaming down her cheeks, she rose abruptly and stood rigidly still, staring hard at the dead boy.

"You okay?" Bishop asked, trying to bring her mind away from it and instantly regretting the stupid question.

Terri pivoted at stared at him with the hardest eyes the Texan had ever seen. "I don't know who or what the Copperheads are, but I sure would like to find them," she snapped with an ice-cold tone.

Bishop was moving to comfort his wife when Grim reappeared, "No one else is alive. There are dozens of dead bodies down in front of what's left of the church. It looks like they were rounded up and massacred."

"There are also drag marks, sir," Butter added. "From the blood trails, it looks like someone removed their dead and wounded from the field. At least some of the villagers fought back."

"Alright. We're done here. Let's get back to Texas," Bishop said after a moment. "Grim, take point. I've seen enough for one morning."

Butter pushed back from the table, almost forgetting to use the napkin spread across his lap. For the fourth time, he complimented May on her cooking. "That was so tasty. Growing up in the desert, I've not had the chance to eat much seafood or fish. What did you call those yummy, little morsels again?"

"Mudbugs," May declared with a content smile. "Crawfish. Cajun Crays. They're like freshwater shrimp. Very popular in Louisiana, even considered a delicacy in New Orleans. My father used to take my sister and me with him on business trips. I learned to love Creole cooking."

"And the rice was so different from what I am used to. What did you call it?"

"Dirty rice. I don't have all the ingredients to make it the right way, but I did the best I could with the wild onions and the few veggies we can scrounge."

"Mudbugs and dirty rice," Butter repeated, shaking his head. "The guys back at the ranch will never believe me."

His reaction seemed to please the young girl, her smile beaming widely. It was the perfect time to suggest what she had planned next. "Want to take an after dinner stroll along the shoreline? The sunset should be gorgeous this evening."

"That would be great!" he responded cheerfully. "Grim says I'm starting to put on weight, and that I'll be fat by the time I'm 25 if I keep eating so much. Walking off some of that wonderful meal is probably a good idea."

"Give me a few minutes to clean up these plates," she said, starting to stack the dishes.

"If we're going to leave the area, I have to get my rifle. Mr. Bishop said no one is to wander off unarmed," he said shyly. "Sorry to ruin the mood by having to carry around a weapon."

Much to the big kid's surprise, May seemed reassured. "No problem. After what we've been through, I'm glad to have a super-sized escort with a nasty-looking gun. I'll see you in a few minutes."

True to her word, May appeared a short time later, finding Butter standing outside with his rifle slung over one shoulder. "Do you remember what it was like to go someplace without a weapon?" she asked.

"Yes," he answered. "Those were better times for sure. That's why I like working for the Alliance. People like Diana and Nick are determined to get us back to that place."

For the next 20 minutes, they wandered and chatted, May pointing out features of the lake and delighting Butter with witty stories. "My sister and I used to sneak down to this cove and go skinny dipping," she confessed at one point. "My daddy never knew. He would have probably grounded both of us for the rest of our lives if he had ever found out."

Butter seemed perplexed, turning to look back at his new friend's nearby home. "Your house isn't that far. Why didn't you just run and get your suits?"

May tilted her head, eventually smiling at his innocence. "Because we wanted to get away with something. We were teenagers and wanted to assert our independence. Rebel against authority a little bit. You can't tell me you never did anything shifty or broke the rules just to see if you could get away with it."

It took him a while, but eventually a wide smirk crossed Butter's face. "One time, when my friend Slim was using the outhouse, I picked it up and turned it over," he admitted. "Then I ran like hell. He'd been making fun of me all day, and I was tired of it."

Smacking him playfully on the chest, she said, "There you go! I knew you weren't a 100% Mr. Goodie Two Shoes."

Now feeling like a member of the club, Butter seemed pleased with himself. "I get in my share of goofing off. Why just the other day, Kevin and I were pestering Grim. We were doing cannon balls off of the bridge ... but then that didn't turn out so well," he chuckled.

"Life is kind of like that," she laughed. "Sometimes things come around and bite your backside."

"Yeah. It's always good to blow off a little steam. Unfortunately, the guys tend to get even with me for my pranks, but I have no regrets," he agreed.

May noticed a dark cloud brewing behind his eyes, and for a second she thought she had done something wrong. "What's the matter, Butter?"

Shaking his head as if to clear bad memories, Butter's voice was sad. "My buddy Slim died in Galveston a while back. I really miss him."

"Oh, I'm sorry. I didn't mean...."

May never got a chance to finish her apology as Butter recovered quickly. "It's okay. He checked out doing what he loved best and for a very good cause. He saved Miss Terri's life that day. He saved all of us."

They continued walking for a bit, the mood still somewhat soured. Butter decided it was his fault and rushed to change the subject. "You mentioned earlier that you have a sister, but I've not seen her around. Where is she?"

The look that raced across May's face told him instantly that he'd made a mistake. "Oh, no, I'm sorry, May," he tried to recover. "Dang it. I'm always saying the wrong thing. I should just keep my mouth shut."

"It's okay, Butter," she said sweetly. "I think my sister April is still alive ... at least I hold on to that hope."

"You *think* she's alive? You're not sure?"

"Yes, my heart says she is still living, but I can't be positive," she admitted, contemplating how to explain. "I've not seen her in over two years."

"Where is she?"

"That's a long story, and I wouldn't want to bore you with it on such a lovely evening."

Butter might have been young, naïve, and lacking worldly experience, but that didn't mean the lad was completely without perception. "I am a great listener," he coaxed his charming companion. "I want to hear. You obviously miss her dearly. She's your sister ... she's important to you. Please, tell me."

The couple meandered in silence, approaching two large rocks perfectly suited for lakeside seating. Only then did May tell her story. Kicking off her sandals, the young girl picked a familiar perch and seemed to briefly enjoy dangling her feet in the cool water. A heavy sigh signaled the start of her tale, her voice a monotone as the narration began. "It was within a week of the last terrorist attacks, when the gangs of raiders started roaming around the lakeshore. My father loaded me, April, and mom, along with as many supplies as we had, onto our biggest house-boat. When the electricity failed and didn't come back on, we motored away from the marina. It was sad, really. This was the only place our family had ever known."

"Sounds like your dad was pretty smart," Butter comment-ed. "Sounds like he was really intent on keeping you guys safe."

Nodding, May continued, "Several smaller vessels joined us. Our little flotilla anchored in the middle of the reservoir, as far from any shore as possible."

May's eyes drifted over the lake's surface, her glazed ex-pression evidence of her mind's transport back in time. "The escape worked perfectly for the first few weeks, our small com-munity of boats well away from the violence that ravaged the shore and Del Rio. I can remember many nights sitting on the bridge, watching the fires burn into the night sky, knowing that people's homes … and lives … were being destroyed. Occasion-ally, if the wind was just right, the distant sound of gunshots rolled across the water. There were a few times I swear I could hear people screaming, like they were being tortured or some-thing."

The recalled memory compelled a shiver down the woman's spine. Butter took her hand, trying to provide comfort. The act produced a smile, but it was fleeting.

"Now I realize we had it pretty well out on the water," May continued. "The big houseboat had a built-in purification system for drinking water, and most of the smaller vessels had BBQ grills or gas stoves to boil additional amounts when needed. Everyone had packed as much food as possible, and there were constantly lines and bait in the lake trying to add fresh fish to our tables."

May chuckled just then, some image from the past bringing the relief of humor. "My father," she began, shaking her head. "He was a creative guy; I have to give him that. He supplemented our dietary intake even further by figuring out how to trap ducks. We were all so tired of fish, and the change really helped improve everyone's morale. Occasionally he would allow us to launch a raft or dinghy and sneak toward the shore. We would gather cattails and other greens from shallow areas. Always at night. Always under heavy guard."

"Smart," Butter nodded, trying to conjure up the images with her.

"You know, looking back now, I'm still not sure exactly what caused our small, waterborne community to fall apart. I guess we didn't realize how good we had it."

"What happened?" he asked, now fully immersed in her story.

"Mr. Johnson became ill, his supply of insulin exhausted after just a few weeks. His wife and son begged for some of the men to go ashore with them to see if they could find medical help or additional medication. No one wanted to take the risk. There were still fires and gunshots. All of the men were certain that pure anarchy ruled the entire area. I think that's what started to divide us. It was as if our group split into two camps."

Butter had heard it all before. Some of the stories detailed while he was working as a bartender at Pete's Place were enough to tear out a man's heart. Still, he could sense the agony in May's voice. The collapse had left a deep wound, and for a moment, he wondered if she would ever heal.

"Mom wasn't in much better shape," May began. "Her supply of cigarettes had run out days before, leaving her sullen, withdrawn, and unreasonable. Initially, she had been the optimistic matriarch of Fiberglass City. When her smokes were gone, the resulting negativity and her short fuse seemed to affect the entire community's spirit."

The couple was brought back to the present when a large fish broke the surface nearby. After straining their necks to catch a glimpse, the story continued. "One day the Howards from Austin got into an argument with the Greenhills from Dallas. You know, today, I can't even remember how the quarrel began. I will, however, never forget the memory of Mr. Greenhill's dead body floating across the lake after Mr. Howard shredded his chest with 12-gauge buckshot. The next night, Mr. Howard's sailboat mysteriously caught on fire."

"Oh, no," Butter whispered. "Not good. Not good at all."

May agreed with her new friend's assessment. "We residents of Fiberglass City began to suffer paranoia, which soon manifested into squabbles, distrust, and a general lack of cooperation. Yet, despite all that, the vast majority of us still felt it was far safer in the middle of the lake than being on land. The arrival of the first raiders changed all of that."

Butter could have almost guessed it. Desperate people, desperate times, no fear of punishment, and empty bellies. The lake wasn't large enough to hide Fiberglass City forever.

Now May's voice was distant, reliving a nightmare that she knew was as real as the warmth of the sun. "They came at night, three rowboats gliding silently. The water was smooth. We didn't hear them coming. Each little boat was full of men with pitchforks, axes, clubs, and a few guns. I can still hear the screams, the fighting, and the sound of people dying. With the sun's first light, I counted 25 bodies bobbing on the surface. There were small pools of crimson running like little mini-rivers through the clear water. Two of our boats were burning; a third was taking on water. Half of the men of Fiberglass City were dead or badly wounded. Only a handful of raiders managed to limp away. They left empty handed."

For the first time during her story, Butter spied a tear rolling down May's cheek. Gently, he reached to wipe it away with his thumb. "I'm sorry you had to go through that," he softly reassured his companion. "I wish I could have been there to help."

"My father had led the defense against the boarders. We found out later that he had been one of the first to die. April helped me fish his body out of the water. We wrapped him in a white bed sheet and used an anchor off the sinking sailboat to bury him out in the lake. That's where he loved to live. That's where he died, and that is where we decided he would be happiest in the afterlife."

"What happened after that?"

Sniffing back the emotion, May continued, "Some of the Fiberglass City citizens blamed the attack on the burning of Mr. Howard's boat. Others thought argument was meaningless. After all, the community's discovery was inevitable as Amistad simply wasn't that big. Whatever the reason, our floating village disintegrated. Everyone was sure the pirates would return with more men. Most of our leadership and able-bodied males had died in the fight. The survivors, mostly widows and orphans, began untying their boats and either sailing or using the last of their precious fuel to head back to the shore. After nearly everyone else had left, Mom felt like we didn't have much choice. We three returned to the marina and home."

Butter understood, and given what he had learned about those days, he thought Hannah had made a very wise decision. The raiders would have returned. They would have brought more men and weapons.

May's voice interrupted his thoughts, "I remember that first step back on dry land. We were so scared, sure that the devil himself was going to rise and drag us down into hell. I felt so exposed. We were no longer protected by the deep moat of water that had surrounded us for months."

Scanning the marina, Butter observed, "It looks like your place didn't suffer much damage while you were gone. Either that, or you're secretly a master carpenter."

His attempt at humor worked, at least for a moment. "Yeah, our property was relatively untouched. Someone had raided the residence, but it hadn't been torched. We found the marina, toolshed, office, and almost all of the docked vessels were mostly unscathed. Someone had broken into the vending machines and made off with all the sweets and chips. The supply closet was missing all of its toilet paper. There wasn't a drop of gasoline anywhere, even the old push lawnmower having been drained bone dry."

"So you guys were all right? No roving gangs of black hats? You had a roof, your old beds, your clothing."

May's eyes became sad again. This time, her reaction seemed different. "We were okay after settling down and getting our land legs back. Those first few days back on shore are a bit of a blur now. It was later that week that the wind shifted, moving around the compass all afternoon. The arrow landed where it normally does, blowing from the southeast and bringing in the humidity from the Gulf of Mexico. It also blew in the corpses."

Butter's eyebrows rose, as May's account increased its pace. "April and I were fishing down at the pier when the most grotesque odor came rolling across the water. Ten minutes later, April gagged, pointing and turning away. When I stepped over to see what had grossed her out, that's when I spotted the first rotting body. There it was, bobbing gently into the marina, covered by a thick, black, layer of flies."

Again, she laughed. "We hightailed it back to the house, screaming like a couple of little girls who had just seen a rattlesnake. We were so freaked out, that we forgot our fishing poles. All that afternoon, the stench got worse and worse. It finally reached the point where mom was considering abandoning the house."

May pointed toward Butter's rifle. "You never go anywhere without that, and I can certainly understand. We were the same way, only with our fishing poles. The day the bodies began washing up, we started worrying that someone would steal our primary source of catching food. Anyway, Mom made us go out the next morning. We all were holding makeshift masks over our noses. The sight was bizarre. There were at least seven bodies pinned against the marina's bulkhead by the wind. The flies were swarming in dense clouds. There was an armada of vultures circling overhead. The smell was nearly unbearable."

"We had to pull them out and bury them," Hannah said, her face twisting in disgust. "We needed the fish to eat and the water to drink and wash. It was too dangerous to wander further around the lake to get more water. We had no choice."

Grimacing, Butter said, "That would not have been any fun. Even with everything I've seen since the collapse, I think I'd still want to toss my cookies."

"April took it the worst," May grinned. "She kept saying, 'Do you really expect us to eat or drink anything out of that water? Ever again?'"

Again a chuckle at the memory. "Mom let her rant for a little bit, but then the protests got old. Mom kept asking her, 'Do you want to live?'"

The storyteller's voice took on a dark and despondent tone as she described the body recovery. She recounted how the next morning, with sheets of painter's tarp and homemade masks smeared in vapor rub, the three of them began the task of fishing out the dead and dragging them to the shallow graves as far away from the house as they dared venture. Some of the deceased were reasonably fresh and whole, other bodies shredding into small pieces or losing entire limbs as the women struggled to pull them ashore.

It was amazing to Butter that May could retell the story, even adding a bit of humor in now and then. He sat and listened, letting her get it all out. Then, after a pause to point out a good-sized turtle surfacing nearby, the young woman's voice turned low and serious. "For the rest of the summer and into the fall, we survived on a diet of fish, roadside greens, and whatever other wild harvest we came across. We never ventured far from the marina, rarely saw any other human beings. When other people did wander down the road or drift by in a boat, we would hide."

"I bet you guys were scared more than not," Butter added, amazed that three, lightly armed women had survived that period.

"We never ventured out at night. From dusk to dawn, we huddled together behind blackened windows and heavily barricaded doors. We spent the time reading or talking by candlelight. It helped keep the fear away."

"How old is April?" he questioned, trying to paint more details into the picture forming from her story.

"April had just graduated from college and landed her first job as an elementary school teacher when chaos exploded in our little world. I was about to become a freshman at the local community college and thinking about joining the Army after I graduated. Both of us were avid readers. Like so many sisters, we were polar opposites when it came to boys, politics, music, and literature. I remember those nights. Sometimes we would fall asleep debating each other over the smallest thing."

"Mom passed the hours playing solitaire with an old deck of bicycle cards and making lists of chores that needed to be accomplished the next day. It was all pretty tranquil until October. The winds changed again, this time shifting to roar out of the north and bringing a deep chill with them," she said, shivering at the memory.

Butter knew that Lake Amistad's southern latitude normally meant mild winters. Snow was extremely rare this far south in Texas, a light frost only the occasional visitor. May seemed to read his thoughts, "Since its creation, this reservoir has never experienced even the thinnest layer of ice," she said. "Just our luck that it almost froze that winter."

"The temperature dipped into the low 40's and stayed there for days on end. I know that doesn't sound like much if you're suffering sub-zero weather in Chicago or Detroit. Hell, our weather would have been considered a blessing to those poor souls. But to us, it was an extreme hardship. Texas homes aren't built for cold weather, and we don't have any sort of wood-burning stove or fireplace. There wasn't a single heavy coat in our closets."

Butter was now hanging on the pain in her words. "What did you guys do?"

She didn't answer for a second, ignoring his question at first. "The worst part was the lack of food. When the temperature dropped, the lake's schools of bass and crappie headed for deeper, warmer waters. Day after day, we returned from the fishing pier emptyhanded. The plants all went into hibernation. The ducks migrated south. Our already bare cupboard soon gathered nothing but dust."

"Ouch," he said, the ache in her words making it obvious what was coming next.

"I'll never forget the hunger," she whispered. "I was already pretty thin, but starvation is a whole different animal. The head-aches came first, followed by the inability to focus, and then the loss of short-term memory. I couldn't sleep. After a while, even accomplishing the simplest task became nearly impossible. I remember crying one morning because I couldn't figure out how to tie my shoes."

Butter's grip on her hand tightened, "You made it. You're here. You survived, and only a very strong person can make it through something like that."

"Thanks," she said quietly. "It got worse. Much worse. It seemed like Mother Nature's cruelty knew no limits that first winter. I am sure it was one of the coldest on record ... if there had been anyone around to keep such statistics. The sky was grey and overcast for days. The wind howled out of the north. Since then, I've learned that staying warm forces the human body to consume more calories. The constant cold made our situation all the more desperate around here."

Something changed in May. Butter felt her frame tense, and her expression became angry. "One morning, April announced that we had to leave the lake. She said that we hadn't seen anyone else in the area for weeks. She argued bitterly that we had to go and find food if we expected to survive."

"Mom kept asking her why she thought every crumb and morsel hadn't already been found and eaten. She kept saying, 'What makes you think we have enough strength left to even walk a few miles? No. We are staying here in our home. The weather will break soon, and the fish will return.'"

Butter frowned, "Where did April think she would find food?"

"I don't know. None of us were thinking clearly. You can't focus your mind when you're that weak. I remember April saying that she hadn't eaten anything but one scrawny frog leg in the last week. She kept saying that by now the raping and pillaging would be over … that people surely had begun to organize and rebuild. There had to be someone that could help us, she argued. Good people must still be alive somewhere."

"Mom didn't buy it. She and April wasted so much energy fighting. I can still hear them, mom yelling, 'What makes you think that evil has played itself out?' And then, 'You and your bohemian attitude. You've been like that since you were a little girl. Never afraid of strangers, always optimistic and hopeful. Always assuming people were good and trustworthy. I love you for it, and yet it has always worried me to no end. Your naivety will get you killed, especially in these times.'"

"I take it your sister didn't listen?"

"Back and forth the debate raged. Mom and I trying to convince April that the world outside the bubble of our little, isolated marina was still a dangerous place. She wouldn't budge though, convinced that we were starving for no good reason, absolutely certain that there must be help out there somewhere."

Now May's voice grew low, telling the story like she was reading from the pages of some novel. "The next morning we found the note. It said, 'I am going to find food and help. I'll be back in a few days. I have to leave now, while I still have the strength to walk. I love you both. April.'"

"Not good," Butter mumbled, now fully understanding what had happened to the mysterious April, and what the sister she had left behind was forced to endure.

"I exploded out of the door after reading that scrap of paper, the adrenaline surge giving me more strength than I knew existed. I jogged down the long lane leading to the marina and began the trek south along the road toward town. In less than a mile, I heard a strange sound drifting past. It was a noise I hadn't heard in months. An engine. A car … or truck. I thought for a second that maybe April had been right. Maybe civilization's recovery hadn't expanded to our little spot on the lake, and we had been suffering for no good reason."

Butter could understand her logic. The three women, holed up in the remote marina, wouldn't have had any idea what was really happening in the world outside.

"I kept going, wandering alongside the road, ready to run for cover or dive into the underbrush. Some little voice kept telling me the situation was dangerous. When the motor sound grew louder, I really got scared. Who had a car? Who had gas? It was all so … so … surreal. Strangers were dangerous; the pirates had proven that. Somehow, I managed to keep going, but every step was hard. I was like an edgy rabbit ready to dash down its hole."

"And?"

"When I crested the next rise, I saw it. A dark spot against the brown and auburn shades of the horizon. I darted off the road to hide behind a small bush. The engine stopped, and then I could hear voices. I just stayed put for a while, listening, trying to get my heart to stop pounding. It was like this tug-of-war inside my head. The strangers might have food. They also might kill me … or worse. If it hadn't been for April's little disappearing stunt, I would have probably tried to run for home."

"So what did you do?" Butter asked, clearly intrigued by her story.

"I had to find April," she answered with conviction. "But I was so weak when the adrenaline rush wore off. I stumbled from that cluster of scrub to a small gully that let me get a bit closer to the pickup without being seen. I don't remember ever being so terrified, but I wasn't about to let the only sign of civilization I'd seen in months drive away before I knew what was going on."

Then the girl changed again, her eyes growing wet before any more words came out. "I spotted a handful of men gathered around the truck, the black barrels of their guns pointing in the air," she sniffed. "They were huddled around a rear tire, almost as if it had gone flat. There was something else in the back of the truck bed, an odd shape. A cage."

Butter's eyes opened wide. He hadn't been expecting that turn of events.

"I could hear them. Spanish words drifted across the sandstone and shale. They were shouting questions like, 'Where did you come from?' and 'How many people are there?'"

"They were shouting at April, weren't they?" Butter asked, already knowing the answer.

Nodding, May replied, "Yes. I couldn't hear her response. Either I was still too far away, or she wasn't answering. Something in the men's tone caused a streak of icy cold to pulse through my core. These men were hostile. They had guns. They were interrogating someone, and in my heart, I knew it was April. Just then, one of them bent over and yanked my sister upright. I was stunned, watching as she was shoved violently toward the back of the truck and then crammed into that damn, awful, horrible cage. The metallic clank of the door slamming shut was so clear, it almost made me puke. I hurried to stand up too fast, became dizzy, and fell to the dirt."

"Oh, Lord, May. Now I understand what you said before about believing she was still alive. Do you have any idea where she might be?"

"They turned toward the south and sped off. I caught one last glance of my sister's horrified face, staring out between the bars. A minute later, the truck had disappeared into the distance. We've not seen or heard from her since."

Chapter 6

Bishop and Terri watched the Blackhawk raise its nose and bleed off speed. Both parents were more than a little nervous about their son's first flight on a helicopter and held their breath as the pilot began the final maneuvers to touch down.

The downdraft kicked up a swirling cloud of southern Texas grit as the wheels gently impacted what had once been a small shopping mall's parking lot. It had taken several moments before the air cleared enough for mom and dad to spot Nick holding their son.

Hunter looked tiny in the big man's massive arms as Nick pointed toward the eager parents, trying to get the lad to wave and smile. The boy refused to cooperate, however, remaining fixated on the pilot's cluttered dashboard of gauges and blinking lights.

Diana's security team was the first to deploy, hustling out of the copter's bay and moving off to augment the perimeter already established by a handful of deputies and the rest of Bishop's team. Since the Alliance leader's visit was unannounced, her protection detail was at the bare minimum.

Despite Nick's famous work ethic and business-first attitude, Bishop noted the big guy scanning the area for his own son. After Hunter had been passed to his mother's anxious arms, the Texan pointed toward a rooftop just over 500 meters away and explained, "He's over there, Nick, pulling counter-sniper duty. I'll bring him down as soon as Diana is in a vehicle."

A few minutes later, they were all loaded into four of Sheriff Watt's SUVs and rolling toward the marina.

The houseboat's main salon was more than spacious enough to host the meeting, which started after Mr. McCarthy's arrival and subsequent search by Diana's bodyguards. Bishop almost laughed as he watched one of the burly security men thoroughly frisk the troublesome fellow. The Texan was sure Nick had ordered the precaution just to irritate the U.S. representative.

"I think the convoy got caught up in some sort of local feud or range war, or perhaps a dispute over territory," Bishop calmly reported once everyone was seated around the dining table. "It's next to impossible to know exactly who or why, and it's for damn sure that bringing them to justice is far beyond our capabilities. Short of a full-scale invasion by the Alliance's military forces, sticking our toe over the border is only going to get us pulled into a dispute that is none of our business. In summary, I recommend an enhanced presence by Sheriff Watt's department and perhaps an occasional military training exercise along the river. Those moves should discourage any violence from spilling over onto our territory. That, sir, is my final report."

"Thank you for that report, Bishop," Nick acknowledged with formality, "Your team did a good job getting in and out of there without leaving a big footprint, and the recovery of an Alliance citizen's property was a bonus."

Mr. McCarthy's palms slammed onto the table as he bellowed, "This is preposterous! A bonus! You call recovering some rickety old, shot-up houseboat a bonus? What the hell is wrong with you people? Do you want the United States of America to fail? Are you wringing your hands in eager anticipation, hoping that millions more of us will starve this winter? Is that what all of this is about?"

Diana remained stoic at the head of the table, her voice betraying none of the frustration that was welling up inside of the Alliance's highest elected official. "Mr. McCarthy, sir, please calm down. I assure you we are utilizing every resource at our disposal. We sent our best people into a dangerous situation in order to discover what happened to that convoy. There's only so much we can do. Even before the collapse, not every crime could be solved."

The U.S. representative's exasperation wasn't going to be quelled so easily. "My nation must secure an external source of agricultural products. There is no other option available to us. We came to the Alliance with hat-in-hand and were promptly kicked to the curb. We were forced to move on and found a viable, willing trading partner in Mexico. Then, all of a sudden, our goods were mysteriously destroyed in Alliance territory. The perpetrators of this crime vanish into thin air, and soon your government executes what I can only describe as a half-assed effort to investigate. An amazing string of coincidences, isn't it?"

"Perhaps," Terri replied. "But a believable one. What is it that you want from us, Mr. McCarthy? Do you want us to invade Mexico? Do you want us to send in tanks and armed gunships? You seem quite adept at pointing fingers, yet I've not heard a single suggestion or potential solution from your side of the table."

"Sending in our armed forces would be a horrible mistake," Nick added. "Tanks rolling across fields tend to destroy crops. Artillery barrages flatten warehouses. Unfortunately, battles often kill civilians. We could probably crush any unorganized resistance in a matter of days, but you would no longer have a viable trading partner. The medicine might cure the symptoms, but it would kill the patient."

McCarty sighed, and then a slight smirk appeared at the corners of his mouth. "I've spoken with the President, and he has approved what we feel is a valid compromise. We want the Alliance to guarantee the next shipment of food."

"What?" Bishop started. "How can we...."

Nick interrupted, stopping his friend before he could finish. "What exactly do you mean by *guarantee*, sir?"

"Washington wants Alpha to deliver 300 tons of foodstuffs to the border at Texarkana. We don't care where it comes from or how it is delivered. If you wish to utilize our original source in Mexico, that tonnage has already been paid for as part of our initial agreement with the people down there. If you want to substitute with product produced in Alliance territory, that's acceptable as well. We don't care what assets you use to secure this shipment or where the food comes from. Such a gesture would dispel any concerns Americans might have about possible Alliance involvement in this incident. We need to be sure that you have our backs."

"So you want us to be your insurance policy and your mercenaries?" Bishop protested as he started to stand. "I got your insurance policy, pal. Right here...."

Terri's hand stopped her husband from rising and making an obscene gesture, firmly pushing him back into the chair.

Diana then dropped a bombshell that evaporated the Texan's follow-on protest. "I think those terms are acceptable, Mr. McCarthy. We in the Alliance sincerely regret this incident and want nothing but continued success for our former countrymen in the U.S. of A. We'll deliver your convoy of food in 25 days."

Bishop was stunned, his eyes wide with shock. In fact, he was so taken aback, he didn't utter another word as the meeting wrapped up and the attendees began filing out of the salon.

By the time he recovered, the Texan had found himself alone with Nick, Diana, and his wife.

"If you think I'm taking my team into Mexico so that asswart doesn't get in trouble with his bosses back in Washington, you've got another think coming," he growled at Diana. "Lady, I would follow you through the gates of hell, but this is bullshit. Pure, grade-A, unadulterated bullshit, and I'm not going to risk a single life on such an ill-advised mission." With that, Bishop rose in anticipation of storming out of the room.

"Bishop!" Diana barked harshly, and then added a softer, "Please."

The Texan did as she requested, his frame stiffening, but waiting for her next words.

Diana's expression didn't change as the Alliance honcho exchanged knowing looks with Nick. She then rose calmly and ambled toward Bishop, gently placing her hands on his shoulders. "I love you like a brother. Your passion is endearing, and your respect for the men in your command is inspiring. You do, however, have about the quickest trigger finger on that temper of yours that I've ever seen. Before you rush off in a huff, please answer one question for me."

Begrudgingly, Bishop nodded. "Okay. Shoot."

"What did the United States use to pay for all that food?"

"Huh?"

"How did they pay for the food?" Nick chimed in, now grinning at his hot-headed friend.

Bishop shrugged, "Hell if I know? Gold? Fuel? Strippers? Beer? What difference does it make?"

"What if they traded weapons for food?" Diana asked, a knowing smirk turning up the corners of her mouth.

It all fell into place, Bishop suddenly realizing that his thinking had, once again, been tactical, not strategic. Still, he had trouble admitting his latest tantrum was unjustified. "What makes you guys think the Colonel... err... the President would do such a thing? He of all people should know that giving whiskey and guns to the savages is a recipe for disaster."

"He may not know," Nick replied. "It wouldn't be the first time someone from Washington had acted autonomously. Remember our friend the ambassador? Just think about this. McCarthy is hiding something, and we're not getting any direct answers from Washington. They know one hell of a lot more about what's going on south of the border than we do, and it's obvious that they aren't concerned with *our* best interests."

Bishop relaxed slightly, stomping to the window to stare out at the lake and digest Nick's words.

It was clear that one or more large, well-organized parties existed in Mexico. It was also evident that they were aggressive and had zero respect for the border with the Alliance. Given the amount of food available for export, it was a reasonable assumption that plenty of manpower existed south of the Rio Grande. A population that could easily be used to raise a sizable army.

"A large, well-armed force could threaten the Alliance," Diana stated as if she could read Bishop's thoughts. "We might be facing raiding parties, organized crime, or even an invasion force. There's only one way to know, and that's to insert boots on the ground ... boots worn by people we can trust."

Bishop pivoted and argued, "I understand the need for intelligence. You'll get no argument from me about that. So why don't we just send in some spies? Bribe some locals to give us information? Governments have been practicing espionage since we lived in tribes – why not do it the time-honored way by being sneaky as hell and going under the table?"

"But that's exactly what we're doing by granting McCarthy's request," Diana explained.

Terri got it. "You're using the convoy protection to give our spies a good cover story. It makes sense. If there's nothing devious going on between Mexico and the U.S., then no harm, no foul. If we do find something's afoot, then you can act on the information without having gone behind Washington's back. As a matter of fact, our friends to the north demanded that we get involved. Brilliant, Diana. Simply brilliant."

Bishop wasn't sold. "Okay. Fine. You want me to protect the convoy and see what's going on down in glorious, old Mexico. I'll be happy to oblige. I need a platoon of M1 Abrahams battle tanks, two companies of crack infantry, and at least two helicopter gunships overhead all the way there and back. Easy as pie, and I promise we'll bring home the bacon."

Nick shook his head, grinning at his friend's antics. "If we go across the border with a significant force, we risk the people on the other side vanishing down a rabbit hole or assuming our actions are an invasion. Either way, we won't learn a damn thing. Besides, everyone in this room knows the Alliance can't afford any sort of long-term military action. If we get pulled into an extended fight down there, both the cost and the political ramifications would be unacceptable. We're still recovering from the property ownership debacle and all of the unintended consequences and disruptions associated with that new law."

"So you want me to take my team into harm's way and play like we're some sort of Hollywood super spies. Shaken, not stirred? I don't like it, Nick. We're not trained for that sort of thing. My guys are the best, but you're asking us to put our round peg in a very dangerous square hole."

Diana countered, "I don't know about that, Bishop. Is what we're asking really all that different than a typical SAINT mission? You're approaching an unknown entity and trying to learn how they're organized, how well armed they are, and who's in charge. Is it really all that dissimilar doing those things in a Texas town versus Central Mexico?"

Bishop held up his fingers and began counting, "First, there is the language barrier. Secondly, we won't have any support or backup close at hand like we do in Texas. Third, we have zero authority down there. Here, we can fall back on the Alliance, an elected government, and rule of law. There, we're just a bunch of cowboys trying to ride shotgun on a convoy of trucks. There's a huge difference in my mind."

Tilting his head, Nick's response surprised everyone in the room. "Yes, you're absolutely right on every count. Tell you what, old friend; you think it over tonight and talk it through with your team and Terri. If you don't want to accept the mission, I'll assign one of the other SAINT teams. Fair enough?"

Bishop nodded but with hesitation. He wasn't quite sure what his best friend was trying to pull. "Fair enough."

Diana walked with Terri on the way to retrieve Hunter from the nanny brought along on the short flight from Alpha. "How's the houseboat working out?" she asked.

"We love it. If it hadn't been for the two massacres and the intense gunfight, it would be a great little vacation spot." Terri smiled at her friend and elaborated, "Heck, I'd have given it four stars on post-apocalyptic-vacations dot com ... if we still had such things."

Bishop and Terri spent the rest of the afternoon playing with their son while Nick and Diana attended a couple of government functions in nearby Del Rio.

After a few hours of peekaboo and roughhousing, Terri decided it was time to address the white elephant in the room. "Penny for your thoughts, Mr. SAINT team boss man. Soooo.... are you going to take the assignment?" she asked, trying hard not to sound overly tentative.

Without pause, Bishop's response shocked his wife. "Yes. If Nick can provide a rather lengthy list of items, I think my team is about the best the Alliance can muster at the moment. The more I think about Diana's little game of spy versus spy, the more it makes sense to me. Besides, I love staying on this boat, and it will take a while for Alpha to gather that many replacement truck drivers and rigs. I figure we can all lounge around in luxury until they do, and Diana will pick up the tab."

It was rare that Terri couldn't read her husband like a book. "What's the real reason, Bishop?"

With a shrug, the Texan retorted, "Like I said, we might as well enjoy ourselves while we can. I can't think of alternative SAINT mission that would include such nice digs on the taxpayer's credit card. Why not take advantage of the perks when we can?"

"Bullshit," Terri countered, her hands flying to her hips. "Spill the beans, tough guy. Spit it out."

The Texan interrupted the tickle fight and held his son up as if making a presentation. In a voice laced with emotion, he admitted, "This is the reason why I'm taking the job. This little guy right here. I made up my mind as soon as we started playing a few hours ago."

"Hunter?" Terri frowned, unable to connect Bishop's dots. "Our *son* is the reason why you've decided to go to Mexico?"

"Yes," her husband answered in his most serious tone. "Seeing that little one die in the village yesterday reminded me of something an old ranch hand told me when I was a kid," he paused to kiss Hunter on his forehead before continuing. "Did I ever tell you about Stubby?"

Terri frowned, "Stubby? No, that name doesn't ring a bell."

"Stubby had lost an arm in Vietnam. I asked him once if he regretted being drafted and having to go fight in Southeast Asia. He said he had volunteered … signed up on his own accord."

"Wait a second. You had a war hero who had lost a limb, and you guys called him Stubby?" Terri asked, not quite believing her husband's tale, and definitely not seeing what it had to do with Mexico. "What a bunch of assholes."

Shaking his head, Bishop said, "There you go again, flying off the handle. We had called him Stubby since high school because he was just over five feet tall, not because of his wounds. Anyway, I asked him why he had joined the Army. He said he went off to war so his sons and grandsons wouldn't have to, and he had no regrets. That child that died in your arms could be Hunter in a few years. If we don't take care of molehills before they become mountains, our child may have to go and wage war on some distant battlefield. I have a really bad feeling about the storm that is brewing south of the border, and I think Diana and Nick are right. It's better to nip this thing in the bud rather than stand back and watch it blossom into a really big problem. Seeing Hunter today reinforced those thoughts. I now understand Stub's logic."

Terri tilted her head and smiled, quickly moving to her husband's side. "It's times like these that remind me of why I love you so much," she responded softly. "You are truly a good man."

The Texan blushed, but only a little. "And you're *truly* a special woman. That's why I want you to go along with us. I need you on this little excursion. I need someone who speaks the language and whose judgement I know that I can trust."

For the second time in only a few minutes, Terri found herself completely surprised by Bishop's words. "Really?"

"Yes, really. I know you're a little taken back by my invitation, but it's true. We're going to be heading into unexplored territory, and I want you by my side. In all the Alliance, you've got the best head on your shoulders when it comes to this sort of thing. I want you there beside me. I think it improves our odds."

Her only response was to kiss him on the cheek, and then she sprang, tackling Bishop and reigniting the roughhousing. The houseboat soon filled with the cackle of laughter and joy, sounds of a happy family playing together.

Hunter, as usual, emerged victorious.

May watched her mother patching the bullet holes in the re-covered houseboat, the glistening white gel coat in stark contrast to the sagging, leather-like skin of Hannah's arm.

"You're not that old," she whispered in a low tone, not intending for her mother to hear.

Indeed, Hannah hadn't weathered the downfall very well. The daily stress of survival, loss of a husband and daughter, and the ongoing saga of life had aged the woman well beyond her years.

May acknowledged that part of the reason for her mother's premature aging was the cigarettes. Everybody knew smoking was bad for the lungs *and* the skin, especially when people had do go to extreme measures to satisfy their habit.

The youngest sister could still remember waking up one morning to find her mother missing. After touring the marina while desperately calling her mom's name, she spied a lone figure roaming in the distance, wandering around what had once been a small, roadside tavern. For a moment, she had thought her mother had finally gone insane with grief over April's disappearance.

As she approached, she was relieved to find Hannah meandering around the parking lot, a plastic trash bag in her hand. "Mom, what are you doing? What's wrong?"

"I'm gathering up cigarette butts," came her matter-of-fact reply. "People liked to smoke and drink, and I'm finding hundreds of stubs around here. I'm going to dry out the tobacco and roll my own."

Watching her mother unwrap hundreds of little tubes of tobacco ... each and every one having been in some stranger's mouth, made May gag. All the while, Hannah seemed unfazed, even giddy at the prospect of once again enjoying the sensation of hot smoke and nicotine. After two days of drying the scraps of brown leaf in the sun, her mother produced the thinnest paper available, twisted a pinch, licked the roll like a cowboy on the range, and lit the makeshift coffin nail.

Now, today, the grotesque habit didn't even phase Hannah's youngest daughter. May had aged as well, morphing into something that neither her parents, nor her sister, would ever have expected.

"Apocalypses have a way of doing that to people," she whispered. "I'm sorry, mom. I have to do what I have to do."

Stepping closer and speaking up so her mother could hear, May said, "I'm going out with Ricky in a while. Do you need anything before I leave?"

Hannah turned to study her youngest, "Are you sure you two are only going fishing? Something about that boy bothers me. He has too much meanness in his eyes for such a young man, and he's way, way too comfortable with that fancy gun of his."

"Mom, you're such a worry wart," May countered, waving a dismissive hand through the air. "Rick and I are going to go fishing, and that's all there is to it. Besides, having a bunch of armed men around seems to be the norm these days," she added, nodding toward the Alliance men on the next pier.

"They're here for a good reason and are professional soldiers. Rick is just a kid from Del Rio who stares at your boobs way too much. Besides, I thought you were a little enamored with that big one from Alpha. He seems like a nice boy. Big as a mountain, but a gentle soul if I'm reading him right."

"Butter? Oh, I like him just fine, but we're just friends. Besides, he'll be leaving in a few days."

Hannah shrugged, returning to her task.

April stared at her mother for a time, a melancholy fog rolling in, eventually dominating the youngest daughter's mood. "I know worrying about April is killing you, mom. I'm going to find her," she whispered. "And then I'm going to bring her home, no matter what it takes."

Turning away, April noted the sun's position. It was time.

"I'll be back in a few hours, Mom," she informed her mother. "If my bike doesn't break down again."

"Be careful, sweetie," Hannah answered. "Please don't be out too late after dark. You know how I worry."

~  ~

May entered the warehouse and scanned the interior, the muzzle of her 12-gauge in unison with her sweeping eyes.

"It's okay," a familiar voice sounded from the darkness. "There are only Quakers here."

May acknowledged the voice by lowering her weapon and continuing down a narrow passage toward the interior.

Rounding the final corner brought the low, yellow hue of several candles perched on a ragtag assortment of old saucers and pans. Strings and gobs of old wax drippings signaled the age and usage history of the lighting.

One by one, May glanced at the pale expressions brightened by the dim illumination. Each one represented a tale of horror, heartache, and woe. There was Ray, her second in command and the group's best shot. Martina was next, her mother having been taken the same day as April. A series of anguished faces appeared, over 30 pairs of tormented eyes staring back at their leader.

A meeting of all the members was dangerous but necessary. Every second they spent in the same location increased the chances of their discovery and capture – an event that would ultimately lead to a ghastly, excruciating death. May, knowing that time wasn't on their side, got right down to business.

"There is going to be a second convoy to Mexico," she announced in a loud and clear voice that was laced with disgust. "Evidently, our friends in the U.S. didn't learn their lesson the first time."

The news brought a low murmur from the gathering, some of the hushed voices angry, some surprised. None were happy.

"This second procession will meet the same fate as the first," May promised. "This time, we will need to be far, far more cautious. The Alliance of Texas will be guarding this second shipment, and they will be expecting trouble. We're going to have to get creative this time."

"Do you know when they plan to move?" a question fired back. "Are you sure this isn't a trap to draw us out?"

May grunted at the inquiry, "No need to worry, my friends. My source is a young man who is quite enamored by my charms. He is a naïve, muscle-bound buffoon. He will tell me anything I want to know. In a few days, I'll have their itinerary, route, and the full composition of their security precautions."

Again, the room was filled with rumblings and whispered comments, but May ignored them. "So far the Alliance doesn't know of our existence. Our efforts to keep a low profile have been successful, but that won't last long if we become careless. The team they have dispatched to Amistad is led by some very competent individuals. They are no fools and are very capable. We should not underestimate them."

"And you're sure they're not siding with the U.S.A. and the Copperheads?" sounded the same inquisitive voice from the darkness. "How we can be sure they aren't the enemy?"

It was a common question and summarized the ongoing debate that had divided the group for the past few months.

The Copperheads had been named after the segment of the white U.S. population who supported slavery before the American Civil War. The parallel was undeniable. Just like the Deep South in the early 1800s, an entire economic infrastructure had blossomed around the slave trade. Those who benefited and supported indentured servitude were assigned the snake-like moniker.

The Quakers who traveled to the New World existed on the opposite side of the spectrum. From the very beginning, their leaders spoke out against the practice of slavery and were the first to formally organize political groups of abolitionists. They played a key role in the Union's anti-slavery sentiment and were considered enlightened by most of Europe and the northern states.

Now, along the eastern Rio Grande Valley, those same lines had been drawn yet again. May was addressing the newest generation of Quakers.

"We can't be sure," May answered. "But we have no choice. The Copperheads will only get stronger and more emboldened if they begin exporting goods … food grown by the hands of slaves … our brothers and sisters and mothers and fathers. In the end, it won't matter if the government in Alpha willingly joins our cause, or not. I don't plan to give them any other option."

May's fiery eyes scanned the Quakers, almost as if she was daring any of them to challenge her position. When no one spoke, her voice softened to a tone of reason and compassion. "We all know we can't defeat the Copperheads with guns and bullets. They are too many, too strong, and now completely dominate the Mexican countryside. I ask all of you to remember how many of our brothers and sisters have died trying to defeat them using force. Until our numbers grow, there is only one way to stop the spread of this evil. We must deny them a market for their ill-gotten gains and turn the Alliance against them. Every time they sell their products, they flex their muscles and their strength increases. Every customer we deny them causes atrophy and furthers our cause. I know it seems like so little, but until we have powerful friends, this is the best we can do."

"Why don't we just approach the Alliance team and explain our situation to them? Why don't we come out into the open? Our cause is moral and just; surely they'll understand and help us," offered another voice.

Shaking her head, May repeated the same answer to the same question that had been asked a dozen times. "We can't take the risk that they'll see things our way. We've all seen local officials, even our neighbors and friends, corrupted by the Copperheads. They spread around favors and bribes. Anyone who doesn't go along is assassinated or abducted for the plantations. This adversary is worse than the drug cartels were before the collapse. If the Alliance doesn't join us, then we haven't exposed ourselves to a potential enemy. If they do take up the fight against slavery, then we've accomplished our goals and will have a strong ally."

Rick picked that moment to chime in, "Besides, with the United States now doing business with the Copperheads, there's no way to predict how Alpha will respond. We keep hearing that Texas is barely keeping their recovery on track. We can't take the risk that they won't join us, or worse yet, will side with Washington."

Several of the gathered heads nodded in agreement, but not all.

"We must pull the Alliance in and get them committed," May added. "The Copperheads did us a favor by butchering the villagers. If the leadership in Alpha starts losing people inside of Mexico, they will have no choice but to get involved."

Chapter 7

Just because Nick wouldn't provide battle tanks didn't mean Bishop couldn't up-armor the convoy's security. He would implement the age-old, proven doctrine of speed-of-action, surprise, and overwhelming force. It was an unbeatable combination.

His first priority was speed, which required mobility. Most inexperienced security contingents made the critical mistake of thinking along the lines of defensive capabilities. Version two of the Mexican gravy train would contain potent, mobile, offensive firepower. If anybody messed with the Texans' trucks, he would take the fight to them, not sit back and wait until the black hats blasted them to bits.

The mistake made by the first group of truckers had been a common one. Their protective elements were anchored to the very assets they were charged with defending. The Texan likened it to guarding a house by carrying it around on your back. Speed simply wasn't an option with such a burden slowing you down.

His first line assets would be two dirt bikes orbiting and scouting ahead of the convoy. In addition to providing a speedy reaction, these off-road machines would deny any foe the element of surprise.

Next in the convoy's entourage would be two 4x4 pickups, each truck's bed lined with sandbags and a crew manning a belt-fed weapon. During the war in Afghanistan, U.S. troops took to calling such machines, "technicals." If someone tried to set up an ambush along their route, Bishop could pull the pickups out of the line and take the fight to the bushwhackers. He prayed they would provide overwhelming firepower.

His final configuration involved attaching long-range firepower on top of the semi-trailers. Kevin, along with a deputy who was a former sniper, would make the trip riding on top of the second and eighth units, surrounded by sandbags, and carrying enough ammo to hold off a brigade.

Once he'd set up the convoy's offensive capabilities, his next task was to train the truck drivers.

"Don't stop if we're ambushed. Always, always push through the kill zone. If the road is blocked, go around. If you can't bypass the obstacle, then and only then you should back out. Never get stalled right where the enemy wants you to be. You're better off running the open road on your own than sitting fat and stupid in the attackers' crosshairs."

For three days, he trained them in the desert north of Amistad, running countless drills and wasting a ton of diesel fuel.

Nick provided military grade, handheld radios. A tech from Fort Hood had given each member a crash course in the operation and usage. If the highwaymen were expecting to follow CB traffic as a tool to track the convoy, they were going to be disappointed.

"Stay off the radio unless you see a threat. Listen; don't talk. Don't bunch up – keep good spacing."

On and on, droned the drills and exercises. Each day ended with classroom debriefings, followed by intense sessions of questions, answers, and suggestions. Bishop was pleased with the general attitude and cooperation of the drivers, but far from surprised. They all recognized the dangers involved, and they all hoped to live through the experience.

Finally, just 20 days after Diana had agreed to provide the replacement convoy, they were ready to go.

"Be in your cabs and ready to roll an hour before dawn," Bishop instructed the gathered men.

They crossed the dam an hour behind schedule, last minute issues causing the delay.

One of the 18-wheelers wouldn't start, a radio carelessly left on overnight having drained the battery. Two of Nick's men had gotten lost in the pre-dawn light and were late arriving at the departure point.

Bishop wasn't nearly as upset as his team anticipated. "Shit happens," he told Butter. "These drivers aren't military, and we put this whole thing together in a matter of days. I thought we'd be lucky if we left before the sun came up."

As the long line of pickups and over-the-road semis crossed the bridge, every pair of eyes was fixed on the string of burned out hulks that still lined the roadway. While crews from Del Rio had worked to clear a path along the road, they hadn't managed to remove any of the wrecks. In a way, Bishop was glad everyone was seeing the carnage. The ambush site served as an excellent reminder that they were entering what was essentially a war zone, and every last man had better be on top of his game if he were going to survive.

In reality, the Texan didn't expect any trouble on the trip south. Whoever had attacked the convoy had waited until the truckers were in Alliance territory with trailers full of goods. Terri had been right in thinking the scrawled message, "SET THEM FREE," indicated a political motivation for the attack. What other possible explanation could there be for intentionally burning several dozen tons of food?

Still, the Texan hadn't survived this long by letting down his guard. As the convoy rolled south, he used the wide-open spaces and lack of population to squeeze in more training for his security detail and to keep everyone alert.

Butter was on one of the motorcycles, the big guy having considerable off-road experience using the 2-wheeled machines to round up strays during his youth on the ranch. One of Sheriff Watt's deputies, a man named Cord, was on the other bike.

"Butter, check out that rise to the east," Bishop ordered over the radio, watching to see how well his defensive scheme was going to work in real life.

A small rooster tail of dust rose in the distance, a signal that Butter had changed direction and was accelerating toward the objective. Just as they had drilled, the second bike followed suit, a small speck of black crossing the arid, Mexican landscape as Cord played the role of wingman.

"The two motorcycles must always stay within visual contact of each other," he had ordered a few days ago. No one goes wandering off alone. You are vulnerable sitting on those bikes. Stay close, and watch each other's back." It was gratifying to see his guys were taking those instructions seriously.

"Nothing but rocks and sand out here, boss," Butter reported a minute later. "Heading back to scout the road."

They traveled three hours without incident and were now starting to see foothills in the distance. Bishop called a halt to refuel the bikes and trucks when they reached an area that was flat with little vegetation. He was pleased to see the truckers circle the wagons, just like they had drilled back in Texas.

Terri, welcoming the chance to stretch her legs, noted her husband's eyes never left their surroundings. "Expecting trouble?" she inquired.

"No, not really. I don't believe anyone will bother us on the way in. If they approach us, it will be on the way home."

"I have to use the facilities," she announced, eyeing the surrounding terrain and looking for a secluded spot.

Bishop nodded toward the area beside the pickup. "Open the door and you would have some privacy at least." Then without waiting for her agreement, called out, "Butter! Miss Terri has to relieve herself. Make sure she is undisturbed."

"Yes, sir," came the big kid's response.

"Boys. Humph," Terri moaned, moving toward the far side of the truck.

"Don't worry, Miss Terri. I won't look, and I guarantee no one will bother you," Butter promised, thinking the lady's displeasure was aimed at him.

Twenty minutes later, the motorbikes were zooming ahead while the truckers were climbing back into their cabs. Bishop and Terri, in the command truck, stayed put alongside the road while the long line of semis began pulling away into the mid-day sun.

Scanning the map, Terri calculated, "About four or five more hours if my numbers are accurate."

"Sounds about right. The next 100 miles are the worst of it. We'll be driving through hilly ground according to the satellite maps Nick provided. If I were a highwayman, that's where I'd earn my keep."

As soon as the last truck had joined the column, Bishop pulled out and accelerated toward the front of the convoy, studying each rig as it passed. "Number 14, back off a little ... you're tailgating," the Texan instructed into the radio.

"You got it boss," sounded the friendly trucker's voice. "I'll pay more attention."

Thirty minutes later, the terrain indeed began to rise and fall, the highway snaking left and right to avoid the higher elevations. Their progress slowed, partly due to the winding pavement, mostly because of the unavoidable grades in the road.

"Go to formation B," Bishop ordered.

The motorcycles were nearly worthless here, unable to manage the steeper hills on both sides of the pavement and forced to run on the road. Two of the pickups took the lead now, the bikes falling back to a secondary position.

It was less than 10 minutes later when the lead scout transmitted, "Movement!"

Just like they'd practiced, all of the trucks instantly dropped their speed but maintained their spacing. The entire convoy moved to the center stripe of pavement so the nimbler pickups and motorbikes could pass on either side at will.

"Talk to me," Bishop said into the mic.

"I've got a small, dismounted party alongside the road at the top of the next grade. Number unknown. They've laid some sort of barricade across both lanes. Their composition unknown. Grim is dismounting to approach on foot to get a better view."

"Butter, Cord, reinforce. Units three and four, to the front. I'm on my way."

After exchanging troubled looks with his wife, Bishop floored their truck and began zipping around the barely-crawling line of semis. Less than two minutes later, they were running out in front of the convoy, quickly gaining on the two motorcycles.

"We are too far north for this to be the checkpoint McCarthy warned us about," Terri said.

"Agreed. This is something different."

"Contact," Grim snarled from the scout truck. "Somebody just shot at us and missed."

"Convoy, circle the wagons. Units three and four, go hot and don't let anybody near those semis," Bishop ordered.

Behind him, the drivers began steering their rigs into a new formation. Going four abreast on the two-lane road as they rolled to a stop, the intent was to at least protect some of the inner trucks with those outside units forming a wall. The pickups would orbit; the snipers became lookouts as well as being able to project power.

A minute later, Bishop was skidding to a halt alongside the scout truck and the two bikes. Grim was already another 50 meters up the road, using a small outcropping for cover and studying the roadblock through his optic. "Butter, you're with me," the Texan barked. "Might just be some locals who don't like strangers. Terri and Cord, stay here and guard our wheels."

"I saw them scramble across the road up there," Grim reported as Butter and Bishop joined the old soldier. "I was just telling my driver to slow down when I saw a muzzle flash, and then the bullet sparked off the pavement."

"Only one shot?" Bishop asked, pulling a large pair of binoculars to his eyes.

"That's all I saw, boss."

Bishop scanned the area ahead, finding a large log lying across both lanes of the road. There weren't any vehicles or people visible, just the big log and a bunch of rocks. He keyed his mic, "Kevin, you got anything moving back by the trucks?"

"No movement, sir. I've got 300 meters of open terrain on all sides, and nothing is moving."

"Stay frosty. I want to know if a jackrabbit scratches his ass."

With a slight chuckle, Kevin came back with a prompt, "Yes, sir."

Bishop visualized Kevin's perch on top of one of the semi-trailers, the kid's long-range rifle and huge optic sweeping the countryside and looking for work. He quickly made the decision that the activity to their front wasn't a diversion intended to draw them out while a larger force attacked the convoy. "Let's go take a look," he announced to his two trusted team members. "Grim, cut 100 meters off the road to the east, Butter, take the West. I'll give you five minutes, and then I'm going to walk right up there and see what they want."

"You sure about that, boss?" Grim questioned. "These guys might be a little trigger happy."

"I don't think so," the Texan replied. "When Terri and I were bugging out from Houston, we ran into a small town that had set up roadblocks to protect their people. This might be the same thing."

"You're in command," the older warrior replied, shaking his head in doubt.

Bishop waited the prescribed five minutes, giving his people time to approach the blockade from the flanks. Taking a deep breath, he stood and began walking toward the roadblock.

Just under 100 meters from the barricade, a shot rang out. The bullet snapped overhead, the sonic boom of the round telling Bishop that either the rifleman had a horrible aim, or a cautionary bullet had just been fired.

Grim had the same inclination. "A warning?" the ex-contractor's voice inquired over the airwaves.

"Either that or they need a little range time," Bishop transmitted.

Bishop took a knee alongside the road, ready to roll off into the drainage ditch if more lead came his way. "What do you want?" he shouted at the men hiding in the rocks ahead.

The Spanish words that floated across the desert were rushed and beyond Bishop's understanding of the foreign tongue. "Habla Inglish?" he yelled back.

"Drop gun. Walk here," the voice responded in broken English.

"Sorry, can't do that," Bishop shouted back.

"You must pay a toll! A toll to pass."

"Nada!" Bishop yelled back. "Ain't happening, Señor!"

Again, the report of a rifle shot ripped through the air. This time, the bullet dropped a little closer. Bishop held his ground.

"We've got four, maybe five hostiles in the rocks along both sides of the road," Grim announced. I think only one of them has a rifle. I see one pitchfork; another guy is carrying what looks like a homemade spear. Orders?"

Without moving his head, Bishop keyed the mic. "Grim, keep their head down. Butter, roll them up. I'm tiring of this little game. These guys are just highwaymen and not very good ones at that. Take them alive if possible."

"Roger that," Grim answered. "Going hot."

From just east of the roadblock, Grim's weapon opened up, spraying the surrounding rocks with short bursts of fire. As Bishop was rolling into the ditch, he spotted Butter surge from the bushes and charge the ambushers.

Grim burst out of the rocks just then, his carbine spitting fire as he hit the thugs from the opposite side. Several panicked voices started begging in Spanish. A second later, Bishop spied several sets of arms rise in surrender after dropping their weapons.

While Grim ordered his new captives to move away from their abandoned rifles, Bishop and Butter swept the area looking for additional adversaries. None were found.

"Search them, Butter. You never know when somebody might get brave and act stupid."

As the kid approached the group of terrified men, Bishop finally took a moment to study the captives. He wasn't impressed.

They were a ragtag lot at best, tattered clothing, extremely thin, and looked like they could all benefit from a shower at the YMCA. The Texan noted the mismatched boots on the largest man in the group, as well as the odd assortment of weapons lying on the ground. Two of the prisoners were actually barefoot.

When Butter approached to search the bandits' leader, the man pulled a large knife and dropped into a combat crouch, apparently ready to fight.

Grim's weapon was up in a flash, but Butter held up his hand and stopped his friend from cutting the aggressive fellow in half.

Tossing his weapon to Bishop, Butter pulled his own blade and flexed his massive arms while executing one of the most bone-chilling growls the Texan had ever heard. The message was clear, "Come on, little man. I love a knife fight."

Seeing the cords and sinew rippling through the towering giant's frame, the prisoner had a change of heart and immediately dropped his own blade while his hands shot skyward.

"He's smarter than he looks," Grim chuckled as Butter stepped closer to finish examining the now demure captive.

When he was within reach, Butter's huge fist slashed through the air. The strike landed on the former knife-fighter's temple, delivering so much force that the unfortunate target was physically lifted off the ground. Bishop winced as the man landed and rolled across the sand, immediately wondering if the guy would ever eat solid food again.

"Pull a knife on me, you little bitch, and I'll rip your head off," the big kid hissed in a rare show of anger.

"Ouch," Bishop grunted, knowing the strike would hurt for days and trying to decide if Butter had really been trying to decapitate the prisoner.

"Butter? Damn, son. I'm right proud to serve with you, boy," Grim laughed. "I think you're finally figuring it out, kid."

"I don't like sneaky people, sir. Makes me mad," Butter answered, his voice now back to its normal, cordial tone.

Shaking his head, Bishop knew they needed to get back to business. "Move them up to the road, Butter. Make those two carry their unconscious friend. Grim, you sweep the area. I'm going to call up the convoy."

"You got it, boss," the older man answered, immediately moving off to make sure there weren't any additional bushwhackers in the vicinity.

Less than five minutes later, Terri, Bishop, and Butter stood beside the road as the procession of trucks began their parade by them. Turning to his wife, the Texan nodded toward the detainees and instructed, "Get their story."

Terri started asking the conscious prisoners questions in Spanish but none would answer. With a nod from Bishop, Butter took a step toward the closer man and drew his blade while flashing an angry scowl.

All of the locals immediately began talking, all at once. With big eyes darting between Butter's blade and the unresponsive man at their feet, Terri had to slow them down more than once.

After a few minutes of exchange, Terri called Bishop aside to explain. "These men are from a village about 100 miles west of here. Sounds like a tiny place. They're trying to reach a cousin's ranch near Brownsville, doing a little looting and the occasional robbery along the way. They are very hungry and scared to death of Butter."

"Who can blame them?" Bishop grinned, staring at the looming giant. "Tell them we will drop off their rifles a mile up the road. Tell them if they ever bother us again, I will let the big guy skin them alive."

Terri seemed puzzled by her husband's words, but knew it wasn't the time or place to question his orders. After hearing the message in Spanish, the prisoners eagerly nodded their agreement.

"Why are they so scared of Butter?" Terri asked as they headed back toward the pickup.

"I have no idea," Bishop answered, shrugging his shoulders. "I guess because he's so large."

Terri nodded with a smile, "I suppose. Little do they know he's just a big, friendly teddy bear under all that muscle. Interestingly, though, one of those men asked if we were Copperheads."

Pulling up short, Bishop stopped and stared at his wife. "Did he say anything else?"

"No," Terri replied, shaking her head. "I could tell he was relieved when I told him we weren't. He seemed to be very frightened of them. He said that everyone they met along the way had warned his little gang about avoiding them. That's all he knew."

Bishop pivoted, wanting to press the bandits for more information, but they had already run away. Turning to assess at the line of trucks now rolling off into the distance, he decided there wasn't time to hunt down his former prisoners. "I've got a bad feeling about these snake people."

Julio's grammar needs a lot of work, April concluded as she scanned the amount of red ink she had just deposited on his paper. "I need to keep him after school for a little one on one tutoring," she whispered.

A quick check of her small desk confirmed that she had indeed saved the worst for last, at least when it came to grading tonight's homework.

Neatly sorting the papers into their respective stacks, she deposited the children's assignments into the canvas satchel and hung the old bag on its hook near the head of her cot.

She next checked her skirt, trying to remember if she had changed to this outfit yesterday or the day before. A quick glance at her only other clothing confirmed that she was wearing the least soiled of her two options. Her analysis was confirmed by the size of the dust cloud that rose into the air when she patted the bottom seam. Laundry day was tomorrow. It would have to do.

Finally ready for bed, she pulled off her clothes and hung both blouse and broadcloth skirt on the same hook as her bag. The next time Castro came by to visit, she would meet his needs with a little more vigor than usual, and perhaps he would remember to install a second hanger in her room. A second candle would help as well.

After pulling back the old wool blanket, she sat on the cot's edge and as usual, planned the next day's agenda. There was the spelling test in the morning … then the children were to take a field trip to one of the remote silos where grain was stored. There, they would learn how some of the machinery worked.

Like most of the curriculum at the plantation, practical skills and life lessons were always intermixed with reading, writing, and math. For a moment, she pined for more books, better equipment, and an expanded education for her pupils, but that simply wasn't an option, and probably wouldn't be for years to come.

Still, the children of the plantation were learning the basics, and that was far and above what most of the world's youth were receiving since the apocalypse. Her students were well fed, had shirts on their backs, were given basic medical care, and had roofs over their heads.

That thought led April to, once again, study her own surroundings.

Her room was really a closet, separated from the main barracks by a partition of scrap wood and a sheet of roofing tin. Three years ago, before the world had gone to hell, she would have considered it a shanty at best. Now, she was one of the few who had her own private space, cramped and drafty as it might be.

Part of her good fortune was due to her need to grade papers and work into the night. Mostly, she had to admit, it was because she had caught Castro's eye, and he liked a little privacy when he came to visit.

A scuffle on the floor outside her curtain drew her attention, her heart sinking at the thought that Castro was indeed on the prowl. The footfalls continued past the old bedsheet that acted as her door, most likely one of the laborers on his way to the outhouse.

An outhouse. Quarters that were barely three feet wide and sported a curtain for a door. A wardrobe that consisted of two blouses and two skirts that felt like they were made of a burlap blend fabric. A man who dropped in for sex anytime he wished, regardless of her state or mood.

April fought the urge to feel sorry for herself. "Stop being such a fussbudget," she reprimanded herself. She was teaching school, the only occupation she had ever wanted. She had shelter. She was part of a community. She was safe. Her stomach was full. She was no longer slowly starving to death.

Hunger.

Recalling that first winter after the apocalypse was always difficult. For a fleeting moment, she wondered how her mother was doing … wished she could sit and argue with her sister, if only for a few minutes. She missed her family terribly and yearned for a simpler time when she would wake up and smell the morning air coming off the lake. As was often the case, she dreamed of the racks of clothes that probably still hung in her closet.

All of those memories were trumped, however, pushed aside by one intense, overriding recollection – hunger. It was a sensation that was impossible to forget ... the gnawing, bone-deep, grinding emptiness that had consumed every fiber of her being. She would never forget how it felt, swore that she would go anywhere, do anything to avoid being hungry again.

"Stop your bellyaching," she whispered to the candle. "You ate today. In this world, what more can you ask? Besides, life here on the plantation isn't so bad. In some respects, it is a lot like how you thought the world should function even before the collapse. A modified communal utopia."

That question directed her thoughts down a different path, a well-worn mental route that she had traveled a hundred times since she had been "rescued" that morning so long ago.

After leaving home before sunrise, she remembered reaching the end of the marina's lane and wondering which direction to walk. The sound of a distant motor made the decision for her, and she turned toward the rare noise.

The men at the pickup seemed surprised to see her meander up to them as if they were giving away free food. "Are you hungry?" they asked.

"Yes. I'm very hungry. Do you have anything to eat?"

"We will take you to a place that has all the food you can eat. You have to work hard for it, but they will feed you."

"Sounds like a plan," she had instantly replied, beyond the point of worrying about where she was being taken, what these strangers would do to her, or the family she was leaving behind. If what these men said was true, she would return for her sister and mother. She would save them.

One of the men handed her two stale pieces of flatbread while they traveled south. She had gobbled down the meager nourishment in a few, very unladylike gulps. A short time later, she was offered water.

After several hours of riding in the back of the pickup, they finally arrived at the pens.

April was amazed at the sheer scale of the estate. There were literally hundreds and hundreds of people being "processed" for a new life on the plantation. Step by step, she was prodded, guided, searched, stripped naked, deloused with some sort of cold liquid, and then finally fed.

During the ordeal, she spotted one man try to escape, darting from one of the holding areas like he was being pursued by the devil himself. A horseback rider thundered across the grounds, his lasso making a perfect circle in the air as his mount quickly closed the distance.

The vaquero's rope encircled the escapee, slamming him to the ground like a stray calf.

April remembered standing at the fence, one of the unwashed multitudes who were pressing their faces against the wire and watching the drama like motorists on the highway slowing to rubberneck at a traffic accident.

The captive was unceremoniously dragged across the gravel, screaming in agony as the rocks peeled away his skin. After two laps around the large area, the rider finally stopped directly in front of the penned audience. Another man appeared holding a large machete. Castro.

Without pause or ceremony, the blade arched through the air, chopping into the escapee's neck and nearly severing the head.

April couldn't pull her eyes away as the almost-headless body jerked and twitched, flopping like the fish she once pulled from the water. It seemed like several minutes before the corpse finally went still.

"You are now the property of the Castle," Castro turned and shouted at the horrified onlookers. "If you try to escape, you will die like this man. If you work hard and follow the rules, you will be fed and sheltered. Our laws are very strict. There is no mercy, leniency, or exception. Live by them or be severely punished."

Even before having studied the language as her minor in college, being a South Texas native had provided April with an excellent grasp of Spanish. Frightening murmurs and hushed whispers began circulating among her fellow detainees. Words like slavers, bondage, and thrall began circulating through the throng.

After being processed like cattle purchased at an auction, April found herself in a line of people waiting for an assessor. An hour later, she was roughly manhandled to stand before a middle-aged Hispanic man who was seated at a cheap, folding card table.

"Name," he barked, scribbling something with a yellow pencil.

"April," she replied, nearly frozen with terror after what she had seen and experienced.

"Take off your clothes," he ordered with a voice containing no more compassion or interest than a man looking under the hood of a used car.

She hesitated, only for a moment, but it was too long.

A searing line of pain flashed across her back as one of the guards whipped her with a length of bamboo. "I said, 'Take off your clothing!'" repeated the man at the table.

She immediately complied, eventually standing nude in front of complete strangers and shaking in fear.

"How old are you?"

"I am 22," she stuttered.

"A gringo? Are you from Tejas?"

"Yes."

Now, she had his attention. Rising deliberately, he came from behind the table and circled her slowly, his eyes traveling up and down every inch of her exposed flesh. "You are young enough and strong enough to be a P," he noted.

"What is a P?" she questioned.

"Silence!" he barked, slapping her hard across the mouth. "I did not ask you a question!"

His composure returned by the time he managed to sit again. "What did you do before everything went to hell?"

"I was a schoolteacher," she exaggerated, more from not wanting to risk a lengthy answer than any measure of pride or ego.

"Is that so? Exactly when and where did you attend university?"

On and on, the questioning continued, April standing naked in front of this stranger who was completely unpredictable and seemingly intrigued by her resume.

"I am feeling benevolent today," he finally announced. "I am going classify you as an S, which is short for 'skilled.' You are fortunate in that others of the refugees processed will be assigned with less desirable job descriptions on the plantation. You could have been allocated for pleasure, and the life expectancy of Group P is nearly as short as those who are designated as L, or laborers."

April was allowed to redress and then escorted to another pen where she found a slightly more refined group of captives. There was a man who bragged about being a dentist, a woman who was a nurse, and a gentleman who claimed to be an engineer.

Over the next few days, April opened wide for a dentist, was examined by a doctor, and interviewed with the head of the plantation's extensive school system. She was issued a set of clothing which consisted of sandals, a broadcloth skirt that had the texture of jute sackcloth, and a single, secondhand blouse. Her new wardrobe was clean and smelled like it had been dried in the sun.

She was assigned what appeared to be a surplus Army cot in an oversized barracks. Nearby, there was a five-stall outhouse that emitted a sickening stench and a three-bay, alfresco shower complete with lye soap and icy water.

Over the next few days, April received what could only be described as an indoctrination into the laws and daily life of the plantation. "You are an American," one of the instructors stated. "You won't last long here. The Yankees never do."

Meals were served in a huge, open-air pavilion that contained row after row of rough, wooden picnic tables. Everyone received all of the vegetables, fruit, and bread they could eat. The meat, normally boiled chicken, was rationed.

April consumed more calories during those early days than she could have ever thought possible in this day and time. Slowly, the pounds returned, along with her strength and stamina.

She was assigned to one of the many small schoolhouses that dotted the Castle's extensive territory. In reality, these facilities were often barns or storage buildings that were temporarily empty, waiting for the next harvest. When the crops began flowing in, the children were moved to an alternate, empty shed. April began her teaching career amid the smell of corn, freshly picked limes, and hay.

She pulled back the blanket to check for scorpions or any of the other nasty crawlies that lived in the region. Finding no unwelcome occupants in her bed, April laid back and tried to slow down her mind so that sleep would come.

"The plantation isn't so bad," she told the candle. "The system works. Lady Bella Dona and her men are feeding thousands of people who would otherwise die of malnutrition or diseases. The children are learning to read and write. There is rule of law and order. This isn't such a bad place."

In fact, before society had vanished, the plantation's system wasn't far from what April had believed would best for the entire world.

Before heading off to college, she had never paid even the slightest mind to politics. During her first semester, when asked by an upperclassman if she was a liberal or a conservative, April hadn't known how to answer.

Like so many campuses across America, April's school was a bastion of left-leaning thought. In Political Science 101, she read about the historic presidential campaign where a self-declared socialist almost captured the national nomination for his party. Her professor boasted how that campaign had inspired an almost religious following. The assurance of guaranteed employment, free education, an extensive government safety net, and a society that distributed its wealth evenly seemed like a far superior alternative. Students gravitated to the promise of a benevolent political system that nurtured its people, eliminated poverty, and educated its young without fear of burdensome student loans.

A few of April's older friends had even abandoned their classes to join the Occupy Wall Street movement. The fervor for change had invaded American colleges and universities from Maine to California. Large corporations were depicted as evil empires, sucking the economic lifeblood out of the many while a few vampires at the top could live in unholy splendor.

Capitalism wasn't working. It seemed that practically every underclassman had siblings, cousins, or friends who had graduated with honors, only to discover themselves under mountains of debt and unable to locate jobs. The 2nd Great Depression simply added fuel to the growing bonfire of disenfranchised youth.

Was the plantation really all that different than the cultural models fancied by her classmates before the collapse? They had envisioned an idyllic system where everyone worked, received basic sustenance, was compensated and treated equally. They believed that issues like race ... gender ... nepotism ... and class distinction could be wiped from the face of the U.S. No child would go to bed with an empty tummy. Diseased folks who could not afford treatment would be things of the past. No doubt, violent crime would evaporate. After all, what would be the motivation if everyone were treated equally? Wouldn't socialism provide a recipe for a perfect, Utopian society?

The activists had droned on and on about the European examples, countries such as Norway and Sweden where healthcare, education, and opportunity were provided by the government. Why couldn't the United States be like those distant paradises?

The plantation provided doctors and dentists. All of the laborers were treated exactly the same. Food was provided, as was a free education. In those respects, there was little that separated the seemingly flawless political system she envisioned in college and the path her life had taken now.

Still, there were some differences, creating a less than pure socialist society. Lady Bella Dona lived in far more luxury than any of the workers. The plantation's matriarch wore better clothing, consumed better meals, and slept in finer surroundings. *But someone has to be at the top of the mountain*, April supposed. There had to be an inspiration ladder ... a motivating goal ... a hierarchy to climb. Leadership was essential and rewarded.

And Castro?

April didn't like having to share her body with the man. It didn't seem right to be forced into such an intimate act. Still, she had finally reached a point of reconciliation with it all. Hadn't the hippies of the 1960s embraced the free love movement? Weren't there cultures all over the globe who viewed sex as a natural biological function rather than an act between two emotionally connected people?

When she considered how many pre-collapse societies had embraced arranged marriages or sanctioned concubines and multiple spouses, Castro's occasional needs didn't seem all that immoral or intrusive.

Sleep finally came, April's rose-colored justification of her situation once again allowing her to drift away.

The convoy reached the checkpoint just over 100 kilometers away from the rendezvous coordinates. McCarthy had warned Bishop that the Mexican suppliers occasionally erected such security measures along the roadways. "You'll know they are friendly if they're flying a solid green flag," the U.S. representative had stated with certainty.

When the scout pickup had reported several vehicles blocking the road, Bishop had again called for the truckers to halt and take a defensive posture.

Sure enough, there was a green flag waving in the late afternoon breeze.

This barricade was a far more sophisticated implementation than their previous encounter. In addition to proper execution, it had been well planned.

There was nowhere to flank the blockade, both the eastern and western approaches offering clear fields of fire for several hundred meters. It was a far more professional and highly effective placement.

Bishop was reasonably sure he was studying McCarthy's suppliers – the people who were to host the convoy and load the freight. Still, the Texan approached with caution.

"Let me borrow your bike," Bishop directed Butter.

Riding solo to a spot within a hundred meters of the barricade, Bishop dismounted the motorcycle and paced slowly toward the curious group of men manning the checkpoint. He stopped well short and stood calmly in the road.

A few minutes passed before a lone man left the blockade and strode toward the Texan.

"Are you with the Yankee convoy?" he shouted in perfect English.

"Yes," Bishop responded. "The trucks are a few miles behind me."

"You can pass. We've been expecting you."

With that, the Mexican turned back toward the obstruction and began shouting orders. Bishop watched as at least a dozen, armed men began climbing aboard the assortment of farm trucks and old pickups. He heard several engines roar to life, and a minute later the road was cleared.

"They appear to be friendly," Bishop broadcast into his mic and then added, "but I want at least one of the automatic weapons on them the entire time we're passing through."

The convoy continued without incident, Bishop noting that the locals closed off the road again after the last semi had passed.

An hour later, they arrived at the designated rendezvous point, a tiny, long-abandoned village in the middle of what was obviously an especially lush, agricultural region.

Terri couldn't help but gawk at the contrasting green that surrounded the convoy as they pulled into the gravel lot of what had been the settlement's church. "Look at all these crops. They're beautiful. I've not seen fields like this since before the collapse."

Bishop had to admit it was impressive.

For as far as the eye could see, the hills were covered with neat, emerald rows of various plantings. The scale of the operation was massive, and in an odd way, the sight was uplifting.

There was so much life springing from the earth, the rich, dark soil thick with the promise of a future. "This makes the farms along the Rio Grande look puny," he observed. "No wonder they've got excess groceries to sell."

After making sure his assets were properly positioned, Bishop instructed everyone to eat and rest while they had the chance. "As soon as we're loaded, I want to turn around and head back north."

It was just under an hour after their arrival that an old, rusted pickup approached from the south. The lone driver was an older man and unarmed. Bishop and Terri headed to the perimeter to meet the visitor.

After a quick round of introductions, the local delivered some bad news. "We were told not to expect your arrival until later today. Your produce is still being loaded onto our trucks. It will be morning before we can exchange your empty trailers for our full units."

The Texan didn't like what he heard but had few options. Spending the night wasn't on his itinerary, yet with the post-apocalyptic world's lack of communications, it was easy to see how the delay could occur.

The messenger seemed to sense Bishop's uneasiness. "Don't worry, Señor. No one will bother you here on the plantation. You are very safe on the estate."

After watching the messenger drive away, Bishop winked at his wife and asked, "How many times have we heard that before?"

Chapter 8

Butter had no complaints about his duties or workload. It was simply part of being on the teams, and that was well worth the hardships. Sure, having to pull guard duty after spending the day on the motorcycle was a pain, but getting to work with men such as Bishop and Grim was a once in a lifetime opportunity. Besides, being a member of a SAINT team really wasn't all that much harder than working a fence line or roundup back on the ranch.

As he patrolled the outer perimeter, he paused and scanned the landscape with Bishop's infrared. It was an amazing technology, turning the dark night into day and virtually guaranteeing that no one was going to approach unnoticed. His back might be sore from eight hours on the dirt bike, but where else would he get to use such cool tools?

Butter heard Grim's voice in his earpiece. "All quiet on the western front?"

"No movement, sir," reported the former ranch hand.

"Kevin will be out to relieve you in 30 minutes. One of the truck drivers threw together a pretty good hobo stew. You can have your fill when you report back to camp," continued Grim.

"Thank you, sir. I *am* getting hungry."

"When aren't you hungry, Butter?"

A year ago, "the kid," as they called him, would have tried to answer the senior man's question. Now, after working with Bishop and the guys, he knew that Grim really didn't expect an answer. "See you in 30, sir."

He continued traversing through the ruins of the old village, his eyes and ears constantly seeking any noise or movement that didn't belong to the still night.

He passed a pile of rubble, a small mountain of oddly shaped bricks and timeworn mortar that had probably been a barn or stable of some configuration. For a moment, Butter wondered why the small community had ceased to exist. He quickly decided that he would probably never know.

After a dozen more steps, he again raised the infrared and scanned the field that bordered the western side of the ruins. His heart practically stopped as the distinct red shape of a woman appeared in the monocle.

Whoever she was, the woman was still a considerable distance away and not venturing directly toward the convoy's encampment. She might be a farmworker or a local just out for a late evening stroll. Reaching for his mic, he started to report the contact but then changed his mind. A lone, unarmed female wasn't any threat. Why get Mr. Bishop and the guys all upset over nothing?

Just in case, the big man swept the area with the scope, making double sure that no one else was with the woman in the field. There were no other heat signatures.

He returned to watching her, noting her random path through the rows of some thigh-high crop that was unfamiliar to the youth from Texas. One of the truck drivers had said it was a variety of bean, but no one was really sure.

Seeing the female silhouette through the eyepiece reminded Butter of May. He wondered briefly what she was doing at the moment, a thought which sent his mind racing. He had decided to see if she would come back to Alpha with him. He was sure she wouldn't leave her mother but wanted her to know how much he liked her company. It wouldn't hurt to ask. Would it?

As the woman walking across the field drew nearer to his position, Butter shook his head to clear the thoughts. The subject in his scope looked like May in shape and movement. "You need to focus on your work, dude. You're thinking way, way too much about that pretty girl back at the lake."

But he couldn't shake the similarities. The image of the now-closer woman was the exact same proportions as May. Her hair was the same length, her breasts had the same seductive curve. "Are you losing you mind, Butter?" he asked himself.

The girl's proximity now left him no choice. She had meandered too close now. He would have to challenge her. "Who goes there?"

The sound of his voice clearly startled the woman, who froze instantly and then remained still. "I'm looking for the convoy from Texas," she explained.

Butter was now sure he'd lost his marbles. This woman even sounded like May. "What is your business here, ma'am?"

"Butter? Butter, is that you?"

It was May! He couldn't believe it. What was she doing here? How did she .... When ....

"May, is that you?"

"Oh, God, Butter. You don't how glad I am I found you. It's a miracle. I swear it!"

She came in now, moving faster toward the sound of his voice. A moment later, she was wrapping her arms around his shoulders and burying her head into his chest.

"May, what in the world are you doing? How did you get here?"

"It's my sister, April. Right after the convoy left, a stranger came by the marina and delivered a message about her. She's being held against her will, being forced to work on this plantation. I took a chance and borrowed a friend's truck and tried to catch up with you and got lost. I didn't know who else to ask for help. I ran out of gas about two miles over the next hill and was wandering … trying to find the main road, hoping I would hear or see the trucks. Oh, Lord in heaven, I'm so glad I found you."

It was all too much for Butter, his head reeling at her story. He reached for his mic, knowing Mr. Bishop wouldn't mind being disturbed given this turn of events. May stopped him, gently putting her hand on his arm and saying, "What are you doing?"

"I need to report this, May. Bishop and Terri will want to know about your sister and the fact that you're in Mexico."

"But you'll get in trouble. You said what you told me about the convoy was a big secret. Won't Bishop be mad if he finds out you told me where you were going?"

Butter instantly understood the quandary, and silently cursed his big mouth. May was right. He had told tales out of school, and loose lips did sink ships.

"You still awake out there, Butter?" Grim's voice piped over the radio and caused the big man to jump.

"All's well, sir. Is there still some of that stew left?"

"No problem, kid. Kevin is strapping on his gear. He'll be there in five minutes. Don't shoot him by mistake."

"Yes, sir."

Returning his attention to May, Butter said, "You need to get out of here before my relief shows up. Can you meet me in 15 minutes over by the church steeple?"

May scanned the area, the outline of the tallest structure in the area clear in the moonlight. "I suppose. Aren't there sentries?"

"Yes, there are. I will flash a red light three times when it's safe for you to cross that open area on the other side," he said, pointing toward a fence line less than 100 meters away.

"Okay," she breathed. "I'll see you there." Standing on her tiptoes, she kissed Butter on the cheek and then melted away into the night.

A few minutes later, Kevin called out, "Coming in."

"Clear," Butter answered.

The two SAINT members discussed the route Butter had been following. Then, as he made to start his patrol, Kevin said,

"Hey, can you leave that infrared with me? I'm sure Bishop wouldn't mind."

"Sure. No problem. Did you bring any batteries? These are getting low."

"Shit. No. I forgot."

"You want me to pop in a couple of fully charged batteries and bring it back to you?"

Kevin thought about his friend's offer. "Naw. It's pretty bright out tonight, and you said it had been really quiet. I'm cool without it."

"Up to you, dude. I'll be glad to run it back out here."

Kevin briefly reevaluated the suggestion. "Don't worry about it. I don't like carrying around the extra weight anyway. I'm good."

"Later then."

"Later."

All the way back to camp, Butter fought the most intense mental battle he had ever experienced. He was so excited to see May, yet waves of guilt raked through his core. Realizing the seriousness of the situation stemming from his breach of security protocols made his stomach hurt. He wanted to tell Bishop what he had just learned yet didn't want to confess his sins. Would the man he idolized ever forgive him? Would anyone on the team ever trust him again?

"Bishop and Terri trust you with their only son," he scolded himself. "What were you thinking?"

He could just hear Grim's blistering criticism. "A short skirt with a pretty face sashays by the boy, and he just loses his mind. Running off at the mouth like that could have gotten a lot of people killed. We don't need men like that on the teams."

Yet, May was so much more than just another pretty girl. She was special, made him feel wonderful inside and was unlike anyone else he'd ever met. Didn't Bishop share secrets with his wife? Didn't a lot of people know where the convoy was going and what route it was going to take?

The conflict continued to rage as Butter made his way into the camp, a large fire still burning in the center of an area now completely walled in by 18-wheelers. Fortunately, given the late hour, most of the drivers had retired to the sleepers and not many people were around.

Grim, however, was waiting on his returning teammate. "The stew is over there, kid. I recommend you break out your mess kit and fill that bottomless pit you call a stomach. I have a feeling you're going to need all of your strength in the morning."

"Yes, sir."

"I'm going to catch a little sack time before I relieve Kevin in a few hours. I suggest you do the same after you eat. Nite."

"Nite, sir."

Butter made a show of filling his plate with the lumpy liquid, but he wasn't hungry. As soon as he was sure Grim had retired, he tossed the stew under the wheel of a trailer and then headed toward the church tower.

Kevin's patrol route wasn't hard to detect, especially given the fact that Butter had just toured the same basic path for two hours. As soon as he was sure his teammate was at the far end of his circuit, the big Texan pulled out his flashlight and blinked the signal to May.

A minute later, she was again in his arms.

Butter found a hidden corner in the skeleton-like frame of the old church where they could huddle and talk without being discovered. The stone floor and walls were cold, but neither of the hideaways seemed to notice.

"You have to help me rescue April," May began. "With your size and gun, it should be easy. The stranger told me where she was being held and said there was only one guard. We have to get her out of there."

Butter was sympathetic but skeptical. "How do you know this man was telling you the truth?" he asked. "And even if we did get her out, how are you going to get home?"

May had to think about that for a moment. "Could you borrow a little gasoline from the convoy? If I could get just enough to get most of the way home, April and I could walk back the rest of the way."

"It's way, way too dangerous to try and get her out with just two of us," he said, shaking his head. "And even if we did manage to set her free, there's no way I can carry enough gas to get you home. That means two women walking across Mexico by themselves, and that is out of the question. We ran into roadblocks and bushwhackers on the way here. This isn't a very safe country. You're lucky you didn't end up like your sister."

The disappointment that crossed May's eyes nearly tore Butter's heart out of his chest. "Yes," she admitted in a sad whisper. "You're right. I'm sorry I've gotten you into this, but I just had to try and set my sister free. I've not seen her for over two years. I had to do something."

Butter tried to cheer her up, "Look, I have to tell Mr. Bishop what's going on. I'm sure he or Miss Terri will come up with some way to get April out and back home. She's a citizen of Texas, and we take care of our own."

May became desperate, "But what if he says no? What if he doesn't want to risk pissing off the U.S. or is so mad at you that he refuses to get involved?"

"Mr. Bishop's not like that, May. He's the best man I know. He and Miss Terri will help, I just know they will."

She turned away in disappointment, whispering, "I'm sorry, Butter, but I've seen so many people in authority do the wrong things since the collapse. I just can't trust anyone these days. There has to be a better way."

Her distressed, emotional state was like a knife ripping through Butter's soul, a pain unlike anything he'd ever felt. For several minutes, they simply sat and held each other, trying to figure out a way forward.

Finally, Butter stiffened with an idea. "I suppose we could sneak off and scout where April is being held. Maybe it will be easy to get her out. If we showed up back here with your sister in tow and explained to Bishop what was going on, he would at least have to take her back with us."

May brightened instantly. "You would do that?"

"Sure," he shrugged. "It won't hurt to at least go scope it out. The one thing I've learned about Mr. Bishop is that he likes to know exactly what he's getting into. He hates surprises."

Smiling slyly, May said, "You're thinking it's better to ask for forgiveness than permission – right?"

Guilty as charged, Butter nodded. "Sometimes a man has to do what a man has to do. Right is right."

May was clearly overjoyed at his words. Taking a quick glance at her watch, she urged, "We'd better get going. She's being held near the main plantation house, and that's almost two miles away from here."

"No problem," Butter responded, checking his own watch. "We have plenty of time. It will be dawn before I will be missed."

Butter caught his first glimpse of the plantation after they had hiked for nearly an hour. While it had been easy to avoid an occasional security patrol using infrared optics, the effort had required an indirect course. More than once, the couple had been forced to hide while a party of sentries passed.

The crest of a large hill, combined with the high moon, eventually provided an astounding view of what appeared to be a mansion straight out of *Better Homes and Gardens* magazine's antebellum edition.

Peering down at the colonial columns and the assortment of outbuildings, the entire setup reminded Butter of pictures he'd seen of pre-Civil War Mississippi or Georgia. May had told him that the locals called the estate the Castle, and now he could understand why.

"She's down there in one of those long buildings according to what I've been told. The stranger said her sleeping quarters were in a structure marked #11," May whispered.

They continued downward, passing through a field of waist-high corn, Butter's head always on a swivel, scanning left and right to avoid any human contact.

Less than half a mile from the Castle, the duo arrived at the first significant obstacle.

A large, wide irrigation ditch blocked their path. Butter thought the waterway would be easy to swim or wade across but quickly determined that wasn't a very good option. "With the bright moonlight, any guard would notice the ripples we would make while crossing. That water is glass smooth, and we would send little waves rolling for hundreds of yards in both directions."

"There has to be a bridge," May suggested. "Let's work our way along the bank."

A short distance later, the pair approached a footbridge, the old wooden structure barely wide enough for two people to pass. Right at the peak of the slight arch stood a sentry, the steel of his machete glinting in the yellow light.

"Shit," Butter growled, studying the lookout. "He's going to be difficult to take out without making a lot of noise."

As the two intruders deliberated the situation, a pair of men approached the bridge from the opposite direction. "Hola," they greeted the sentry, who promptly stepped aside to let them pass.

"We need to look like the locals," May whispered. "We need to look like we belong."

Butter glanced down at his load vest, carbine, and high-tech optic. "That's going to be a little hard to accomplish. My gear doesn't exactly fit in with this year's fashion line."

"Maybe not yours, but I think I could fake it in the dark," May offered. "If I distract him for a second, can you do the rest?"

Butter didn't like it. "That's really, really dangerous. You might get hurt, or he might be shout out a warning. I don't think it's a very good idea."

Another few minutes passed while both of them tried to think of an alternative. Finally running out of patience after checking her watch, May maintained, "We have to try my plan. It's the only way we're going to find out if they are holding my sister."

May began pulling out her shirt and rustled her hair. Next came the undoing of the top two buttons of her blouse. "I'll get his attention and try to make him turn his back to you," she said, and then was gone, sauntering casually toward the bridge.

Shaking his head in disgust, Butter moved down into the shadows near the bank, trying to get as close as possible to the passage and be ready when May put on her show.

"Hola," she greeted, strolling casually onto the crossway.

Like before, the guard merely nodded as she came closer, not identifying the lone female as a threat. May continued past the sentry and then paused a few steps to his rear. "Nice night," she continued in passable Spanish. "It's a shame we both have to spend it alone," she added with a sultry tone.

The guard turned, suddenly intrigued by her words. Butter, despite his enormous girth, was up and moving, his boots hardly making a sound.

By the time the guard heard the big kid's footfalls, it was too late. The heel of Butter's palm slammed into the man's neck just as he began to turn, the blow so powerful it nearly knocked the sentry over the railing.

Butter effortlessly scooped the unresponsive fellow onto his shoulder while May retrieved the guard's blade. Less than 10 seconds had passed before the two were scrambling off the opposite side of the bridge and darting into the shadows.

Producing a small role of duct tape from his kit, Butter quickly bound and gagged the unconscious sentry, dumping the man's body in a shallow draw were it wouldn't be discovered until daylight, praying they would be long gone before either the guy woke up, or someone stumbled across his prone frame.

The rescuers encountered no additional security as they made their way toward the main compound. It took them only a few minutes to locate the building labeled #11. There were no lights, and the building was quiet.

Butter went in first, his carbine high in one meaty fist, his flashlight in the other. He was hopeful neither would be necessary. Inside, the two Texans found themselves staring at two long rows of cots lining the walls. There had to be over 200 people sleeping inside the moderate-sized building.

The fact that it was extremely dark inside was a two-edged sword. Butter and May's un-plantation-like appearance was somewhat hidden from the occupants. The duo was, however, going to have a very difficult time identifying April amidst the rumpled blankets and belly sleepers.

May took the lead, walking down the center aisle, scanning desperately right and left. Some of the occupants were easy to eliminate due to facial hair or clearly-male shape. More than once, she stepped closer to a particular cot, anxiously searching for the familiarity of April's face.

Some minutes later, they arrived at the opposite end, May beginning to get desperate. "I didn't see her," she murmured in the lowest of voices.

In the narrow space, Butter started to turn, thinking they should take a second pass. He would risk using his flashlight. As he tried to pivot his large frame, an elbow caught in April's curtain-door, revealing a dim candle lit inside.

"What's in there? Another room?" May whispered. She pulled back the curtain and froze.

April heard the footsteps outside her threshold. When her drape was pulled back, she expected Castro's lust-filled face to come barging in.

Instead, the doorway was filled with the shoulders of one of the largest men she had ever seen. While April hadn't visited every part of the plantation, she knew instantly that the giant in her doorway wasn't one of Castro's men. His clothing, bulging vest, and futuristic-looking weapon were as out of place as if he were wearing an astronaut's spacesuit.

Another face appeared over the Goliath's shoulder, bobbing up and down on tiptoes to see past the big man's frame. In the dim light, she couldn't be sure ... thought it was impossible ... it had been so long ... May!

April's silence had nothing to do with a desire to avoid alerting the sentries or arousing her dorm mates. She was simply too stunned to breathe, let alone speak.

May burst into the small space, pushing past Butter and nearly knocking the big fella into the rickety wall. "April! Oh my God, Sis. I can't believe we found you!"

The sisters embraced, both pairs of eyes growing damp with emotion. Butter kept by the doorway, his eyes and ears working overtime, worried that the noise would draw unwanted attention.

"What are you doing here?" April finally whispered.

"We came to rescue you. To take you home."

April seemed taken aback by the concept, a scowl asserting itself on her face. "To take me home? Rescue? Why? I'm just fine, can't you see? I'm teaching school and eating every day...."

"You're a slave!" May hissed in disbelief. "All of these people are slaves. I've come to set you free and take you back home to Mom and the lake."

Confusion manifested itself April's eyes, her sister's words coming far too fast. The entire encounter was just so unexpected – so weird. "But, but, but I'm fine. I miss you and mom, but can't you see that I'm happy here?"

"I saw them put you in a cage the day you disappeared. You've been in a cage ever since. Can't you see that?" May pleaded.

April shook her head, "What are you talking about? There was no place else to ride in the truck. I volunteered to get behind the bars."

Standing near the opening, Butter began to worry about the racket they were making. "Can we hurry this up?" he asked nicely. "These people out here are starting to take notice of the noise."

May flashed him a dirty look and then said, "She's suffering from Stockholm Syndrome. Give me a minute."

Tilting his head, Butter considered his partner's statement, Bishop having mentioned the condition before during SAINT training, briefing his team that the condition was sometimes called capture-bonding. Basically, those held against their will for extended periods could begin to identify, empathize, and defend their captors.

He didn't care. "Can we have this conversation somewhere else? Like back at our camp? If we don't get out of here quickly, we are going to be knee-deep in shit in short order."

"I don't want to leave," April shakily countered. "But he's right. You two had better run like hell before Castro and his men discover you are here."

"Come with me, April. Please. If you want to come back later, that's fine," May pleaded, trying to reason with her sister.

"No!" she responded, panic apparent in her tone. "Being out after hours is against the rules. Leaving the plantation is against the rules. The punishment is swift and severe."

Butter was at the end of his rope, now regretting the entire adventure. With a move as quick as lightning, he pushed May out of the way and scooped up April onto his shoulder. "Come on," he growled, "We're out of this pop stand."

April, for her part, was so shocked by the behemoth's brash move, she didn't make a noise until they were nearly a third of the way down the aisle and rushing for the door. Finally, she found her voice, "Put me down, damn it! Right now! I demand you put me down."

When Butter didn't comply, she tried to wrestle away, clenching a fist and striking the big man in the back. When that didn't have any effect, she kicked and squirmed, trying to wiggle out of the vise-like grip that held her fast.

As it became clear that Butter wasn't going to comply, April started pleading with her dorm-mates, "Help me! These people are kidnapping me! Help me!"

There was a mixed reaction from the residents, some ignoring the ruckus, other rolling over to see what all the fuss was about. Many thought that it was just Castro coming to visit the shapely, young gringo woman who taught school. Others were convinced that April had violated the rules and that the plantation's security forces were taking the woman away for punishment.

Realizing that none of her roommates were going to do anything to assist her, April's desperation reached a new level – she started screaming at the top of her lungs.

In some recess of her mind, April was stunned that none of the plantation workers were moving to help her. For a flash of time, she wondered what was wrong with them. Why wouldn't they help one of their family? It all served to motivate her struggling.

Butter was about to pull the kicking, loud-mouthed woman off his shoulder and knock her out cold when May stepped up and slapped April hard across the face. The blow temporarily stopped the older sister's earsplitting pleas, but only for a moment. Blinking the shock from her face, April inhaled deeply and began shouting for help as they bounced out the door marked #11 and burst into the plantation's courtyard.

Moving quickly toward the unguarded bridge, Butter could sense movement around him. In the distance, he could hear alarmed voices – somewhere a horse's hoofs pounded the earth. It was obvious April's shouts had been heard.

He was less than 100 meters from the crossing when two men stepped out from a tree line, blocking the direct route. The cold steel of long machetes was clear in their hands. Butter could hear more people chasing them from the cluster of barracks and outbuildings to their rear. A horse's unhappy whinny wasn't far away. People were yelling Spanish words from what seemed like every direction.

With his head spinning left and right, Butter raised his carbine with his one free hand, hoping the threat of a firearm would make the two guards retreat. They held their ground.

Out of the darkness came a sound that sounded like a sizzling, pissed, super-sized insect. The last four feet of a bullwhip instantly wrapped around the barrel of Butter's weapon and then jerked with significant force. The action pulled the big kid's finger tight against the trigger and the thunder of gunfire rolled across the plantation.

Barely managing to hold onto his weapon, Butter dropped April unceremoniously to the ground to free his other arm.

The man with the whip kept pulling hard on Butter's rifle, so the kid decided to go with the flow.

Charging like an enraged bull, Butter rushed directly at the whip-wielder. The surprised sentry didn't have time to react before the Texan's shoulder slammed into his chest, crushing his solar plexus and breaking several ribs. He let go of the whip.

Pivoting to bring his weapon back into the fight, Butter was struck in the thigh by another guard intent on tackling the intruder. The angle was bad, barely knocking the rescuer off balance.

Two more guards arrived just then, both of them having the same idea. One was introduced to Butter's rifle butt, the other easily tossed aside like a hamburger in a greasy spoon.

Now, there were at least a dozen guards rushing into the fight. A second bullwhip hissed through the air, slashing squarely across Butter's back. The sentry seemed stunned by the lack of reaction, realizing too late that his leather had no effect through the thick body armor protecting the introducer's torso. By the time he had recoiled the length of rawhide, a huge fist had crushed his jaw.

Still, the sentries poured in, a half-dozen rushing the stranger that had been so bold to trespass onto their plantation. One man managed to wrap his arms around Butter's legs as another hurdled onto his back. A second later, a wall of sentry-flesh bowled the big kid over.

Landing in a heap of entangled limbs and struggling muscle, Butter's priority changed from making an escape to surviving. Nearly 300 pounds of highly skilled, desperate strength began wreaking havoc on any body part that came within his grasp.

He snapped one man's neck, broke another's arm. Howls of pain and agony came from the dog pile as Butter's feet, fists, and elbows crushed bone and tore tendons. In seconds, the pursuers began crawling and scrambling, trying to get away from the fury of hammering blows.

Flinging the last body aside, Butter stood and found a grip on his rifle, the weapon's sling keeping it within reach. Despite their number, the guards began backing away. None of them were armed. None of them had ever encountered anything like this mountain of flesh rising like a Phoenix from the earth.

"Stop! Stop, or I will kill the girl!" shouted a voice in clear English.

Butter pivoted to see a man holding a pistol to May's head, the revolver's hammer already cocked and ready to fire.

For a second, Butter made eye contact with the gunman, boring into his soul and trying to gauge if the local would actually pull the trigger before he could aim and fire his own weapon.

Castro's gaze was empty and cold, his eyes holding less emotion than someone who was preparing to swat a fly. *This man is a killer*, Butter realized. *He doesn't care. May's life means nothing to him.*

The kid then glared at the pistol's barrel, the metal so dark against May's fair skin. The girl was terrified. The muzzle was rock steady against her temple.

Butter relaxed, holding out his weapon in surrender, the barrel pointed downward. "Okay, mister. You win. Please don't kill her."

Castro's mouth curled in a cruel smile, and then he nodded at the ring of guards. A moment later, Butter was knocked to the ground. At least a dozen boots began kicking and stomping on the kid's prone frame, the recovering sentries now extracting their vengeance.

Grim's voice carried alarm. "Bishop, our local contact is approaching in that old pickup. He doesn't have any trucks with him."

It took a moment for the sleep to vacate the Texan's eyes, a bit longer before Bishop blinked in confusion. "It's probably nothing. He's probably just stopping by to let us know the day's schedule."

"There's more, sir. Butter is missing," Grim reported, justifying his urgent tone.

"Huh? Missing? Where did he go?"

"No idea, boss. I saw him after Kevin relieved him of guard duty. He was going to eat and catch some rack time. No one has seen him since. His bedroll is nowhere to be found."

Again, the Texan wasn't quite sure there was an issue. "He's probably off digging a cat hole. After that terrible stew last night, I'm surprised the entire camp doesn't have a bad case of the runs."

"I don't think so," Grim replied, trying to make his groggy boss understand. "We heard some distant gunfire a few hours ago. At first, I thought it had nothing to do with us. Now, I'm not so sure."

"Why didn't you wake ..." Bishop started to scold, but Grim interrupted.

"You've been working double shifts planning and getting the convoy ready. I decided to let you get a full night's sleep unless I had proof there was trouble afoot. Our perimeter remained quiet."

Standing, the SAINT leader scanned the area and then began strapping on his kit. "Let's go see what our host wants at such an hour."

By the time the old pickup had meandered to the convoy's perimeter, Bishop and Grim were waiting in the road.

"Hola," the Texan greeted.

Bishop could tell instantly that something terrible was wrong. The normally mellow fellow driving the truck exited the cab sporting the deep scowl of someone who was delivering bad news.

"One of your men trespassed last night. He tried to rape one of our women and killed two of our sentries when they tried to intervene. Several of our people were injured before he was apprehended. He said his name was Señor Butter, and we now have him in custody," the driver announced.

"What?" Bishop stammered. "Butter? Rape? I don't believe it. There must be some sort of misunderstanding."

The stoic local shook his head, "There are several witnesses, Señor. There is no doubt. My superiors are furious. At this time, they are undecided how to proceed with the shipment. I was ordered to come and inform you of the incident so that no more of your people would trespass looking for your missing soldier."

"And what do you plan to do with Butter?" Grim asked.

"He will be executed at sunset, Señor. It is our law," the chilling words hung in the air.

Terri, stifling a yawn and stretching high, joined them at the roadside. It took Bishop only a moment to fill in his wife. "Butter? Butter wouldn't hurt any innocent person. What the hell is going on?" she barked.

The local shrugged, seemingly not caring. "I will return after my superiors have made their decision regarding the shipment."

The driver turned to leave, but Terri stopped him. "Wait, please. Will Butter get any sort of hearing or trial? Can we see him? Can I talk to your superiors?"

For the first time in their brief amount of contact, Bishop saw something flash behind the Mexican's face. "Your soldier-friend killed two unarmed men who were doing nothing more than trying to rescue the women he was assaulting. There were dozens of witnesses to this atrocity. Our law is very clear. He will be executed. As far as your having any discussion with the plantation's jefe, I will relay your request. Please order your people to stay within the area we have designated so there are no additional incidents. If any more of your party is found outside of this village, we will consider all of you criminals and act accordingly. Do you understand?"

Bishop and Grim didn't like the man's tone, the Texan bowing up as if he were about to unleash a verbal assault of his own. Terri stopped the onslaught with a firm hand on her husband's shoulder.

Smiling at the local, she said, "You have our word that we will honor your wishes. I would, however, suggest that your leaders take a few moments to speak with me. The man you have in custody is a highly regarded citizen of the Alliance and has personally been decorated by our highest elected officials. For the sake of ongoing diplomatic relations, I think it would be wise for everyone to calm down and have a reasonable discussion. Wars have been started over circumstances far less complex than this."

The messenger tilted his head, not sure if Terri had just issued a threat. Again, Bishop thought he saw something more in the local's demeanor.

After staring at Terri for an uncomfortable period, the local finally shrugged his shoulders and answered, "I will relay your request."

Without another word, the liaison spun and climbed into the pickup's cab, driving away and leaving the stunned group behind.

"This is bullshit," Grim bellowed first, summing up what everyone was feeling. "No way Butter just wandered off, tried to rape some farm girl, and then killed innocent men. That boy has a lot of growing up to do, but I'd bet my life there's more to this story than what we're being told."

Exchanging hard looks with his wife, Bishop ominously announced, "You may just have to do that, Grim. We all may be betting our lives."

"What are you going to do?" Terri asked her husband.

"What can I do? I have less than 10 good fighting men and a bunch of willing, but unskilled truck drivers. Given the size of the operation around us, I would assume we're completely out-numbered and outgunned. Add to that the fact that we have no idea where Butter is being held; we don't know the terrain, and we've got Washington breathing down our necks to deliver the groceries. I don't see what else we can do but sit tight and wait for their response."

"You can't let them just execute the kid," Grim stated. "We never leave anyone behind."

It was clear from Bishop's expression that he agreed, but the team leader offered no solution. After a bit, he asserted, "Let's get everyone up and spread the word about what has happened. Let's hope our new Mexican friends will give diploma-cy a chance."

Chapter 9

April walked from Castro's office, exhausted, confused, and wanting desperately to wake up and realize the events of the last few hours had all been a terrible nightmare.

For over an hour, the plantation's security chief had drilled her with probing questions, threats, and even two, open-handed slaps across the face.

April had told the truth, repeating the same story time after time after time. It had probably saved her life.

Toward the end of the interrogation, Castro had grown frustrated, reaching a new level of spitefulness. He had yanked her up by the hair and pulled her roughly to the back room where May was being held.

Her sister was naked, arms suspended in shackles hanging from the ceiling. May was bleeding from the corner of her mouth, one eye nearly swollen shut. Her breasts showed bruising, and one nipple appeared to have been burned. There was a puddle of urine on the floor.

"Do you see what we do to lawbreakers?" Castro had barked. "If you don't tell me everything, it will be you hanging in this cell and receiving the attentions of my most sadistic interrogator."

"I am telling you the truth. I don't know how May knew where I was. I sent no message, and I've had no contact with the outside world. I didn't know she was coming. I didn't ask her to rescue me."

"Perhaps you would be more forthright if you watched a dozen of my men satisfy themselves with your sister? Maybe your tongue would speak honestly if you watched her brutally violated over and over again?"

The situation merely deteriorated when she had tried to justify her sister's actions. "I ran away from our home. My family had no idea what became of me. Wouldn't your sister … or brother … or parents come looking if you had simply disappeared?"

Castro wasn't buying it. "She is a spy, sent by the Quakers. The gringos have been meddling in Mexico's affairs for hundreds of years. Those terrorists are no different. If we are not diligent, they will come and take everything we have worked so hard to achieve here on the plantation."

"She's no more a spy than you are. She is a stranger to this land and is unfamiliar with the laws and customs. Surely, she is deserving of mercy," April had desperately pleaded, but to no avail.

"Your sister will be executed with the other Yankee infiltrator," he pronounced. "She will be hung until dead. Go back to the barracks and stay there. Do not talk to anyone. You will be summoned in time to watch your sister's final moments."

Now, as April trudged back to the barracks, she struggled to make sense of it all. Sure, plantation society required harsh rules and unbending discipline to survive and maintain the rule of law. Post-collapse anarchy had threatened to destroy what few fragments of humanity remained. She had experienced hunger personally, a poignant lesson that most of the residents had learned firsthand. She lectured her students on the value of a system that allowed them all to eat.

Yet, during the entire time she had been at the plantation, she had never seen or heard of any serious external threat. The operation was enormous. The fields now produced an excess harvest. There was order and a society. Why were Castro and Lady Bella Dona being so punitive? Why execute a young girl whose only sin had been a misguided attempt to rescue a beloved sibling? May hadn't killed anyone, hadn't destroyed any crops or harmed any of the operation's assets.

Finally entering building #11, she paused upon reaching the center aisle, the harrowing journey on the big stranger's shoulder returning to the forefront of her thoughts.

"My sister kept calling me a slave," she whispered incredulously to the empty rows of cots. "May was insistent that I was a slave. Why did she think that? How did she know where I was? Why did she choose that label?"

The questions continued to flood her thoughts as April plodded slowly back to her closet-room, her sister's use of the term "Stockholm Syndrome" rolling through her brain with every step.

By the time she pulled back the drape, April had reached a conclusion. May was simply mistaken. "I'm not a slave," she informed the cubicle. "I receive food, water, shelter, medical care, and clothing as a paycheck. I am compensated for my labor. I am provided for, the same as everyone else here at the plantation. May just doesn't understand."

For the next few hours, Bishop kept busy organizing the truckers and deploying his limited assets to bolster their defenses. It was a pitiful exercise.

Despite having brought two belt-fed weapons and their larger-than-normal supply of ammunition, the Texan knew that against even a modest assault, it was impossible to defend their tiny swatch of Mexican soil for more than a few hours.

Still, he had to try. That and the activity kept his mind from dwelling on Butter.

Over and over again, Bishop asked himself what in the hell had happened to his man? He mentally played out every possibility, finding none of them plausible. Had someone managed to infiltrate their lines and kidnap his team member? Had Butter somehow been lured away from the camp and then been taken prisoner?

None of it made any sense, and after a period, Bishop gave up trying to figure it all out. He needed to speak with Butter. He needed to interview the kid and uncover the truth.

Just as Bishop was ordering three of the semis to change their position, Kevin's voice boomed over the radio. "Movement. 110 degrees magnetic. Something big up is moving on that hill."

Everyone that heard the broadcast stared where the sniper had indicated, straining their eyes to see what was surely trouble.

Bishop headed for that side of the compound, running into Grim on the way. Before they could reach the outermost edge of their defenses, the rumble of a large diesel engine vibrated through the surrounding fields.

"I sure as shit hope that's not what I think it is," Grim huffed as the two men dashed for the perimeter.

Bishop had just pulled up his binoculars when the silhouette of a long tube crested over the distant hill. A moment later, the roundness of a turret appeared, soon followed by the outline of a tank.

"Oh, shit," Grim said. "That's what I was afraid of. Where in the hell did a bunch of farmers get a fucking tank?"

It was a few moments before Bishop responded from behind his optic. "I see old markings of the Mexican army on the side. At least that answers that question. It's not a tank, though. It's an armored personnel carrier."

"Sure as shit looks like a cannon on top to me," Grim countered. "It has armor and tracks. Might as well be a tank."

"It's only a 20mm cannon," Bishop continued. "I think those are French surplus units Mexico purchased years ago."

"*Only a 20mm cannon?* That might as well be a nuke compared to what we're carrying," Grim replied, clearly unhappy with being completely outgunned.

"Movement, 130 degrees magnetic, same profile," Kevin transmitted, followed less than 20 seconds later by, "Movement, 150 degrees magnetic, same profile."

Indeed, two more of the monstrous machines soon appeared, their cannons pointing directly toward the Texas convoy's encampment.

Over the next ten minutes, the three armored behemoths rumbled across the countryside, eventually encircling the camp and blocking the road back home.

Once more, Kevin's voice sent a chill down his boss's spine. "Movement, all points. Infantry. Dismounted. At least two hundred troops, all armed. They're surrounding us."

Bishop watched the deployment, praying that it wasn't a prequel to an assault. "If they come in, we're screwed," he said to Grim.

"Now I know how Bowie and Travis felt at the Alamo," Grim whispered. "And it sucks."

Shortly after the final armored vehicle had settled into position, Kevin's voice again set Bishop on edge. "Movement on the road. It's the same pickup truck as before. One person, the driver, is visible."

The Texan exchanged looks with his wife, and then held up his crossed fingers. "You're our way out of this, darling. I hate to put on the pressure, but from a military perspective, we're out of options. If this gets violent, we're all dead in less than twenty minutes."

"No pressure, huh?" she grinned. "Let's see what our friend has to say."

They met the truck at the usual spot, the same local exiting the cab as Bishop and Terri approached. There was no friendly greeting this time.

"I have spoken to my superiors, and Lady Bella Dona has agreed to meet with you," the messenger explained.

"Lady Bella Dona?" Terri asked, wanting to make sure she had heard the man correctly.

"Yes. She is the matriarch of all that you see around you. Her family has owned this land for nearly 200 years."

"Why the heavy equipment?" Bishop asked, nodding toward the tracked war machines sitting atop the surrounding hills.

Grunting, the Mexican explained, "They are here to protect you. Considering last night's events and the fact that there are several organizations that oppose us, we felt it prudent to protect your trucks and men so you wouldn't meet the same unfortunate end as the first convoy did. We have positioned our security forces to guard your assets against such an attack."

Bishop thought the man was lying, trying to get the Alliance team to drop their guard. Before he could protest the need for such a massive response, Terri stepped between them.

Flashing her husband a glance that said, "Don't press it," Terri redirected the conversation onto less controversial ground. "When will we have the pleasure of meeting Lady Bella Dona?"

"Right now. I have permission to bring two of you back to the Castle ... the main house ... with me. No firearms or weapons will be allowed."

Bishop didn't like it, thoughts of Hunter losing both of his parents flashing through the Texan's mind.

Sensing the discomfort, the messenger said, "You have the good lady's personal guarantee that no harm will come to either of you."

The Texan's gaze moved to the armored vehicles on the hilltops, then switched to images of Butter's scheduled demise. Shrugging his shoulders and flashing his wife a look of helplessness, he responded, "What choice do we have?"

After handing Grim his weapon and load vest, Bishop submitted to a quick frisk. As a show of respect, Terri was allowed to merely spin in a circle with her arms spread wide.

"Any last words of wisdom if you don't come back?" Grim asked in a low voice as Terri marched toward the pickup.

"Get as many of them back to Texas as you can. Have the snipers take out the two APCs blocking the road home, and run like hell for the border."

Bishop then joined his wife in the old truck's cab, the interior smelling like a combination of fresh hay and motor oil.

The road was bumpy, the two passengers jolted left and right as their escort seemed unconcerned with avoiding any pothole or rut in their path. After a few kilometers had passed, the truck crested a small ridge, exposing an enormous valley below. There, like a diamond set in a ring of green, was what the driver called the "Castle."

Despite the stress and seriousness of the situation, Terri remarked, "It's beautiful. Gorgeous. I had no idea anything like this existed outside of the Deep South."

The old pickup bounced and bumped its way down into the valley, the fields growing greener as they descended. Before long, the Texans began seeing the occasional outbuilding and barn, as well as dozens and dozens of workers tending to the crops.

The density and number of structures continued to increase as they approached the main house, eventually looking like a small settlement or village by the time they reached the valley's floor.

It was like any small colony. Bishop spotted large, metal buildings where the flash and spark of a working welder strobed through a doorway. He noticed stacks of tires and piles of engine parts, most likely used to repair the machinery required by such a huge, agricultural operation.

Another warehouse accommodated a factory that evidently produced large, woven baskets – hundreds of the post-apocalyptic dump trucks lining one wall. It was a sight Bishop had grown accustomed to, farmers requiring an innovative method to haul harvested produce since the economic collapse.

All in all, it was a thriving, energetic place. People were hurrying here and there with a purpose – hauling, working, cleaning – carrying out the day-to-day activities of the community. In a way, the place reminded Bishop of Meraton or downtown Alpha. The landscape was different, but the energy was the same.

Before long, the truck arrived at the main gates and pulled into a huge, circular drive.

The truck stopped a considerable distance away from the broad porch. "Stay here," the driver ordered as he exited the cab.

A small squad of security men appeared, rushing up to the messenger. It didn't surprise Bishop one bit when the man who had escorted them onto the plantation began issuing orders. "I thought he was a little too self-confident to be just a delivery boy. I'd bet he's actually pretty high up in whatever hierarchy exists here."

"Odd," Terri replied, ignoring her husband's speculation. "None of the security types have firearms. That doesn't fit with the armored units that surrounded our camp."

Bishop nodded, "I see machetes, and what the hell … does that guy over there have a bullwhip hanging from his belt?"

Terri spied it as well. "Isn't that a pretty strange weapon for a sentry or guard?"

"Damn right it is. In all my days, I've never seen the like. What possible purpose could that serve? This place is just boiling with weird."

The security contingency formed a line, and then their escort opened the truck's door. "This way please."

The couple walked toward the front porch, passing by the sentries almost as if they were dignitaries inspecting an honor guard. It all seemed so surreal to the visitors.

As they drew closer to the house, a stunning woman appeared, her dark hair pulled high into a bun, a flowing, white cotton dress covering her tall, slender frame. Terri couldn't help but glance down at her own jeans, plaid shirt, and hiking boots with a frown.

"You look damn hot to me, babe," Bishop whispered to his wife. "The *belle* of the ball."

"Thanks," she grinned, still not happy with the formality mismatch.

Evidently, Bishop wasn't the only one impressed with Terri's appearance.

Smiling widely as the duo stepped onto the verandah, Lady Bella Dona virtually ignored the leader of the SAINT team, instead sizing up Terri from top to bottom with an incredibly intense stare. *What is that all about?* Bishop wondered. *What am I, chopped liver?*

The Texan's confusion began to clear once their hostess nodded approvingly at the female Alliance diplomat while wetting her lips. "Yummy," Bishop thought he heard the woman whisper.

Terri's virtual undressing complete, Lady Bella Dona offered her hand and said, "Welcome to the plantation. I am Bella Dona, the manager of this facility." Her English carried a bit of a British accent, Bishop noted. Probably educated overseas.

She seemed genuinely surprised when Terri introduced herself as the official diplomatic envoy of the Alliance of Texas. Again, Bishop saw a definite sexual attraction flicker in the other woman's eyes. *Yeah, that's right, lady. My bride has beauty and brains*, he thought, a smidge of jealousy surfacing. *And she can also shoot pretty damn well, too. Keep it up, and you'll find out why the gents refer to her as the 'Annie Oakley of the Alliance.'*

Bishop shifted in his boots and cleared his throat loudly. "Ahem."

"Oh, and this is Bishop. He is responsible for convoy security," Terri quickly recovered.

"I had no idea we were entertaining an official delegate," the hostess responded with a musical tone, her eyes fixated on Terri and completely ignored Bishop. "I apologize for our lack of formality. I thought your compatriots were merely here to transport our produce back to the United States?"

"The Alliance asked that I make the journey with the trucks to ensure that goods procured by our close ally in Washington were delivered without incident," Terri clarified. "I must apologize for my informal appearance. I had no idea that we would be meeting with any of the local dignitaries."

Bella flushed, waving a dainty hand in dismissal. "I'm hardly a dignitary, my dear. I'm just a farm girl who inherited a large parcel of land and struggle to keep my workers fed."

Terri's gaze swept the surrounding hills before replying, "It looks like you are a very successful farm girl to me. This is an extremely impressive operation."

Bella Dona ignored the compliment, stepping aside and motioning for her guests to enter the house. "Please, let's get inside out of the sun. Surely you must need refreshments after traveling that dusty, old road?"

The couple entered through the gargantuan doorway, finding themselves immediately surrounded by opulence and the sure indicators of vast wealth. From the impressive, crystal chandelier to the broad, sweeping double staircase, the Castle was every bit as impressive on the inside as out. "You have a beautiful home," Terri cooed. "I'm very impressed."

"Thank you. It is so rare these days that I receive visitors. Your words are too kind."

The Texans were then guided into a sitting room off the main hall. Inside were floor to ceiling bookshelves, all of them filled with expensive-looking leather volumes and lavish collectibles.

No sooner had they been seated, than two servants appeared with trays. One was filled with an assortment of beverages, on the other stacks of smoked meats, a rainbow of cheeses, and at least five different varieties of bread were piled high. Bishop noticed that the tray-bearers didn't make eye contact with anyone in the room and that their hands were shaking with fear as they deposited the platters on the table. In an instant, they were gone, exiting out of a side door without even a "Thank you," from the hostess.

Bishop also noted that the pickup truck driver stayed very close to the lady of the house, the man constantly on edge and seemingly always ready to intercede. *He's her bodyguard*, the Texan realized. *How many times have I played the same role?*

Bella Dona noticed the object of Bishop's attention and with a twinkle of a laugh, said, "I see birds of a feather do flock together. Castro is my loyal lieutenant … what you would call 'my right-hand man.' His family has served the plantation for six generations, and I would be helpless without his loyalty."

136

Before Bishop could comment, Bella continued, her attention now back on Terri. "So what is it *I can do for you*? Castro explained your urgent request to meet with me. How may I be of *service* to you?"

Terri ignored the sexual overtones, her voice remaining even and official. "First of all, I would like to extend a hand of friendship from the Alliance. We had no idea that an organization such as yours had survived the collapse. Secondly, we are still investigating the demise of the first convoy, and would appreciate any information you can share regarding that ambush. And finally, we would like to discuss the unfortunate events of last night and the involvement of one of our people."

The plantation's mistress waved her hand through the air in a signal of dismissal, "Yes, I've been informed of that unpleasantness. I suppose our species is even more unpredictable these days. Given the current-day pressures of survival, I'm surprised we don't experience a greater number of criminal acts. I'm sure that man's actions last night weren't sanctioned by you or the Alliance."

Inhaling to speak for the first time, Bishop never got the chance to respond, as his wife was quicker with her words. "I agree. We, however, know that man quite well. In fact, he is a personal friend of ours and a highly decorated member of the Alliance government. We're having a difficult time believing him capable of such crimes."

Bella Dona's expression flashed white-hot, but for less than a second. When she spoke, her voice retained its formal, almost musical quality. "I realize this must be extraordinarily stressful for you. I can't tell you how many times I've had well-grounded, trusted employees suddenly fall completely out of character. I suppose the hardships we all have endured are to blame. Some people simply can't handle stress and reach their limits."

"Not Butter," Bishop replied evenly. "He is one of the most level-headed individuals I've ever commanded. He's really nothing more than a big-hearted, innocent kid."

Again, something cold and dark appeared behind Bella Dona's eyes. Like before, it passed before Bishop could zero in. "We are peaceful, simple farmers here at the plantation," she cooed. "But we will defend ourselves and have grown quite adept at doing so. What choice does anyone have in these troubling times? The only real option is to rise from the anarchy and thrive. That being said, I assure both of you, the man we have in custody did indeed commit the offenses as Castro reported."

After flashing her husband a look that said, "Let me work this," Terri returned to Bella with a smile of innocence and promptly changed the subject. "This morning we found our camp surrounded by heavily armed men and tracked machines of war. I'm sure you can imagine how concerning this development was."

Bishop saw it clearer this time, but like before, the emotion in Bella Dona's eyes passed very quickly. His wife's question also prompted a new reaction as well. This time, there was a hint of fear in their hostess, immediately followed by a thinly veiled, seething fury. Still, her voice remained sweet and smooth. "Yes, I ordered our security forces to act after consulting with Castro," smiled the plantation's mistress. "We have recently learned that an organized group of hostile individuals is active in this area, and I ordered our men to protect your encampment so that no harm befalls this shipment."

"Are you referring to the Copperheads?" Bishop asked.

Bella Dona seemed truly puzzled by the question, glancing at Bishop as if he'd lost his mind. "No. I think you're confused, sir. A lot of the locals refer to my security forces by that foul moniker."

The two Texans were stunned, but after the shock had passed, it all was starting to make sense to Bishop.

When neither of her guests commented, the lady took it upon herself to expand. "I've always despised the term, but it is understandable in a way. As I was saying, we've had to meet force with force in order to hold our ground. When our barns were raided, Castro and his men hunted down the thieves and administered justice. You must understand that we have endured roving bands of violent, animal-like men who had no conscience. We've survived raiders, scavengers, warlords, drought, pestilence, and marauders. I suppose it's no surprise that the locals fear us and thus call us childlike names and spread vicious, unfounded rumors."

Wait until she finds out about the latest water cooler gossip making the rounds. These unfounded rumors now include massacring an entire village, Bishop thought.

"I'm afraid you're right," Terri countered. "We clearly don't know who the players are. So if your employees are the Copperheads, then who are the other groups you spoke of?" Terri continued.

Bella Dona seemed bored now. "Given the events of last night, we felt the additional security was judicious. There are numerous organized groups that oppose us. As a matter of fact, we are quite certain that the one called the Quakers is based in Alliance territory. To be blunt, that's the real reason why I invited you here today. I wish to formally request that you arrest these

138

terrorists and turn them over to us so that we can administer proper justice."

The surprises continued, Terri now wishing she had a program so she could keep all of the actors straight. "An organized group? Out of the Alliance? Are you sure?"

Castro stepped forward, "Yes, we are quite certain. We are positive that their home base is in Del Rio. They call themselves the Quakers, and they are the most vicious of all who would like to take for themselves what Lady Bella Dona has built."

Quakers? Bishop thought. *Copperheads? Where have I heard those two names used together before?* Before he could consider the question further, his wife began speaking.

"I assure you, Madam, the Alliance has no knowledge of any such organized group, nor would we sanction any activity in a foreign land. I, as an official representative of the government in Alpha, would be very interested in what proof you have of these serious allegations."

"So you are saying that the Alliance isn't really in control of what was Texas before the collapse?" Bella Dona countered. "I'm afraid I'm the one who is confused. Is your government in control, or not?"

It was a stinging point, obviously intended at undermining Terri's authority and diminishing the influence she was trying to leverage. Keeping her best diplomatic expression intact, she responded, "There are some regions of the former state where we are just beginning to rebuild order and an elected government. In most regions, the rule of law is well established, in other remote parts of the territory, we're only beginning to make inroads."

Bella sighed. "So I am to believe that Del Rio, as well as the area along the eastern Rio Grande Valley, are not firmly under your government's control?"

"I wouldn't agree with that statement," Terri responded. "While it is true that the Alliance hasn't established as strong a presence there as we have in many of the major metropolitan areas or in the western part of Texas, there is law enforcement and local leadership that reports to our capital."

"I see," Bella Dona sneered, her demeaning tone obvious. "We thought as much given the threats we face from the north. I say, however, that I look forward to the day when we don't have to expend so much of our limited resources on security."

I bet that maintaining armored personnel carriers and a private army ain't cheap, Bishop considered. *I wonder if the Colonel knows about that.*

Terri kept her cool, pretending to sympathize with their hostess. "I understand exactly what you are saying. Since society fell off the edge, we all have been forced to embrace violence in the name of self-defense and to establish the rule of law. Which brings us full circle back to our friend. If our man committed these heinous acts, we would fully support his punishment as per your rules and regulations. I ask, however, that you try to look at the situation from our perspective. Like you, we've seen the worst mankind has to offer. Over and over again, we've been involved in situations where miscommunications, invalid interpretations, and incorrect assumptions have led to all sorts of difficulties."

"What is it you ask of us?" Bella Dona countered, clearly growing impatient.

"We would like to speak with our man," Terri answered simply. "We would like to understand how these events transpired, both so that we can accurately report the incident back to our government, and so that we can take steps to ensure such issues never occur again."

"I'm afraid that's not possible," Castro barked from his perch at the doorway. "We had to sedate the accused. He continued to resist us with the strength of the insane, and I couldn't risk injury to any more of my men."

I bet you had to sedate him, Bishop thought, conjuring visions of an irate Butter beating the crap out of anyone who came within reach. *He would definitely be a handful.*

"You don't believe us?" Bella Dona spat after observing her guest's reaction. "I find that offensive, to say the least."

Terri tried to recover, "It's not that we don't believe you. We simply are trying to understand how and why this all occurred. We are not making any accusations of dishonesty or foul play."

An unspoken message passed between Bella Dona and Castro, a silent communication that only they understood. The lady of the house then seemed to make a difficult decision. "Let us show you something. Perhaps it will help with this lack of understanding you profess."

The Texan noted Castro clearly didn't like his boss's direction, the bodyguard visually tensing. Before he could protest, Bishop saw a look from Bella Dona that could melt iron. *There's a lot more to this woman than meets the eye*, he concluded. *She's scary as hell, and obviously completely in control here. I wonder how? She doesn't look all that tough to me.*

Bella Dona rose abruptly, almost in a huff, and motioned her guests toward the door. Following the couple outside, she then gestured towards a group of buildings a short distance away.

The security squad that had greeted the pickup appeared, the group of muscular men forming a perimeter around the plantation's mistress like she was the President of the United States strolling through a hostile crowd.

No words were spoken as the sizeable entourage crossed the grounds. A few moment later, Bishop spotted a large gathering of what appeared to be farm workers. Upon spotting Bella Dona, the throng parted while all of the men removed their hats. Every single pair of eyes looked away.

Pointing toward the ground with an angry, stabbing finger, Bella Dona spat, "Does this help with your understanding?"

Terri and Bishop followed to see five bodies laid out beside freshly excavated graves. "This is the work of your friend, that *decorated* government servant. Those men lying there were fathers, husbands, and brothers, murdered by this man you came here to defend," Bella Dona hissed.

Bishop removed his own hat in respect for the dead. Much to Terri's dismay, the Texan then moved forward and knelt close to examine the deceased.

The first cadaver had obviously suffered a broken neck. No other injuries were visible. It was the sort of demise Butter was more than capable of delivering.

The second body showed signs of a completely different form of death. A single bullet hole was visible in the man's temple. No exit wound showed on the other side. As Bishop looked closer, he noticed a ring of raw skin around the man's wrists. *This guy was bound and executed with a small caliber handgun*, the Texan surmised. *Now how would Butter have managed that?*

Moving down the row of dead men, Bishop discovered two other questionable victims, both having been bound and shot in the head. One of the corpses had the sticky residue of duct tape across his mouth.

The Texan also noted that all of the deceased wore the same utility-gray shirts as Castro's security crew.

The last carcass was lying face down. As he started to rise, Bishop noted an unusual marking on the dead man's back. Pulling back the collar of the poor fellow's shirt, the Texan almost gagged when he saw that the man at his feet had been severely whipped a short time before his demise.

"Satisfied?" Castro asked from the edge of the crowd, almost as if he was daring Bishop to question the evidence at hand.

Before he could answer, Bishop's attention was drawn to a nearby barn. There were two ropes dangling from the high, sturdy beam normally used to winch hay into the loft. A pair of hangman's nooses swung in the afternoon breeze. Castro followed the Texan's gaze.

"Why two ropes?" Bishop asked.

"There were two individuals involved in last night's transgressions. Both are to be executed this afternoon at sunset," answered the local muscle.

Terri picked up on Castro's admission immediately. "Two people? Why weren't we told about this? Are both of the accused from our convoy?"

Bella Dona stepped forward, "You weren't told because it isn't significant. One of the perpetrators admits that she traveled here independent of your convoy. She has confessed that you had no knowledge of her presence or intent."

"She?" Bishop asked, tilting his head.

"Yes," Bella Dona answered with a nonchalant response. "I believe her name is May."

Terri's shock at the name of Butter's coconspirator passed quickly. Bishop saw it and hoped he was the only one who took notice.

Stepping toward their hostess, Terri's tone became very undiplomatic. "So you expect me to believe that a 20-year-old girl traveled several hundred miles across hostile lands so she could meet up with our friend and try to kidnap and rape another woman? I'm struggling with this, partially because it doesn't make a lick of sense, but mostly because new facts keep coming to light. You must realize that May is a citizen of the Alliance as well."

Everyone but Castro seemed to have forgotten about the throng of people that still surrounded the Texans and their hosts. Bishop was reminded of their presence when several of the onlookers inhaled sharply as his wife's words challenged Bella Dona.

Castro appeared about ready to explode, the purple-faced strongman taking an aggressive step toward Terri with murder in his eyes. Bishop intercepted, moving in front of the local, his posture making it clear he was ready to fight.

Bella Dona regained control of the situation quickly, "I think we should all step inside before continuing this discussion. Please, let's get out of the heat and give everyone's emotions a chance to simmer down."

With their guests in tow, Castro and Bella Dona took the opportunity to have a quiet, private discussion as they strolled back toward the Castle. Bishop decided to do the same, drawing close to his wife and leaning into her ear. "Butter didn't kill all of those guys back there."

"How do you know?"

"They were shot in the head with a small caliber handgun, probably a .32. Butter carries a .45 like mine. There would be an exit wound the size of a golf ball if they had been shot with one of our pistols. Plus, our guide initially told us that Butter had killed two of the sentries, remember?"

"Perhaps May shot them? She could have brought a weapon with her."

"Could be, but the guys who were executed had been bound right before they were killed. One of them had most of the skin whipped off his back. I think Castro had his incompetent guards killed and is blaming Butter."

Terri nodded, then added, "Did you see how all of the farm workers wouldn't make eye contact with Castro or Bella Dona? It was like they were scared to death of our hosts. What have we stumbled into here, Bishop?"

"I don't know, but this whole mess reeks of evil. It's everywhere. There's something else that's bugging me – where have I heard of the relationship between Copperheads and Quakers before? I just can't quite place it...."

"A conservative religious group and a breed of snake?"

"No, I am sure someone coupled the two groups of people in another conversation, and it's driving me nuts trying to remember. It's like those times when you can't think of a word."

The group arrived back at the main house, the two Texans escorted into the library, no one speaking a single word. Again, they found themselves alone in the room with Castro and Lady Bella Dona.

The lady of the house didn't take her seat, however, choosing instead to stand beside her previous perch. After everyone was settled, she began speaking as if the entire affair was nothing more than a social Sunday tea. "It is obvious by the look on both of your faces that you don't believe we are being forthright about this situation. So be it. If you'll excuse me for a brief time, I will make arrangements to have a key witness to last night's events brought here so that you can interview her. In the meantime, I will have additional refreshments brought in."

As Bella Dona turned to leave, she had another thought. "And please, don't try to leave this room. Our security people are extremely tense given last night's trespass, and I wouldn't want any harm to befall my guests."

The couple found themselves alone in the library, looking at each other, both questioning just exactly what was about to happen next.

Grim lowered his binoculars and turned to Kevin. "Bishop was right. Those armored vehicles are old French surplus models they sold to Mexico years before the collapse. I'm stunned they're still running."

"They look pretty potent to me," Kevin replied, still scouting the closest APC through his scope.

Shrugging, Grim said, "Their armor isn't all that thick. Oh, don't get me wrong – it will stop anything we have with us, but if you had a .50 caliber, it would blow through that plating like it was made of cardboard."

"But we don't have a 50. Mr. Bishop told me to only bring along my AR10, and it doesn't have near the same punch."

Grim rubbed his chin, "That's true. Hindsight is always 20/20. Still, now that I've had a good look at them, I'm not nearly as concerned."

Studying the senior man, Kevin's eyebrows bounded towards his hairline. "You've got a plan."

Smiling broadly, Grim nodded. "Come on. Let's get back to the camp. We've got a little prep work to do. If push comes to shove, I want to be able to get these truckers out of here."

The two SAINT members stalked back to the camp where Grim immediately began to issue orders. "I want 20 gallons of gasoline carried between those two trucks where our friends up on the hill can't see what we're up to. Kevin, get a couple of the truckers and have them start pulling bullets apart and putting all the powder into some sort of dry container."

Grim then pointed at one of the deputies and commanded, "Grab another man and start scavenging through those old buildings over there. No telling what you will find, but I already spotted some scrap irrigation pipe. Be discreet, but bring me as much of it as possible. Assume those guys up on the hill are watching your every move, so be sneaky."

Grinning at his comrade, Kevin nodded while stroking his chin between his thumb and forefinger in a knowing gesture. "You're going to make pipe bombs," the rookie operator surmised. "Are you sure they will penetrate their armor?"

Shaking his head, Grim cracked a smile, "You're close, kid, but no cigar. I'm going to make something far, far more potent than any little, ol' firecracker. Watch and learn, my young friend. You never know when some of Uncle Grim's dirty tricks might come in handy."

The two Texans were beginning to think that their hostess had forgotten them when Bella Dona suddenly appeared in the doorway. Behind the regal plantation owner was a younger woman, followed closely by the always-present Castro.

April was immediately introduced as May's sister and one of many schoolteachers who taught in the plantation's expansive system of schools. Upon hearing of the sibling relationship, both Bishop and Terri immediately understood Butter's actions. Large pieces of a complex puzzle were finally falling into place.

After everyone but Castro was seated, Bella Dona got things started, "April is one of our most valued employees," the matriarch explained. "She came to us just over two years ago without hope and near starvation. You may ask her anything you wish."

Terri didn't hesitate. "Did Butter try to rape you?"

The question seemed to surprise the educator, her frightened eyes darting between Bella Dona and Castro before she answered. "I'm not sure how to answer that," she stammered. "He lifted me onto his shoulder and was carrying me outside. I tried to fight him off, but he is so fast and strong. I'm not sure what his intentions were."

Despite desperately wanting to press the young woman seated across from her, Terri held back. *You catch more flies with honey than vinegar*, she thought. *Pour on the honey.*

"I'm sorry you've had to endure what was obviously a troubling series of events," Terri said softly. "I wish there was some other way we could continue our investigation without making you relive that trauma."

"It's okay," April nodded, sniffing back a tear. "It was all so … so … fast. My life here at the plantation has been quiet and routine. I'm still getting over the shock."

Reaching across to gently pat the distraught girl's hands, Terri chose a different path. "Tell me about the downfall and how you and your sisters survived," she said. "I'm always curious to hear the survivors' stories."

For the next 15 minutes, April complied with Terri's request, relaying the story of her family anchored on the lake, her father's horrible death, and the hungry months that followed. It was clear from the teacher's choice of words that her memories were tempered by her near starvation scare. Like so many other survivors,

145

malnutrition was an experience that would likely dominate her thoughts until she died.

Both Bishop and his wife had heard similar tales from countless refugees welcomed into Alliance territory. Starvation was a cruel master, driving its servants to the brink of mental anguish while their physical bodies failed them. The famished might have to wait as long as 70 days before death's welcome release. The process was harsh and demeaning, always stealing victims' humanity long before stealing their lives.

"She came to us thin and frail, barely able to function ... a stick-figure of a human being," Bella Dona interjected. "We fed her, clothed her, provided medical care, and nursed her back to health. Now she is a productive individual who contributes to our revival."

"So why did your sister think you needed to be rescued?" Terri asked.

April seemed to be growing comfortable with the two strangers and the fact that she was inside the Castle – a place she had never been allowed before. "May called me a slave. She said I was suffering from something called the Stockholm Syndrome. She was convinced I was being held here against my will."

"And are you?" Bishop asked, regretting the question the moment it left his throat. *No way she'll answer honestly with my buddy Castro looming over there.*

April's brow knotted tightly as she considered her answer, "Of course not. I simply choose not to leave. Where else would I go? What else would I do? I left a world where I was starving ... where every morsel of food I put in my mouth was robbing my mother and sister of nourishment they needed so desperately. Here I can eat all I want. I have a job where I help children learn, something which is very gratifying. Why would I want to leave this and return to a living hell where I have no resources?"

Terri sat quietly for a bit, contemplating what she had just heard. Everyone in the room was surprised when she turned and directed her next question directly as Castro. "Can she leave? Can we take her home to visit her mother? I'll be happy to provide her an escort back here after they say a proper goodbye. I am sure you can appreciate how worried she is about her."

For the first time since their visit, the plantation's strongman couldn't seem to find his voice. Bella Dona came to the rescue, "No, she isn't allowed to leave until her contract has been fulfilled."

"Contract?" Terri asked.

"Yes, all of our workers agree to a contract. In exchange for our nursing them back to health, they agree to stay and work here in our community until they have paid us back for that investment," Bella Dona explained.

"The company store," Bishop mumbled, referring to a practice implemented by coal companies in West Virginia during the early 1900s. The miners were paid in a currency that was only usable at a store owned by the parent corporation. The money was never enough to cover living expenses, so the miners became permanently indebted and could never leave the mine. Another piece of the puzzled fell into place, and the Texan didn't like the picture that was being to emerge. "Indentured servitude," he added, loud enough for everyone in the room to hear.

Bishop's words set Bella Dona off, the once-hidden core of fire and brimstone now on public display. "You Texans, always so judgmental, always so smug with your hypocrisy and pretense of holding the moral high ground. Let me tell you something, sir. We had no choice but to implement our contracts. We had thousands of refugees at our doorstep, all of them begging for food. You have no idea how many would take our charity and then run away. No one wanted to stay and plant the fields. None of them were willing to work at harvesting the crop. No, hundreds and hundreds of them would accept our benevolence and then leave us with empty silos and barren fields. They were like locusts, descending on the plantation and consuming everything before they left to swarm the next victim."

Terri could tell her husband was about to unload on their hosts, and in a way, she didn't blame him. Still, his loss of temper wasn't going to get Butter out of hot water or get the United States the food they so desperately needed. "We aren't here to judge your system or impose our own morals on anyone. We're only trying to understand what happened with our friend and why a resident of the Alliance traveled all this way and ended up in this mess. How your affairs are conducted is your own business," she stated calmly.

Bishop looked at his wife as if she had lost her mind, yet knew her well enough to sense that she had some unknown objective in mind. Bella Dona seemed surprised as well, looking at Terri as if she were trying to determine her guest's sincerity.

"So you're not going to start lecturing me on the evils of slavery?" Bella Dona asked, still doubtful. "You're not going to recite a manifesto supporting the rights of the individual or the advantages of freedom of choice? I must say, I'm surprised. Perhaps my own prejudices have clouded my judgement."

Shrugging, Terri continued, "We understand desperate times call for desperate measures. I've looked around and have witnessed scores of well-fed people who seem healthy enough. April is teaching school. Medical care is being provided. In reality, your plantation is light years ahead of most of North America. What my husband or I might personally think about your methods is irrelevant. How you administer, manage, or retain your work-force is none of the Alliance's affair."

Bella Dona still wasn't buying Terri's spiel but didn't seem to care all that much. Abruptly standing, she said, "Good. So we are done here. You have your answers, and I'm afraid I must get back to running the plantation."

"One more question, please," Terri said, sitting put and obviously not intending to leave just yet, "When is April's contract paid in full?"

"I would have to calculate that," Castro answered smugly. "It would depend on her contribution, her condition when she arrived, and how many disciplinary issues are on her record."

"Fair enough," Bishop nodded. "How many of your work-force have ever satisfied their contracts?"

"Enough of this," Bella Dona snapped. "You are no longer welcome in my home. Please leave immediately, or I will be forced to revoke my personal guarantee of your safety."

"Set them free," Terri whispered, remembering the message scrawled on the earthmover. "So April, is your sister one of these Quakers?"

The school marm's confusion returned, "May? A terrorist? I can't ... there's no way.... May just got out of high school a few years ago. She's not like that. She's not a violent person at all."

"Leave! Immediately!" Bella Dona barked.

"I don't think you want us to do that," Terri said with certainty. "If we leave without resolving this issue, I will guarantee that the United States will never purchase another ounce of food from your plantation. I can also promise you that if you execute our man without satisfying our reasonable requests for information, the Alliance will return in force and find the answers we seek. That would be an unfortunate occurrence for all involved."

For a moment, Bishop was sure Bella Dona wasn't going to fall for Terri's bluff. While his wife had done an excellent job of selling the threat, the Texan was sure the woman standing across from them would see it for exactly what it was – desperate posturing.

Bella Dona, however, had a different idea. "I see," she began, a long, thin finger pressing against the dimple in her chin. Finally, after a very short period, she brightened with an idea.

"A compromise," announced the plantation's jefe. "I will release your two felons upon fulfillment of two conditions. First, you will bring me proof that the Quakers will no longer threaten our operations. This is critical as we are offering to return the female terrorist to you. Secondly, I want a treaty with the Alliance that states your government will not meddle in our affairs. In exchange, I will fill your trucks and allow the convoy to return home, and I will pardon your citizens. I will give you 10 days to fulfill your side of the bargain. In the meantime, your trucks and their drivers stay here, under our protection."

Terri considered the offer, "And exactly what kind of *proof* would you require?"

"I want their heads on a pike," the matriarch unemotionally replied.

For a second, Terri thought her host was trying to make some sort of bad joke. When Bella Dona maintained a straight-face, the Alliance representative shook her head, "That's impossible. We don't execute even the most heinous criminals via evisceration. Besides, if you don't know who they are, how would you know we had eliminated the Quakers?"

"We'll know," Bella Dona answered with a sure smile. "Of that, you can be certain."

"And if we can't deliver what you request in that time period?" Bishop asked.

"Then I will execute your friend and confiscate the trucks," Bella stated without hesitation. "Both of you and one other person will be allowed to leave and return to Texas to fulfill your side of the agreement. The rest of your party stays right where they are."

"That is unreasonable," Terri protested. "We have no idea who these Quakers are, or where to even begin looking. They would have to stand trial ... be given due process. We don't just walk up and shoot suspects in the head."

"They are murderers," Bella Dona countered. "They ruthlessly attacked the first convoy, massacring those innocent men without mercy or remorse. For the past year, they have destroyed our crops, burned our barns, and sabotaged our equipment. They have butchered dozens of our workers in the fields. If the Alliance is as morally high and mighty as you profess, wouldn't your government want to vigorously prosecute these criminals regardless?"

Both Bishop and Terri had to admit Bella Dona had a point. While they were sickened by the methods and practices used on the plantation, the charred remains on the Amistad dam were black and white evil.

"Prove to us that our people are still alive and being well-treated, and we have an agreement," Terri said, standing abruptly. "We will be back within ten days."

Chapter 10

After being allowed to see Butter and May from afar, Bishop and his wife were escorted back to Castro's truck. The couple decided to ride in the pickup's bed because Terri couldn't stand being next to the plantation's strongman in the cab. "I'm afraid some of his slime will rub off on me," she explained to her husband.

The open-air transport also provided the couple a chance to talk without prying ears.

"I sure hope you've got some plan cooked up," Bishop declared as they bumped and banged along the old road. "I understand she had us cornered, but how in the hell are you going to find these Quakers and dispose of them in 10 days?"

"I don't have a plan, and I have no idea what we're going to do. When we get back, I'm going to call Alpha and get Diana and Nick down here pronto. I also would like to have a little chat with your ex-boss. This whole situation extends well beyond just us and a load of groceries. Saving Butter and May's lives is critical, but the scope of the problem far exceeds that one matter."

The Texan shook his head, "I'll leave all of the strategic thinking to you and the brain trust in Alpha. Right now, all I want is to get my people out of this hellhole and back on Alliance soil."

"What about the other Alliance citizens that are stuck on the plantation? How do we know they weren't kidnapped or forced into bondage? How can we be certain that as her power grows, Bella Dona won't decide to expand her territory? What would stop her from advancing across the river and expanding her workforce?"

Bishop wasn't sure he agreed. "What makes you think they are forcing people into slavery?"

"Do you remember when I first approached the two young fishermen? The first thing the older boy asked was if I was by myself. He told me that I was in danger because I was older and pretty. He said bad men would come and take me away. Doesn't that sound like job recruitment via gun barrel?"

Nodding, Bishop acknowledged, "Yes, I suppose if you could take the words of a child at face value. But, for all we know, that kid's parents told him wild stories so that the boy wouldn't wander off or get in trouble. Parents have done that for years."

"You might be right, but that boy's story was just one part of the equation. Why did the villagers attack the men in the pickup? Why did the Copperheads massacre the village? Why would a young girl like May travel all the way into Central Mexico and attempt to rescue her sister? The words on the side of the earth-mover said, 'Set Them Free,' and now we know why."

"So you're convinced that the Quakers formed their militia because of widespread kidnapping and forced labor? I'm not so sure, but let's assume that's true. Why wouldn't they come to the Alliance and ask for our help?"

Terri had to ponder his question for only a moment, "You heard Sheriff Watts. He said that this region had suffered corruption, racial infighting, and all kinds of other issues. Maybe the Quakers didn't trust the Alliance. Maybe they tried, but none of the local leaders would listen. Who knows? One thing for certain is that we need to hear their side of the story, and that needs to happen *yesterday*."

Bishop hopped up on his soapbox, worried about the logistics of this new objective. "Where do we even begin? Take out an ad in the *Militia Gazette*? I can see the header now, 'Are you or someone you love trying to overthrow a new order Mexican government? Aspiring to destroy a socialist paradise?' I'm having a hard time seeing folks flock to answer that advertisement." He paused for affect and then snapped his fingers as if a brilliant idea had just come to him. "I know," he continued in a cynical tone, "What if we go door to door in Del Rio? We could hard question every resident."

Terri seemed oblivious to his tirade, her eyes fixed on the passing landscape, her mind on darker matters. Bishop, determined to shock her back to the problem at hand, added, "Terri, we've only got 10 days to pull all this off before Butter and May have their necks stretched, and we lose those trucks."

The Alliance diplomat stirred slightly, the glazed expression fading from her face. When she finally spoke, she exposed her innermost fear, "I wonder what she intends to do with the drivers if we don't fulfill our part or the bargain?"

Bishop shuddered, "I don't think I want to know."

With Castro behind the wheel, the pickup finally arrived at the encampment, stopping well short of the perimeter. Jumping down from the back of the truck and then taking a moment to brush the dust from their clothing, the two Texans glanced up to see their driver standing nearby.

"I will issue the orders to allow one of your vehicles and three people to leave this place and head north," Castro announced. "That same number will be allowed to return at any time in the next ten days. If we detect any sizable force moving south toward the plantation, I will order my men to crush this camp. Is that clear?"

"Yes, we understand," Terri replied. "The truck drivers don't have enough food to last ten days. Will you resupply them?"

"Yes," Castro nodded and then turned to climb into the cab.

Bishop spied Grim and Kevin hurrying toward him, the old soldier carrying the Texan's carbine in the cradle of his arm. He smiled at his friend's perception, having felt naked without his weapon during the excursion. "Oh sweet, baby girl," he whispered after seeing his firearm. "You don't know how badly daddy has missed you."

Following her husband, Terri was passing Castro when the local strongman paused with an afterthought, half in and half out of his truck. Reaching out, he grabbed Terri's arm roughly and pulled her close. "I know your kind – know how you think," he hissed. "Don't come back here without satisfying Lady Bella Dona's terms. Don't be clever or attempt even the tiniest deceit. If you do, she will have you for a plaything in her bed until she tires of you, and then I will take over from there. I know from experience that you wouldn't last long."

Terri didn't look away, nor did she fight the man's crushing grip on her limb. With eyes equally as cold, she surprised the plantation enforcer by stepping in closer and putting her weight against the truck's door, pinning Castro's fingers in the opening.

He grimaced, but didn't acknowledge the agony shooting up his arm in any other way. It was a showdown of sorts, a game of chicken to see who would concede first. Terri pressed more of her weight into the door and growled, "And I know your kind and how you think. I'm coming back for our citizens, and they better fresh as fucking daisies, or you'll be my plaything. And I promise … you will last a good, long time before I finally let you die."

More of Terri's weight leaned against the door, one of Castro's fingers cracking audibly as a bone gave way. Still, he barely flinched at the pain. Removing his hand from Terri's arm, the now-irate man reached for his waistband, obviously going for a weapon.

For a moment, Terri thought she had just made a huge mistake, stepping back just as Castro got a grip on whatever he was reaching for. She was readying to turn and run when the muzzle of Grim's rifle appeared out of nowhere, the cold, black steel pressing against the local's temple.

"I wouldn't raise that hand, friend. You won't make it," Grim warned.

Castro grunted and then shook his head as he climbed into the cab.

Watching the old truck drive away, Terri's color returned to normal, but her eyes never left the pickup as it faded into the distance. "I don't like that guy," she stated.

"No? Really? I wonder why," Bishop responded, his voice thick with sarcasm.

Grim and Kevin were disappointed when they realized that Butter was still being held. Their expressions soon degraded even further as Bishop and Terri debriefed the team on the morning's events and what they had discovered at the plantation.

"What the call, boss?" Grim finally asked, sure he wasn't going to like the answer.

"Terri, Kevin, and I are going to head north," Bishop answered. "We'll huddle with Nick and Diana and hatch a plan. In the meantime, I need you to stay here get these truckers ready to defend themselves. I have no idea how this is going to go down."

Grim understood, but Kevin clearly wasn't in agreement. "Sir, if it's all the same to you, I would like to stay here and help Grim."

Bishop's thoughts immediately went to Nick and how he would explain leaving the big man's son behind as a hostage. "Terri and I need you, Kevin," he urged the anxious kid. "We've got to travel through some pretty rough territory on the way back."

"I respectfully request that you allow me to stay here, sir," he firmly responded. "My teammates are here. Butter is my best friend, and it wouldn't seem right to just run off and leave him. Besides, sir, we both know that my dad wouldn't allow me to come back with you."

As he digested Kevin's words, Bishop was torn between his friendship with Nick and the heartwarming loyalty the rookie was displaying. On one hand, as a parent, he would want his son out of harm's way no matter what the cost. On the other, the kid's bravery and grit would make any father's chest stick out with pride. Anyone who had ever commanded men would give his right arm to obtain such comradery within the ranks.

"Besides," Kevin added, sensing Bishop's indecision, "My skills would be far better utilized here than on the road. I would recommend you take one of the deputies instead. One of them was telling me that he has six kids at home. I think he would be a better choice. Don't you, sir?"

In the end, Bishop nodded his agreement. "Based solely on what is the best use of your skills, I have to agree," the Texan admitted. "You stay here and help Grim prepare the defenses."

Kevin's smile challenged the morning sun, "Yes, sir!"

The trip back to Texas passed without incident. The top priority on the couple's long list was to brief Alpha on what they had discovered.

"My sixth sense was right," Diana stated over the shortwave. "Sounds like we've got one hell of a mess down there."

"We need help," Terri said, stating the obvious. "I think this warrants all hands on deck."

"I agree," the Alliance leader responded. "I'll get Sheriff Watts and some of his people headed that way ASAP. I've got commitments for the next few days that just can't be put off. After that, Nick and I will be there. In the meantime, I'm going to call the President in Washington and get his point of view on this mess. Maybe he has some influence or can come up with a brilliant idea."

"Bishop and I will get started trying to find these Quaker people. The clock is ticking."

"Nick is going to be a wild man with Kevin in the middle of all this," Diana worried. "I may have to tie him down to stop him from rushing off and making things worse. You know how hot headed that man can be."

"It always sucks when kids are involved," Terri acknowledged. "As a matter of fact, my next task is to go speak to April and May's mother. I'm hoping she can point me toward the Quakers."

"Help is coming," Diana repeated. "We'll be there soon. Good luck."

Terri looked at Bishop and shook her head. "I'm going to go talk to Hannah. Maybe she can help."

Bishop didn't envy his wife's job. "Like the boss lady in Alpha said, 'Good luck.'"

Hannah Lee was hard at work repairing the damaged houseboat when Terri cleared her throat.

Jumping with a start, the marina owner exclaimed, "Oh, Lord, you scared me!"

Terri didn't have time to be polite. "Hannah, I'm afraid I have to talk to you – right now. Why don't you put down that paint brush and come on over to our boat?"

For a moment, it appeared as though the older woman was going to argue, but the seriousness etching Terri's face convinced her otherwise.

Once seated and sipping on a cool glass of water, Terri broke the bad news.

For a long time, Hannah just sat and stared at her glass, finally offering, "I don't know whether to be happy or bust out in tears," the older woman responded with a shaky voice. "You've answered my prayers by finding April alive and healthy. My little May, on the other hand, seems to be in deep trouble. I'm not sure what to do."

Reaching across the table and taking the shocked woman's hand, Terri said, "Don't worry just yet. The Alliance is putting their best people on getting both of your girls back. Right now, if you want to do something to help, I need you to think hard about May, her friends, and what she did in her spare time."

Wiping away the water from her eyes, Hannah inhaled deeply and nodded, "Of course I want to help, but I really don't know much. May's only friend was a kid from Del Rio named Ricky. I didn't care for him at all. He was a little too cocky for my taste."

"Tell me about Ricky."

"He and my May rode their bicycles with some other teens in the area. I didn't like it … almost made her stop hanging out with them on more than a few occasions. But, in the end, I felt sorry for the kids. After the collapse, a huge portion of their lives vanished. All of their social media, cell phones, texting, and music simply disappeared. Us older folks, we didn't grow up with all that, so we didn't miss it as much. For the young ones, it was their way of life. All of a sudden, poof, it was gone."

Nodding her understanding, Terri tried to gently steer Hannah on topic. "Where does Ricky live?"

"To be honest, I just don't know. He always rode his bicycle and met May at the end of our lane. She would dawdle outside, sometimes for over an hour, waiting to see him coming down the road. Now and then, three or four others tagged along. Most of the boys carried guns, so I felt she was reasonably safe."

Terri continued to question the marina's owner for another 15 minutes, but it was clear that Hannah didn't know anything else that was going to help. Still, if May was indeed involved with the Quakers, this boy Ricky might be a solid lead.

155

Standing to signal the end of the interview, Terri hugged the marina owner and said, "Thank you, Hannah. I promise; we'll do everything we can to bring your girls back home."

Sheriff Watts, along with a handful of deputies, had arrived a short time later. Bishop welcomed the senior lawman's insight and experience. "Let's go find some Quakers," the tall officer had shrugged after being briefed on the situation.

It was easy to find where May's cycling friend lived, Bishop simply walked the road, following the signs left in the sandy shoulder alongside the pavement. Bicycles had narrow tires and there was no shortage of imprints. When the indentations stopped after a particular driveway, it was a pretty sure bet that young Mr. Ricky lived in the small home visible at the end of the private drive.

Standing alongside the pavement, the Texan pointed toward the gravel and dirt lane that was thick with the imprints of bicycle tires. "I think we've found our fugitive."

Sheriff Watts agreed, "I would say so. Let's go see if he's home."

Shaking his head, Bishop had a better idea. "If we storm up there and make a big, official fuss, our young suspect might clam up. His parents might not like the law appearing on their front doorstep and advise the young man to keep his mouth shut. I spied a cluster of sage about a mile up the road. Why don't you drop me off there, and I'll radio you after I've had a chance to chitchat with Ricky."

Watts knew what was on the line, having been ordered to "provide any and all cooperation to Bishop and Terri." He also understood where the SAINT lead was coming from. People felt comfortable at home, and that would often make them more difficult to interview in that environment. Catch the same person away from their primary residence, and they often would sing like a Blue Jay.

"If you say so," the sheriff remarked, tipping his hat to Bishop. "I do hope that citizen will still be able to walk after your so-called, chitchat."

Bishop's eyes suddenly grew dark, "He is a known terrorist, after all. So much is riding on this; we don't exactly have time for a beer." He shook his head to clear his thoughts of the dark mental image of Butter and May's demise, returning to the unpleasant business at hand. A moment later, Bishop grinned, "I'm not going to *hurt* the young man. I might, however, *scare* him just a smidge."

The lanky sheriff nodded, "And there's just no telling what might frighten the average citizen. As far as I know, that's not a violation of an individual's rights."

A short time later, Bishop was waving goodbye as Watts drove off. He then turned, and began finalizing his plan.

Either wind or rain had washed a few inches of silt across the pavement here, and the local county highway department obviously wasn't performing much maintenance these days. The barricade wasn't any big deal for a car or pickup, but for Ricky's two-wheel transport, it was a serious obstacle. The sand was too soft to navigate safely while riding, the footprints next to the tire tracks making it clear that the young man had to dismount and walk his bike across the wash.

According to Hannah, May normally rode with her friend shortly before dusk to avoid the heat. Since automobiles were still a rarity, cycling after dark wasn't nearly as hazardous as before.

Bishop chuckled, "Conspirators like the darkness, but so do bushwhackers." The Texan then began setting his trap.

Just as the sun dropped low in the west, Bishop spotted a sole figure peddling toward his hide. Hannah had described young master Ricky as hard to miss in a crowd.

"He has the brightest, rust-red hair I've ever seen on a boy," Hannah had reported. "And more freckles than any three kids should ever be allowed."

Sure enough, Bishop spotted a mop on the approaching rider that left no doubt he had the right guy.

As predicted, Ricky slowed and then dismounted his bike immediately before the sandbar. Just as the tracks indicated, the kid pointed his bike toward the side of the road where Bishop was hiding.

Ricky was almost through the obstacle when the scrape of a boot caused him to turn. Before he could execute the maneuver, however, the world went black as Bishop pulled a dark pillowcase over the lad's head.

"Hey, what the hell…" the protestor snarled from inside the hood. Before he could finish, Ricky was on his ass, and then a heartbeat later, an incredibly strong pair of hands yanked on his arm, twisting it viciously until his body flopped face down into the sand.

Ricky barely felt the boot on the small of his back, the pain shooting through his shoulder being so intense. "Oh, God! Who are you! Stop! Please!"

"Shut your mouth," came a harsh, low growl as Bishop torqued just slightly on the kid's arm. "Shut up before I rip off this arm and shove it up your ass."

"Okay, okay, Mister. Take the bike … it's all I've got."

"I don't want your bicycle, boy. I want to know where the Quakers are meeting tonight."

His prisoner's hesitation was too long, telling Bishop instantly that he had the right man. Still, Ricky tried to play it dumb. "The who?"

Again, Bishop torqued on the arm. Not enough to dislocate the lad's shoulder, but almost. "Don't try to bullshit me, son. May sent me to find you and your other friends. Where do you meet?"

The mention of May's name caused another lengthy pause before the muffled answer came from under the hood. "You know May?"

Bishop didn't have time to play nice. Still, he was a bit surprised at the youth's resilience. Normally, the ambush and hood were enough to motivate all but the most disciplined tongues. Pulling his sidearm, he pressed the weapon close to Ricky's masked head and cocked the hammer. Without any warning, he fired a shot into the sand.

In a way, the Texan felt sorry for the kid. The .45's report was enough to make a person's ears ring for hours. Without any warning, inside the dark confines of the hood, he was sure Ricky's brain was just about to go into convulsions. The smell of urine soon confirmed that fact. On the other hand, there were accusations that he had participated in a massacre and torched food bound to the famine ridden U.S.

"The next one goes into your right kneecap," the Texan shouted. "I carry a .45 automatic with 200-grain hollowpoints that have a velocity of 980 feet per second. I will fire at an upward angle so that the lead shatters your tibia, crushes your patella, and shreds every tendon between the femur and your asshole. You will never ride that bicycle again. Where is the fucking meeting?"

Inside the darkness of the cloth, Ricky was trying to cry, breathe, think, and lie all at the same time. The resulting gibberish didn't answer Bishop's question.

The Texan shook his head in frustration. The kid at his feet was being stubborn. He touched the tip of his boot to the back of the prone kid's calf, sure that it felt like the barrel of a pistol to his hostage.

It was like a bolt of electricity shot through Ricky's convulsing body, a clear, "Nooooo!" escaping from the terrified lad's throat.

"Where is the meeting?"

"It's at the warehouse, you son of a bitch," he sobbed.

"What warehouse?"

"The one just outside of town, next to the water tower."

Bishop loosened his grip on the boy's arm, then pulled the weak-kneed youth to his feet. A moment later, the red mop of hair was exposed, Ricky blinking rapidly as his eyes adjusted to the light. "Come on, son. You're going with me."

As expected, the removal of hood stiffened the boy's constitution. "Fuck you, Copperhead. I'd rather die than be a slave. You can kill me right here and now, but I ain't going anywhere with you."

"I'm not a Copperhead, dumbass. I work for the Alliance," Bishop stated with a serious voice. "The second thing you should know about me is that I've killed more men than you have hairs around your pussy. I strongly suggest that you show me a little more respect."

When the youth didn't respond immediately, Bishop pointed to the widening, damp stain that darkened the front of Ricky's pants. "And lastly, you should really work on controlling your bladder, baby boy."

Embarrassment was now added to the whirlwind of emotions clogging Ricky's brain. Bishop didn't care. Lucrecia's hourglass was running out of sand. There were hundreds of lives on the line, including Butter's.

Reaching for the microphone, the Texan broadcasted, "I've got him, Sheriff. I would appreciate a ride."

"Everything okay?" Watt inquired across the airwaves.

"Yes, everything is fine. By the way, you wouldn't have a spare pair of trousers in your trunk, would you?"

Having dry jeans didn't seem to help Ricky's attitude. Nor did learning that May had been captured by the Copperheads.

"She knew the risk," the defiant youth stated boldly. "We all know the risks."

Terri was playing the role of good cop. After Bishop's initial encounter with the lad, there was no need for a bad cop. "Why didn't you come to the Alliance? Why didn't anyone come forward and report that slavers were ravaging the countryside?"

The suggestion seemed to offend the young man. "We did. When the Copperheads first started taking people from their homes, several folks went to the men who were running the town. The next night, the whistleblowers disappeared. It was several months before we found out that the slavers were bribing the local cops and the man who called himself the mayor."

Sheriff Watts spoke up from the corner, "That's believable. From what I've been able to ascertain, these Copperheads used the same old tricks as the cartels. Bribes and threats were common along the river."

Pointing a finger at Watts, Ricky spat, "Bribes? Graft? Tell the truth, Mr. Honest and Upright. Hell, half of the people that ended up in Bella Dona's meat market were delivered by your deputies."

For the first time since Bishop had known the good sheriff, Watts showed embarrassment.

"Sheriff?" Terri asked. "What is he talking about?"

"Ma'am, what did we do with criminals back in the early days of the recovery?"

Terri tilted her head in thought and then answered. "We exiled them. We ran them out of Texas with a stern warning not to come back."

"Yes, ma'am. That was about our only choice. There weren't any jails or prisons, so my men were ordered to take people to the border and kick them out of the Lone Star State. What few deputies we had here along the border did the same thing, forcing criminals into Mexico."

Bishop rolled his eyes, "So we were using Bella Dona as a warden, her plantation as a prison? Wonderful. That's just great."

Watts shook his head, instantly becoming defensive. "My men didn't know anything about slave labor or any plantation. They were ordered to kick offenders out of Texas, and they did. What happened to them on the other side of the river wasn't our concern."

Spreading his hands, Ricky barked, "Homeless criminals roaming from house to house, terrorizing our community. No wonder the leaders struck a bargain with Lady Bella Dona. And when the supply of felons was low, they subsidized their catch with locals. Now do you understand why we didn't come to Alliance and ask for help? Hell, from what we could see, you people were in bed with Bella Dona and her lot, feeding them a ready source of human flesh."

Terri studied the redheaded young man sitting in the corner, eventually shaking her head in disgust. "So you take it upon yourselves to murder a bunch of innocent truckers?"

"Innocent, my ass. They were warned. We went to the guy gathering the convoy and explained how they were buying food grown by the hands of slaves. Captured and imprisoned citizens. Jeb ... or whatever his name was, didn't believe us or didn't want to. He pulled a shotgun on us. Said if we didn't get away from his truck, he'd cut us in half."

"So you murdered them," Watts stated with disdain.

"We are fighting a war. There are causalities in war. As soon as those truckers left Texas with their trailers loaded with equipment ... equipment that the Copperheads use to build weapons, they became combatants. Hell, there are tanks rolling around the plantation now. All thanks to the good ol' U.S.A. We couldn't just stand by and let Bella Dona and her henchmen get stronger and stronger. What else were we supposed to do?"

"How did May find out where her sister was being held?" Bishop asked.

"One of the slaves escaped and managed to make it to the settlement on the lakeshore – the one that was burned a few nights ago. The villagers had been fighting the Copperheads for months, just like us. They handed the fugitive over so we could hide him. He told us where April and several other gringos were being held."

"So May, a 20-year old girl, takes it upon herself to go and rescue her sister?" Terri asked, still not believing the kid's story.

Grunting, Ricky shook his head. "You underestimate May. When she first joined our cause, we all made the same mistake. Within three months, she was our leader, and no one has questioned her since. She is the strongest person I have ever met and one of the smartest."

Bishop shook his head, "She must not be too smart. She managed to get herself captured along with one of my men."

The kid grunted with a light laugh, "You think that wasn't intentional? May knows the only way we can destroy the Copperheads is to turn the Alliance against them. She played that dumbass hulk on your team like a cheap fiddle. And guess what? Now you're in, like it or not. Mission accomplished."

Terri had to admit, the young man was right. The Alliance was in knee deep and sinking further into the quagmire with each passing hour. Nick and Diana were on their way. The Army was sending a general from Fort Hood. Sheriff Watts was voicing rare complaints about the draw on his limited manpower.

Bishop sensed his wife's growing frustration. Returning his attention to their guest, the Texan decided to try to intimidate Ricky, "Bella Dona wants us to bring her the Quakers' heads. There are dozens of innocent lives that will be lost if we don't comply. Why shouldn't I just round up your friends, put you on a school bus, and deliver you to the plantation?"

"There's little we could do to stop you," Ricky answered with a shrug. "But then again, what would our families and friends say? Do the people in Alpha really want it known far and wide that the Alliance supports slavers over its own citizens? Go ahead, lady. Wrap the Quakers up in a neat, pretty, little package and put a bow on top if that's the reputation you want your government to have. May predicted that the Alliance would fall within six months once people knew that our blood was on your hands."

Terri struggled to keep her temper from boiling over. Combined, the Alliance members involved in the convoy operation had decades of experience dealing with everything from international relations to law enforcement. Yet, despite their knowledge and history, a second-string bunch of locals had pulled the organization into the middle of a conflict that could result in a hot war and hundreds, if not thousands of causalities.

Ricky seemed to relish her dilemma. "What is your problem? Why are you mad at us? If someone kidnapped your family and you knew they were being forced into slavery, wouldn't you do everything within your power to set your loved ones free?"

He then turned and glared at Bishop, "You're a tough guy. Mean and capable. How many people did you say you had killed? And yet you sit there staring at me as if I'm some sort of monster or criminal. You threaten to shoot me. Why? From where I'm sitting, I'm the white hat in this drama. We were doing the right thing! Why aren't you and the all-mighty Alliance rolling south to wipe this scourge from the earth?"

Bishop just sat, staring back at the kid with a blank expression. When it became clear that the Texan wasn't going to answer, Ricky threw up his arms in disgust. "You people make me sick. I'm not the criminal here. You are. Who sits around intimidating a kid when there are citizens you're sworn to protect laboring in bondage? Since we've been sitting here, Bella Dona and her crew have probably worked another half dozen innocent people into their graves."

162

"Why is it every time I have a conversation with you people down in Texas, it blossoms into some huge international incident?" the President's voice boomed over the radio.

Diana glanced at Nick and rolled her eyes, "Believe me, sir, we're not any happier about this than you are."

"Slaves?" the voice from Washington barked. "That's a pretty broad term, Miss Brown. A term often twisted to encompass all kinds of business models. If I recall, before this new world order, there was a media exposé about slave labor in China being used to produce imported goods. I also remember headlines about factories burning in India where child labor was supposedly involved. And wasn't there some huge scandal in Texas about the sex trade and illegal immigrants?"

"Yes, sir, I do remember reading about all of those events."

"While personally, I am outraged by such practices, the downfall of society has moved the bar when it comes to individual rights and human dignity. You said Bishop and Terri reported seeing thousands of well-fed, productive people on this Mexican plantation. Is that correct?"

"Yes, Mr. President."

"Well let me tell you, ma'am, when the snow starts flying this winter, I'm going to have about two million starving souls in the upper Midwest who would gladly sign up for hard labor in exchange for a mouthful of food. I don't know about your administration in Alpha, but we fight this same moral dilemma practically every, single day here in Washington. Which is more important, human dignity and freedom, or a belly full of food? It is easy to mount a philosophical debate while enjoying a four-course meal, but a little dicier conversation out in the real world. The choice is never easy or clear."

Diana nodded, able to relate to what the man on the other end of transmission was saying. "I understand, sir, but that's really not what I wanted to speak with you about. We requested this conversation hoping to learn what the United States had used to procure the food from Mexico. What form of payment did you use?"

There was a pause, and then Diana heard the rattling of papers in the background. "I'm looking at the inventory sheets, Miss Brown. Looks like a bunch of farm equipment to me. I see a long list of diesel and gasoline engine parts, tractor treads, wheels and tires, welding supplies, and a host of other industrial goods. Why is this information important to you? I don't understand?"

After throwing Nick a questioning look and receiving a confirming nod, Diana responded, "Because we believe they are building an army, sir."

Again, Washington was silent for a considerable period. Finally, "I suppose the stuff we sent them could be used to repair military equipment. But, it could also be implemented to maintain a farm or a food processing plant or a factory that makes tennis shoes."

"I understand, Mr. President."

"So, if you don't mind sharing, what are your plans, Ms. Brown? Obviously, we both have a lot at stake here."

"At this time, sir, we don't have any viable solution to the issue. I have my best people working on it, but so far I've not heard any reasonable plan of action."

A low grunt sounded over the airwaves before the Commander in Chief spoke again. "You have my sympathies, Diana. This is a deep quagmire if ever one existed. I'm sure you're well aware what will happen if widespread starvation rears its ugly head among our population."

Diana sighed, "Yes, sir. They will come south ... to Texas, and I'll have more mouths to feed."

"You may get caught in a refugee vice, Ms. Brown. You could have millions of ravenous people from the north and the south coming to rest on your doorstep."

"Yes, sir, we are well aware of that potential. We all want to avoid causing any more suffering or hardship."

"I wish you the best of luck, Diana, and please, give my best to Bishop and Terri, if you would. Tell them I look forward to seeing my godson soon."

"We could wipe out the entire plantation with a single air strike," Nick stated evenly. "Four F-15 Eagles could probably do the job in less than a minute. Unfortunately, dozens of Alliance citizens, as well as Butter and the truckers, would probably be killed by the bomb's collateral damage."

"That would leave us with thousands of unorganized, hungry refugees at best," Diana said, shaking her head. "I don't think that is a viable option."

The big man's focus then settled on Bishop, "Could we insert a Special Forces team and attempt to pull Butter out?"

"Doubtful," the Texan replied with a frown. "Castro isn't stupid. I'm sure he's moving the hostages around every night. He's probably doing the same with his own worthless carcass, as well as Lady Bella Dona. The facility down there is the size of a small city. We'd never find our people before being discovered and engaged."

"What about an airborne assault?" offered the general from Fort Hood. "We could transport in with a few dozen Blackhawks full of infantry and take over the entire place in a matter of minutes."

Bishop stood and stepped to the wall map, pointing with a pencil. "The hostages are in at least two different places. We know they have armor here … and here. It would take a huge invasion force to control both locations, and even then, there's no guarantee that we would find our people. No, General, my read is that an invasion of any sort is out of the question. Those people down there are absolutely ruthless. They will kill our citizens the moment they sense anything is wrong."

"Would they accept any other form of ransom?" Diana asked. "Can we offer something other than the Quakers?"

Nick didn't like the idea. "Negotiating with radicals is never a good move," he stated firmly. "Even if there were something we could provide that would get our people out of there, in six months they could just snatch a few more citizens and make further demands. We would find ourselves facing the same problem."

"Lady Bella Dona wanted in my pants pretty badly," Terri chuckled, trying to lighten the mood. "Maybe I should offer to have sex with her in exchange for releasing the hostages."

"Hell, if it would avoid a war and a bunch of people getting killed, I'd go hop in her bed with ya," Diana added.

A virtual menu of snarky comments immediately formed in Bishop's mind, including an offer to be the event's photographer. Then an image of a badly beaten, suffering Butter formed in his brain, evaporating all wit and humor. *For once, I'm not the person throwing out the bad joke at the wrong time*, he thought. *I want that boy home.*

Glancing across the table at his friend, Bishop found Nick waiting for it. Only mild disappointment flashed across the big man's face when the Texan shook his head, "No, sir. I'm not saying a word."

"Negotiate, free our people, and then go wipe them out?" the general suggested. "We could station troops along the border to block the flow of refugees and wouldn't have an ongoing blackmail problem."

No one liked the military option, yet there didn't seem to be any better solution. "First of all," Diana began, as the meeting was losing steam, "the Alliance cannot afford a protracted engagement. Secondly, the general's idea assumes we can negotiate some other solution."

"It's not our fight," Bishop added. "I'm as morally outraged as anyone over what we saw down there, but is it really any of our business? Before the collapse, I'd wager that everyone at this table had a pair of shoes in their closet that had been made by forced labor somewhere in Asia. I hated it then, and I hate it now, but like the old American politicians used to say, we can't be the world's policeman."

Nick nodded his agreement, "When the Alliance first began the recovery, we bussed thousands and thousands of people out of the inner cities and put them to work in the fields. We set up entire communities made of tents and dug trenches for latrines. The conditions were deplorable. If someone had wandered into our territory and witnessed those events, they might have easily concluded that we were using slave labor to grow our own food."

"But that was different," Diana countered, now on the defensive. "We didn't force those people to work. Any of them could have declined, moved on, or found a different way. We didn't deny individual free will."

Shaking his head, Nick said, "Back then, if you wanted to eat Alliance food, you had to go work in Alliance fields. It was the only option our government had to provide food for a famished populace. Is what this Bella Dona lady is doing in Mexico really all that different?"

"I think that was April's point ... why she didn't want to leave," Terri added. "Bishop's right, it's none of our affair. Hard times call for hard measures. We shouldn't be so quick to judge."

Bishop spoke again, "Does anyone remember Fort Stockdale and D.A. Gibson? We kept hearing they were using slave labor, kept hearing that same story from refugees wandering into Alpha. And what did we find when we finally 'invaded?' It just goes to show that there are two sides to every story, and I think it's a very bad idea for the Alliance to get involved with either side of this coin."

Terri nodded, the slight redness of embarrassment n her cheeks. "Yes, I remember. I was bound and determined to kill anyone who abused the downtrodden. I've learned a lot since then ... some very difficult lessons."

A prolonged, silent pause prompted considerable contemplation, all of the gathered debating both the tactical and moral paradox they faced. No one liked the apparent evil that lurked just south of the Rio Grande, yet there were no workable alternatives.

Bishop was the first to speak again, "Maybe this isn't any of our business, but that doesn't mean we have to support slavery. No matter how this problem is resolved, I hope the clever people at this table find a way to deny Bella Dona a market for her ill-gotten gains."

"That's going to be a hard sale to the president, Bishop," Diana said. "He's as desperate for groceries as we were just a short time ago. If this decision comes down to mass starvation versus procuring food grown by slaves, a full belly is going to win over individual rights every single time."

"They will eventually fail, no matter what we do," Bishop shrugged. "They are experiencing the same problem that all utopian societies eventually encounter. I don't care if you call them socialist, communist, hippie communes, or Plato's Republic, they all suffer from the same basic flaw. When the people are handed everything by the government, they become dependent on that government. Freedom evaporates; individuality disappears. Before the collapse, the United States and its welfare safety net created generational poverty and dependence. Those folks became slaves in their own right, unable to break the cycle and trapped in virtual poverty. Their master was the government, pretending to be the generous benefactor, just like Bella Dona. And yet, politicians with socialist leanings generated popular support right up to the collapse. It's been tried over and over again, and the results are always the same. You would think our species would learn," Bishop grumbled.

Nick nodded his agreement, "Most people don't know that Carolina, Georgia, and Pennsylvania were all founded on some English philosopher's cockamamie vision of a Utopian paradise. Even Thomas Jefferson had his visions of the Yeoman Republic. This isn't anything new, yet it has never worked."

It was Terri who brought the meeting back to its original purpose. "This conversation is interesting and informative, but we are out of time, folks. If no one has a better solution, I propose Bishop and I go back down there and see if we can talk some sense into Bella Dona. It doesn't matter if we're dealing with a Utopian paradise or inhuman slave pit, we still have to get our people out of there. That has to be the top priority. I just don't see any other way."

"Just remember," Bishop muttered with an icy voice. "Evil feeds on benevolence."

Chapter 11

April shooed the last of the children from the shed and then glanced at the sun to judge the time. She was getting them out late, again, and wondered if Castro would punish her for being too soft on the little ones.

She didn't blame the kids for wanting to stay, couldn't bring herself to snap and shout at them like the other teachers. *They crave learning*, she thought, trying to justify the daily lingering that occurred after class was over. *They're just little sponges, wanting so badly to soak up knowledge.*

At least, that's what she wanted to believe.

Deep down inside, April knew that her justification wasn't entirely truthful. Demanding chores, wretched quarters, and hard labor waited at the end of every school day. The older the child, the more that was expected of him. Some of the larger boys were already reporting to the fields.

Turning to find the one student left, she sighed deeply and approached Julio.

"We need to have a word about your grammar, young man," April began, trying to find the middle ground between serious and supportive. "You're struggling with punctuation, and I do not see enough effort on your part."

Looking up shyly, the preteen boy merely shrugged and mumbled, "I'll try to do better, ma'am."

April sat down on the bench next to her prize student and took his hand gently in hers. "Of all the children I have taught, you are the most gifted, Julio. Your writing is beautiful, and it touches me more than anything else I've ever read. I want to squeeze every sentence to get every last drop of joy out of each word. Please, don't throw this away. You could be the next Shakespeare or Twain or Tolstoy."

Large, sad, chocolate-brown eyes peered up at April. "I'm sorry, ma'am, but I ... I just.... There's no use."

The teacher disappeared from April's posture, replaced by the nurturing friend. "What's the matter, Julio? Is something wrong?"

"I will be 12 next month. You know the rules. I am to report to the fields on my birthday," sounded his weak, faltering voice. "What good does it do to learn about writing when in less than three years, I won't be able to stand without pain? I see how my mother and father suffer. I know my future."

Reaching down to brush back a lock of his dark hair, April tried to keep a positive face. "You don't know that things will be the same in three years, or next year, or even next month for that matter. Besides, you can still write after coming home from the harvest. You can still express that wonderful way your mind looks at the world."

The adolescent's trepidation turned to anger. With eyes flaring and breaths short and hard, he snapped, "You don't see my parents. You don't see the blisters on their hands and feet, see them wince with every step. How many people in your family have been scarred by the whip?"

On the outside, April weathered his verbal outrage without any reaction. On the inside, his words aggrieved her deeply. "I know our lives are a struggle right now. I'm sorry you have to grow up in such a difficult time. Still, we have food, shelter, and protection from evil men. We're making progress. Things will get better, I promise."

"Food," he spat. "The harvest. The crops. Plow, plant, weed, pick, stack, and store. That's all I ever hear, see, or will ever know. My stomach may be full, buy my mind is starving."

There it was again, a brilliance way beyond the adolescent's years.

"We have to eat, Julio," the teacher reasoned. "I am sure you've heard the stories about life after the collapse. I was there. They are true. We have no choice but to work together and sacrifice to survive. We all must do our part if things are going to get better."

"My dad doesn't think things will get better. Neither does my mother. I hear them whispering at night. They say that there is plenty of food for everyone here at the Castle. They say that Lady Bella Dona is working everyone into their graves so that she can build an army and rule all of Mexico. I believe them."

April was shocked at the ordinarily docile, young man's inflammatory statements. "Don't say those things, Julio," she mumbled, looking all around to make sure no one was within earshot. "Words like those can get you and your parents into a lot of trouble."

"What about words that I write? Will those get me into trouble as well? Will my words ever set me free?"

His questions left April feeling unsettled, and yet she immediately realized that she shouldn't be surprised. Julio didn't think like the other children – his mind worked in its own beautiful, unique way. She was positive his intellect placed the child in a class far and above common measurements such as genius or prodigy. He had exceeded her knowledge of mathematics over a year ago. He could read and retain any material. It was his writing, however, that was indescribably exquisite, his insight inspired.

"Julio, please, don't give up. I know it's difficult to understand right now, but...."

"My father says that writing isn't going to put food on our table," he interrupted. "My mother loves to read my words, but then she starts crying and sobbing. She says that I should be going to a university ... not out to pick limes and melons in the mud."

April squeezed his hand with affection, "The universities will reopen one of these days, Julio. I promise. Now, you must go before we both get in trouble. I will see you tomorrow, okay?"

He stared at her with wide, wet eyes, finally muttering, "Yes, ma'am." He scampered away, each landing of his bare feet raising a small puff of dust from the dirt path.

The entire episode served to deepen April's already heightened sense of despair. The past few days had been the most difficult she had ever experienced, including those unforgettable weeks of starvation back at the marina. As if May's pending death sentence were not bad enough, a man had tried to abduct her, she had been interrogated at the Castle, and Castro was in a dangerous mood. It was as if her warm, safe world was crumbling into tiny pieces.

Inhaling deeply to clear her mind, April began tidying up the schoolroom, stacking the books onto an old barrel, making sure none of the children had left anything behind. She had been promised this shed for the next three weeks, after which, it would be filled to the rafters with bales of straw.

Finally feeling like her duties were complete, she followed in Julio's footsteps, ambling back toward the main cluster of buildings that surrounded the Castle. Castro, despite his frayed nerves and short temper, was allowing her to visit May each evening. She would drop off her satchel, brush her hair, and then go and see her sister.

It was over three miles back to building #11, the old path leading April through the seemingly endless fields, most being attended by hundreds of workers. "My stomach is full, but my mind is starving," she repeated the student's words. "I wonder how many more of them feel the same way."

It was a shame, really, a tragedy that the world was so cruel as to deny children like Julio the opportunity to realize their full potential. Her student belonged in the classroom where he could refine and develop his gift, not carrying baskets of vegetables on his shoulders.

More and more buildings now dotted her route as she drew closer to #11 and the heart of the plantation. Some of the metal structures were enormous, and for a second, she wondered about their purpose.

The rare sound of an engine drew her attention to another of the monstrous facilities, the deep rumble soon followed by the appearance of a huge, tracked vehicle with a cannon on top. April had no military experience, but even she recognized the tank.

"What are you doing here?" a harsh voice barked behind her on the path.

April turned to see one of Castro's grey shirts approaching with a scowl on his face, his club slapping the palm of his hand.

Looking down as she'd learned long ago to do, April answered, "I am a teacher, jefe, on my way back from class."

She could feel the man's intense scrutiny as he judged her response. "Teacher? Class? School was scheduled to have been dismissed over 30 minutes ago. I see no reason why a teacher should be standing around, watching a restricted building. So I will ask again, what are you doing here?"

"I am on my way back to my barracks," she said with the humblest of tones. "I had to hold a student over."

"You didn't appear to be hurrying anywhere just a moment ago. You were standing, gawking like a spy. Are you a spy, schoolteacher? Are you a Quaker?"

"No, I'm nothing of the sort. Please, allow me to be on my...."

Without warning, the security man slapped her hard across the face. "Now answer my question, missy. What were you doing looking at that restricted building?"

The blow was harsh, April stinging from both the impact and the humiliation. She didn't know how to answer his question, afraid that any response would draw another painful strike – or worse. "I was ... I said...."

Like a striking cobra, his fist slammed into her stomach. April doubled over in pain, collapsing to her knees as she gasped to replace the air that had been knocked from her lungs.

"Who is your unit master?" he shouted, raising the club.

"Castro," she managed. "I report to Castro."

The name of the plantation's head of security took her antagonist aback, but only for a second. Yanking her up by the hair, he bellowed, "If you are lying to me, I will have you whipped. Now walk, schoolteacher. We will find Castro and verify your story."

171

Being pulled by the arm, April noticed Julio standing in the shadows, watching the entire affair. His lips moved without sound, mouthing the words, "Things will get better."

By the time they arrived at Castro's office, April was sure her arm had been jerked from its socket, the brutal security man never loosening his grip or allowing the circulation to return to her limb.

Castro appeared mildly amused until the guard mentioned the restricted building. April shivered when she noticed the security chief's eyes go cold. "I will handle this. Thank you for bringing it to my attention."

After the subordinate had left, Castro turned to her and said, "With your sister being a self-confessed terrorist, you really shouldn't be around restricted spaces. It just doesn't look good."

"I – I didn't know," she said honestly.

"Do you think that matters? Our entire operation is on edge right now. We have armed, hostile men less than 5 kilometers away, the Quakers are increasing the rhythm and ferocity of their attacks, and we expect the Alliance to invade at any moment. Don't make me regret trusting you."

April nodded her agreement, "Yes, sir."

"Go on about your business. By the way, after your stellar performance with the outsiders, I ordered one of the carpenters to install a door on your quarters," he stated with pride. "It should provide additional privacy. We do reward loyalty. I may even visit this evening to celebrate."

Looking quiet and demure, April left, making her way toward #11 and her closet-quarters. With each step along the beaten trail, her anger boiled, threatening to develop into a full-blown, seething rage.

The fact that she now had to keep her head down and eyes forward was infuriating. Her arm ached, her core still throbbing from the impact of the guard's fist. She was even too intimidated to acknowledge the people passing by, paranoia causing more achiness in her gut than the brutal punch. "What is happening to our community?" she questioned silently. "Why am I being treated in this way? I did nothing wrong, yet I'm being made to feel like a criminal."

For a moment, the distraught woman considered fleeing. Castro was out of control, he and his men growing more and more tyrannical with each passing month. She had no belongings to pack. She could simply walk away, cross the fields and hills, and go home to Texas.

She began creating a mental framework of her escape and journey, using the same outlining methods she taught Julio to use when writing a long paper. She would need water, some food, a spare set of clothing, and a map. She then added a rucksack, or basket to carry her traveling supplies.

It then dawned on April that her plan was deeply flawed. She had no vessel to carry water, as the plantation always provided hydration to its workers via pump wells and young men carrying large buckets on their shoulders. There was no way to cache or carry food, the kitchens serving as much as a person could eat, but no more. A map was impossible.

May.

Even if she could manage an escape, she couldn't leave her sister behind. "You ran away once," she whispered. "Look at all of the trouble that has caused. No, you can't just up and leave."

Remorse welled up inside April. She was completely dependent on Castro and Bella Dona for even the most basic of human needs. Her mere survival was in the hands of others. She had become completely dependent on the 'utopian' machine that was the plantation. She was no longer a functioning individual capable of free will and independent action.

Anger soon began to morph into frustration. There was no place to go, no appeal or higher authority. "You want to come by and celebrate?" she hissed, remembering Castro's words. "You consider that a reward?"

As she made her way up the main aisle of #11, she noticed a man with a tool belt standing outside of her quarters. He seemed perplexed. "I was instructed to install this door, but there's no wall to hang it from. I will have to build a wall or forget about the door."

"I'll gladly take a wall," she stated, thinking her day might finally be getting better.

"I will get permission. It may take a few days. Nothing moves quickly around here."

As the man turned to leave, April realized that he had left the large, wooden door partially blocking her entrance. "Sir! Sir, could you please take this door with you?"

"I can't," he stated with a shrug. "I have to leave it here."

"Well, can you at least move it somewhere else so I can get to my bed?"

Blinking once, then twice, he said, "I could, but then why would I? If you want to move it, go ahead, be my guest. I will be fed this evening whether or not you like where I left the door."

He then pivoted and walked away, leaving April steaming mad. She shouted in Spanish, "What is your problem, asshole? Why are you being such a jerk?"

"Because I wasn't born a pretty, gringo woman who the boss likes to fuck. My wife and I sleep out in the open, just like everyone else. So shut up, Yankee bitch, and enjoy your privacy. I've been around here a long time, and I've never seen Castro use a woman for more than a year. How long has he been doing you?"

April was furious. Now, not only was the heavy, wooden obstacle blocking her entry, she would probably be moved to the bottom of the carpenter's list.

Sighing, and squeezing through the narrow opening, her frustration grew. "The problem with this place is that there is no motivation to perform," she grumbled. "Like it or not, there's no accountability, no annual reviews or salary increases. The carpenter was right; he will eat the same tonight whether or not he accomplished what he was instructed to do."

Realizing that it was near time to go and visit her sister, April began to brush her hair in the small section of a broken mirror she had found in the trash heap. She remembered Julio's repeating of her own words, "It will get better."

Setting down the brush, she had her doubts. Julio's parents had gossiped that Lady Bella Dona was building an army, and she had seen some sort of tank pulling out of the workshop. Were those rumors true?

Her mind then jumped to the hundreds of working laborers sweating in the fields. "There isn't any diesel fuel or spare parts to fix the tractors," the bosses always said. Yet, she had seen a tracked vehicle that by itself could pull a plow or tow a huge wagon of grain. Why was the plantation wasting such a valuable commodity?

Putting away her things, April decided she wouldn't mention what she had seen to May. Castro had warned her, and she would heed his words. Espionage was a capital offense.

Butter stared at the old concrete ceiling, trying to make shapes out of the stains and discoloration.

His mind then drifted away from the cramped confinement of his cell, wondering for a moment what Grim and Kevin were doing. He would miss Kevin the most.

"At least the beatings have stopped," he whispered to the dank, concrete walls. "At least you don't have to endure more pain."

Adjusting his massive frame, he grunted at the putrid mattress that served as his bedding. For two days, he wouldn't venture near the thing, the smell of urine and feces grossing him out. Now, he didn't even notice the stench. It beat trying to sleep on the cold, cement floor.

Other than the legless-bunk, the only other fixture in the room was a bucket that served as a toilet. Once a day, for 15 minutes, he was allowed to carry it outside to a trench where he emptied his waste. Encumbered with heavy, iron shackles that cut into his thick limbs and under the scrutiny of at least 10 guards, the excursion was Butter's only contact with the outside world. Had they come for him yet today? What day was it anyway? Why didn't they just kill him and get it over with?

At least the beatings had stopped.

He could feel his body beginning to heal. Salt, what little was in the watery gruel that he was served, no longer burned his mouth. He could see clearly out of one eye now, the other not feeling as puffy and inflamed but was still swollen shut.

Butter began tightening his muscles and limbs, one by one, doing an inventory to check the status of his injuries. Had he done that yet, today? Or was that yesterday? He couldn't remember. It didn't matter.

Every now and then, he could hear voices. Once, he would have sworn it was Mr. Bishop. "He's come to rescue me," the big kid had thought. For an hour, he had stared hard at the thick, wooden door, waiting for his teammates to barge in.

When his cell door hadn't burst open, Butter hadn't been disappointed. Eventually, hope began to flicker, and remorse became his master. "What do you expect?" he had eventually chided himself. "You violated orders. You disobeyed Mr. Bishop. Why would he come rescue such a loathsome example of humanity? Why would any of your teammates even care? You put all of them, the mission, and the truckers in danger. Why were you so stupid?"

May.

For the hundredth time, he wished he could take it all back. Now, replaying the events in his head, he realized how ignorant he had been. He had made a mistake and then gotten into more trouble by trying to correct it.

His tortured brain conjured up an image of his old friend and mentor, Slim. "When you find yourself in a hole," the tough cowboy had advised, "Stop digging." Yet, he hadn't followed that sage counsel. He'd continued down the wrong path, getting himself deeper and deeper into trouble.

At least the beatings had stopped.

175

May.

Despite his physical pain and tortured mental state, he could forgive her. The SAINT team was like his family. He'd always imagined Kevin and Slim as his brothers, Grim the mean, old uncle that secretly loved them all but was afraid to admit it, and Mr. Bishop as the father figure. He would gladly give his life for any of them, just like May.

If his loved ones had been taken against their will, would he have acted any differently than May? Wouldn't he lie, cheat, and yes, even kill, to set Kevin free? Or Grim? Or Mr. Bishop? He knew he would – he had already done as much in defending Slim. It was difficult to hate May given the realization. Besides, if his limited understanding of Spanish was accurate, she was going to be hung as well, at least according to a conversation between the guards he'd overheard.

Reaching up with the arm that hurt the least, Butter felt his throat, wondering what the noose would feel like with all of his weight pulling on the rope. A tear rolled down the big kid's cheek, leaving a trail of slightly cleaner skin in its wake.

"At least I won't have to face Mr. Bishop after I'm gone," he declared to the empty cell. "It will be a relief not to lay here and rehash all my regrets."

Grim turned a page in his notebook and began to scratch another diagram with his pencil.

Beside him, Kevin whispered, "You called it, sir. They are changing their sentries, right on schedule."

Nodding with a smile, the senior man finished his sketch and then scribbled a few notes. "Let's get back to our lines," he responded, flipping the small pad closed.

With Grim in the lead, the two Alliance men began backing slowly down the hill. Below them, just over 300 meters away, they could identify the outline of the semi-trailers illuminated by the numerous campfires.

Slinking from rock to bush to gully, the two experienced fighters took their time descending back to friendly lines. The local militia wasn't entirely without skills, and more than once, they had sent out a random patrol.

Kevin saw his partner drop suddenly, Grim going prone with amazing speed. Less than half a second later, the younger man was eating dirt as well. Neither of the Alliance members dared breathe or make even the slightest sound.

The four-man patrol was less than 20 feet away, the sound of an occasional footstep the only sign of their passing. Still, it had been enough to give Grim enough warning to avoid being discovered. After a minute, he gradually raised his head and scanned the area, eventually signaling Kevin that the area was clear.

"They're getting better," Kevin whispered once he was sure the team had passed.

"A little," Grim replied. "Bishop would have their ass for making that much noise. They're still far from first class, and frankly, that might be the only thing that saves our asses."

Just over 100 meters from the outermost truck, Grim changed directions again. Kevin knew instinctively that it wasn't a Mexican patrol this time but one of their own.

It wasn't the first time Grim had worked extra hard to avoid friendlies. "We are being watched every minute of every day, and our foe has the high ground," the elder trooper had explained. "If those people up there see our sentries challenge someone, they're going to know we are violating the rules and going outside the camp. So we avoid everyone, friend or foe."

It made sense to Kevin, another one of the seemingly endless lessons he was learning by working with such an experienced man as Grim. Between Bishop and his second in command, he felt like he was attending the University of Survival, majoring in Covert Activities. He loved it.

"Besides," Grim had added with a smirk. "If we get around them and into our own camp without being detected, look at all the fun we can have rubbing it the guards' faces. Trying to catch us will keep them sharp."

The remainder of their egress passed without incident, Kevin relieved to return to the friendly confines of the encampment.

"So what did we learn tonight, my young friend?" Grim asked as he began removing his equipment.

Kevin had to think about it for a bit, "We confirmed several things, but I don't know of anything new."

Chuckling, Grim pulled his notebook and began reviewing the evening's observations. "We learned a lot tonight, Kevin. Enough, I hope, to get at least some of these truckers back home to their families."

The questioning look on the younger man's face made Grim sigh. "We can now be certain of exactly when they have a shift change. We know how and when their supplies are delivered, and we can be absolutely positive which of the two armored vehicles houses their commander."

"But, sir, we already knew most of that, didn't we?"

Grim shook his head, trying to be patient with his teammate. "Look, Kevin, if you see a midnight change of the guard once, you were just in the right place at the right time to make an initial observation. If you confirm it at the exact same time twice, that can still be random circumstance. When you see it the third time, that is actionable intelligence. As the old adage goes, the third time is the charm."

After storing their packs, the two men continued toward the center of what the truckers had taken to calling, "The Diesel Riviera."

Indeed, the way Grim had ordered the trailers positioned was like the streets of a small town, complete with blocks and intersections. This was true for all but the innermost area, which was a narrow rectangle. Here was where the secret business of preparing for battle was being conducted, away from the prying eyes on the hillsides.

The preparations had been difficult at best. Not only was Grim trying to construct a plan with nearly zero resources, few weapons, and mostly untrained personnel, he had to do so without giving the militia surrounding them the slightest hint that something was amiss.

Any supplies they scavenged from the abandoned village had to be smuggled in at night. Any assembly had to be restricted to the confines of the "Freightliner Square."

It was frustrating work, fraught with peril.

"Bishop and Terri are supposed to return in two more days," Grim informed his hastily assigned commanders. "We have to be ready tomorrow, just in case they come in a little early."

"And if they don't show up?" asked one of the deputies.

"Oh, they'll be here," Grim answered with confidence. "Of that, you can be sure. What we can't count on is that they'll be bringing help."

"What are going to do if they don't have the military with them?" asked another driver.

"Then we're going to head home emptyhanded and pray that we don't have too many flat tires from driving over the piles of scrap metal that used to be armored vehicles."

Grim's bravado drew a round of laughter from the gathered men, the seasoned warrior's self-confidence and experience making them all feel better.

Deep inside, however, Grim was full of doubt. He had a couple of belt-fed weapons, a few carbines in the hands of experienced men, and a bunch of shotguns wielded by out of shape civilians who may or may not be able to fight.

He and Kevin had counted just over 600 men in the surrounding hills, as well as 6 heavy machine gun emplacements and 2 APCs. Not all of those gun barrels were pointed at the Texans, however. It was clear that many of the garrison surrounding them were facing north, almost as if they expected an invasion.

The Mexican forces appeared to be reasonably well disciplined, but already Grim had found several weaknesses with their deployment, positioning, and leadership.

Their patrols were as predictable as the rest of their schedule. The hill to the north always enjoyed lunch first, followed by the men to their south. Both groups changed their sentries and the men staffing the cannons on top of the APCs at the exact same time every day.

While all of these observations were the sign of an inexperienced military unit, it was what they did with their best weapon system that gave Grim a badly-need boost of optimism. They did not move their armor from position to position, instead choosing to sandbag the two tracked machines into a fixed emplacement. "That is one of the stupidest things I've ever seen," Grim told Kevin as he watched a platoon of men filling hundreds of bags. "Those are tracked units. They are designed to move ... and move quickly while spitting death. Why on earth would anyone anchor them down? It doesn't make any sense. They should be keeping us guessing, wonder where their big guns are going to be next."

Kevin had to agree. While the Mexican forces had selected an excellent tactical location for the heavy units, he was going to give their crews hell with his sniper rifle if it came to a fight. He already had the range zeroed in.

Grim continued to tour Freightliner Square, cracking a joke here, thanking someone for their extra effort there, and once stopping to make a suggestion. As he watched his boss move from group to group, Kevin was amazed at the transition. Who knew the always-griping, stubborn old-timer had such leadership capabilities?

It was inspiring, Kevin decided. "And we're going to need every ounce of it if we are going to get out of here alive."

Castro was at his desk, using some foul smelling liquid while cleaning a weapon on the scarred wooden surface.

"A trophy," he announced after looking up to see April passing through the threshold. "This is a fine carbine with an unusual design and excellent optics. It belonged to the Alliance prisoner, but now it's mine," he boasted.

"I didn't think firearms were allowed near the Castle?" she asked innocently. "Is the threat from the Alliance so dire that the law has been changed?"

"Only for a select few," he responded. "Even the emperor had his well-armed, private guard. Our leader is showing good judgement by allowing a few loyal servants access to superior firepower."

April started to question him further but then reconsidered. According to what she had been told, Bella Dona had long ago outlawed any armed security forces within five kilometers of the Castle. "It is like Rome," the matriarch was quoted as saying. "No Roman general would ever bring his forces into the capital city. It was a sign of disrespect, or worse, treason. We shall model our operation here at the plantation just like the longest lasting empire the world has ever seen. It worked for nearly 1500 hundred years for them. Why would we change a thing?"

Now, here in Castro's office, Rome had evidently fallen to the barbarians.

"Let me see inside your basket," Castro ordered. "You know the drill. I must perform a detailed search before anyone is allowed access to the prisoner."

Detailed search, my foot, April thought. *You just want to feel my boobs and ass.*

Castro began by opening the small basket hooked on April's arm. After finding nothing but food inside, he then reached to search her person.

The young woman suffered through the indignity as his hands explored and groped her body. Long ago, she had realized that Castro's acts had nothing to do with sexual gratification. No, like so many sexual sadists, he merely used violation as a weapon to leverage his power over her. If he wanted, he could have commanded her to undress and submit on the spot, but he didn't. There was, however, no lust or need for a physical release within the man, only a sickening hunger for dominance and submission.

Today, Castro finished quickly, waving her through the door leading to the cells after only a brief pat down. Obviously, he wanted to return to his newest plaything, the black parts of the rifle still lying disassembled on his desk.

Another guard was inside, marching up and down the short hall lined with heavy cell doors. It was a dark, evil place, fouled by the stench of human body odor, aged urine, and pungent feces. April often thought she could feel pain emanating from the walls as if the rough planks had absorbed the agony of the prisoners.

The inner sentry recognized her and knew exactly which cell she intended to visit. Reaching for a key that would open the heavy padlock securing the door, he said, "For the past few days, I thought you were wasting all of that food on this prisoner. I guess it pays to have the inside scoop."

April didn't understand, her brow wrinkling in question.

"I hope she ends up a breeder," he grinned. "I'll have to visit her and see if Castro's claims about gringo lovers are true."

Ignoring the man's sneer and the fact that Castro had been bragging again, April asked, "What are you talking about? Isn't this woman going to be executed with the giant man?"

The guard shook his head, "Not any more. And the boss told me today that Lady Bella Dona no longer desires to sell her at auction tomorrow either. She is young and firm. She'll be a pleasure bitch or a breeder. Whatever her classification, I'm going to be the first in line."

Stunned, April just stood there, trying to comprehend what it all meant. If what the enforcer said was true, May wasn't going to hang. That, however, wasn't exactly good news.

Being assigned to the Pleasure House meant being a whore, a sexual plaything for any man on the plantation who was being rewarded. From what April had garnered, it was mostly Castro's security forces who were allowed to frequent the den of debauchery.

Officially dubbed the "Nursery" or "Vivero," the Breeder House was a recent addition to the rapidly expanding plantation infrastructure.

Originally, the Breeder House was supposed to be a facility for young women who were pregnant out of wedlock. With a workforce well over 100,000 strong, such occurrences were inevitable. From April's point of view, its creation had been one of the few uplifting developments and a sure sign that Lady Bella Dona did indeed care about her workers.

Within a few months, however, the schoolteacher's perspective changed.

In reality, the Nursery was nothing more than a higher quality bordello, a step up from the common man's Pleasure House. Women of childbearing age and exceptional beauty were assigned there. Their "contribution" to the community was to satisfy the plantation's upper management while supplying a future labor force. The concept disgusted April, reminding her of the NAZI Lebensborn program during WWII.

While the guard fumbled for the right key, April considered her sister's new fate. May was from a different world, and because of that, she wouldn't last long at either facility.

Before the collapse, in an environment that fostered such progressive concepts as social justice, wealth redistribution, and equal rights, facilities like the Nursery and the Pleasure House would have generated outrage and protest.

How many nights had the two siblings debated into the wee hours, the younger sister staunch and unmoving in her conservative beliefs? May believed everyone should carry a gun, hated government social agendas, and thought those who utilized safety-net programs were nothing but a bunch of lazy freeloaders who wanted to live off the hard labor and achievement of others.

April supported strict controls on firearms, a free college education for all, government-provided healthcare, and tolerance.

The guard managed the door just then, a small corridor of light flooding the otherwise dark confines. Her sister was exactly where April expected her to be, lying on the soiled mattress with eyes closed.

"Hello, April," the younger girl whispered.

"Hi, May. How are you feeling?"

May ignored the question, unmoving on the filthy bed.

"I brought you food," April offered, holding out the basket as the sentry closed and locked the door. "Why don't you sit up and eat a little? It will make you feel better."

"They're not going to hang me, April," May's monotone, robotic voice responded from the darkness.

"I know. I just heard. My prayers have been answered, sis. And I was praying hard."

May moved then, managing to lift herself and lean on one arm. Her eyes were hollow and empty, "Why, April? Why did you ask God to torture me even further? I wanted to die tomorrow. Now I'm going to be stuck in a living hell, day after day of some sweaty, fat bastard violating me hour after hour. Why do you hate me so? Will you enjoy my suffering?"

April was shocked, her sister's words stabbing like a knife, "I don't understand, sis. You want to die? Why would I pray for you to be killed? Things will get better. Each day that you're alive is another chance that your life will improve!"

Rolling back to her prone position, May stared blankly at the ceiling. "Give me liberty or give me death. I would rather die than live in slavery like you."

April studied her sister, taking in the bruising, lacerations, and filth that covered May. For a moment, she attributed the younger woman's attitude to the treatment she had suffered after capture. No doubt, Castro and his goons had roughed her up pretty badly.

Yet, May wasn't one for theatrics. There had been no malice or emotion in her voice, the words coming from her sister's throat almost mechanical.

"I'm so sorry, May. You have to believe me, I didn't ask anyone but God to intercede or show you mercy. I had no part in this last minute change of plans," April pleaded.

"I believe you," the weak sister answered from the dark. "I don't hate you. I'm sorry that I said those mean things."

"Why don't you eat something? You'll feel better with something in your stomach; I promise."

"No. I want to die. I'm not going to eat. I want the end to come as soon as possible."

It was then that April noticed the bowl of jailhouse gruel lying near the door. It was untouched. "Really, sis, you're going on a hunger strike? If anyone knows how horrible that is, it should be us. After what we went through...."

"No, I wanted them to hang me ... I prayed for my suffering to end. It doesn't matter, though, the end will come – maybe slower, but one way or the other, I will escape. I bet not even these Mexican bastards enjoy fucking skin and bones."

"May," her sister began to protest, but the already-dead voice from the mattress interrupted. "Don't bother bringing any more food, sis. Don't bother coming back. I love you, and I don't want you to see me like this. Always remember, mom and I both love you more than anyone. Now go ... please."

Again, April started to speak, but the prisoner stopped her. "Go! Please! Now!"

Sitting in silence, the bastion of April's soul was slammed by waves of guilt and remorse. She knew her sister better than anyone, was certain she wasn't playing any sort of head game or putting on an act. Her sister preferred death over life, and that was the saddest thing she had ever felt.

It is all my fault, April thought. *This is my doing. I should have left with her the other night. I should have gotten word back to my family so they wouldn't worry about me. I shouldn't have been so selfish.*

Like a mallet striking the head of the nail, the blows hammered her, driving April's mind into the depths of anguish. She wanted to grab May and shake some sense into her, slap her across the face until sanity returned.

183

Harsh words formed in April's throat, the older girl ready to scream and shout at the stubborn woman with her in the darkness.

But the torrent of awareness bombarding her mind stopped her.

A single, unavoidable truth compelled the older sister to re-examine everything about her existence. While April had chosen to come to the plantation ... had chosen this lifestyle ... May had not. April understood the rules, agreed to them at some level and bought into this social code. But the unfairness of her little sister's sentence, the reprehensible treatment of her by the guards ... these things could not be justified.

April found that as her mind opened, she found herself feeling again – not due to any realization of the gross injustice done to her, but a desire to protect May, a sensation she had denied for so long, an awareness finally strong enough to override the numbness that had enslaved her very soul. Yet, April knew May was right. The realization came slowly, only a dim flicker at first, eventually building into a blinding, white-hot illumination of truth. Her sister was brave and honest. April was a coward and had been lying to herself since arriving at the plantation.

Once acknowledged, those feelings welled up inside the school marm. Castro's abuse. The floggings and hangings. The horrible working conditions and quarters. No due process. No rights. No liberties. And the worst part ... the most egregious act of all – beating the plantation's plowshares into swords, converting their pruning hooks into spears. Could it be possible that Bella Dona was raising a mighty army to rule all of Mexico?

It took all of April's self-discipline not to storm out of the cell and go for Castro's throat. She wanted to help her sister and hurt her abuser in the process, to claw his eyes into bloody holes. She wanted to make him understand the pain he so easily inflicted on others.

With labored breathing and a new resolve, April turned to the door and rapped lightly. It opened a moment later, the same guard tilting his head at her quick exit and still full basket of food.

It was probably fortunate for April that Castro was no longer at his desk when she exited through the front office.

As she plodded back toward building #11, the world around her took on a completely new perspective. Taking special notice of the laborers she passed, she observed a population devoid of joy and laughter, evidence of a crushed, submissive society that no longer seemed alive. Her senses now on high alert, she realized an unusual stench that hung in the air, the sickening odor lodging in the back of her throat. It was the reek of death, the gradual wasting away of human souls.

Her quarters were just as shocking. *How had she lived like this?* April thought, throwing the basket of food on her cot. *May had been right – she had been suffering from Stockholm syndrome. She was truly a slave.*

Tears of helplessness rolled down April's cheeks as she laid on her cot. Eventually sleep came, but not before the hours of torment and regret had changed her forever.

Chapter 12

Grim lowered the binoculars and turned to Kevin, "I told you they would come back."

"I never had any doubt," the younger man replied.

After multiple searches, Bishop's truck was allowed inside the truckers' compound. Grim didn't waste any time, "What's the plan, boss?"

For the next hour, Bishop outlined the trials and tribulations that occurred during the eight days he and Terri had been absent.

"That's it? That's all you guys could come up with?" Grim responded, clearly disappointed.

Bishop shrugged, "Every other option played out to a dead end. We've got no choice unless you've cooked up something since we've been gone."

Grim took his turn, explaining to Bishop what had been accomplished and learned since the Texan had headed north.

Bishop nodded, patting his buddy on the shoulder. "Excellent work, my friend. Better than I expected. I'm glad at least one of us made some progress."

For another 30 minutes, Terri and the SAINT team huddled, reviewing their options. When every possibility had been hashed and exhausted, Bishop stood and said, "It's time. Let's see if we can get as many of these guys home as possible."

"That same pickup is on the way into camp," called the lookout. "One driver, the same guy with the ponytail."

"That would be Castro," Bishop informed his wife. "Right on time."

The couple chose to ride in the back, and after Castro had frisked Bishop and scanned Terri, they were again on their way to Bella Dona's lair.

The planation's matriarch met them on the porch as before, this time dressed completely in black. Terri wondered if it was an omen.

After being escorted into the sitting room, the lady of the house got right down to business. "Our people in Del Rio tell us that the Quakers have been detained but are still alive. The deadline is midnight. Why are you here?"

"We are not going to execute the Quakers, Bella Dona," Terri replied. "You weren't honest with us, and now we know the other side of the story."

"And what would that be? What lies have those terrorists been spouting now?" the estate's queen hissed.

"You led us to believe that all of your workforce came to you begging for food. We now know that isn't true. In fact, there are dozens and dozens of Alliance citizens that were abducted from their homes and businesses, and we believe they are here."

"That is preposterous!" Bella Dona snapped. "We have never forced anyone to come to the plantation. Lies! Nothing but lies from the mouths of those who want nothing more than to see us fail."

Bishop swiveled in his chair and faced Castro. "Do you deny that your men have been raiding along the Rio Grande and rounding up people to work here?"

The henchman just stared at Bishop. "It is none of your business, Gringo. I don't answer to you."

Slowly and deliberately, Bishop reached into his jacket, removing a thin stack of papers and offering them to Bella Dona. "This is photographic evidence we have that proves otherwise."

Snatching the pictures from the Texan's hand, Bella Dona peered at the first image with a scowl. It showed Castro in his pickup, along with three armed men. In the bed of the truck was a large cage. Between the bars was clearly visible the bloodied face of a very frightened, young man. "His name isn't important," Bishop began. "That picture was taken two miles north of Del Rio just seven months ago. A group of hunters had found a supply of batteries and were using them to power a game camera. The boy in the bed of the pickup was out checking the machines when he disappeared. The family initially blamed raiders or vagabonds until they found this image was captured."

"This proves nothing!" Bella countered. "For all I know, Castro was helping that young man find his way home. I should've known you would side with the terrorists. Besides, we have no need to kidnap anyone. We have thousands and thousands of desperados arriving on our doorstep each month."

"The next photo," Terri continued, "was taken from an Alliance surveillance drone."

Clearly angry now, Bella Dona flipped to the second image and found herself staring at a cluster of people working in a field. All of them were staring skyward, as if they had just seen a UFO or other strange aircraft.

"The third man from the right was identified by his wife. He has been missing and presumed dead for several months. She stated that kidnappers broke into the home and pulled her husband out at gunpoint. That picture was taken here, less than 1 kilometer from where we sit," Bishop said coldly. "You can keep flipping through the photos if you want, but the story remains the same. You have been abducting Alliance citizens, dragging them from their homes in the middle of the night."

Bella Dona tossed the papers back at Bishop, "This proves nothing. I would never endorse such criminal acts. These are nothing more than wild, unfounded accusations. That man could have been unhappy with his wife and left home intentionally for all I know."

Terri shook her head, "Either you're deceiving yourself, or someone is doing it for you. The Quakers merely want their loved ones back and want the abductions to stop. The Alliance government is in agreement with their cause. We can end this peacefully."

"They murdered your own truck drivers!" Bella growled with fury. "You would harbor homicidal maniacs? Grant protection to confessed killers? Castro was right. I should have eliminated you all when I had the chance the first time."

"Can you hear yourself? Don't you see how your words sound like just like a murdering megalomaniac?" Bishop snorted.

Coming in to support the cause, Castro finally spoke. "We do have Alliance citizens here," he chuckled. "They were exiled by your own law enforcement, kicked out of their homes for minor offenses or unproven accusations. We have rescued dozens of them, dying of thirst or hunger in the desert. Yet, you accuse us of being barbarians. You gringos haven't learned anything from the downfall. You're still a bunch of racist bastards, convinced that you hold the moral high ground. It is sickening."

Ignoring Castro's words, Terri was clearly done with the debate. "Release Butter and May ... and any Alliance citizen that wishes to go home. In exchange, we will guarantee that the Quakers will no longer cross the Rio Grande and that the Alliance will not invade Mexico."

Bella Dona grew ice cold in less than a second, her voice like a winter wind, "This conversation is over. Your people will be executed immediately. Castro will order his men to seize the trucks and all the personnel accompanying them. Both of you are under arrest."

Terri laughed, "If you do that, Bella Dona, the Alliance will invade your lands with armor, helicopter gunships, and thousands of crack troops. Jet fighter-bombers will fill the skies over your beloved plantation, and this house will be nothing more than a smoldering pile of rubble. Your security forces will be crushed in less than 48 hours and thousands of people will die."

"I don't think so," the lady smugly replied. "I don't think the people in Alpha will do that if we have both of you and dozens of truckers here as our guests. I also don't believe the President of the United States will be too happy if his food supply is suddenly destroyed by the Alliance's military. No, that was a worthy bluff, but it is not going to work."

Bishop looked at his wife, a glass of water halfway to his lips. Terri shrugged and then fixed her gaze on Bella. "I was afraid you would say that."

With a swift, smooth motion, Terri reached into her boot and withdrew a small automatic pistol. When Castro spied the weapon, he immediately reached for his waistband.

Bishop reared back and threw the heavy crystal tumbler. Just as Castro's hand was bringing his pistol up, the whizzing, glass missile smashed against his head with enough force that the bodyguard stumbled backward while grunting with pain.

The plantation strongman shook his head to recover but not fast enough.

In a flash, Bishop was on him, three rabbit punches landing in a drum-like cadence. Reeling backward, trying to get away from the stinging blows, Castro stumbled and dropped his weapon.

The near-fall gave the security chief some much-needed space between himself and the charging Texan, Castro putting it to good use. Recovering from the speed and surprise of Bishop's assault, Castro now set himself, ready to meet the attack on more even terms. Rolling his weight to a back foot, the Mexican's left leg sailed through the air in a perfect roundhouse kick, the arch of his boot on a perfect trajectory for Bishop's chin.

The Texan, however, wasn't there, and Castro's powerful strike found nothing but empty air.

Bishop was already moving again, sidestepping the incoming kick and moving closer to Castro as the enforcer tried to regain his balance.

A brutal punch landed against Castro's ear, and then the heel of the Texan's boot struck the larger man in the side of his knee with bone shattering force. Howling in agony, Bella Dona's bodyguard dropped down, withering in pain as he collapsed to the floor.

Like a wolf smelling blood, Bishop bounded in for the kill. Stepping on Castro's wrist, the Texan raised his other foot, clearly taking aim at the downed man's throat and preparing to unleash a vicious coup de grace.

"You're not very good," Bishop stated with emotionless eyes. "But then again, your kind never are."

"Stop! Please!" Bella Dona whimpered, ignoring Terri's pistol pushing against her head.

"How tender," Bishop grunted, never taking his eyes off the prone man under his boot. "Honor among the evil. How many of your slaves begged for mercy? How many souls pleaded for their lives right before this piece of shit killed them?"

Not waiting for an answer, Bishop reached down and grabbed a handful of Castro's ponytail, dragging the groaning man across the floor. The enforcer's pistol was in Bishop's hand a moment later.

No sooner had the guard backed out of the door than Castro found his voice, "You'll never get off this plantation. You are already dead. Even if you kill us, my men will tear you apart."

"Perhaps," Terri shrugged. "If that's true, then we have nothing to lose – right?"

Bella Dona said, "Stop this, please. If you let Castro and me go, I will free the prisoners and allow all of you safe passage from the plantation."

"It's too late for that," Terri replied. "You had your chance. I can't trust you, and I'm the one holding the gun."

"So what happens now?" Bella Dona asked.

"We wait," Bishop replied, pulling up a chair where he could keep an eye on Castro. "I hope you didn't have big plans for this evening because we're not going anywhere."

"It's time," Grim stated, peering at his watch.

"Now or never," Kevin nodded, turning to hustle away for his assigned position.

"Good luck, men," Grim said to the gathered truckers.

The sleepy encampment suddenly came alive, hustling shadows moving in every direction at the edge of the campfires.

For the past week, Grim had ordered the truckers to start their engines every night at dusk, pretending to charge the rig's batteries and keep the engines lubricated. To the plantation's militia in the surrounding hills, the cranking motors were nothing new.

Kevin found his sniper rifle right where he left it 30 minutes ago. Slinging the long-range weapon, he began climbing to the top of a trailer.

Reaching the roof, he crawled to the low ring of sandbags that had been his station during the drive south from Texas. It was a well-constructed nest, with good cover and excellent bracing. His motions were smooth and confident, practiced every night since Grim had hatched their escape plan.

As he chambered a round into the rifle's breech, the audible whoosh of a huge fireball rolled across the camp. Men were scurrying along the perimeter with torches, setting gasoline-soaked brush and gathered firewood ablaze. Grim had called them blocking fires and smoke screens.

A wall of flames rose between the Diesel Rivera and the surrounding forces. In moments, the blaze began to die down, but that was by design. A thick, grey smoke began to rise, blocking the plantation men's view of the encampment on the north side.

With even, measured motions, Kevin adjusted his aim, bringing the armored unit to the south into the crosshairs of his optic. The high outcropping was an anthill of activity now, the images of men darting here and there indicating that the alarm had been sounded.

Kevin watched a man climbing on top of the tracked gun, heading for the cannon that protruded like an insect's stinger from the turret. For a passing moment, he was tempted to knock the man off the machine before he could reach the deadly weapon, but that wasn't his job tonight.

Instead, he lowered his aim slowly, moving down the steep, rock face under the APC's tracks. He bypassed a machine gun emplacement, several sandbagged fighting holes, and dozens of scrambling men.

Finally, the crosshairs happened upon a single, tiny, glowing strip of tape. The fluorescent green hue was less than an inch square, yet its ghostly presence was like a neon sign in the powerful optic.

Kevin had done the math over a dozen times. He knew the exact distance to the target, had measured and verified the angle. There was no wind. The humidity wasn't a factor.

He centered the crosshairs on the tape and moved his finger to the trigger. A roll of socks was taped to the rifle's buttstock, the padding designed to keep as much of the twitching, throbbing, shaking, inhaling human body away from the weapon as possible.

Only Kevin's cheek and trigger finger touched the long-range tool. He began to control his breathing and relax every muscle in his body. He was a puddle of goo, a boneless, muscleless bag of liquid with one moveable part – his finger.

He squeezed gently on the trigger, gradually building the pressure. The shot was just over 800 yards. Not an incredible distance for a man of his skill and training, but the target was very small.

The rifle roared, the powerful bullet splitting the air at supersonic speeds.

The distance and elevation required a lobed, arching trajectory, gravity and air friction bleeding the energy from bullet the moment it exited the muzzle.

Almost a full second later, Kevin knew his aim had been true.

Grim had mixed the fuse, a concoction of chemicals, gasoline, and rags. It had taken the old warrior three nights of sneaking through the enemy's lines to carry and plant the explosives.

Kevin watched the telltale spark and flash as the fuse burned. Soon the strobing illumination increased in intensity as multiple lines of burning cloth branched and forked their way to the bombs.

"Pipe bombs aren't very potent against armor," Grim had informed the younger man. "Smokeless powder, like we removed from the ammo, doesn't accelerate enough to generate much of a kill radius. Against armor, it is practically worthless."

Grim, however, had a better use. "Ever heard of a Bangalore torpedo?"

Kevin had indeed heard of the weapon. "Isn't it a tube of explosives used by engineers to clear mine fields and other obstacles?"

"Yup, sure is. We're going to make our own Bangalore torpedoes, son. And we're going to remove one big-ass obstacle."

The 25mm cannon on top of the APC opened fire just then, distracting Kevin from the sizzling fuses. Quickly adjusting his weapon, the SAINT shooter found the outline of the tracked war machine and soon had his crosshairs centered on the man-shape at the top of the turret.

Squeezing the trigger as before, Kevin was about to send the shot when his optic was bleached white by the explosion.

Over 100 pounds of tightly packed gunpowder exploded at that instant, compressed into nooks and cracks within the rock face. A curtain of earth, stone, and dust erupted from the beneath the heavy armored vehicle, blasted into the air by Grim's Bangalore pipes.

The explosion was a sign for the truckers to roll. At the same moment, the convoy's two belt-fed weapons began peppering the surrounding militia with automatic fire, a shroud of deadly lead showering the now confused troops in the hills.

Kevin's job was to engage the armored vehicle to the south, just in case Grim's improvised explosive device failed to do the job. The SAINT sharpshooter felt the trailer beneath him begin to roll, relieved that the convoy was moving.

When the dust finally began to settle, Kevin had to smile. The tracked APC was still on the hilltop but was no longer a threat. Half of the outcropping that had been supporting the heavy armored unit had been blown to bits. The earth could no longer support its weight. The armored vehicle was lying helpless on its side, a great wounded beast in its final throes of death.

Gunfire raked the convoy, the plantation's forces now recovering from the shock and awe of Grim's pyrotechnics. The pickups surged forward, raking the dismounted troops with deadly fire. Kevin and the other trailer top shooters joined their comrades as the trucks began to pick up speed.

The incoming fire grew intense, bullets sparking off the metal trailer and whacking into the sandbag wall that surrounded Kevin. One of the lead semis was on fire now, another swerving side to side and finally slamming into the ditch and erupting in a ball of flame. Grim had warned that causalities were inevitable.

Neon lines of red and green fire filled the air, tracers coming in and going out. There were shouted orders, the screams of the wounded, and explosions all around.

Kevin was working his weapon as fast as he could find targets, firing at muzzle flashes, shadows, and anything that moved along their path.

The lead trucks had been modified, up-armored with sand bags, shielding the doors of their trailers and even spare tires and wheels. They needed every inch of plating, every extra pound of protection.

Then, much to the surprise of the militia commanders, the lead truck made an unexpected move.

Rather than turning north and making a run for Texas, the column of rolling iron ventured south toward the plantation.

So shocked were the local troops, they temporarily stopped shooting and began staring at their officers with puzzled, confused eyes.

The pace and rhythm of battle changed in that moment. Despite being outnumbered and outgunned, the convoy shooters managed to get over the top, pouring more rounds into the enemy than were being received.

Under Castro's strict orders, the ring around the gringo trucks had been far stronger along the northern side. That's where the trucks would attempt to run. That was the direction where help from Texas would arrive. That was where Castro concentrated his assets.

The first truck slammed into the two pickups forming the roadblock at 40 miles per hour, shredding the lighter vehicles into scrap and throwing the defenders over a hundred feet through the air. The convoy poured semi after semi through the newly created opening, guns blazing in every direction.

Kevin knew they had punched through when the blizzard of lead suddenly stopped. Now, nothing but fresh, cool night air was flying past his head.

"I sure the hell hope you know what you're doing, Grim," the kid whispered to the moon.

Still, he had to admit – it was good to be going on the offensive. He just hoped the militia they had left behind wouldn't catch up too quickly.

April awoke with a start, her groggy head trying to determine if the noise had been a dream or reality. Before she could even rub the sleep from her eyes, another muffled explosion rolled across the fields like a distant thunderstorm approaching from the north.

In fact, April would have thought the noise was nothing more than the weather if it weren't for the nearly continuous crackling and popping sounds. Any survivor of the apocalypse recognized gunfire. A memory burned into the brain's core, it was a sound no one ever forgot.

Her deepest fears were confirmed when she rushed to her door and peered into the barracks. There she observed dozens of frightened faces staring toward the north. There were hushed whispers laced with fear, a few of the braver souls actually standing and staring toward the source of the noise.

April's first thought was of the huge man being held prisoner with May. Were the Texans coming to rescue their friend? It was clear from the noise outside that a battle was being fought. Would the fighting come to the Castle?

Without any sort of plan or forethought, April threw on her clothes and sandals. Some unexplainable force was drawing her toward May. She had to help her sister.

From building #11 to the detention center was only a distance of a few city blocks, yet April stayed in the shadows and advanced carefully. Being outside after hours was against the rules. If she were discovered, the punishment would be severe. Only the security forces were allowed outside of the barracks.

The occasional torches that served as streetlights only illuminated small pools of earth here and there. April was careful, lingering in the darkness, peeking carefully around corners before crossing any open spaces.

Pounding footsteps gave her a fright, but the two security men running past didn't even glance her way. In the distance, she could hear shouting but couldn't make out the words. A cloud of stress hung over the plantation.

By the time she was enroute to Castro's office, the distant gunfire had ceased. However, she quickened her steps when she noticed the foreboding glow from a large inferno on the north horizon. Suddenly, chaos ruled the night ... more shouting, followed by another group of hurrying men, the distant rumble of an engine, and then eerie silence.

For the first time since she'd been in Mexico, April found Castro's office vacant. Even if the headman weren't on duty, there was always someone sitting at the heavy, oak desk. The chair was empty and cold.

Mustering every ounce of courage she had, April ventured further inside toward the metal door that led to the cells at the rear of the building. Again, she was stunned. No one was guarding the hall. "What on earth is going on?" she whispered. "Has the whole world gone insane?"

A radical thought then occurred to April, a concept so foreign to her thinking that she worried for a moment about her own rationality. Even if she could open May's cell, there was no place to take her sister – no place to hide a fugitive.

Yet, this was an opportunity. She had never seen this building unguarded. She had never felt such a sense of panic surging through the plantation. She had to act.

In desperation, she struggled to recall minute details of the last time she'd last seen Castro. He had been seated at his desk, cleaning the big Texan's rifle. There were no clues in that previous conversation. No threats, hints, or predictions.

April stared at the desk hard, noting the bottle of cleaning fluid still sitting exactly where it had been before.

Her mind traveled back in time, to an evening not long after her arrival at the plantation. Castro had brought her to this facility, partially to impress her, partially to assert his authority, but mostly to frighten the new woman that held his interest.

He had given her a tour of the cells, shown her the interrogation room complete with its horrible array of saws, pliers, sharp instruments, and a wooden floor stained purple from the blood that had been spilled. She remembered how the walls stank of pain, suffering, and fear. She briefly wondered why such a place was necessary. "Follow our law, be accommodating to me, and you will never have to visit this room," he had warned.

When they returned to the front office, he had grabbed her roughly, bent her over his desk, and begun to satisfy his needs. So vigorous was his pounding into her flesh, the desk had begun to scoot and scrape across the floor.

When he had fallen off her, exhausted and panting, April had noticed a floorboard had been jarred loose. There was a compartment hidden there. She could see the handle of a pistol, some papers, and a ring of keys.

She had forgotten about Castro's secret vault until now. Not knowing what else to do, she ducked behind his desk and began searching for the stash.

A minute later, she discovered the opening, easily lifting the two slats of wooden flooring away to reveal a sizeable partition. Inside she found the Texan's rifle, along with several magazines of ammunition and a variety of personal effects. A set of keys was resting under the heavy weapon.

She had seen the huge man from Texas in combat, had watched horrified as he had thrown Castro's enforcers around like they were children fighting a wild bear. He had been trying to take her some place. He and her sister had a plan of escape. Did the big soldier know how to get out? Would he still be willing to help?

She grabbed the keys and the weapon, struggling to lift the heavy rifle and ammunition. A moment later, she was at his door, fumbling for the right key to undo the lock.

Butter had heard the distant battle as well, rising from his bunk as the muffled sounds of gunfire and explosions had drifted through his cell wall. "Is Mr. Bishop really coming for me? Is he going to give me a second chance?"

The thought gave the big kid a renewed optimism, the need to survive now rushing through his core. "Everyone makes mistakes," he announced to the empty room. "Miss Terri knows I'm a good person."

The hope of rescue fueled Butter's mind with positivity. He wanted to set things right and enjoy his life again. He wanted to live.

The rattle of the keys outside his cell sent him back to his bunk. He would play possum, draw the guards in, disable them, and make his escape.

Instead of the beefy security types barging in, Butter noticed a smaller, frail shape outlined by the lantern light in the hall. A timid, female voice whispered, "Hello? Are you in here?"

What kind of trick or torture is this? Butter thought, lying absolutely still as if he was asleep. Through slotted eyes, he observed April peek inside, holding a lantern in one hand, something dark in the other.

"Are you okay?" she asked, once the light had found his face. "Can you walk? I have your gun."

Butter looked to see his carbine in her hand and immediately rolled off his mattress. It took him less than a minute to check the weapon, his mind still screaming at the impossibility of it all and wondering if his captors were playing some sort of cruel joke.

His weapon was perfect, as were the full magazines April carried in a bag. Never before had he held anything that felt as wonderful as that rifle. "Where are the guards?" he asked.

"I don't know. I heard the gunfire from the hills and came here to make sure May was okay. There isn't anyone around," she stammered.

"Where is May?"

April pointed at the cell across the hall and held up the ring of keys. "I knew where Castro kept these and your gun. Can you get us out of here?"

"I don't know, but I can try," Butter responded. "Let's get your sister out of here."

It took May twice as long to believe her eyes and her sister's words. The fact that Butter was hovering in the doorway holding his carbine finally persuaded the weakened girl.

"There's another gun," April thought to say as the trio entered the front office. Butter hastily rummaged through Castro's stash, looking for anything of value. Luck was with him, and he recovered an old .38 police special and his .45 automatic. He handed the revolver to May while he stored his blaster into his waistband.

A few moments later, they were out the door and rushing for the shadows.

Butter had never breathed sweeter air.

197

Never one to fully trust subordinates, Castro had never fostered a strong middle management team. Those few individuals who did have some level of competence had been assigned to guard the convoy. Once the Alliance mounted its attack, the plantation's security forces accelerated from mere alarm to pure hysteria. Castro's men had been scrambling to find their leader among the sounds of the firefight, the few static-filled radio transmissions that had been broadcast from the militia, and the pulsing glow of flames on the horizon.

The headman himself wasn't in a much better frame of mind.

Castro had been on edge when the ruckus of the battle first reached the sitting room. Bishop had watched his captive's eyes as they nervously darted back and forth, the Texan ready for any attempt at escape.

The enforcer's situation had grown even more desperate when the firefight had suddenly stalled. Bishop spotted his captive's hands shaking, a thick layer of perspiration now forming on Castro's skin. "The cavalry is coming," Bishop whispered to torture the man. "The Alliance isn't very happy with you and the lady of the house. You should have taken the deal."

"Fuck you," snarled the prisoner. "We are ready. I will enjoy pissing on your graves."

Before Bishop could respond, one of the room's hidden doors squeaked open, the face of a timid guard poking through the opening as if he was hesitant to interrupt.

The man's eyes opened wide when he realized Terri and Bishop were holding the guns. Before he could withdraw, Bishop's pistol roared, the sentry dead before he hit the floor.

"Our little secret is out," the Texan remarked to his wife. "If Grim doesn't arrive shortly, things are going to get a little dicey."

Terri shrugged, never taking her eyes off Bella Dona. "Grim will be here. But if not, then *she* gets the first bullet."

The fact that there was only one route in and out of the plantation was a two-edged sword. While Grim didn't need to worry about anyone outmaneuvering him using a side road, the facility's security forces knew exactly where he was going.

Bishop had reported a series of irrigation canals crisscrossing the fields. "There are pedestrian crossings all over the place, but only one series of bridges that will support trucks. That's where they're going to try and stop you. That's where the choke point is. Be careful," he advised.

Now, rolling toward the plantation with his column of shot-up trucks, Grim was growing more concerned with each passing minute. It was taking them too long, their progress slowed by the uneven surface, narrow passes, and washed out pavement.

Riding in the lead pickup, the convoy commander finally reached for the microphone and keyed the talk button. "Prepare to stop ahead. We're approaching a flat area. I want to unload the bikes."

"We're going too slowly … giving the other side time to set up an ambush or barricade the bridges. We need to send out scouts," Grim whispered.

It was a difficult call.

On one hand, the grizzled old veteran wanted to hit hard and fast. Every minute he delayed reaching the objective gave the defenders more time to prepare. Bishop, Terri, and Butter were there, most likely under siege and waiting desperately to be rescued.

Yet, rushing head first into a kill zone would be the end of them all.

Even worse than being ambushed was the possibility of being sandwiched between two enemy forces. Grim had no doubt the militia they had just left behind was trying desperately to regroup. How long would it take before they and their armored vehicle were giving chase?

If he had to, Grim would turn and fight. Their chances were better facing one foe, either ahead or behind, than trying to fight in two directions at once.

Ultimately, Grim's decision was based on the experience of his men. These were truck drivers and officers of the law, not infantry or assault troops. While he didn't question their bravery or grit, there was only so much they could do.

Three minutes later, the long stripe of trucks was idling as the two motorcycles were rolled off one of the empty trailers. Turning to Sheriff Watts' most trusted officer he instructed, "Scout the bridge ahead first. If it is defended, then come back to report to me while your buddy finds us some way to flank the bridge. Is that clear, Cord?"

The two riders, both deputies, nodded their understanding and then roared off.

"We're going to stay right here for a few minutes," Grim informed the rest of the convoy over the radio. "I'm not going to roll into another ambush or get pinned down while those guys we left back there hit us from the rear."

Butter and his two female cohorts were huddled in the corner of an unused barn. May was weak, from both physical abuse and her self-imposed hunger strike. Finally, after managing to put some distance between themselves and the detention center, Butter had called for a 10-minute rest.

While the girls regrouped, Butter kept a watchful eye on their surroundings. They were far from being out of trouble, the area still thick with numerous large structures and dozens of security men.

As he rose to get the girls moving again, the sound of cloth scraping against the barn's wall made the big man freeze. Someone was out there. Someone was moving.

Butter's training took over, the big man moving his carbine to his back as he lifted a nearby length of pipe. Dropping into a combat stance, he prepared to dispatch whoever was approaching. It would have to be done silently. A gunshot would bring every guard within a kilometer running.

The moonlight glowed in the space between the old barn's wall-planks, Butter's aroused senses detecting the night shadow of someone gradually making their way toward the opening.

Without a sound, the big man raised the pipe like a baseball slugger readying to swing for the fences.

A shape appeared in the entrance, and Butter sprang. As the pipe started to descend, something in Butter's brain stopped the assault at the last possible moment. The person standing in the doorway wasn't a man or a woman. It was a child.

The two of them stood staring at each other in the moonlight for several seconds, the child absolutely terrified by the image of a giant holding a club over his head.

Butter, realizing he had almost killed a small boy, was trying desperately to gather his wits.

"You … you … are you the gringo from Tejas?" the kid finally managed to stutter in Spanish.

Not understanding the language, Butter didn't know exactly how to respond. As he slowly lowered the pipe, April appeared at his side. Staring at the child, she said, "Julio? Julio, what are you doing here?"

A flicker of recognition brightened the boy's face as he rushed toward April's waist. After a reassuring hug from his teacher, the lad peered up at her and said, "Everyone in our barracks has heard the fighting and shouting. My father and the

200

other men are arguing over what to do. My mom is so scared, I decided to sneak out and see for myself. I come out at night all the time. It's the only chance I ever have to be alone and think about writing."

With a reassuring pat on the head, April explained, "I think the Texans are coming to rescue their friend. If everyone stays in the barracks, they should be safe."

Julio glanced between April and Butter, a question forming behind the young boy's eyes. "Will you take me with you, sir? Will you take my family back to Tejas?"

Butter was checking the direction of his moral compass ... trying to decide the best way to respond when the sound of a diesel motor reached the barn. Pushing everyone back into the shadows, Butter raised his weapon and again was preparing to fight.

A few moments later, it became clear to the big man that his carbine wasn't going to be much good. The path was filled when first one, then several more armored vehicles roared by. All in all, Butter counted a dozen of the war machines.

"Where in the hell did those come from?" he asked April.

"They've been working on them in the big maintenance barn for months," Julio responded in English. "My dad said they found them at a deserted military base. The trucks from the United States brought enough parts to repair them."

While he hadn't been privy to the Alliance's plan, Butter had a pretty good idea of what was happening in the hills above the plantation. A battle had been waged, and it didn't matter if it were tanks from Fort Hood or some other Alliance force trying to take control of the valley – those armored personnel carriers that had just rolled past the barn were going to be a problem.

Butter also understood that the column was heading for the bridges. It didn't take a tactical genius to figure out that those war machines were going to cause a lot of Alliance troops to go home in a body bags.

Julio saw his own opportunity, jockeying for an opportunity to leave the plantation. "Señor, please take my family out with you. My father and the other men in our barracks will fight with you. I swear it. So will the men in the building next to ours. We can help you. Please, sir, take us with you."

It was almost too much for Butter to comprehend. May was barely able to walk, and he still didn't trust April. He didn't know what was going on with the Alliance or the convoy. All of this was compounded by the fact that he wasn't even near 100%, his body and mind still suffering from the beatings and poor quality nutrition. After all, the plantation's finest cuisine had not been reserved for the man who was expected to swing by a rope anyway.

"I don't think your father and his friends can do much against tanks," April said, trying to intervene after sensing the big man's uncertainty. "I think all of the workers would be safer if they stayed in their barracks and waited until the Texans arrived."

"But I know where the armory is!" Julio spouted, upping the ante. "A lot of the workers were in the old Mexican Army. They have had training. They know what to do! If they had guns, they would fight! I know it!"

"Armory?" Butter asked, his attention perked.

"With your gun," the boy continued, pointing at Butter's carbine, "You could shoot the guards, and then the men from my barracks could fight. Please, Señor. I beg you. If we stay here, we will surely die. We must leave this place."

May's groaning interrupted the hushed conversation. "She's dehydrated and weak," April stated, rushing to comfort her sister.

"Don't get me wrong. I understand, but we have got to keep the noise down," Butter countered. "If somebody hears her, we're going to have the entire security force coming down on our heads."

"Take her back to my barracks," Julio suggested. "You can meet my father. You will see that he is a brave man. We can help."

After exchanging looks with April, Butter agreed, "I can't come up with a better plan. Let's go before someone figures out we've escaped."

With May hefted onto Butter's shoulder, Julio led them out of the barn and along a zigzagging route back to building #19.

Nearly identical to the layout of April's home barracks, the group entered to find a sea of frightened faces huddled in small groups.

"Julio, what have you done?" a male voice called from the masses.

"This is my teacher," the boy answered with an unwavering voice. "The giant gringo from the jail and her sister have escaped. It is their friends fighting Castro. They need our help."

A lantern appeared, held out by a middle-aged man who focused immediately on Butter's carbine and the pistol in his waistband. "What do you want?" he asked the big kid in passable English.

"I want to go home," Butter responded honestly. "Your son said that a lot of you wanted the same thing."

A murmur arose from the throng, half of the voices frightened by stranger's punishable words, but many expressing support. The father's words silenced them all, "We all want to leave this place, but Castro's men have weapons; we do not. They are young and strong; we are old and worn down."

"He can kill the guards at the armory," Julio spouted, "There are dozens of weapons housed inside. You could all have guns. This is our opportunity at life … at freedom."

The child's treacherous suggestion set off another round of whispered debate, many of the gathered residents inhaling sharply with fear. Even speaking of such things could bring down the enforcers and result in the skin being whipped off the offender's back.

For his part, Julio's father didn't speak, instead turning his lantern to study the faces of several other males in the room. Butter spotted many of the men nod their support. "It may be our only chance," whispered one of the older slaves.

"How many will come?" the father probed loud and clear. "Step forward if you will fight. Go back to your bedsheets if you are too frightened or feeble."

Initially, April was stunned at the number of men and women who came forward. A moment later, she understood. There was excitement, plenty of fear, and another emotion she hadn't seen in a long, long time. The lantern's dim glow exposed hope in the faces of the people around her, a beaming optimism that the teacher hadn't experienced since the apocalypse.

"Okay," Butter nodded. "Where is this armory?"

"This way," Julio declared with glee.

Chapter 13

The motorcycle's reflector gave Grim the first hint that the scout had returned. "Stopping here," he broadcast to the truckers behind him. "Maintain your spacing."

A few seconds later, Grim was out of the pickup and jogging to hear a report.

"Bad news, sir," Cord began. "The main bridge is a mile up the road, and I spotted at least one of those damn armored cars rolling toward the crossing. There's already a bunch of infantry all around the other side of the ditch."

"Shit!" the convoy commander erupted. "Any chance we can get across before their heavy weapons arrive?"

"Maybe … if we hurry … I don't know how long it will take them to get into position."

Thinking to rush back to the pickup's radio and order the convoy to make a mad dash for the bridge, Grim was halted by the arrival of the second scout. "That APC and about 100 men are coming up behind us fast. They're less than two miles back and hell bent for a piece of our ass."

"Damn it!" Grim exploded a second time in less than a minute. His worst nightmare was coming true. He and his charges were going to be stuck between a rock and a very hard place. "We have to get across," he snarled, turning to run for the truck and its radio. "No other option."

"Let's go!" he began shouting into the mic the moment he bounded into the cab. "All out. Full speed ahead! We have to get across that bridge before the bad guys get there. Move! Move! Move!"

Spacing no longer mattered, the pickups spitting dirt as their wheels spun in acceleration. "Use your headlights," he ordered into the radio. "They already know where we were. We need to make some time."

Illumination facilitated the convoy's speed, the long line of 18-wheelers now rolling down the uneven lane toward the valley below. Grim ordered the machine gun-equipped pickups to the front of the line, hoping they could slow the defenders who sought to block the bridge.

"We need room to maneuver," he whispered. "We need buildings to hide behind," he continued, the list of things necessary for their survival growing by the second. "We need God's help," he finally surmised.

While runners dashed to the neighboring barracks to spread the word, Julio and his father led dozens of men through a large field of avocados and over a hill. As Butter and his new friends negotiated the neat rows of crops, more and more people joined them, seemingly approaching from all directions.

After nearly two kilometers of hiking, they finally arrived at their destination. There, isolated on three sides by irrigation ditches, was a stout-looking concrete block building.

Butter studied the complex, noting the razor wire and high fence surrounding the facility. There was a heavy gate across the dirt path leading to the only entrance. The Texan could identify two tall guard towers, as well as a sandbagged nest on the roof. The place reminded him of a federal prison.

"How many men protect this place?" Butter asked, sizing up the defenses.

"As many as a dozen ... as few as six," someone answered.

"How deep is the water?"

A man stood and held his hand shoulder high, "Like this, Señor. In most places."

It was clear to Butter that the armory's security had been designed to repel an attack launched by a large mass of un-armed men. The two, elevated guard shacks were poorly placed, both on the front gate's side of the complex. The fortified post on the roof wasn't even manned, but probably would be at the first sign of trouble.

In less than a minute, Butter had made up his mind. Draw-ing the two pistols from his belt, he handed one to Julio Sr., the other to a capable looking comrade. "Do you both know how to use these?"

"Sí, Señor," they eagerly responded.

Using a small rise to hide their huddle, Butter drew a quick diagram in the dirt as another man held a small candle close to the ground. "I want the two men with pistols here and here," the kid instructed, stabbing the ground with his stick.

After scanning the faces of his troops and confirming un-derstanding nods all around, Butter continued, "The rest of you come with me. When Julio's father is set up here, he will shoot at this guard tower. The other pistol shoots at the second tower. You don't have to hit anything, just keep them occupied. I'll take care of the rest. Understood?"

Again, the Texan received a hardy round of nodding heads.

"Okay, let's go."

It took the revolting slaves just over five minutes to get into position. Butter took cover behind a low berm, less than 100 meters from the armory's perimeter. Behind him, ready to charge on his command, were at least 150 men.

A single pistol shot rang out, quickly followed by another, and then several more. Alarmed voices sounded from inside the armory as a sentry fired an AK.

Butter thanked the bright moon, flipped the safety off his carbine, and loosed a volley at the left tower, and then another group of rounds at the right. Before the last piece of ejected brass had landed in the soft soil, he was up and charging the gate.

A man was screaming in pain from the left target, so Butter concentrated his wrath on the right. He fired three shots, ran ten steps, and then cut right. Five more shots, then cut left. Rinse. Repeat.

A screaming body fell from the right tower, and now Butter was the object of the guards' attention.

Despite his size and lack of cover, Butter was a difficult target in the darkness. His aim was deadly, and the towers were simple plywood structures with thin walls. No one had ever thought to provide any sort of bullet stop. After all, the slaves didn't have guns.

When he was within 50 meters, Butter flipped his blaster to full auto and slammed home a fresh magazine. Taking a knee, he sprayed the right tower with a potent blast, and then directed his lethal discharge to the left.

Waving for his comrades to rise and follow, Butter screamed, "Hit them! Kill them! Charge!" Without further ado, he pivoted and charged the gate full out, praying that no one was left alive in the towers.

A hundred voices sounded from behind the Texan as the slaves rose, their throats filled with a pent-up bloodlust that had simmered for years.

Almost reaching the heavily fortified gateway, Butter observed the outline of two human shapes exiting through the armory's door. Puffs of dirt erupted as bullets thumped into the path at his feet. He rolled hard to the right, coming out of the desperate dive with his weapon pointing at the defenders and loosed another volley.

The wave of surging workers passed Butter, screaming battle cries at the top of their lungs as they rushed the entrance. They began to fall as the few remaining guards tried to stem the tide.

A wall of humanity hit the front gate and fence, as men pushed, climbed, and scrambled to get inside the perimeter. More of them fell bloody to the earth, but that didn't seem to matter.

Butter laid back, pumping lead into the reinforced nest of the roof, hoping to keep the defenders down and minimize the damage they could inflict.

The metal barrier collapsed inward from the weight of the crowd, the now frothing mob raising their voices of fury to a new pitch. They were motivated by the realization that their lives and the fate of their families, depended on a single event. They had to take the armory – any other outcome meant a horrible end to their existence.

It was all over in less than two minutes, the few remaining guards torn limb from limb as they were overrun by the shouting, vicious throng of slaves.

Butter strolled through the entrance, his body weakened by the exertion and a week of brutal captivity. Still, there was energy in his step as he watched dozens and dozens of rifles being hauled hand over hand and distributed to the growing number of rebellious workers.

Soon after, two wagons arrived, and the rebels began loading cases of ammunition and more weapons. A sea of torches appeared on the surrounding hillsides, hundreds more revolting slaves coming to get their weapons and their revenge.

Standing and watching as hundreds of guns were passed out, Butter wondered how many of the revolutionaries would survive the night. It didn't matter, he decided. They would die free men, struggling for a worthy cause. Compared to all of the SAINT missions he'd been assigned, Butter experienced a higher sense of fulfillment than he had ever realized. That warmth was only heightened when he felt a tug on his khakis and peered down to see Julio's smiling face beside him. "Thank you, sir," the boy earnestly beamed.

Smiling, Butter patted the child on the head and then glanced up to see a ring of anxious faces surrounding him. No one said a word as more and more armed men joined the circle. It took the Texan a moment to realize that they were all waiting on his orders.

"Where do we go?" Julio's father asked. "What now?"

Butter was about to respond when the sound of another battle rumbled through the fields. His head snapped to scan north, realizing that he'd forgotten all about the column of armor that had rolled by the barn. "Oh shit," he whispered. "I sure do hope the Alliance brought plenty of firepower."

The front, up-armored semi swerved, sparks and slivers of metal flying from the truck as the driver drew his last breath behind the wheel.

Across the dark line of water cutting through the moonlit field, Grim spotted hundreds of twinkling, white flashes erupt.

As his foot slammed on the brake pedal, the driverless truck ahead jackknifed, the trailer arching into the air as a blizzard of hot lead shredded the diesel fuel tanks and engine block. A huge fireball turned night into day as trailer tumbled and rolled across the field.

They were too late.

With his pickup still skimming across the roadside dirt, Grim pushed the microphone's button, "Circle the wagons!" he screamed. "Circle the wagons!"

Not that it was going to do them any good.

Dirt, blacktop, smoke, and lead filled the night air as the plantation militia unleashed a deadly barrage of fire at the convoy. Grim could feel the rounds smacking into his pickup's sheet metal as he dove from the cab. One of the convoy's gun trucks erupted in a fireball, the machine gunner's flame-engulfed body shooting across the night sky as the doomed truck somersaulted across the field.

Grim fast-crawled to the ditch alongside the road, his gut instinct telling the old trooper to get his weapon into the fight ... to return some of the hell that was raining down on his men ... to do something.

Survival instinct prevailed a moment later. He was in command. His people were dying by the second. He had to lead.

The truckers were doing better than expected given the wall of death that slammed into their ranks. From his prone position, Grim watched as the semis assumed a defensive formation. Kevin was firing from his position on top of a trailer. A few others had managed to get their weapons into the fight.

Darting low from position to position, Grim did his best to maintain control. "Conserve your ammo," he shouted to one group, "Let's make them come in and get us."

The driver of the second gun-truck had watched his twin die and was playing it smart. Racing across the field, he managed to make it to cover behind one of the crippled trailers as the man working the belt-fed blaster sprayed round after round back across the water.

As drilled, the drivers jumped from their cabs, armed with an assortment of rifles and shotguns. Scrambling for wheels, low spots in the dirt, or anything that would provide refuge from the relentless hailstorm of lead, the rate of return fire released from the beleaguered convoy gradually began to rise.

The 25mm guns atop the militia's armored units were wreaking havoc. Firing shells that were over an inch in diameter, the plantation's security forces had somehow acquired exploding ordnance for their mini-cannons. Large holes began exploding through the fortress of trailers that now surrounded Grim's constituency. Deadly shrapnel whizzed and screamed through the night air, creating bedlam amongst the defenders.

Were it not for Kevin and Cord's sniper rifles, the affair would have been wholly one-sided. Within minutes of engagement, the plantation's crews were learning a hard lesson about exposure.

The surplus French war machines weren't designed to fight at night, their optical aiming systems several generations old. That mean that the gun commanders had to control the weapons from the turret to guarantee any level of accuracy. This provided the Alliance marksmen with plenty of prime targets.

Despite the deadly accurate fire from the convoy's long-range shooters, Grim knew they couldn't hold out for long. His 30 rifle barrels were no match for the hundreds on the other side of the canal. He didn't have any way to knock out the tracked cannons. His team was basically fucked.

Just when he thought it couldn't get any worse, another wave of gunfire rose from the convoy's rear. "Shit!" Grim spat, knowing that the militia chasing them had finally caught up. Now they were completely surrounded, being squeezed from two sides. There was no place to go, no possible egress, no place to hide.

"Alright, Bishop. I did my best. Now it's up to you and God," Grim said, looking toward the plantation.

As the sounds of the second battle rumbled into the Castle's sitting room, Castro tilted his head heeding the random shouts of his unit.

Picking up bits and pieces of conversation as the fighting raged, the plantation strong man grinned at Bishop. "My men have the truck drivers surrounded. Your friends have no escape and are dying by the scores."

"Let us go," Bella Dona offered with venom. "End this now, and I will spare their lives."

Terri glanced at her husband and then shook her head. "I have a better idea," she announced, motioning with her pistol barrel for Bella Dona to stand. "We're going to sashay out there and tell them to drop their weapons, or I'll blow your head off. How's that for a fair trade?"

Shrugging, Bishop added, "Doesn't sound like we have much of an option. We might as well sweeten the deal with Castro."

Using the two hostages as shields, the couple moved toward the sitting room's main threshold. Bishop pushed open the door and quickly retreated behind Castro's shoulder.

Outside in the hall, a half-dozen security men stared up in surprise. "Back off or they both die," Terri warned.

The royal guard did as instructed, slowly retreating toward the front door. Bishop spied a man who appeared to be in charge of the small team. "Go find whoever is in command of the fight," he ordered. "We want to make a deal."

"What is it you propose?" the brawny man retorted, pausing at the door.

"An immediate cease-fire. We all walk out of here ... or the lady and Castro receive a lead injection," Bishop threatened.

"Now stop wasting time and find whoever is in charge," Terri hissed. "I'm nervous, and that makes my finger twitchy," she added, pressing her pistol's barrel hard against Bella Dona's temple.

Nodding, the beefy bodyguard rushed off, soon disappearing into the night.

The couple and their hostages remained in the foyer, Bishop taking comfort in being able to peer out through the large glass windows that lined the exterior. Beyond the wide front porch, he could watch a ring of grey-shirted men at the edge of the grounds. Someone had issued them weapons.

The Texan could also see the strobe of battle flashing in the night sky. From the sound of things, Grim was taking an ass whooping. Bishop briefly wondered if his friend was still alive and how many of the truckers would make it home.

It seemed like an eternity before the low throb of a diesel motor reached the Castle's foyer, followed a few moments later by the appearance of another French APC rolling through the courtyard, eventually rolling to a stop in front of the verandah.

As a single man hopped down from the huge machine, two squads of armed infantry followed, spreading out on either side of the tracked APC. "Now we're getting somewhere," Bishop stated from inside. "Let's hope this guy is reasonable."

"Inside!" shouted a voice in accented English. "My name is Tito. I command the militia. Show yourselves, and we will talk."

Bella Dona and Castro were shoved out first, Bishop and Terri following behind with weapons pressed into the captives' backs.

Again, Bishop repeated his demands. "Call an immediate ceasefire, Commander, and let all of us go. In exchange, we won't harm Bella Dona or Castro."

Bishop knew immediately that something was wrong. With an evil sneer, Tito tilted his head and then turned to his troops. "Kill them all," he ordered. "The plantation is now mine."

The militia shooters were confused, acting as if they didn't understand the order. The hesitation was just long enough for Bishop to move.

Grabbing Terri and shoving her hard toward the entrance, the Texan then managed to pull Castro down as bullets began tearing into the porch and door.

Realizing that a coup was in progress, the grey-shirts tasked with guarding Bella Dona started firing at the militiamen. In seconds, absolute mayhem filled the courtyard.

Bishop and Terri no longer had to worry about Castro and Bella Dona, both of their hostages diving for cover as bullets ripped through the Castle's walls.

Glass, paint, wood splinters, and lead filled the foyer as the foursome crawled, scampered, and scooted deeper into the house, desperately trying to escape the maelstrom of deadly lead.

The group found a reprise, ducking behind the broad staircase and its shielding structure. "Those traitorous bastards!" Castro hissed, "I can't believe they would turn on us!"

"Evidently, your benefits package leaves much to be desired," Bishop quipped, trying to catch his breath. "The shareholders are unhappy."

Outside, Bishop could discern an intense firefight between Bella Dona's royal guard and the militia troops. He didn't want to hang around to see who was going to come out on top.

Terri was thinking the same thing. "We have to move," she announced calmly.

"Okay," Bishop replied. "Let's shoot both of them and then get out of here."

"I like that idea, but unfortunately, we have to take them with us. They are our ticket out of here."

Bishop's eyes bored into Castro, spewing visual hatred and disdain, "How about we shoot him and use her as a hostage? I think she's the lesser of two evils."

The lady of the house offered a better idea. "I know a way out. A secret passage."

The two Texans exchanged a glance, both of their eyebrows shooting skyward. "Is that so?" Terri asked Bella Dona. "And just why should we believe a word you say?"

"She's telling the truth," Castro chimed in. "There is an escape tunnel, created long ago when banditos roamed these hills. Only my sister and I know of it."

Bishop shook his head as if trying to understand. "Your sister?"

"Yes," Bella Dona admitted. "My father had an affair with Castro's mother. She was a servant here. He confessed this sin on his deathbed many, many years ago."

The Texan wasn't interested in anyone's family history at the moment. "Where is this tunnel?"

"In the kitchen," Bella Dona pointed. "I will show you."

Waiting for a lull in the skirmish outside, Bishop nodded and waved Bella Dona and her brother out. The foursome made a mad dash for the back of the Castle, eventually arriving at the kitchen. After opening a small cabinet, the plantation's master reached for a small lever and yanked hard on the device.

A panel in the wall popped, revealing a narrow, low opening. Mounted on the wall were a torch and matches. Stone stairs led down into the darkness.

"I need one of these," Bishop told his wife. "This is like super-villain stuff. Very cool."

Chapter 14

It was the strangest army Butter could have ever imagined.

The armory had been stuffed with a variety of different weapons, ranging from cases of brand new AK47 battle rifles to box after box of U.S. M16s. Intermingled with the military grade weapons were just about every brand, caliber, and style of hunting rifle, shotgun, and pistol.

For nearly 15 minutes, the first men into the facility had handed out the weapons and ammunition to a wall of eager, reaching hands. It seemed like every laborer on the plantation now wanted a gun.

They kept coming even after the supply of firearms had been exhausted, the late arrivals relegated to pitchforks, axes, and shovels.

Large baskets, originally used to haul the harvest from the fields were converted into supply packs, scores of women carrying heavy loads of ammunition on their heads and shoulders.

Butter secretly prayed someone had thought to bring along the first aid kits. They were going to need them.

It was April who pointed the young Texan in the right direction. "The battle is being waged over the main bridge," she informed the new army's de facto general. "That crossing has to be the key to the entire valley."

"I guess we take the fight to the bridge then. Let's get moving."

Butter recognized the men who had helped him storm the armory, nominating Julio's father as his second in command. It took less than a minute to explain where they were going, and why.

Soon orders were being shouted to the masses, the verbal instructions repeated until they reached the edge of the ever-expanding mob.

"We are ready," replied Julio, Sr.

"Let's move," Butter decided, waving his hand toward the sound of the battle.

It took them nearly 10 minutes at a fast jog before they could see the match raging at the bridge. In the brilliant flashes of gunfire, Butter recognized the semis just across the water. "What the hell are they doing here?"

It was clear that they had been heading toward the plantation, which confused Butter even more. What he did know was that somebody had ordered them into defensive positions. That meant Grim or Bishop was still in command.

It was also pretty obvious that the convoy from Texas was getting its ass kicked. Butter spotted the tracked armor arrayed against the trucks, along with hundreds of plantation militia.

Waving over his insurgency counterpart, Butter took a knee and drew a quick diagram in the dirt. "Take as many men as you can and sneak along the water's edge. Hit them from the side. I will take the rest as they arrive and hit them from the rear."

A moment later, the Mexican was up and shouting orders to dozens of eager faces. While Butter could see fear in their eyes, there was something else as well. These were men overflowing with years of repressed anger and hatred, and it was all about to boil over.

More and more of the endless line of armed men arrived after Julio had left, Butter waving them to assemble between two rows of shabby barracks. When at least 200 were gathered, he shouted, "Let's do it. Follow me!"

It was the first time the kid from Texas had ever led men into battle, but his SAINT training and months of working with Bishop and Grim were now paying dividends.

"My gosh, we've got a serious vacuum on the leadership side," Butter whispered to no one as they hustled to engage. "These men deserve someone who won't falter. They need someone to rally around. It has to be me."

Only once did he turn to glance over his shoulder, emboldened by the sea of brave faces that were still there, following him into the breach of hell.

Over a slight embankment rolled the wave of slave soldiers, following the tall gringo. Butter spotted one of the French machines ahead, the vehicle surrounded by dozens of infantry, all of them firing at the trucks across the water.

Snapping up his carbine, Butter sprayed eight shots into a cluster of militiamen and then immediately emptied his magazine into the man operating the APC's cannon. Before he could switch magazines, his troops opened fire with devastating effect.

Hundreds of former slaves hit the militia's rear, screaming ferocious battle cries and shooting at anything that moved. The militia forces were stunned, many of them unsure who was behind them. They fell by the dozens, victims of confusion and poor training.

In a matter of seconds, the slaves were among them, small clusters of close quarters battle breaking out all along the water's edge.

Just then, Julio's forces struck like a sledgehammer against the militia's right flank, propelling a wall of deadly lead into an already beleaguered foe. Butter could feel the battle's momentum swinging their way. If they could knock out the armor, it would be over quickly.

He was also well aware that taking out those APCs was the key to keeping their casualties low. Spying the nearest tracked cannon, the big man charged like a rampaging bull.

Two militiamen appeared through the grey smoke that now drifted across the field in choking clouds, both of them moving to intercept Butter's bold advance. The Alliance man dropped his first adversary only a few steps away, his momentum carrying him into the second before he could adjust his aim.

Butter's shoulder slammed into the remaining man, knocking the Texan off balance and sending both of the combatants rolling over the ground.

Regaining his feet first, Butter tried to bring his rifle into play but was too slow. The steel of an arching machete blade flashed in the light, the big kid barely managing to block the vicious stroke with his barrel.

As the local fighter coiled for a second swing, Butter's massive fist sailed through the air, landing square on his foe's jaw with bone crushing force.

Staggering, the Mexican backed away, trying to regroup.

Butter moved like a big cat, closing the gap between them in less than a heartbeat. Again, the native raised his blade to slash at the behemoth towering over him.

Butter caught the man's wrist on the down stroke, stopping the machete cold in midair.

Twisting hard on his foe's limb, Butter stepped into the man while pulling hard. When he felt the opponent's weight shift, the Texan rammed his shoulder into the man's solar plexus and lifted with both arms.

It was a scene no witness would ever forget, a giant holding the kicking, squirming militiaman high above his head, roaring with the intensity of combat, charging at the APC.

Straining with every ounce of his mass, Butter launched his human cargo at the armored war machine. The machete wielder slammed into the side of the steel plating with a sickening thud, instantly going limp as he slid to the ground.

Butter scrambled to the top of the machine, bringing his carbine around and into the fight. Another grey-shirt appeared at the front of the APC, managing a single shot before the Texan snap fired two rounds into the enemy's chest.

Bending to the armored deck, Butter pulled open the main hatch and loosed a deadly spray of high-velocity death at the interior. The cannon went silent.

Two more militia charged the Texan, his form clearly visible given his perch on top of the APC. Butter killed both of them, countless hours of range time paying dividends of instinctive accuracy and lightning-fast target acquisition.

As the firefight raged all along the irrigation ditch, Butter's presence atop the APC became a beacon to his men. Like the flags that had been used on the battlefield since prehistoric times, his easily visible presence became a waypoint for the slave army. He was the rally point, the unit's colors, and a reassuring sign that his side was still in the fight.

So intense was the fighting, magazines were soon emptied, bolts and slides locking into battery with empty breeches. Like so many battles, the fight degraded into a primitive, whirling fur ball of violence complete with blades, rifle butts, and fists. The enemy was too close to reload. There wasn't the time or the space to chamber a round. The two sides were so intermingled, it was impossible to use gunpowder and high-velocity lead without the risk of friendly fire killing one of their own.

Again and again, the militia tried to remove Butter from the APC, many of the plantation's officers understanding the meaning of his presence and how it served to embolden the rebellious slaves.

Like a child playing king of the mountain, Butter was a whirling storm of punches and kicks, slicing with his blade or grappling bones until they snapped. He was insane with bloodlust, impervious to pain and determined to maintain his position atop the war machine. Countless times machete steel whizzed past his body, a few of the lucky attacks managing a shallow cut or glancing blow. None of it seemed to have any effect.

More than once the big kid had two or three men hanging off his limbs in a desperate attempt to dislodge him. Butter used every trick, hold, and ounce of his strength to dispatch his adversaries.

Two militiamen managed to get behind the frenzied gringo, both readying their deadly blades as their target was busy snapping the neck of another man.

Butter noticed the movement over his shoulder and pivoted as the duo sprang for the kill. For a brief moment, the Texan thought he would finally fall. Blocking one of the militiamen's stroke left the big man's right side was exposed, an opening the other combatant pressed.

Just as Butter winced in anticipation of his foe's knife slicing through his rib cage, the machete wielder's chest exploded, showering the Texan with a spray of gristle and hot blood.

Following the life-saving shot's trajectory with his eyes, Butter wanted to thank the shooter with a nod. He found nothing but water and open fields in the direction the bullet had traveled. Finally letting his eyes travel further, the Texan could detect the outline of semi-trailers illuminated by the trucks that were burning. "Kevin?" he wondered for a moment. "Thanks, buddy, if that was you."

"Grim, you better get up here. Something's happening to our front."

What now? Grim winced at hearing the transmission. "I'm kind of busy down here, kid."

"You'll want to see this, sir."

"Hell fire and damnation," Grim cursed, as he scampered for Kevin's sniper perch. "This can't be good."

A minute later, he was climbing up to the top of Kevin's trailer, belly crawling along the top to avoid the heavy fire rounds zipping and buzzing overhead.

Finally reaching the kid's sandbagged "hole," Grim flung himself over the edge and demanded, "Okay, what's so all-mighty important."

"Look," Kevin said pointing toward the distant irrigation ditch. "Butter and a bunch of ragtag looking guys are taking out the APCs and militia."

"What?" Grim snapped, raising a pair of binoculars to verify Kevin's unbelievable report.

Sure enough, the old warrior spotted several skirmishes in progress.

"Check out the APC closest to the bridge. That's Butter. I just knocked a guy off his back."

"Holy mother of God," Grim whispered, "If that big, dumb kid isn't a sight for sore eyes."

Without wasting another second, Grim turned to his sharp-shooter and said, "I want all but a few men to turn and face those shitbirds riding our ass. That includes you and that long-distance dialer you're holding. Go back to Cord's truck. I want both of you reaching out and touching someone. Got it?"

"Yes, sir," Kevin grinned.

A moment later, Grim was transmitting orders that had all but a handful of his men moving to the convoy's rear. If Butter could keep those assholes on the other side of the irrigation ditch busy, his shooters could hold their own against the smaller force behind them. "We actually might survive this clusterfuck," he grumbled.

The dead and wounded began to pile up around Butter's perch, the carpet of bodies making it difficult for friend or foe to climb onto the Texan's personal slice of the battlefield. The steel plates and sides were slick with blood and human gore. Those who did manage to achieve the armored deck were soon addressed, adding to the bleeding, withering heap of flesh beside the tracks.

During a brief lull, Butter found himself with a moment to scan his surroundings. Four of the APCs were burning, five others, including the one beneath his boots, were no longer firing their deadly cannons. That left three more that still survived.

Butter peered down into the open hatch at his feet, the dead face of the former commander staring back up at him with lifeless eyes. "I wonder if this gun is big enough to kill one of its own kind?"

Kicking the dead body out of his way, Butter dropped down into the hatch to study the cannon's controls. They were nearly identical to the M2 machine gun he'd fired at Foot Bliss. Was it really that easy?

A pair of buttons near the butterfly trigger were labeled with right and left arrows, another level printed with up and down indicators.

With a touch of a button, the motorized turret rotated left. Another test sent the cannon up, and then down. Butter smiled for the first time in over a week.

Spinning the gun, he took aim at the closest operational APC. The sights were very similar to the irons on his carbine. After taking aim, he pressed the trigger.

The big gun barked much louder than Butter expected. Again, he fired, this time making sure to see if the round landed high or low.

Within seconds, men were fleeing from the targeted APC, a small column of smoke rising from the rear engine compartment. Shortly thereafter, flames licked the hatch, followed almost immediately by a massive explosion that thrust pieces of the doomed machine soaring into the night. "Damn," Butter whispered. "I gotta get me one of these."

Making sure to close the panel behind them, Bishop had forced Castro down the slick stone steps. Bella Dona followed, with Terri the last to descend. Ten steps down, they reached a damp, foul-smelling, brick floor. The torchlight exposed a low tunnel leading off into the blackness.

"My gosh!" Terri grumbled. "You'd think with all the dough these guys spent building this place, they would have included a secret passage that could have accommodated more than a Hobbit."

There wasn't any option but to crawl through the claustrophobic tube, the effort reminding Bishop of the time he visited a cave in the Texas Hill Country.

Not long after they began their subterranean journey, water dripped from the ceiling, and the occasional tree root made the space even tighter. Still, the old structure had been well constructed, maintaining its integrity for many decades.

Their journey passed in silence, all ears focused on the muffled sounds of battle, the occasional rumble or explosion managing to penetrate the earth around them.

An intense detonation shook the ground, sending a shower of earth and mortar from the roof. Castro, in the lead, hesitated, coughing the grit from his lungs.

"Keep moving," Bishop grumbled from behind. "It's tight enough in here without us having to crawl over your dead body."

After scrambling through the spooky confines for several minutes, Bishop noticed that the tunnel was beginning to ascend. It was only a slight, barely noticeable, upward grade, but it helped calm his nagging fear of being trapped underground.

Castro's lead torch soon indicated a wall, and for a moment, Bishop worried that they had encountered a dead end. The enforcer knew the secret, however, and pushed hard against one edge.

The barrier moved on old hinges, swinging outward like a door. Sticking his head through the opening, Castro disappeared through the opening.

Bishop was so distracted with finally being out of the crushing passageway, he didn't see Castro waiting in ambush. Just as the Texan's head cleared the opening, the plantation henchman struck.

Only cat-like reflexes saved Bishop's life, his last-second move of ducking back into the underground structure allowing the Texan to absorb a glancing blow. Still, it hurt like hell, bells ringing inside his head.

Leveling his pistol to send a round Castro's way, Bishop paused before pulling the trigger. He didn't know what was on the other side of the hatch, didn't want to announce their presence with a gunshot. Besides, firing a pistol in the tight confines of the underground shaft would leave him completely deaf for several hours.

Ducking his head quickly out and back, Bishop didn't see Castro. "Shit!" he barked over his shoulder to Terri. "He's making a run for it! Stay here with the lady. I'll go find his ass."

Bishop lunged through the primitive entry, finding himself in some sort of small root cellar. He spied a ladder in the corner and began climbing.

Nearing the top rung, Bishop could make out a trapdoor blocking his passage. Expecting Castro to be on the other side, Bishop pushed cautiously against the hatch, finding himself peering out at an old barn. The plantation's head enforcer was nowhere to be seen.

Climbing out into the night air, Bishop took a moment to scan his surroundings. Gunfire still raged down by the water, but the pitch of the battle had clearly declined. "Grim, I hope you're still with me buddy. Hang on; I'm working on getting you out of this mess."

The Texan heard a scrape, a sound like cloth being pulled across wood. *There you are*, he thought. *Let's play a little game of hide and seek.*

Castro, given the revolt that just occurred on the Castle's front verandah, had apparently hidden inside the barn versus taking the chance of running for the protection of his own men. Bishop didn't blame him.

Yet, the escape tunnel had deposited them outside of a huge facility. *There's only one way to do this*, he thought. *Walk around until he either tries to jump me, or I find him first.* From Bishop's point of view, both options sucked.

The Texan's natural instinct pointed him toward the huge barn's open end to his right. On that side, there was freedom, the great outdoors, the best possible escape. Instead, Bishop turned the opposite direction, thinking to draw Castro out and retake his hostage without attracting any unwanted attention. Besides, if

Bella Dona's brother had made it outside, the chances of finding him in the wide-open spaces were greatly reduced.

He ventured slowly along the barn's outer wall, choosing his footfalls with great diligence. Stopping often to listen, the Texan was confident that his field craft was far more practiced than Castro's.

The shed was a large rectangle, nearly 50 yards on each side. The further Bishop traveled from the door, the darker it became. Old farm machinery was stored here, a rusting plow there, some sort of dilapidated sprayer alongside. The place smelled of used engine oil and musty earth.

Bishop had to admit, Castro had no shortage of hiding places. Between the lack of light and the piles of junk laying around, the Texan could have walked right past the man and not known he was there.

As much as he wanted to retake the vile hatchet man, Bishop recognized that Bella Dona was the key to their escape. His thoughts returned to Terri, probably still in the root cellar with the plantation's mistress. He needed to get back to her. He would settle with Castro later.

Bishop pivoted, his mind now working on the next step after rejoining his wife. A sound registered in his mind … a movement of air … someone had inhaled. A bolt of lightning shot through his right arm as something hard came from the darkness. The pain was unbelievable, his hand no longer able to hold the pistol.

It was pure instinct that caused Bishop to duck as the axe handle whizzed over his head, so close the wood actually brushed hair. Castrol growled, pissed that he had missed and resetting for another blow.

Bishop bolted.

In Castro's world, bravado dictated that Bishop should hold his ground. He was a man, wasn't he? He had been attacked, assaulted, challenged. He should fight.

The local strongman was absolutely stunned when rather than turn and defend himself, the gringo had scurried away like a young maid being chased by a wolf.

Bishop already had a four-step lead by the time Castro recovered from his surprise. Ducking his head, the enforcer gave chase. "Are you running to your wife? Does she protect you?" he snarled as his target accelerated.

Ignoring the insult, Bishop was trying to regain control of his right arm as he ran. The pain was getting worse, and a quick check via his good hand revealed a bone protruding from the skin between his wrist and elbow. "Fuck," he grunted, now understanding the searing, white-hot agony that bored into his brain.

Castro had managed to gain the element of surprise, reduce his enemy's capabilities, and a now held a weapon with the longest reach.

"Coward!" Castro taunted while giving chase, "Stop and fight, little girl."

I'm going to stop soon enough, ass clown, Bishop thought. *On my terms, not yours.*

A large piece of machinery provided the Texan the opportunity he was looking for. He cut hard around the rusting hulk and then stopped and ducked.

Castro barreled around the corner a moment later. Bishop was waiting.

The Texan sprang at his nemesis, bounding out of the shadows like a striking snake. With his good arm wrapped around Castro's waist, the two men when down, a heap of straining, grunting, cursing, tackling flesh.

Bishop, despite his handicap, now had surprise on his side. Grappling eliminated his opponent's advantage. *It's tough to swing an axe when you're rolling in the dirt*, he thought.

As the two combatants struggled for the upper hand, elbows flew, fists jabbed, and muscles strained. Both managed to deliver their fair share of punishment, but the Texan's strength, conditioning, and skills were too much for Castro to handle.

Time and again, Bishop punched with his good arm, each blow draining more of Castro's energy and focus. The Mexican was getting sloppy, his timing off, his balance wobbly.

Somehow, Bishop managed to roll away and stand, panting hard from the pain and exertion. Castro remained on his back, beaten and moaning in pain.

Out of the darkness, Bella Dona emerged, her brother's axe handle wielded held high above her head. Snarling like a tigress trying to protect a cub, she launched a vicious downward strike at Bishop's head. He turned, partially blocking the blow with his one functional arm. Again and again, she hacked and swung, driving the Texan back until he finally stumbled and fell.

With eyes glaring with hatred and stringy hair glistening with perspiration, she looked like a crazed demon as she towered over Bishop. He tried to rise, strained to roll away, but his body was at its limits. The pain from the broken arm and exertion of combat were inducing shock.

"Now, you die," Bella snarled and coiled for the final strike.

The barn was filled with a thunderous roar, the front of Bella Dona's chest exploding outward in a crimson cloud of blood, flesh, and bone.

Again Terri's pistol fired, the second bullet spinning the plantation's mistress a quarter turn. The third shot knocked her over, tearing out another section of lung, rib, and flesh.

Before Bella Dona's body had hit the ground, Terri was rushing to Bishop's side. One look at her husband's arm and battered face nearly sent her into a panic. He finally smiled, whispering weakly, "Hello there, pretty girl. Come here often?"

"How bad?" Terri asked, running her hands up and down his torso, checking for blood ... or holes ... or both.

"Just my arm," he replied. Then added, "And my chest, and my head, and my shoulder, and my...."

"I'm sorry, Bishop. She got away from me as we made the root cellar. She threw the torch into a puddle in front of me ... and then ran like hell up the ladder, knocking it back into the room once she reached the exit. I couldn't see ... didn't know where Castro was, or you, or her for that matter ... and had to regroup very carefully."

"It's okay," he managed. "Just let me sleep a while."

"No. You can't go to sleep. We need to get you help. Right now."

"But I'm sleepy. Let me rest. I'll be fine."

Blood was pouring from his arm. Several small cuts and lacerations added to the drain on his system.

Terri wondered where she could get help. She had no idea of the layout of the plantation, nor was there any way to ascertain who was winning the battle outside.

Something rustled near the shed's opening. Someone was coming. Terri raised her pistol. She couldn't run with Bishop in his current condition. She wasn't about to leave him. The barn was their Alamo.

The outline of a small boy appeared, and Terri exhaled. Her relief was only temporary. More and more shapes began to emerge from the darkness, at least a dozen men standing outside.

Someone produced a lantern and then called out a demand in Spanish. "Surrender with your hands in the air, or we will shoot you."

Terri didn't know what to do. If she called out, they might simply fire at the sound of her voice. If they were Bella Dona's supporters, the sight of the lady of the house's dead body wasn't going to win Terri any brownie points. If they were the rebellious militia, she was dead anyway.

"Come out!" the agitated man ordered. "This is your last chance."

Castro managed to stir with a grunt, startling Terri. She had forgotten all about him.

Bracing for a fight, Terri managed to palm her weapon, but Castro limped right past her and headed for the barn's door. "Put down your weapons, you idiots. It is Castro. The gringos are inside the shed. Kill them," he growled.

From the ring of shadows outside, Terri noticed a large shape emerge as Castro strode into the moonlight. "I know you," a voice declared in English. "You like to beat and rape prisoners."

"Butter?" Terri whispered, "Can it really be?"

Castro recognized the mass of muscle at the same moment. Turning to escape, he managed two steps before the flash and roar of a rifle's blast split the night.

"Revenge is mine, sayeth the guy with the gun," Butter announced.

A freight train was rumbling through Bishop's head, its massive engine rattling every cell between his ears. The pain was nearly unbearable, but it told the Texan he was alive.

Terri noticed her husband squint with discomfort. "Hey there, are you finally awake?"

The sound of his wife's voice managed to penetrate the wall of agony inside his head, its tone helping relieve some of the pain.

"Yes, but I wish I wasn't. God, what a headache. How long was I out?"

"Almost a full day," her words reassuringly jingled. "Some guys will do anything to get out of work."

Still uneasy in anticipation of the additional misery that was sure to come if he opened his eyes, Bishop ran a mental check of his body. He was sore practically everywhere. When he tried to tighten the muscles in his right arm, the train in his head revved its mighty engine.

One thing he did manage to ascertain was that the plantation had the most comfortable jail beds he'd ever felt.

"Now or never," Bishop groaned, forcing his eyes to open.

As expected, the light hurt, but it was a different discomfort. Terri's smiling face was worth it.

"Hi, babe," she grinned. "Welcome back."

Without thinking, Bishop tried to raise his right arm and touch her face, but the train sounded its angry horn in protest. His left hand, however, managed to rub her cheek.

Bishop took in his surroundings. Instead of bleak, grey confines and prison bars, he found white walls, a large window, and the softest sheets that he'd ever encountered. "Where?" he started to ask.

"While you were out, I moved our reservation to the Castle," she grinned, brushing his hair with tenderness. "Room service ... king sized bed ... a bathroom with so many showerheads, it looks like a Home Depot ... and valet parking for the convoy right outside," she teased.

Bishop smiled at her effort to brighten his day. "And the damage?"

"Your arm is badly broken, and you went into shock. You've lost a good bit of blood, but there is a doctor here, and he seems to be taking good care of you."

"Grim?"

"Grim is just fine, running around here fussing and griping at everyone and everything. He's trying to get some of the convoy's trucks repaired and loaded with food."

"Butter?"

"Butter saved us all," Terri stated. "He managed to lead the slaves in revolt. None of us would have survived if it weren't for him."

She began her high-level account of the events that had occurred at the plantation the previous night. When Bishop learned that Bella Dona and Castro were both dead, he merely nodded. When she told him that the lunatics now ran the asylum, he managed a smile.

"Wow, I missed out on everything," Bishop commented after she was done. "How many did we lose?"

Terri stared down, sadness in her voice as she reported, "We lost 14 very good men."

For the next 20 minutes, Terri reviewed the casualties, both she and her husband fighting back the tears as she reported the dead. Bishop had grown to like the truckers during the weeks they had trained together. A still melancholy overtook the mood.

"Brave men, going above and beyond," Bishop stated, finally breaking the silence.

"The Alliance will take care of their families just like fallen military," Terri stated with certainty. "I'll see to it. A lot of people do, and will, owe their lives to those men."

"And the wounded? There have to have been a lot of wounded?"

"The worst of them are in bedrooms right down the hall. April has ordered the Castle be turned into a hospital for those wounded during the battle."

"April?"

"Yes, April the schoolteacher. She and May, along with a man named Julio, have been running the show since the fighting stopped. I don't think any of them have slept a wink for two days, but they're trying to hold things together in the vacuum."

"And the militia? I can't believe they're all dead."

Terri shrugged, "Some of them fled into the hills; some surrendered. I think April wants to grant them amnesty, but I think a lot of the former slaves want blood."

The door to Bishop's room opened, Grim sticking his head inside. The SAINT member was freshly shaven, his fatigues crisp and clean. "You're back among the living, boss! That's great news."

After a quick greeting, Grim glanced at Terri and announced, "The final count of Alliance citizens is 214. So far, April has scrounged up four plantation trucks that can make it back to Texas, as well as a dozen trailers. She wants them back."

"Final count?" Bishop asked. "You mean 214 causalities?"

Shaking his head, Grim said, "Oh, Lord, no, boss. That's 214 former workers here at the plantation that are Alliance citizens and who want to go home. They've been coming in droves since the battle ended."

"I'm surprised there aren't more," Terri replied. "Last count I heard is there were over 1,000 Texans here. Why only a few hundred?"

Grim shrugged, "Evidently, some don't want to leave. I talked to a few of them, and they said that there was food here, education for their kids, and medical care. More than one said that there was nothing for them to go to in Texas. Now that Castro and Bella Dona are out of the picture, a lot of the former workforce is looking at this plantation as a great career opportunity. I heard someone was drawing up plans for new housing, and even a permanent school for the kids. April is outside right now, talking about giving over parcels of land for private ownership. She's quite the whirlwind."

After taking a minute to digest all that had happened, a nagging question popped into the forefront of Bishop's thoughts. "Butter?"

The Texan knew something was wrong after the look exchanged between Terri and his second in command. "Well? What's wrong?" he asked. "Where's Butter?"

"He's under house arrest," Grim responded with a grimace. "He turned himself in and pretty much demanded that I file charges."

Nodding, Bishop responded, "Good. That was the right thing for him to do."

"Bishop, you're not going to pursue this are you?" Terri asked.

Terri recognized a grimace accompanied by deep pain flash across her husband's face. She had never seen him look like that.

"I have no choice," Bishop mumbled.

Three days after the battle, Bishop was finally deemed strong enough to make the trip back to Alliance territory.

After gathering his equipment and belongings for the journey home, he issued the order that he had been dreading for days.

A knock on the door brought a sigh to the Texan's throat. "Come in."

Kevin entered first, his carbine held at port arms. Behind the SAINT team member trudged Butter, followed by one of the surviving deputies.

Butter looked like hell warmed over. Wearing a face thick with stubble, the man was covered with lacerations and bruises … along with the saddest eyes Bishop had ever seen on the kid.

"Reporting as ordered, sir," Butter stated, standing stiffly at attention.

Bishop ignored the big man, instead turning to Kevin and saying, "Leave us."

"Yes, sir," came the automatic reply. A moment later, Bishop was alone with his youngest team member.

"We are going back to the Alliance in a few hours, Butter. You know that you'll face some very serious charges once we are back in Alpha."

"Yes, sir."

"I'm so pissed at you, young man. You violated standing orders, displayed a clear disregard for my command and for the safety of your teammates. You endangered everyone on this mission, and perhaps even the future of the entire Alliance."

"Yes, sir."

"Yet," Bishop said, softening his tone, "you also saved all of our asses, as well as the tens of thousands of people working on the plantation. In the past few days, I've interviewed a dozen witnesses to your heroics the night of the battle, and if even half of what I heard was true, your bravery and actions were worthy of being taught to school children."

"Thank you, sir."

"So here's the deal, Butter. You are well within your rights to go to May and request asylum. I will have little choice but to honor that demand. You can stay here with the girl who is evidently very important to you and be with people who think you're a great man and a hero. You can avoid a court martial, and the possible punishment if found guilty. Do you understand?"

"Sir, yes, sir. But I decline. I am a Texan, sir. I am not a coward. I need to deal with the consequences of my actions."

"I see," Bishop replied. "Then I have no choice but to formally place you under arrest and file charges. You *will* face a court martial in Alpha when we return, son."

"I understand, sir."

"One last thing, Butter. You have the right to representation. I would highly recommend that you secure the services of a military lawyer at Fort Hood. I will try to ask around and make sure you are assigned the best."

"That won't be necessary, sir. I've already picked someone to stand beside me," the big kid stated.

"Oh? And who might that be, son?"

"Why, Miss Terri, sir. She agreed to represent me just this morning."

Bishop was stunned, a stream of hot protest forming in his throat. Butter, noting his commander's dam was about to burst, added, "After all, sir, you've told me repeatedly that she was a mean woman. That sounds exactly like what I need when I face these charges."

"What on earth were you thinking?" Bishop snapped at his wife, clearly upset.

Shrugging in innocence, Terri looked like the cat who had just swallowed the canary. "Because I think this whole military tribunal thing is absolutely ridiculous. That kid made a mistake of the heart. He didn't act in the name of personal gain or wasn't trying to deliberately harm the Alliance or his team. He was hoodwinked by a pretty face and an honorable cause. Diana should be pinning a medal on his chest, not putting him on trial."

Bishop shook his head in frustration, "You don't understand. The rules Butter violated have been a necessary part of military life for hundreds and hundreds of years. Armies can't be effective without that kind of discipline and restriction. Their governments wouldn't trust them. The entire system would fail."

"SAINT teams aren't the Army," Terri countered. "You may be paramilitary in form and function, but you also play the role of law enforcement, diplomats, and trade envoys. On this specific mission, you were providing security for a foreign trade delegation, while secretly playing the part of intelligence agents. How can you possibly try to impose such narrow rules on men who fulfill such a wide variety of missions?"

Bishop didn't want to have the trial right then and there. His arm throbbed constantly, his team was exhausted, and there were still hundreds of individuals and tons of food to deliver. He had at least a dozen reports to write one-handed, and would be answering Nick's questions for hours. "If you want to represent Butter, that is your decision. As long as you don't get so deeply involved that it affects us, I'm good."

She waved a hand through the air, dismissing his concerns. "This will be easy," she smiled. "I got this with one hand tied behind my back," she teased, pointing toward his slung limb.

At first, Bishop thought his wife was making a huge mistake. Diana and Nick were their friends, yet both of the government officials had taken an oath to serve the Alliance. The families of the fallen deputies and truck drivers deserved justice.

During the drive back to Texas from the plantation, Terri informed him of her strategy. "We are going to plead guilty," she announced. "I'm going to save all my powder for the punishment phase of his hearing."

As she continued to describe her plan, it was easy for Bishop to visualize the circus-like atmosphere that was sure to surround the event. The courthouse in Alpha would be overflowing; newspapermen from all over the territory would flock to write their articles. He could see Nick entering the courtroom, forced to dress more like a businessman than the Alliance's top military commander – the necktie and jacket looked odd on the big man, his finger repeatedly seeking to loosen the restrictive top button of his shirt from his massive neck.

General Owens would be there, his formal dress greens glistening with awards and ribbons. Sheriff Watts would no doubt be involved, his flawless uniform projecting authority and service. Yet, if Terri got her way, they would all end up looking like fools.

Yes, it would be a widely publicized event, drawing a packed house and dominating conversation in the capital for days.

"I'm going to call you, Grim, and Kevin to the stand first," Terri announced. "Then we'll bring April and May up from Mexico to tell what happened down there. Oh, and we'll have Mr. Beltran testify as well. This is going to take a long time, but Butter deserves justice."

Bishop groaned at the prospect, fully realizing what a huge series of problems his wife was about to create.

Terri would stress the seams of military law, basing her arguments on the unique nature of the SAINT organization and its cross-foundational reach. Diana would want no second-guessing of the due process being administrated by the Alliance and would have to give the defense plenty of leeway.

Butter was well known and popular, yet the families of the truck drivers and law enforcement officers who had lost their lives in Mexico deserved the best the government could offer. The whole thing could easily get out of control.

"Why are you going to do this?" Bishop finally protested. "You know this could seriously damage the Alliance and hurt Diana in the next election. Is that what you want?"

"No," she pushed back. "I want our law to protect the individual, not the institution. If we don't respect individual liberties, we're no different than Bella Dona's plantation."

"There's a huge difference!" Bishop snapped, now growing angry.

"Is there? Really? Other than the pay scale, what is the difference? We have trials. They are fair, regardless of whether the government likes it or not. Butter's rights are more important than the Alliance, and the minute we let that slide...."

"Stop the truck!" Bishop snapped in frustration.

"Huh?"

"I said stop the truck."

Terri, worried something was wrong with her husband, did as ordered. Before the lead pickup had even rolled to a stop, he was climbing out the passenger door.

The entire convoy pulled to the side of the road, the drivers in the follow-on vehicles staring at Bishop with questioning faces.

Down the line of trucks Bishop stormed, his fuming gait heightened by the restriction of his arm that in the sling.

Grim met the procession commander four trucks back, the old soldier scanning right and left, thinking there were bandits or trouble coming from the surrounding countryside. "Bring Butter up here, right now!" Bishop ordered.

"Sir?"

"What is everyone's fucking problem today?" the Texan growled. "Am I not speaking loud enough? I said, 'Bring me the prisoner.' Now!"

Terri, worried that Bishop had lost his mind, rushed up. Her husband pivoted and said, "This is a private meeting."

"What are you doing, Bishop?"

"I said this is a private meeting! Do all of you people have wax in your ears or something?"

Grim and Kevin arrived just then, a very confused looking Butter between them. "Reporting as ordered, sir!" the big kid announced.

"Leave us," Bishop instructed his wife and the two guards.

When they were alone, Bishop stepped close to the big man. "Of all the bullshit we have to deal with. Of all the crap that seems to fall on our heads, I find myself having to deal with your stupidity."

Butter didn't respond, now wondering if his boss had finally cracked under the stress.

"So here's the deal, young man. I have the right to prosecute charges in the field. As a sworn officer of rank, it is well within my prerogative to administrate justice if a proper hearing and court martial aren't practical. Do you understand?"

A look of fear crossed Butter's face. He'd never seen Bishop like this, didn't know what to expect.

"Do you understand?" Bishop barked, seriously wondering if everyone around him was deaf from the battle.

"Yes, sir," Butter responded sheepishly.

"Good. Now, I have one question, and one question only for the accused. If you had it to do all over again, would you still have gone down the same path?"

Butter had to think about his response, and Bishop gave him plenty of time. After more than a minute of consideration, the big kid nodded, "Yes, sir. If I had to do it all over again, I would still have had to help those folks."

"Why?"

Tilting his head, Butter said, "Because it was the right thing to do, sir. I felt it in my gut. My heart and head were in agreement. It was the high road, the moral thing to do. I have only one regret, sir... one bad call that is eating alive from the inside out."

"And that bad call was?"

"I didn't come to you, sir. That was a mistake, and I will never forgive myself for it."

Bishop nodded, sure that Butter had just spoken with a pure, heartfelt honesty.

231

Pacing back and forth on the side of the road, Bishop finally reached a decision. "By the authority granted by my commission, I hereby find you guilty of all charges. You will receive a reduction of two pay grades for a period of one year. If no further transgressions are committed, your pay will be reinstated after that time. Do you understand?"

Blinking rapidly as he digested what had just happened, Butter finally acknowledged his commander's question, "Yes, sir, I do."

"Attention!" Bishop barked, moving to stand within an inch of the taller man's nose. In a cold whisper, he growled, "If you ever violate my trust again, son, we won't have a hearing … or defense lawyers, or a trial. I will personally kick the living shit out of you and throw you off my team. Is that clear?"

A huge smile broke out on Butter's face, "Does that mean I'm still on the team, sir?"

Bishop remained stone cold serious but didn't say anything. Finally pivoting smartly to the nearby huddle of Grim, Terri, and Kevin, he snapped, "Get this man his weapon and assign him to one of the security posts. He is now officially reinstated, and make sure he earns his pay. There's been enough sloppy discipline in this unit, and we are turning over a new leaf as of today. Do I make myself clear, gentlemen?"

"Yes, sir," the team crisply responded.

As Bishop passed by his wife, he winked and whispered, "Benevolence can also feed loyalty."

THE END

CPSIA information can be obtained
at www.ICGtesting.com
Printed in the USA
LVOW13s0009210217
524838LV00016B/1093/P